You are warmly invited to

The Inaugural Meeting of the Fairvale Ladies Book Club

Sunday, 25 June 1978
Ten o'clock

RSVP to Sybil Baxter – ask the operator for 'Fairvale'

Take the Victoria Highway from Katherine, drive for about an hour then look for a wooden sign saying 'Fairvale Station'

THE INAUGURAL MEETING OF THE

FAIRVALE LADIES BOOK CLUB

SOPHIE GREEN

hachette
AUSTRALIA

hachette
AUSTRALIA

First published in Australia and New Zealand in 2017
by Hachette Australia
(an imprint of Hachette Australia Pty Limited)
Level 17, 207 Kent Street, Sydney NSW 2000
www.hachette.com.au

This edition published in 2018

10 9 8 7 6 5 4 3 2 1

A catalogue record for this
book is available from the
National Library of Australia

ISBN 978 0 7336 4040 7 (paperback)

Cover design by Christabella Designs
Typeset in 12/17.4pt Sabon LT Pro by Bookhouse, Sydney
Printed and bound in Australia by McPherson's Printing Group

The paper this book is printed on is certified against the
Forest Stewardship Council® Standards. McPherson's Printing
Group holds FSC® chain of custody certification SA-COC-005379.
FSC® promotes environmentally responsible, socially beneficial
and economically viable management of the world's forests.

For my mother, Robbie, who taught me to read

*And in memory of her parents, Amy and Tom Hille,
and the stories they told me*

1978

13 February   A bomb explodes outside the Hilton Hotel in Sydney, Australia, killing three people

5 March   'Wuthering Heights' by Kate Bush becomes a number 1 single in the UK

18 April   The US Senate votes to give control over the Panama Canal to Panama

30 April   The Democratic Republic of Afghanistan is proclaimed

15 May   Former Australian prime minister Sir Robert Menzies dies

15 June   King Hussein of Jordan marries American Lisa Halaby, who becomes Queen Noor

16 June   The movie *Grease*, starring John Travolta and Olivia Newton-John, is released

25 July   Louise Brown, the world's first IVF baby, is born in the UK

16 October   Pope John Paul II becomes the 264th pope

27 October   The Nobel Peace Prize is awarded jointly to Egyptian President Anwar al-Sadat and Israeli Prime Minister Menachem Begin

CHAPTER ONE

The morning sky was its usual muted dry-season blue as Sybil paused to gaze out of the kitchen window. Before she'd moved to the Northern Territory she'd thought it would be a land of perpetual brilliance: blood-red dirt, sapphire skies and emerald trees, and a luminous, pendulous sun reigning over the land. All of that was true – just not at the same time.

The palette of the place changed with the seasons. The light of the dry season was pallid at dawn and dusk, and during the wet the sky was often so heavy with cloud that it was hard to say what sort of blue it was. When it rained – and rained and rained – the trees turned so bright and the earth, even the rocks, became so alive with new growth that it was like living in a greenhouse; but during the dry season the colours of the trees seemed subdued, almost as if the persistent foliage felt like it didn't have permission to be any more vibrant. The wet season was the star up here: it had the power to turn the Katherine River into a swollen force, waterfalls cascading down the sides of the gorges; it made the air leaden with moisture and turned people into molasses. And it could kill.

Everyone knew of someone who had died trying to cross a river during a wet, or a child who had wandered off

3

to a waterhole or creek they thought they knew well, only to discover that the usual friendly trickle was now a roiling torrent in which lurked traps for small feet: tangled branches, rotting animal carcasses, strong currents. It was too easy for the wet to claim an unwary child – or adult. That's what had shocked Sybil the most when she'd arrived here. She'd grown up in Sydney, with all its traffic and bustle and urgency, but she'd never known anyone to die because of the weather. Yet in her first year here on Fairvale Station, she knew two. It had been an unwelcome lesson: the Territory would always be the boss. Humans could try to bend the land and the seasons to their will, but they would fail. They would fail forever. All they could do was surrender completely and make the best of what was there. And the best was plentiful.

It was impossible not to fall in love with the place. So many colours and contradictions; so many secrets and surprises. She had been here for twenty-six years, since she was twenty-five, and she knew enough to realise that she would never know the Territory completely, even though it felt like the Territory knew her. It knew her weaknesses, that was for sure; it also brought out her strengths. Of all the relationships in her life, this was the one that seemed to contain the most challenges and rewards. Not that she'd tell her husband that.

As if on cue, Joe walked into her field of vision. She smiled as she saw him lift his battered Akubra and scratch his head. He did that a lot, usually when he was trying to work out how to say something stern to a worker without actually sounding stern. He was a gentle man, in so many ways. She was lucky to be married to him; lucky that he had taken her away from a life that was pressing in on her. She hadn't loved him then but she loved him now. And it was time to call him in to breakfast.

4

She waved vigorously through the window, hoping to catch his eye; his lifted finger was the sign that she had. She saw him turn towards the cattle yards and cup his hands to his mouth, no doubt calling to their son Ben, who had also started the day early. Everyone on Fairvale was up with the sun, if not before, and they worked long after the moon rose. Sometimes Sybil wondered whether she'd have chosen this life if she'd known that it was relentless: seven days a week, so many hours a day. There seemed to be very little time even to read a book, because they were all so tired they'd fall into bed at night. Except they did end up making time for the things that mattered, and if Sybil thought she was missing out on being a lady of leisure she was also aware that life wasn't made for sitting around and doing nothing. Human bodies were built to work, and the hard, long toil of each day made the snatched hours of relaxation all the more precious.

Sybil watched as her husband and son pushed open the gate to enter the garden. Despite the fact that they lived in the middle of hundreds of thousands of hectares with apparently no need for fences, where the land threw up its own natural barriers, the gate kept out the working dogs and any stray cattle that might trample through the green-lawned garden that Sybil had defied nature and good sense to create. That garden still carried the signs of the lush growth of the wet season just past. Before too long, though, the dry would start to bite and she'd need to draw on the bore water to keep the garden at its best.

She'd fashioned it – perhaps ridiculously – as if it was a garden belonging to a quaint English cottage instead of a large, squat outback home. Fairvale's big house had a generous verandah that wrapped around three of its sides, but it was no more genteel than that. The garden was Sybil's attempt at bringing something refined into her immediate world. She had fashioned long garden beds to border the lawn. A bird bath sat in the middle of the grass; instead of swallows dipping their beaks into it, however, the local cockatoos used it as a swimming pool, raucously announcing their activities every time. It often sounded like they were laughing at her – laughing at her delusions of order and grace – and they probably were. She'd started this garden as a bride, trying to bring something of her old, organised life into her new. If she'd waited five years, it wouldn't have mattered so much. By that point in her marriage she had realised that she would never be able to control anything much around here, apart from herself.

After the beds had been dug she had, at great expense, ordered poinciana saplings and a jacaranda tree from a supplier in Darwin. African trees, she'd thought, might have a chance of surviving here. She had installed some camellias, hoping they would reach a fair height even if this wasn't their natural habitat. They had survived, although they weren't always happy about it.

Maidenhair ferns hugged the ground; she'd planted them hoping they would keep the beds together, and moist, to encourage the other plants to grow. The ferns loved the wet season and hated the dry; some years Sybil thought she'd lose them all, yet they'd endured. She supposed that plants that had been growing on earth for millions of years could outlast the tough seasons.

The lawn had been the hardest part. It was a risk, when the wet season was likely to turn it into mush, but Joe had gone to Darwin one day and returned with enough lawn to cover the patch of dirt that was left after the beds had been planted. Sometimes he'd laugh at her, slowly shaking his head, as he watched her curse the weather and offer up the occasional prayer that her lawn would be saved.

'Why are you laughing?' she'd said once, irritated that he could be so amused while she was so annoyed.

'Because that lawn is the only thing that can make you believe in God.' He'd laughed more heartily then and she'd wanted to stomp away from him – because he was right. Instead she'd pressed her lips together, turned away and started pruning a camellia.

The garden had been many things to Sybil over the years: a source of pride and frustration; a refuge when she needed a few minutes to herself; a place for her children to learn to take care of nature; and a spot where she and Joe could sometimes sit quietly as the sun set on a dry-season day, listening to those cockatoos, still laughing at her.

Mainly, though, the garden was her work of art – the only one she had. Out here on Fairvale, two hours from the nearest town and a long way from the culture and sophistication of her childhood, Sybil needed something to gaze upon. Something that wasn't stampeding cattle and mangy dogs, coals in a fire or a creek bed full of animal skeletons.

As the two men approached the flyscreen door, she could hear them talking about one of the workers. It was as she'd suspected: Joe needed to pull the man back into line and he didn't have the heart to do it.

'If you don't, I will,' she could hear Ben saying. 'And I won't be half as nice as you.'

'Now, now,' came Joe's deep, measured tones; he sounded just as he had when Ben had misbehaved as a boy and Joe had tried to discipline him. *Now, now, Ben*, he'd say. *You don't really want to do that, do you?* Amazingly, this tactic had often been effective. As it no doubt would be with the worker.

'Hello, love,' Joe said as he opened the door, removing his hat and hanging it on the hook by the door. Sybil liked the way he always greeted her as if he hadn't seen her just half an hour ago, wrapped in her towel as she exited the shower, her hair wet, her face unadorned. He always made it sound as though seeing her was an occasion.

'Smells good, Mum,' Ben said as he pulled out a chair and sat.

'There's nothing cooking yet, Ben,' she said.

'I know.' He winked. 'Get a wriggle on.'

'You can go and eat with the others in the dining room if you don't like it,' Sybil said. The residents of Fairvale – the community of stockmen, workers, and their wives and children if they had them – usually ate together, with all the food cooked by Ruby, who had been with them for years. Sybil always liked to make breakfast for her family in their home, however. The days could become so frenetic for Joe – so many people wanting to talk to him, to ask him things, to have him do things for them – that providing him with a quiet start, with a meal where he could eat in peace, was, she felt, important.

Joe tapped his son on the shoulder. 'Be kind to your mother,' he said. 'We're lucky to have our breakfast made for us.'

'Yeah, yeah.' Ben grinned at his mother, taking off his own dusty Akubra and putting it on the table. Sybil knew that grin: it was Ben's good-luck charm, his means of getting out of trouble. He'd been using it on her since before he could talk and she always fell for it, even though she tried not to let him see that.

'Do you reckon the rain's finished?' Sybil said, turning her head briefly towards the kitchen window.

'Could be a bit more.' Joe squinted at the sky. 'Sometimes we get fooled. It's been a good wet, though, so we shouldn't be greedy. The bores are full. We'll last through the dry.'

'Where's Katie?' Ben said to his mother.

'She's your wife, Ben,' Sybil replied. 'How should I know?' Her son was twenty-three years of age – old enough not to be lazy. Although she had a motherly impulse to want to take care of everything, he was a grown-up.

'Because you've been in the house together.' He tried his grin again.

'And I've been in here,' Sybil said.

'All right,' Ben said, sounding weary and getting to his feet. 'I'll get her.'

'Thank you,' Sybil said, turning to a loaf of bread next to the stove, picking up the knife so she could start to hack out the many slices she'd need just for this one meal.

'Ka-aaate!' Ben called as he walked through to the rest of the house, and Sybil turned to Joe and raised an eyebrow. Only he could understand the paradox of loving Ben and being exasperated by him at the same time.

Joe smiled. 'Cup of tea, love?' he said and Sybil nodded.

'Thank you,' she said as she started to slice.

Another day on Fairvale was beginning.

CHAPTER TWO

Sallyanne sat in the car with the ignition off, turning her wedding ring round and round on her finger, feeling the sun already burning through the side window. It wasn't even ten o'clock.

The car was almost new, although that didn't make her love it any more. It had been her husband's choice, but Mick rarely drove it; he had a ute for work and he'd drive that on weekends too. Sallyanne would rather have had one of those little Japanese numbers instead of a burnt-orange 1976 Kingswood station wagon that felt as wieldy as a truck and was as hot as an oven inside.

She sighed and kept turning her ring. She didn't know why she did that when she was nervous; it wasn't as if the ring looked any different whichever way she moved it.

The ring was a plain platinum band. Platinum, her mother had once told her, was more valuable than gold. That had been years ago, of course – her mother had been dead for half of Sallyanne's life. She never forgot anything her mother told her, though. Or anything her mother did.

Sallyanne remembered arriving home from school and finding her mother cackling – yes, actually cackling, almost bent over with laughter – in the presence of other women who crowded their small sitting room. There were cups of tea in her mother's best china and half-full plates of Arnott's biscuits. Lemon Crisps, Scotch Fingers and Venetians. Her mother had barely noticed her only daughter arriving, apart from saying, 'Hello, darling, it's just the CWA,' before she continued laughing.

There had never been another meeting at their house but her mother had remained a member of the Country Women's Association until she died. Sallyanne had always thought it was an organisation for women far older than her who wanted to talk about their grandchildren, but her mother hadn't been that old. Not that much older than Sallyanne was now.

The blast of a horn made her jump and she looked up to see a woman waving at a car in the street. It was the same wave her daughter, Gretel, had given her as she'd left this morning, her fingers waggling as she'd chewed on some of her hair, a new habit that Sallyanne would have to stop.

She'd left Gretel with Mick's mother, who was a reliable babysitter, if a somewhat unenthusiastic one. Colleen had never been keen on watching Gretel's brothers, Tim and Billy, declaring boys to be 'nothing but trouble – and *exhausting*, Sally, they're *exhausting*', although she'd softened once Gretel had arrived. However, Sallyanne reflected with another twist of the ring, the woman had never learnt to call her daughter-in-law by her proper name.

The boys were at school now. Probably looking forward to recess. And here was their mother, acting like it was her own first day of school.

Sallyanne had thought about doing something with her days ever since Billy had started kindergarten. With only Gretel at home, she'd really had no excuse not to try to make better use of her time. So when she'd seen the little advertisement in the local paper, announcing the next CWA meeting and welcoming new members, she had called the number in the ad and stammered out her question about whether she could attend. Of course she could, a kindly lady had told her.

'And you sound young, dear,' the lady had gone on to say. 'We need some young ones.'

Sallyanne was glad she sounded young because she had been feeling so old lately. Her body was worn out from carrying and feeding three babies, from running a household of five people. This morning had been like all the others: she was up early to make Mick his tea and toast, never receiving any words of thanks, just the glowering that now seemed to be a fixture. He was drinking more and smiling less, and she didn't know why – she knew only that he'd decided it was her fault that he needed six beers in quick succession at night, which was probably why he was morose in the mornings. That was her fault, too, apparently. He'd always had a temper, arriving quickly and violently and gone in the same way, but this latest turn in his personality was settling into his foundations and she didn't like it. Didn't like the way he looked at her, as if she was provocation and prey. Didn't like the way he snapped at the kids, when their only offence was to be young.

So she made the best of it: she would be chirpy with the children as they woke and tumbled into the kitchen for their breakfast and Mick grunted his goodbyes. She would bustle around, packing the boys' lunches, making sure their shoes were polished, answering Gretel's constant questions about why puppies barked and trees were green. It was exhausting and she always felt there was nothing left over for her. No time, no energy, no motivation.

Still, she had to make an effort. Thirty-four years of age was too young not to try. Not to live.

She'd decided to drive past the front entrance of the building on the main street. She could have parked out the front. Instead, her throat feeling like someone's hand was on it, she'd turned left at the corner and gone around the block to First Street, thinking she'd park out the back. She wouldn't feel so exposed if she was waiting there.

Yet she could see there was a rear entrance to the building, and now two women walked past her car, laughing, as they headed for it. They had the short haircuts that were so practical in this hot place and the short-sleeved cotton dresses that were also advisable, but she was sure they were wearing stockings. Sallyanne looked down at her own cotton dress and her bare legs. Was she meant to have worn stockings? Was that what proper CWA ladies did? Even in a place where the air was so stifling that people sat in the hot springs – a pool of water that was thirty-eight degrees Celsius – in preference to being on dry land?

It was too late now for stockings so she'd just have to hope no one would notice. Maybe this particular cotton dress hadn't been such a good idea, though: her belly, so slack after three babies had grown in it, was pushing out prominently with nothing to hold it in. If she'd worn a different, more structured dress – if she wasn't so fond of biscuits and cakes – she wouldn't look so plump. Those other women didn't look plump. They looked like they'd been working out in the sun every day of their lives: sturdy and strong and hearty. She'd never been hearty.

Feeling sick with uncertainty about what would happen once she stepped inside the building, Sallyanne pushed open the creaky car door and put one tentative foot onto the road.

She tucked her wispy blonde hair behind her ears, licked her lips, and then sent a silent plea to her mum to give her strength as she emerged fully from the car and slammed the door shut – it was the only way to get it to stick. Trying to remember to keep her shoulders back, she walked across the sparse lawn at the back of the building, then, falteringly, opened the screen door that took her into a room that was smaller than she had imagined.

Sallyanne guessed that there were about twenty women standing around – she'd never been good at estimating the size of a crowd, though. They were all older than her, although some not by much. There was an array of dresses in various unremarkable patterns, and sturdy handbags placed on or next to the large table that dominated the space.

Almost to a woman they had short or shoulder-length hair, which made Sallyanne conscious of her own long locks, which she had wanted to cut for years except Mick kept telling her not to. She looked like Rapunzel, he'd say; certainly there were days when Sallyanne felt like her, too.

Sallyanne realised that a moderately tall, middle-aged woman was looking at her curiously. She was sure she'd never seen the woman before – she'd have remembered such a striking face. The woman looked like Ava Gardner before Frank Sinatra got to her. She had short grey hair cut close to her head and she was wearing something no one else in the room was: boots, and a Western shirt tucked into her slim waist above a pair of sensible-looking pants with a flare at the hem. Sallyanne had seen those shirts in cowboy movies, always worn by men. A large silver buckle adorned the woman's belt. She looked like she was about to go to work on a property, which meant she probably wasn't from town. Sallyanne was sure she'd have noticed her if she was – she knew pretty much everyone by sight. That's what happened when you'd lived your whole life in one place.

'You're Sallyanne Morris, aren't you?' the woman said.

'Yes,' Sallyanne replied cautiously. 'How did you know?'

The woman smiled enigmatically. 'I'm Sybil Baxter. From Fairvale.'

Sallyanne knew about Fairvale. Everyone in the area did. The Baxter family had lived on Fairvale for so long that no one in town could remember them not being there. Well, no one except the local Aboriginal tribe, but people didn't really talk about that.

'And you're joining us?' Sybil's smile was more generous now.

Sallyanne nodded and let out the breath she didn't know she'd been holding onto.

'It's my first meeting,' she said, sure she was spluttering.

Sybil nodded towards the women gathering around a table laden with cups, saucers and scones. 'Shall we?'

Sallyanne felt herself relaxing, just a little.

'What made you want to join us?' Sybil said, walking slowly.

Because I need some new friends, Sallyanne almost said but realised how that would sound. 'I heard that you talk about books sometimes,' she said instead, and was rewarded with a look of delight on Sybil's face.

'You like to read?' Sybil said, stopping before they reached the table.

Sallyanne nodded vigorously. 'I love it,' she said. 'It's my escape. It gives me—'

She bit her lip. She would sound loony if she told this woman that she loved books because they let her exist in different worlds, far from the dusty, hot town in which she'd grown up. In books she could live in London and Crete and New York City; she could inhabit the eighteenth century or

New Kingdom Egypt. In books she could find tips on how to be a proper lady, what it felt like to have a grand romance, how to say 'fiddle-dee-dee' when you really wanted to tell someone to *get lost*. Not that Sallyanne said 'fiddle-dee-dee' to anyone. She'd tried it when she was a teenager, convinced that Scarlett O'Hara was her role model, and her friends had teased her for a week.

The quizzical look Sybil was giving her told Sallyanne that she'd let her mind wander again, in full view of another human being. Her mother always used to say she was 'off with the fairies', which she'd never quite understood – fairies didn't interest her so much as pharaohs.

'Sorry,' Sallyanne said quietly.

'For what?' Sybil now looked amused.

'I lost my train of thought.'

'That doesn't need an apology.' Sybil smiled sympathetically and Sallyanne felt a pang of something she recognised from her earliest school days: the desire for a friendship.

'So you've grown up in Katherine?' Sybil said, although her intonation suggested she knew the answer.

'Yes. Born here. Raised here.' Sallyanne grimaced. 'It sounds boring when I say it like that.'

'Not at all,' Sybil said. 'It's a fine town. I wish I could spend more time here.'

'And you're from . . . ?' Sallyanne guessed it was some-where far away. Sybil held herself as if she knew her place in the world and was comfortable with it. It wasn't the sort of confidence that came from growing up in a country town – one glance around the room at the slightly rounded shoulders and the universally deferential postures, even on the most robust-looking women, could tell anyone that. All these women, with lives and families they'd made their own, holding themselves as if they had something to apologise for.

'Sydney,' Sybil said.

'I've always wanted to go there,' Sallyanne said. 'Some of my favourite books are set there.'

'Oh? Which ones?'

'*Harp in the South* is the main one. I—'

'Sybil!'

A short, wide woman with a rigidly set perm was waving at them, and Sallyanne felt immediately disappointed that her conversation with Sybil Baxter was clearly about to end.

Sybil gave her an apologetic look and touched her arm lightly.

'Come and I'll introduce you to Peg,' she said, waving briefly at the other woman. 'And . . . I may have an idea.'

Sallyanne frowned.

'A book-related idea,' Sybil said. 'I'll ring you, if that's all right?'

'Shall I give you my number?' Sallyanne said, not daring to hope that it was this easy to make a friend.

'I don't need it. I'll just ask the operator to connect me.' Sybil squeezed her arm. 'Come on. Peg's a hoot.'

Perhaps it *was* that easy. Or perhaps Sybil felt sorry for her. Whatever the truth, Sallyanne allowed Sybil to lead her into the CWA fray.

CHAPTER THREE

In the stillness of the evening the house was quiet – apart from the noise of her husband's heavy feet coming down the hallway. Kate smiled and felt the same thrill she always did whenever Ben was near.

The door creaked open and there he was: six feet one, dark curly hair, skin tanned dark brown and the biggest smile in the Northern Territory. She loved the way one of his eyes almost closed each time he smiled at her – as if he was trying to make his smile even bigger, pushing it as far up his face as he could. His teeth were improbably white against his skin and his eyes danced.

'Aren't you a picture,' he said, walking in and closing the door behind him, starting to pull his shirt over his head.

She glanced down at herself: her long hair, also dark, tumbling over her chest, her nightdress almost threadbare because she needed to buy a new one and there hadn't been a chance to go into town for months. Her skin was drying up now the wet season was over and she felt as though the red dirt that seemed to get into everything on Fairvale had seeped into every pore. When she looked in the mirror – less often than she used to, because increasingly it seemed a ridiculous vanity in a place where everyone was subject to the same

18

conditions – she would loom close, checking to see if there was dirt inside her upturned nose, or inside the rims of her eyes, which used to look so big and round, and which she now squinted against the sun so often that she worried they'd turn into slits. She lamented the high forehead that she'd once thought aristocratic: now it seemed like just another location for dirt to collect.

Kate could hardly believe she'd survived her first wet season, but she had, even though it had meant ending every day feeling like a limp tea towel that had been used to mop up one too many messes. Before they'd arrived in Australia Ben had told her how the seasons in his part of the Northern Territory worked: there were not four seasons but two. The wet season lasted from November to April and brought with it torrential rain and the probability that creeks and rivers would keep people trapped on their properties. The dry season was a blessed relief but sometimes it was too dry, and their water supplies could run down. Then there were two unofficial seasons: the build-up and the build-down.

'The build-up,' Ben had said, shaking his head and starting to laugh, 'it makes people go troppo.'

'Troppo?'

'Short for "tropical". The place is tropical so the weather makes people . . .' He'd shrugged.

'Go troppo,' she'd finished. 'But what does it mean? What happens?'

'You go a bit crazy. The humidity gets . . . It's hard to describe.' He'd grinned quickly. 'You're the first person to ask me.'

She'd found out for herself when they'd arrived in that October of 1977. The humidity had shocked her, the first week it came. She'd spent a bit of time in France, growing up – the ferry to Calais had been as close to a rite of passage as she'd ever managed – but she'd never been anywhere else, let alone anywhere tropical. She'd never even thought about tropics beyond what she'd read of British colonies in Singapore and Malaya and India, and in those stories the English people were always being fanned by servants and given cooling drinks. There were no servants on Fairvale – there were 'workers', not even Ruby the cook was to be called anything else – and they couldn't keep anything cool because they didn't have a refrigerator.

Somehow, she'd made it through that build-up without going troppo – looking back, she suspected she was simply too shocked at how different everything was to properly succumb – and the wet season had come and gone. Now that the dry had arrived she had to learn to adjust to that as well.

'I wouldn't say I'm a picture,' she said, thinking that it was Ben who looked as if he was not so much picture as sculpture, his chest and arms so perfectly proportioned that sometimes Kate suspected a joke was being played on her: he was too attractive to be real.

'I look frightful,' she added.

'You'll never look frightful to me.' Ben pulled his jeans off and then he was naked, jumping onto the bed beside her and kissing the tip of her nose. 'You're my English rose,' he said. 'Always blooming.'

'Ben,' she said. 'That's so corny.' She rolled her eyes.

'Not if it's true, baby.' Now he kissed her cheek, and her neck. She sighed as his lips moved to her collarbone.

'The English part is,' she said, giggling as he tickled her belly.

'Just take a compliment, would you?' He kissed her on the lips, hard, undoing something in her. And as he kissed her arms, her fingers, her feet, back up to her neck, along her jaw, she felt the work of the day leaving her.

Kate had travelled a long way to be here, with Ben. Some days she felt it more than others. Some days her body ached with the effort of living in this strange country that was so far from what she knew that at first she had almost thought she'd moved to another planet rather than a different hemisphere.

Instead of the fabled woods and lawns of England that she was used to, her home was set in a landscape that was embedded in red – or was it more of an orange? The colour of the ground changed depending on the sun's location. There were no dense stands of trees here; no gentle light, either. Everything was bright and there was a hardness to it. She hadn't loved it at first sight – not the way Ben told her she would. He had rhapsodised about the land of his upbringing, about the beauty and wildness of it. He'd told her how fascinating it was, how full of secrets and discoveries. All she saw were trees that looked like they were barely hanging on and earth in dire need of rain. She'd hoped she would adjust but she was sure, then, that she would never love the place the way Ben did.

The day they'd arrived on that ragged flight from Sydney after staggering off the plane from London, they'd been picked up at Darwin airport and driven more than four hours down the Stuart Highway and out along the road to Fairvale. It was the longest she'd ever driven in her life; she was sure that they must have crossed a border somewhere, but Ben told her that, no, it was still the Northern Territory. Stan was their driver; she didn't think a stockman was meant to be a chauffeur but Stan had said, grinning, that he'd missed Ben too much so he'd volunteered to pick them up.

Stan was the first Aboriginal person she'd met, but only one of the community who lived on Fairvale. Kate had tried not to stare at him on that long drive – he looked so different to anyone she'd ever seen. She was sure he'd worked out what she was doing, though, because just before they left Darwin to take the highway south to Katherine he'd turned around and winked at her in the back seat.

'You're gonna see a lot of strange things, missus,' he'd said, laughing. 'Including me.'

She'd felt mortified, then Ben had started to laugh.

'You're not wrong, mate,' he'd said. 'But keep your eyes on the road and off my missus, eh?' Ben had laughed again. Kate had felt like she was missing something: a joke Ben and Stan shared. Or maybe she was being overly sensitive. Her mother said she could do that sometimes.

When they'd arrived at the homestead – the big house, as she now knew it was called – Kate had almost leapt out of the truck with excitement. But as the door to the house opened, and Sybil appeared – her face beautiful and stern – Kate had felt nerves overtake her. What had she been thinking, coming to live with parents-in-law she hadn't met?

Climbing the short steps to the house, she'd approached Sybil, who had held out her hand instead of offering a cheek as Kate had hoped. It was the way things were done where she was from: one kiss, or two.

'Hello, Kate,' Sybil had said. She smiled with her lips together and she seemed calm – clearly not as nervous to meet Kate as Kate was to meet her. Sybil had looked into her eyes for a few seconds then looked down; she'd taken Kate's hand, shaken it, then glanced at Joe, who'd appeared beside her and proceeded to wrap his arms around Kate and noisily kiss her cheek.

'Welcome to Fairvale,' he'd said. 'We're excited you're here.'

As soon as Joe had let her go those nerves had returned. She remembered that she had looked around the verandah, her eyes not settling on anything; perhaps she had a strange expression on her face because Ben had wrapped his little finger around hers and tugged, causing her to look at him.

'You all right?' he'd mouthed and she hadn't known how to answer. Everything had felt right from the moment she'd met him but here, standing in her new home – his parents' home – she felt askew.

Given how alien Ben's life was to hers, they had met in a fairly mundane way: at a dinner party held by Kate's cousin Georgia, who just happened to be engaged to Ben's friend Charlie. Ben and Charlie had met as teenagers at boarding school. Charlie had been doing his stint in the 'old country' – it was expected of young Australians, Ben had told her that night as he sat next to her, his broad, tanned hand resting close to her own on the table, her heart beating more quickly than it should as she watched his fingers playing on the tablecloth, shifting the cutlery around.

'So Charlie,' he'd glanced over his shoulder at his friend, who was carving a leg of lamb, 'said he was going for a year. His dad had lined him up a job in a bank and he was going to come here, work hard, have some fun and go home. Except he met Georgia, didn't he?'

Ben had grinned in Georgia's direction.

'And that was that. He's stuck here and now he's managed to drag me over for the wedding.'

'But it's not for another month,' Kate had said, confused.

'Yeah, I know.' Ben had fixed his eyes on hers and that's when she knew she was in trouble. He kept looking at her – looking *into* her – and as much as she felt exposed, she couldn't look away from him.

'But Charlie said I might as well have a holiday.' He shrugged. 'I need some time to think about things.'

'Oh – what things?' she said, more to check that her voice still worked than anything.

He waved a hand. 'Family things. My brother is meant to take over the family property and I'm meant to shove off.'

She heard something in his voice – irritation?

'But you don't want to?'

'No,' he said, then he started to laugh. 'Bloody Lachie doesn't care about the place and I care about it too much. Isn't that the way?'

'So you can't . . . take it over?' She had no idea how such things worked: her family lived in the village, not on a farm, and although she was aware that there could be succession issues within families, she was one of three girls and it was unlikely to happen in hers.

'Not unless Lachie steps aside. And given that he's not qualified to do anything else, I wouldn't mind betting he won't.' He smiled tightly. 'But there's a stockman's job for me there as long as I want it, and Dad's been good enough to give me some time off so I can be here. Charlie said I might get to meet a nice English girl.' He winked. 'What do you think my chances are?'

She'd almost hiccuped with surprise. 'I, oh . . .' She swallowed.

'You don't have to answer that,' he said. 'I think I already know.'

As his eyes remained locked on hers Kate could see no trace of his easy mirth; instead she saw only intention. She swallowed, hoping it would dampen down whatever was bubbling up through the centre of her chest – the light, fluttery feeling that only intensified as she watched his eyes grow slightly rounder and the corners of his mouth lift. For a second she was terrified – truly gripped by the idea – that he was going to laugh at her. Why wouldn't he? Who was she, after all, to feel attracted to this handsome man with his big life? But there was no laughter: just the warmest smile she'd ever seen.

'So where are you from, Miss Kate?' he said, picking up his knife and fork, giving her a chance to gather herself.

'Oh, um . . .' She swallowed again. That fluttering wouldn't go away. 'Nowhere special.'

He cocked an eyebrow as he looked at her. 'I find that hard to believe.'

She felt herself blushing, which she was confident she hadn't done since she was about thirteen years old.

'I'm from Gloucestershire,' she said. 'But I've spent a lot of time in London. My sister and I lived with our grandparents here while we went to school.'

'No schools in Gloucestershire?' he said, cutting into the meat on his plate.

'Not schools my parents liked.' Her own meal wasn't so much unappetising as impossible: she couldn't eat with him sitting beside her. She didn't even feel like she could move her hands to take hold of her cutlery.

'So my . . .' She quickly took a sip of water. 'My grandparents offered to have us live with them while we went to school. It probably saved my parents' marriage.'

'Oh?' He frowned.

'I mean – they have a wonderful marriage. I tend to think it's because they didn't have us around much when we were being awful teenagers. They could enjoy each other without us being in the way.'

He nodded. 'I think mine are a bit the same. Lachie and I went to boarding school. And when we were home we didn't spend too much time in the house.'

'Why not?'

Ben's laugh was short. 'I was always on a horse. Lachie was . . .' He shrugged. 'Who knows? Pulling the wings off flies, probably.'

She couldn't see any indication that he was joking but he looked away from her so quickly that perhaps she didn't catch it.

'So that explains your posh accent,' he said lightly. 'Posh schools.' He grinned.

'I'm not so posh,' she said quietly. 'If I were properly posh I'd have a better job. Or no job at all.'

'Posh girls don't work?' he said.

She sighed, more loudly than she'd intended. 'Not for boring bank managers, they don't.'

'What would you rather be doing?' He put down his cutlery and swivelled so that his body faced hers, as if he was issuing an invitation to tell him the truth. Kate wasn't sure what her truth was, though – she had never, she realised, stopped to think that there might be something else she'd rather be doing. She had recently become aware that she had been waiting for something to happen to her – waiting for her life to become more interesting – when she should be taking steps to *make* it more interesting. She wished that she'd been taught how to do that at school instead of being pounded with the incantation that *marriage, babies, family, home* were her destiny. Were the destiny of every girl. She wanted those things but she'd always wanted more, too. *More* had been what she couldn't define or quantify and no one she knew could help her do that.

'Seeing different places.' It had popped out of her mouth without her even forming the thought.

His eyes encouraged her to keep going.

'I don't know,' she said, faltering in the face of his clear interest. No one had ever been so curious about her.

'Yeah, you do,' he said quietly but firmly. 'Tell me.'

Kate was aware that she was breathing more quickly than normal; aware, too, that she liked this feeling of possibility and excitement that was infusing her whole body.

'I don't want my whole life to be staying at home doing the ironing and baking cakes,' she said, then suddenly worried that he'd find her less attractive if she didn't conform to what was expected of her. 'I mean, I wouldn't mind doing those things. But there are other things I want to do too.'

He grinned at her.

'Is that funny?' she said.

'Maybe.' He started to laugh. 'I don't know any women who stay at home doing anything, so I'm wondering where you got your ideas from.'

'You don't?' Almost all the women she knew either did that or seemed to aspire to that. There were days when it appealed to her too, and other days when she dreamt of a life that was filled with new things to learn and new skills to develop; a life that required more of her than doing what other people wanted and needed. It was a life she didn't quite know how to shape yet but a life that she knew was out there, somewhere, if only she had the opportunity to find it.

'Not where I come from,' Ben said. 'Mum's too busy for that stuff. The other women on Fairvale – well, they have jobs too. Dad irons his own shirts. We have a cook to make the cakes.' He grinned again. 'It's different, I guess, from what you're used to.'

'What does your mother do?' she said.

Ben grinned at her conspiratorially. 'She runs the place,' he said. 'And lets Dad think he's doing it.'

Immediately Kate was even more intrigued by this robustly masculine man who had grown up with such a mother, but for the rest of the dinner she'd had to talk to the man on her other side, who had loudly proclaimed that 'the colonial' had taken up enough of her time and it was his turn.

Ben had called her the day after the dinner, a Sunday, to ask if she would like to go for a walk that afternoon; he preferred being outdoors to inside, he'd said. He'd come to her flat in Sloane Square and they had walked straight towards Kensington Gardens. They had talked so easily, both laughing, and when the sun had finally emerged from behind the day-long clouds she had felt it was shining only on them.

They had stopped beside the Serpentine, Ben taking her hand in his as they stood by the lake. She had felt warm and safe yet thrilled.

'So what are we going to do?' Ben had said.

'It will be time for dinner soon,' Kate had said, glancing back in the direction they'd come from. 'There's a nice little bistro near home. We could go there.'

Ben had looked amused. 'That's not what I meant,' he'd said, pulling her closer towards him.

'Oh?' She felt like she was blinking so rapidly that he'd think she had a tic.

He put his other hand against her cheek and she wanted him to keep it there forever.

'I meant what are we going to do for the next fifty years?' he'd said. Kate had wanted to explode with laughter, relief, happiness – and love. She had fallen in love with him already, this man from half a world away, and although she'd never loved anyone before she was sure this sense of absolute convic-tion and courage and promise, not to mention surging desire, was that. Or, if it wasn't, she was prepared to take the risk that she was wrong, simply to be with him.

He'd lowered his lips to hers and she felt none of the reticence she'd felt in the past when boys and young men had kissed her.

She didn't feel that she was transgressing rules, that she would be found out and her reputation ruined; she didn't feel repelled that her own need to be liked, to be found *pretty* or even *beautiful*, had led her to do something she didn't really want to do.

As Ben kissed her, it felt like the most natural thing in the world, and also the most dangerous. As his arms wrapped around her and his body pressed against hers, Kate felt at once at home and in the most exhilaratingly foreign land she could ever visit.

Eventually – minutes later, maybe an hour – the kiss ended.

'I think we'd better keep doing that,' he'd said, and his smile was kind and cheeky all at once.

'I agree,' she'd said, sliding her hand into the crook of his elbow as they wordlessly turned to take their first steps into their future.

He hadn't gone back after that month. He'd told his father that he had something important to do in England. By his account Joe had been unworried, although Sybil had written to tell him that Lachie was behaving erratically and she'd really feel better if Ben returned. That's when Ben had asked Kate to marry him. That's when she had said yes.

It had been a quick courtship – Georgia, for one, had cautioned her against marrying Ben so quickly. But there were so many reasons in favour of it and so few against. Kate was, as she liked to say, a good Catholic girl and she had resisted other men in the past – she had no wish, however, to resist Ben. Nor did she want to think about how dull life would be if he returned to Australia and she didn't go with him.

'I think it's time we made a baby,' Ben said, his voice muffled against her chest, interrupting her thoughts.

'We've been giving it a good try,' she said, although she didn't mean it lightly. She thought she'd be pregnant by now and as each month passed without a change, she felt a little more despondent. Kate had surprised herself by how much she wanted to have Ben's baby while still not wanting to have her life defined by motherhood. She still believed what she had told him about wanting to do other things with her life yet there was a force inside her stronger than any belief. She supposed it was biology – Mother Nature wanting to make a mother of her – or perhaps it was something just as powerful and primal: love. Whatever the urge was, she had given in to it – even if it hadn't yet yielded to her.

'We sure have.' He moved up to kiss her mouth, his lips full and a bit rough. All that sun made them peel from time to time. She didn't mind it. In fact, she liked his ruggedness. It was just one of the many things she found attractive about him.

'I love you,' she said as he smiled down at her.

'You bet you do,' he said, patting her hip. 'And I love you right back.'

As his lips found hers again she tried not to think about the months that had elapsed without her fulfilling what should be the most natural thing in the world: having a child. Once they had married she thought it would just happen. Georgia had fallen pregnant on her honeymoon; Kate couldn't understand why it was taking so long for her.

'Kate,' Ben whispered.

'Yes?'

'I can hear you thinking,' he said, and his hand slid over her hip, down to the inside of her leg.

'I'll try not to,' she said, and she meant it, even if she only tried for a little while.

CHAPTER FOUR

Some horses were easy to read. Some horses were easy to read on certain days and impossible on others. But this horse – this horse that Della had been riding for months now, this horse that should have known better – was impossible on all days. She was stuck with him, though. She'd tried to swap. She'd asked for a more compact quarter horse instead of this big lump of part-Clydesdale she'd been given. She'd been told no.

'Arthur, stop it,' she admonished as he shoved against her, again, as she pulled his saddle tight.

'Ar-thur, *stop it*,' mocked a high-pitched voice behind her. She knew who it was: Ross Watson. He thought it was funny to mimic her accent. Like Texan accents were inherently funny. She thought his was funnier. Weirder. He barely moved his mouth when he talked and his vowels disappeared into his nose. But she didn't make fun of him. Mostly because that was how she'd been raised; partly because he was twice her size. She was small. *Teeny-tiny*, her father had always called her. He'd meant it affectionately. Ross used it like a weapon.

'Shut up, Ross,' said Bob as he came in carrying a saddle. Bob was a bit older and he'd been on Ghost River Station for a while. Most of the younger men listened to him.

'You shut up, Bob,' Ross said, keeping his voice high.

Bob shot Della a look – and not for the first time. It wasn't a look of sympathy so much as resignation. So a weak smile in return was all she could manage. She and Bob knew the truth: she could pay Ross no attention but he'd demand it. She couldn't say anything about Ross to their bosses, either.

Ghost River was owned by a man called Augustus Major. Bob had told her that the station's name came about because when the riverbed ran dry – as it sometimes did during the dry season – the ghosts of a young man and woman who had died trying to cross the swollen waters during a wet season many years ago could be seen on the far bank, beckoning for help. She hadn't known whether to believe him or not, especially when one of the stockmen had told her a different story – that a previous owner thought the trees by the river were ghost gums, before he realised that they didn't grow this far north. She wasn't sure which explanation she preferred.

While Aug, as he was known, was the owner, it was his wife, Felicity, who everyone called the Major General. Felicity was in charge; Aug did what he was told. So it was no use going to Aug about anything, and Della knew that Felicity would just tell her that if she wanted to work with men, she had to put up with men.

'Del, you right to go out for a few days?' Bob said, running his hand along Arthur's flank.

'Sure,' Della said, patting her saddle bag. 'I have what I need.'

'What – lipstick?' It was Ross, cackling.

'If I know Del,' Bob said, his voice low and steady, 'it'll be a book. You like reading, don't you, Del?'

She smiled at him, grateful. If Aug and Felicity couldn't help her, at least Bob stood up for her.

'Where's your pack, Ross?' Bob said and Ross looked alarmed. 'Forgot your own bloody lipstick, did ya?'

Ross took off from the stables, heading for the men's quarters.

'He's got a kangaroo loose in the top paddock, that one,' Bob said, shaking his head. 'Sorry he gives you such a hard time.'

Della shrugged, scratching Arthur's neck. She still hadn't given up on trying to win the horse over.

'He doesn't,' she said. She didn't want to appear weak. She was already a woman doing a man's job and she had a lot to prove.

'He does,' Bob said, frowning. 'But I'm keeping an eye on him.' He started to turn away from her. 'I have to go to the house before we leave. You right?'

She nodded. She was right. Despite Ross's bad behaviour, Della was where she wanted to be and she wouldn't change anything about it.

Each time a new stockman appeared at the station or a drover came through, they'd always ask her how she came to be here, so far from home. She'd always say she didn't really know, and she'd be stuck here until she figured it out. But she did know: Della had spent her whole life in her home town in Val Verde County in rural Texas and by the time she'd finished high school she knew it wasn't going to be big enough. In school she had learnt a quote by Helen Keller, and she was determined to live by it: 'Life is either a daring adventure, or nothing.' Della didn't want her life to be nothing. But she hadn't known how to make it something until her father had hired a worker who was Australian. Johnno, his name was, and he was from Far North Queensland, he'd told her, saying it like it was its own country and she should know where it was. They had worked together on the ranch for weeks before he'd asked her a single question about herself. They were out on horseback, checking that there weren't any animals injured in a recent mudslide.

'You seem to know what you're doing,' he'd said slowly. If she thought Texans had a drawl, Johnno beat them all every time.

'Is that a compliment?' she'd said, steering her mount around a hole.

'I reckon,' he'd replied. 'You're the first sheila I've worked with. I wasn't sure if you'd be any good.'

She bristled. 'Sheila?'

'Girl. Woman. I forget that some words don't travel. Anyway – most sheilas are off having babies by your age.'

'I'm only twenty-two.'

'Yeah. That's what I mean. Don't you want 'em or something? It's not like you're ugly – plenty of blokes round here must fancy ya.'

'Gee, thanks,' she'd said, now feeling as if spikes were growing through her skin. 'If you must know, my daddy told me I'm the best worker he ever had, so I'm doing him a favour by working here instead of having babies. And one boy did ask me to marry him but I said no. I don't want to be stuck here having a small life with some boring man and his wailing brats. I'd rather die.'

He'd laughed then – thrown his head back so far that his hat almost fell off.

'You're all right,' he'd said. 'And I was just teasing ya.'

They'd become friends after that, and she'd found out that Johnno was far more decent than he'd initially led her to believe. When it was time for him to return to Australia – he'd had his adventure, he told her, and wanted to go back to Cooktown – he said she should come and visit. He'd show her the sugarcane fields and the rainforest. They'd eat soursop and star fruit, and go to a place called Port Douglas where they could walk on Four Mile Beach.

Della wasn't interested in him as a beau but she wasn't foolish enough to ignore fate when it was extending her an invitation, even if she was often sceptical about the concept of it. So she saved her money and after a few months she had enough to get a bus to San Francisco and then an aeroplane to Sydney.

She never made it to Far North Queensland, because not long after her arrival in Sydney she'd discovered a newspaper called *The Land* and, in it, an advertisement for a station hand at Ghost River Station, 'near Katherine, NT'. She'd asked the lady at her boarding house what a station was and the explanation made it sound like a ranch. Then she'd asked where Katherine was and the lady had snorted and said, 'You don't want to go there, love – they have crocodiles. And it floods half the year. The other half it's so bloody hot that you can't open your eyes or your eyeballs dry up. And I've heard that the mango trees have so much fruit that people turn orange from eating it.'

Della had wanted to go there, though. It sounded exactly like the sort of strange new place she wanted to visit. So she'd written in response to the ad, giving the telephone number at the boarding house. Two weeks later – after she'd given up hope of hearing anything – the call had come.

Felicity Major, the woman had said her name was. She'd quizzed Della about why 'a girl' would want the job – 'We don't usually have girls here,' she'd said with no trace of irony – and Della had told her about the ranch and the cattle. About riding horses since she could walk. About how her father had begged her not to leave because he'd never find someone who worked as hard as she did.

'All right then,' Felicity had said. 'If you can get up here by the end of the week, you've got work.'

Della still wasn't sure how she'd managed to get herself to Ghost River in time, putting it down to blind faith and determination. She was good at applying herself when the situation called for it.

That had been a year ago. She'd lasted through the wet season, when the other station hands left, making herself useful to Felicity. She knew how to bake and sew – her mother had taught her, saying that even if Della wanted to spend her life on horseback she still had to know how to take care of herself – so when Felicity needed help in the big house, Della volunteered. It kept her in work. It kept her on Ghost River, which she had fallen in love with in a way no human had ever inspired. And it allowed her to pick up her old job when the dry season started again.

As she gave Arthur one last pat she could see Ross heading for the big house, his odd loping stride taking him past the cattle yards. They'd be out mustering for days and she'd have to put up with his stupidity. Only when Bob was out of earshot, though. And she could handle it the rest of the time.

'Are you Della?'

Della jumped – she hadn't even heard anyone approaching the stables. That was the trouble with the stables being open at both ends: someone could sneak up on you. She turned and saw a fairly tall woman with short grey hair smiling at her in a curious way. She looked like someone who was always busy: she was wiry, and there was a slight pinch around her eyes, as if she had spent her life looking beyond whatever was in front of her.

'Yeah,' Della said slowly, holding out her hand for the lady to shake. Shaking hands wasn't the conventional thing for ladies to do, but she liked to do it.

'I'm Sybil,' the lady said, and her handshake was firm even as her smile was broad. 'Felicity told me I could find you here.' She nodded towards the big house. 'I'm visiting for morning tea. I live about an hour away. Fairvale Station.'

Della nodded. She'd heard of it. Bob had a brother working there. 'Can I help you, ma'am?'

Sybil's face brightened and she held out a piece of paper.

Della took it, noticing that its contents were hand drawn, the writing bold and clear. *The Inaugural Meeting of the Fairvale Ladies Book Club*, it read. *Sunday, 25 June. Ten o'clock.*

'Felicity told me you like to read,' Sybil said.

'I do.' Della moved to hand back the paper.

'No, it's yours,' Sybil said. 'I'm starting a book club – well, that's obvious.' She gestured to the paper. 'We're all a bit isolated out here, aren't we? It's good to have some other people to talk to.'

Della scowled. Had Felicity made her out to be some charity case?

Sybil rushed on, as if reading her mind. 'I got the idea from a woman in town. She knows someone in Melbourne who does this kind of thing. Initially I thought Felicity might want to join but she suggested you instead. Said you read more than anyone she knows. And I thought . . .' Sybil smiled quickly. 'I thought you might know some books I don't. Being American.'

'Okay,' Della said slowly.

Sybil looked relieved. 'My daughter-in-law, Kate, will be there. And my friend Rita. Plus a woman from town, Sallyanne. The first book we're going to talk about is . . .'

She fumbled in the large canvas bag on her shoulder and pulled out a thick tome. 'The Thorn Birds by Colleen McCullough.'

She held it out to Della. 'You can read this copy,' she said.

'You don't need it?'

Sybil shook her head. 'I've already read it. Twice.'

'Guess you'll have some opinions, then.' Della turned the book over and scanned the back cover copy. She looked up at the sound of Sybil's laughter.

'I guess I will,' Sybil said. 'So you'll come?'

Della looked at the size of the book and calculated the time left between now and the twenty-fifth of June. She had a few weeks – easy. She could probably read it twice herself. Did she really want to join a book club, though? She'd always kept her reading to herself. A friend of hers back home had a book club with two other women and it sounded like all they ever did was argue about how they'd have written the book differently.

She had, however, left home so she could experience new things. 'If I'm not out with the cattle, sure,' Della said at last.

'Felicity said she'll make sure you won't be,' Sybil said, grinning. 'I'd really love you to come.'

'All right,' Della said, looking at the book again. 'Thanks.' She smiled at Sybil for the first time.

'See you soon,' Sybil said. 'I should get back to the house.'

Della gave a half-wave as Sybil left and watched as she took confident steps up to the house, where Della could see Felicity standing on the verandah.

CHAPTER FIVE

As RAAF Base Tindal appeared like a speck below the plane, Rita couldn't help grinning while she craned her neck to look out the window. Small as the plane was, she didn't mind: it was her office, after all. She felt as though she'd already seen the entire length and breadth of the Territory from this plane, travelling to stations and Aboriginal missions and outpost towns, all in the name of the Royal Flying Doctor Service. When she'd moved to Alice Springs several months ago the only part of the Territory Rita knew was the small town of Katherine, the road that led from Katherine to Fairvale Station, and the station itself, when she went to spend time with Sybil. The last time she'd flown up here they'd landed at the airfield in Katherine. Now that was closed and all civilian flights put down at the RAAF base twenty-five kilometres out of town. Rita would have thought that an inconvenience if she hadn't known that twenty-five kilometres in a place like this was equivalent to going around the corner.

She didn't get up to this part of the world often enough – didn't see Sybil enough. Their lives conspired to keep them apart. Yet their friendship was long enough established that decades could pass and they would still pick up a conversation as if they were in the middle of it.

They had met when Rita was seventeen, starting her training as a nurse and doing a stint at the children's hospital in Sydney's Camperdown as part of the compulsory rotation through hospitals. Sybil was more senior; she was twenty and young to be promoted as far as she had been, which immediately signified that she must be very good at her job. Rita's class was the first she'd supervised and at the start she'd been too officious, too keen, it seemed to Rita, to prove her authority. With the benefit of time, and their friendship, Rita could tell that Sybil was simply inexperienced with authority and hadn't really known how to lead, or to teach. That friendship had not been a logical development, given their different places in the hospital hierarchy, and it might not have happened at all if they had not been on duty together one bleak winter's night when the corridors of the hospital felt like channels to the Antarctic.

They were standing together, looking into the cot that held a baby who had been born prematurely, hours earlier, and transferred to the children's hospital for specialist care.

'He's so little,' Rita had whispered.

Sybil had nodded. 'We were worried he was going to fall through the cot.'

'And he's . . .' Rita had tried not to shudder, but the child was so deformed that she found it hard even to call the baby 'he'. He seemed to be an 'it', and she felt like a terrible person for thinking it.

Sybil had sighed. The sound was soft, almost regretful. 'Yes, he is,' she'd said. Her arms were folded and her face impassive. 'Poor little thing.'

'So . . . what are we meant to do?'

'We wait,' Sybil had said, and Rita saw the smallest of grimaces.

'For what?'

As Sybil half turned her face, Rita could see the barest trace of tears.

'For him to die,' Sybil had said, her voice firm.

Rita felt the shock of pragmatism, and the realisation that Sybil must have had other nights like this when she had waited for a child's life to end.

'There's nothing that can be done?' Rita whispered. 'To . . . save him?'

Now Sybil looked at her fully. Her eyes, usually so guarded, were wide open but in the half-light of the ward Rita could not read them.

'No,' she said, and Rita could see her swallowing.

'But—' Rita felt her breath catch, sharp in her chest.

'It sounds harsh, I know,' Sybil said, and as she looked at the baby Rita saw her forehead relax. 'It sounded harsh to me when I had my first experience of it.' She turned to Rita again. 'I'm not a religious woman but there are things I've seen . . . There are moments of grace, Rita, even in the toughest of circumstances. This child isn't meant to live long, and what we can offer him is a good death. He will be here for a moment, then he will be gone, and his parents will mourn and they will live with their grief and they will carry on. That is where our job is: helping people adjust to things that they cannot control and that will affect their lives forever. We have to offer them that grace, even if it doesn't last for long.'

Rita hadn't quite understood what Sybil meant that night. She had been too young and too full of zeal to change the world and make everything better. A year on the job had, however, brought her to the place that Sybil occupied. And after that night Sybil had always had a smile for her, and a nod; after that year was over they would seek out one of

Sydney's few cafés if they had a shift ending at the same time. On their rare days off they would go to Wylie's Baths in Coogee and lie on the warm cement, soaking up as much sun as they could before plunging into the sea.

'Just about to put down, darl,' Darryl, the pilot, yelled to Rita over his shoulder, and Rita remembered where she was: high over the Northern Territory, not at a Sydney beach. 'Are you strapped in?'

'Yes!' she yelled back over the considerable noise of the single-engine plane.

Rita kept her grin as Darryl pitched them towards the landing strip. The first few flights in this little plane had seemed like a nightmare – Rita had never flown in anything so small and loud, so seemingly fragile. But she'd done enough trips now to know that one engine was sufficient to keep them in the sky, and this hardy little aircraft and its hardier pilot had conquered the Territory as they transported the Flying Doctor's team to far-flung places and, sometimes, brought patients back to the Alice.

There were days – fewer now than there had been – when Rita completely regretted leaving Sydney to move to Alice Springs. Sydney was her home; she'd been born, raised and lived all her life in Punchbowl, a suburb of big back gardens, vegetable patches and corner shops. She'd had a sheltered upbringing in a moderately large, well-kept house, attending a girls school nearby, walking in the bush on weekends, playing tennis, taking piano lessons. She'd gone swimming at Cronulla Beach in summer and in winter her mother would take her and her brother to the Southern Highlands or the Blue Mountains for vigorous walks. Her friends all lived the same way.

In the thirty-odd years since she'd left the family home and worked mainly in hospitals, Rita thought she'd seen all there was to see. She'd had no pressing reason to leave the job she'd taken at the Royal Alexandra Hospital for Children. She loved paediatric nursing and she had worked at the hospital for so long that it felt like a second home. Yet she was in danger of becoming complacent. If work was to be the great love affair of her life – given that no other candidates had presented themselves, not for lack of her now-abandoned hope that she might meet a husband someday – she needed to keep the spark in it.

Rita had known from a young age that she wasn't interested in being married for its own sake. She loved her work and she knew that she was unlikely to enjoy housework and mothering work as much. So if she was going to give up her vocation it would have to be for a passionate relationship with a man who had more to offer than just being male. Some of her friends had chosen husbands because they had reliable incomes and they were mildly handsome, and those friends were happy enough – but that wasn't what Rita wanted. She would rather stay alone forever – and risk the disapproval of everyone she knew or met – than be 'happy enough'.

She had made several attempts at forming relationships but the men had always been inadequate, mostly because they were lacking in the sort of vigour she hoped for and because they were unkind. Those attempts had stopped when she was in her late thirties; since then she'd mostly been untroubled by well-meaning friends, or unkind men. Over the past couple of years she had realised that if she wasn't to live the way she was supposed to – the way everyone else did – she could liberate herself further from the expectations that other people had placed on her.

A new colleague told her that she'd once worked for the Royal Flying Doctor Service, based in Queensland. Rita had heard of the Flying Doctor but knew nothing more; she soon found out and then one day she was calling their head office and enquiring about vacancies. Within a fortnight she had resigned in Camperdown and started to make plans to move to the centre of Australia, to a town that was unlike any part of Sydney she had visited.

Where Sydney was beautiful and growing busier than she was used to in her childhood, Alice Springs was sparse and mysterious. They had in common the brilliant blue skies that seemed to stretch further than the horizon, but Rita was never allowed to forget that Alice Springs was in the desert. The lush harbour foreshores, the gorgeous purple smattering of jacarandas in spring and the tree-lined streets of Sydney could not have been more different to the yellows, oranges, browns and reds of the Alice.

Her spirit of adventure had brought her to the centre of Australia but it had also caused her to overlook the fact that she knew no one in the town. She missed her life – the rhythms of it that were so familiar to her. She missed going for walks along Bridge Road in Glebe, looking at the old houses and the grand trees. She missed the smell of biscuits from the Westons factory across the road from the hospital. She even missed the hospital's seemingly endless corridors, which she had stopped noticing after a while.

On her most homesick days, however, Rita tried to remind herself that if she had not come to the Alice she would never have known that Australia could hold such difference, or such wildness. Sydney was vast but even it did not contain the landscape she saw around her in the centre. Nor was it as quiet, ever.

'Did ya like that?' Darryl called back to her once they were on the ground.

'Are you fishing for yet another compliment?' she said, laughing.

'Of course,' he said as he kept his gaze firmly ahead, his hands steady on the controls as he taxied along the runway. Darryl could act the larrikin but when it came to flying he was always professional. 'It's because my ego's bigger than Ayers bloody Rock.'

'If you expect me to disagree with you, you're going to be disappointed.'

Darryl grinned and brought the plane to a stop. Rita tucked her book into her handbag. She'd told Sybil that she'd read *The Thorn Birds* 'ages ago' but she'd been fibbing, because she was sure she'd be able to read it in time for this meeting of the reading group – the Fairvale Ladies Book Club, as Sybil had told her it was to be called; she'd even sent a rather quaint invitation in the post. Rita had had to quickly skim the last chapters of the book in the plane and try not to get motion-sick at the same time.

She could see why Sybil had chosen it as their first book: the setting wasn't strange, for one thing, so they wouldn't have to spend time talking about that. They could, instead, talk about the characters – not that Rita believed her opinions would be welcome. She thought Meggie, the heroine, was a bit of a sap for falling in love with Father Ralph – a man she clearly could never have. Rita far preferred the feisty Justine, Meggie's daughter, who, Rita believed, worked out that her mother was a sap before she was even out of nappies.

Book stashed, she quickly pulled out a mirror. She might be living in the bush these days but she still cared about her appearance, and she didn't mind if anyone thought her vain because of it. She knew someone would be waiting for her at the airstrip – Sybil always sent someone else if she couldn't get away herself – and she didn't want to look a mess.

Rita tilted the mirror so she could check her hair: dark brown, now streaked with grey, it was cut bluntly at her shoulder and she was still unsure about the fringe that one of the Alice hairdressers had talked her into. It might hide the lines that were starting to traverse her forehead but it wasn't practical for a hot climate. She was stuck with it, though, at least until she could grow it out.

She closed one eyelid then the other, checking to see if her brown eyeshadow was still in place. Brown make-up to match her brown eyes – she'd long ago decided that it was easiest to stick to one look if it suited you. She drew the line at brown lipstick, though; pink was just fine.

Close to the tarmac Rita could spy Ben Baxter leaning against his dirt-covered ute. She hadn't seen him for at least a couple of years; he was more handsome than she remembered but he was definitely Sybil's son. She'd know him anywhere.

'Auntie Rita,' he called as he loped towards her, meeting her halfway between the plane and the car, stretching out his hand towards her suitcase.

He pecked her on the cheek and she squinted up at him, remembering that she'd packed her sunglasses into the case.

'Ben,' she said. 'I've told you not to call me that. It makes me feel a hundred.'

'Aren't you?' he said, looking confused. Then she reached up to ruffle his hair and he laughed. 'I don't know what else to call you,' he went on. 'Round these parts "auntie" means you're someone special.'

'I know,' she said, pretending to sound resigned. 'I'll accept my fate.'

They walked a few steps in silence.

'It's good of you to come,' Rita said.

'Mum made me,' Ben said quickly, then they smiled at each other. He'd always liked to tease her, from the time he could talk. Their relationship was affectionate and easy, and Rita sometimes felt like Ben was the son she never had. She'd just never been able to feel that way about his older brother.

'How's married life?' Rita said as he opened the passenger door for her.

'Great,' Ben said, shutting her door before swinging her case into the tray of the ute.

As he hopped into the driver's seat, Rita looked over. 'That's all – great?'

'We're newlyweds, Auntie,' Ben said, turning the key in the ignition. 'We're still in the honeymoon period. It's all great.'

'Kate doesn't mind living on Fairvale?' Rita kept her voice light. Sybil had written letters to Rita saying she was worried that Kate would find it hard to adjust to Territory life.

Ben was concentrating on the road now, though, and she'd be talking to his left ear for the long drive out to the station.

'If she does, she hasn't said.' He wound down his window.

Have you asked her, Rita wanted to say, but it would sound like an interrogation, and she didn't want to spend the next two hours with a defensive Ben. She wanted to hear stories about what had been happening since she'd last visited. About the life she would never want to live but which interested her nonetheless. Then she'd tell him some horror stories about her work. He'd shake his head and say they were lucky they hadn't had such a terrible thing happen at Fairvale; Rita would murmur her assent while knowing that it was probably only a matter of time. She knew from things Sybil had told her – and what she'd seen in her short time working for the Flying Doctor – that everyone who lived on one of these stations would see their share of injury and maiming and accidental death; of babies born too soon and mothers too far away from hospital; of heart attacks in the home paddock and a doctor nowhere in sight. Ben hadn't been alive long enough to know that these things tended to go in cycles, as if nature sorted itself into a peculiar rhythm.

The two hours passed quickly as Rita looked out the window at the termite mounds and the short trees stretching across earth that looked the same to the untrained eye. Her time in Alice Springs had taught her that land which some people described as 'dead flat' was actually a vibrant canvas that could reward close attention.

Ben filled her in on the comings and goings of Fairvale: the scandal that erupted when one of the stockmen was discovered to be having an affair with the teacher – who had subsequently left – and the even bigger story that the stockman's wife was not only turning a blind eye but letting him stay in the marital bed while the teacher had left the next day; the safe arrival of babies in the camp of Aboriginal workers; and, finally, he reiterated what Sybil had already told Rita in a letter: his brother, Lachie, had not returned from Melbourne, where he'd moved a couple of months before to 'study'. Sybil had been sending letters and telephoning the number he had left whenever she was in Katherine – the Fairvale radiotelephone was not up to the task of interstate calls – but there had been no response. She knew that Sybil wasn't concerned – yet. Lachie had been a bad correspondent when he was at boarding school, and he was prone to fits of pique that meant he would refuse to talk to his parents or his brother for days on end if one of them disagreed with his opinion or otherwise said something he didn't like.

'You don't sound upset,' Rita observed.

'How could I be?' Ben said, and Rita thought she saw his jaw clench for the narrowest of seconds.

'What do you mean?'

'Rita,' Ben said, drawing out her name, taking his eyes from the road for a second so he could roll them at her. 'Everyone knows he's a pain in the arse.'

Rita started laughing. 'I thought it was just me.'

'Nah. He's a dickhead to everyone, I can assure you.' Ben's shoulders heaved as he let out a sigh. 'We're better off. So is he, probably.'

'So you're the heir apparent?'

'Some would say "hair apparent".' Ben ran a hand through his thick locks.

'Except you've got your mother's hair, not your father's.'

'Who says I can't be *her* hair apparent? Dad's going bald anyway.'

'And is he well, your father?' Rita had always been fond of Joe. He was a good husband to Sybil – all she could want for her friend.

'Yeah,' Ben said vaguely. 'He's got a few aches and pains. Getting old, that's all. He was a bit breathless last week.'

'Really?' Breathlessness wasn't something to be ignored.

'Yeah. He's all right. Nothing serious. Mum's keeping an eye on him.'

Ben pulled the car to a stop at the gate that marked the start of Fairvale's long driveway, turning to Rita as he opened his door.

'We're better off without Lachie,' he said darkly. 'You'll see what I mean.'

CHAPTER SIX

The room was as neat as Sybil could make it after decades of use and being crammed with the mementoes of several Baxter lives. The room – the house – had belonged to Joe's parents first, and even though they had long ago left the place and died since, Sybil sometimes felt that her mother-in-law, Una, was hovering in the corner, judging her every time she added a photograph frame or moved a lamp.

This house had been Una's domain for the first few years of Sybil's married life. Sybil had had to unlearn what her mother had taught her about housekeeping so she could do things Una's way. For those years Sybil had felt as if she was permanently on parade, never able to relax. The house hadn't been hers and, often, her marriage hadn't felt like it was either. Only her children had allowed her to feel as though she had something that belonged just to her. After Una had moved out she'd reverted to her own mother's methods, which were less militaristic but no less effective.

Sybil cast her eyes over the long, low coffee table, where the tea cups and saucers were ready to be filled from the pot that she would make as soon as Sallyanne and Della arrived.

She bent down to fluff the cushions on the old couch. That had been Una's, too. Sybil had wanted to buy a new one as soon as she moved out but Joe had resisted. The couch was his favourite place to sit in the house, one end of it dimpled where he had spent years reading at night. So she'd had the old piece of furniture upholstered anew, convinced that the pale mustard colour she chose would age well, except now even that was fading, as everything tended to here. The conditions were harsh on bodies and worse on furniture.

All cushions plumped, she stood and glanced over at the array of family photographs. One of Joe as a boy, grinning, holding a horse by its lead as a dog licked his feet. His parents, looking grim. Ben and Lachie as children, holding hands as they stood in the garden. It was probably the last time they'd been so affectionate. Even then, Lachie had never seemed comfortable on Fairvale, or in his family.

Sybil remembered something that happened when the boys were nine and ten years of age. One of the Aboriginal stockmen, Tommy, had watched them as they moved around the yard and had slowly nodded his head before turning to her, his eyes serious.

'That big boy, he doesn't belong here,' Tommy had said.

'What do you mean?' Sybil had asked, thinking that Lachie had done something naughty.

Tommy had shaken his head. 'He has never been here,' he said, and Sybil had grown more confused. 'He belongs somewhere else.'

Sybil had stared at him, not knowing what to say.

'That young fella.' Tommy had jerked his chin towards Ben, who was hanging off railings at the cattle yards, upside down and giggling. 'He has been here long time.'

Tommy had grinned. 'You'll see, missus,' he said, then he'd lifted his hat to her and ambled off towards the stables.

Sybil had told Joe about it, wanting him to say that it was nonsense – how could Tommy know anything about their children when he'd barely spoken to them? Instead Joe had looked thoughtful.

'Maybe he's right,' he'd said.

Tommy had been right; so had Joe. It was clear as soon as Lachie finished school that he didn't want to be on Fairvale, and certainly wasn't interested in spending the rest of his life working with and for his family. Still, none of them had been prepared for him not to be around. To leave them the way he had.

'Everything ready?'

Sybil jumped as Rita spoke.

'Where did you come from?' Sybil said.

Rita looked at her strangely. 'From my bedroom.' Her eyes flickered to the photograph that Sybil had been gazing at. 'Are you all right?'

'I was wondering,' Sybil said, her eyes once more going to the image of her sons, so young, so carefree.

'Yes?'

'Should I have noticed earlier?' She tried to smile, an attempt at making light of a situation that was becoming more serious. Sometimes she would be clutched by the thought that she might never hear from her son again. She'd tell herself she was being ridiculous, but there was a stab of dread in her that told her she wasn't. 'We tried to make them who they weren't. The exact opposites of their natures.'

'I don't think that's true, Syb.' Rita shrugged and raised her eyebrows. 'You were just trying to do what you thought was best.'

Rita's tone was reassuring, and Sybil loved her for it. But she had responsibility in all of this.

'I didn't pay attention,' Sybil said. 'There were signs everywhere and I didn't notice them. When the boys were boarding, Lachie never wanted to come home for holidays. But Ben—' She couldn't stop the smile as she remembered her second son arriving home after an absence. 'He'd barely wait until the truck stopped before he ran around to see who was home. Who was in the camp. Where his mates were. Where Joe was. Lachie . . .' She remembered his face like thunder, stomping away from the truck, leaving his bags there for someone else to carry inside. The little prince, just as they'd created him.

'It's done now, Syb,' Rita said. 'You're never going to change Lachie's mind about being here.'

Sybil nodded, even though she harboured a kernel of hope that Rita was wrong. 'I just don't think that not being here should mean that he doesn't talk to us at all,' she said.

Rita put her arm around Sybil's shoulders and squeezed. 'You've been a terrific mother,' she said. 'And he's a grown-up now. Let him make up his own mind about things. Isn't that what you taught him?'

Rita was right, of course. But Sybil wondered: would a good mother have a child who didn't want anything to do with her? Who had ceased contacting her and was not responding to her own attempts to contact him? These were questions that would drive her mad if she let them. So she wouldn't.

It was time, therefore, to stop wallowing in her regrets, to put the kettle on to boil and to hold the inaugural meeting of the Fairvale Ladies Book Club.

CHAPTER SEVEN

'Hello, Sallyanne,' Sybil said as she opened the door, standing back and gesturing for the young woman to enter the house.

'Hello, Sybil,' Sallyanne said, sounding breathless, offering her hand then quickly pulling it back. In the other hand she held a plate that contained what looked like an iced loaf cake.

Sallyanne was nervous, Sybil realised, so she kissed her on the cheek. She wanted Sallyanne to feel welcome. She had heard the town gossip that her husband could usually be found in local hotels at night, rather than home with his family, and she knew that Sallyanne didn't have a mother she could turn to. She could use a friend or two in her corner; it was the reason Sybil had been looking out for her that day at the CWA meeting.

'You weren't meant to bring anything,' Sybil said as Sallyanne gave her the plate, although she didn't want to sound too stern. Sallyanne had gone to some trouble and it was a country custom always to bring a plate to someone else's house. It was also a custom for the hostess to gently protest, and that way everyone felt like they'd been suitably grateful for attending and receiving.

'I like to bake,' Sallyanne said, her voice light – almost giddy, Sybil thought. 'It gives me a bit of time to myself.'

'I know what you mean. Please, sit down and – oh, that's who I was looking for. Sallyanne, I'd like you to meet my daughter-in-law, Kate, and my dear friend Rita, who's flown in from Alice Springs.'

As the women greeted each other, through the open door Sybil saw one of the Fairvale trucks coming up the drive. That would be Stan bringing Della from Ghost River. She'd been pleased he was available to drive her – his reliability as a stockman was matched by his skills behind the wheel, and she knew he'd get Della here safely. There was an hour of unpaved road between the two properties and it helped to have someone experienced to manage it.

She watched as the truck stopped and Della exited and started to walk towards the house. Sybil could have sworn Della was smiling, although her first encounter with the young woman had suggested that smiling wasn't something she did readily.

'Thank you, Stan!' Sybil called, and was rewarded with a wave as Stan headed for the shed by the cattle yards.

'Welcome, Della,' she said. Another kiss on the cheek, although she noticed that Della seemed reticent to receive it. She might be shy, or diffident – Sybil had thought that the first time she met her – but that wouldn't stop Sybil trying to make her feel welcome.

'Della, I'd like you to meet Kate, my daughter-in-law.' Sybil watched as the two women nodded at each other.

'I like your shirt,' said Kate.

'Oh – thanks,' Della said, her face colouring a little. She tugged at the shirt's hem. 'I brought it from home.'

'Where's home?' Kate gestured to the couch and the two women sat.

'Texas. Near San Antonio.' Della smiled vaguely. 'My folks have a ranch.'

'So . . . it's not that different to here, then?' Kate said. Sybil watched as she smiled sweetly. She didn't see Kate smile that often when she wasn't in Ben's company – perhaps Fairvale wasn't giving her enough reason to. In the bustle of running the place each day, she knew there were things she overlooked.

Della's smile broadened. 'It's different, all right,' she said.

'Yes, it is – isn't it?' Kate's eyes were bright.

'Where's home for you – England?'

Kate nodded. 'Yes. I grew up in the country – but not country like this.' She laughed, a little strangled sound, and Sybil wondered if she was nervous.

'There ain't no country like this,' Della said. 'It's a strange place.' Her smile was brief and mysterious.

'So you work at Ghost River Station, Della?' Rita jumped in.

'I do. I'm a stockman. Stock lady?' She frowned. 'I'm not really sure what I am.'

'How unusual.' Rita sat forward on the couch. 'I didn't think women did that kind of work.'

'I worked for my daddy at home. We had cattle.' Della glanced around quickly at the other women. 'But I don't want to talk about me. I'd rather hear about y'all.'

'Oh, Sybil's boring,' Rita said, wrinkling her nose. 'You don't want to hear about her.'

Sybil narrowed her eyes at her old friend and Rita winked back at her.

'Sallyanne and I met at the CWA,' Sybil said, and she noticed Della's confusion. 'The Country Women's Association. It's a . . . what should we call it, Sallyanne? A group? A gathering?'

Sallyanne's cheeks were red and she glanced down at her lap, where her hands were playing with her thin cotton skirt. She was pretty, Sybil thought, and younger looking than her years. In another place – in Sydney – Sybil might think that she was too young and pretty to stay with a husband who preferred getting drunk every night to going home to her, but there were fewer options for a woman in Katherine than there were in Sydney. Perhaps there weren't any options at all.

'I – I think it's a gathering,' Sallyanne said, looking up and around. 'I had fun. It was good to . . . to meet all those ladies.'

'And here you are,' Sybil said, beaming at her. 'I'm hoping to persuade Kate to join me at the next meeting.' She glanced at her daughter-in-law, who looked mildly surprised. 'I didn't bring her last time because I thought everyone else would be too old and talking about their grandchildren. But now that you've joined, Sallyanne, we won't have that problem.'

'Oh.' Sallyanne's cheeks were further inflamed and she glanced shyly at Kate. 'That would be lovely. To have you there.'

Kate smiled brightly at Sallyanne and Sybil felt something click inside her: she would like to think it was the sound of things shifting into place but perhaps it was merely relief. Everyone was smiling. No one looked as if they wanted to head for the door. This meeting might just go well.

'Now, before I go and make the tea, shall we say a few words about the book to get started?' Sybil said. 'As it's our first meeting I think it's all right if we plunge in. I suppose there are meant to be rules for this sort of thing but I don't know what they are.'

'Right,' Rita said, her voice loud and clear. 'Let's talk about that old bitch Mary Carson. And Meggie. I want to know if you think poor little Meggie should ever have fallen in love with that creepy priest.'

'He was not creepy!' Sallyanne said, looking aghast. 'He truly loved her!'

Rita patted Sallyanne's hand.

'All opinions are welcome here, Sal,' she said. 'May I call you Sal?'

Sybil slipped away to the kitchen. As she waited for the kettle to boil she could hear chattering and laughter coming down the hallway. She didn't remember ever having it in the house before – not like this. There hadn't been much laughter when her parents-in-law lived here, and when she and Joe entertained it was usually when another family came to stay. There was, no doubt, laughter at those times. But she'd never had a group of women here. It had never, actually, occurred to her before. Women in her position worked seven days a week to keep their households going and then when the work slowed, during the wet season, it was almost impossible to visit anyone else's property. On the stations most of the socialising happened with the other people who lived there. However, she'd become conscious that Kate might not be as content with that arrangement. She'd come from London and she had mentioned going to museums and galleries. Sybil couldn't give her these; talking about books was as close as she could manage, even if she wasn't sure if there was a proper way to do that.

Walking back into the sitting room with the teapot, Sybil felt her heart lift as she watched the four women's faces alight, their bodies perched on the edges of their seats, leaning forwards.

'Sallyanne has decided that Della is a real-life Meggie,' Rita declared as Sybil put the teapot down.

'Without all the drama,' Della added, laughing drily. 'I really don't want that kind of drama in my life.'

'And why are you Meggie?' Sybil said, sitting in her favourite chair.

'Because she rides with the men and works the land,' Sallyanne said, looking at Della with a certain wonder. 'It's so exciting.'

'Do you ride?' Kate asked.

'No!' Sallyanne laughed, then her smile faltered. Sybil wondered if Sallyanne ever got to be happy for long. 'Never been on a horse in my life. Do you?'

'Yes.' Kate's smile was accompanied by a dreamy look in her eyes. 'Every chance I get. I love it.'

'Perhaps you and Della should ride together one day,' Rita said, giving Sybil a pointed look. Sybil had briefed Rita on her motives for creating the book club, and finding Kate some new friends was chief amongst them.

Kate and Della glanced at each other shyly.

'Perhaps,' Kate said.

'That would be fine,' Della said.

'Good,' Sybil jumped in, then a thought occurred to her, prompted by the memory of Della's smile as she arrived at Fairvale. 'Stan can drive you to Ghost River, Kate. It's time you saw a bit more of the country around here.'

She watched as Della's eyes flickered ever so slightly and felt a flash of satisfaction that she had read the situation correctly: Stan had been the cause of Della's smile.

'Now,' Sybil said, 'let's talk about whether or not Meggie was a good mother to Justine.'

Sallyanne was the first to leap to Meggie's defence and Sybil was pleased to see how animated the younger woman became. She'd been right to ask Sallyanne today; her initial reason might have been prompted by pity but that evaporated now. The more Sallyanne spoke, the less shy she was. It was clear she was passionate and whimsical, and Sybil was glad she'd have the opportunity to see her more. Provided, of course, everyone wanted another meeting of the book club.

Actually, she wasn't going to give them a choice: she would convene another meeting before the wet season began in November and she would make sure Kate visited Della at Ghost River. She would give them that push, but she couldn't meddle further, even if it was her inclination to do so.

'Syb?'

Rita was staring at her.

'Yes?' she said.

'This is your party and you're off with the fairies,' Rita said. 'Come on – we're talking about Rock Hudson now.'

'Rock Hudson?'

'Sallyanne thinks he should play Father Ralph if there's a movie of *The Thorn Birds*.'

'Not now!' Sallyanne said, sounding quite indignant. '*Younger* Rock Hudson.'

'That's a better idea,' Sybil said. 'Now – who'd like some more tea?'

The pot was empty, and Sybil started back to the kitchen. On the way she saw Della and Kate exchange a conspiratorial smile and Sallyanne's hands flying as she and Rita started to discuss whether the young Paul Newman wouldn't be a better choice for Father Ralph.

Outside, she could hear Joe calling to someone about checking a saddle strap. He was probably heading her way; he said he'd stop in to see 'your book ladies'. She felt, as always, happy that she was going to see him.

CHAPTER EIGHT

It had been a long, interesting day at her first book club and Della let her head rest against the closed window as Stan drove her home from Fairvale. She'd spent several hours talking about books and Texas and the Flying Doctor Service, then Kate had given her a tour of Fairvale, which had fewer buildings and people than Ghost River but sometimes felt more grand. She'd learnt that the town of Adelaide River, about three hours up the Stuart Highway, had been a thriving camp during World War II. She'd learnt that Darwin had been bombed during that same war.

When Della had first arrived in the Northern Territory on her way to Ghost River, she'd had to stay two nights in Darwin before she could get on a bus to Katherine. She hadn't known anyone, and hadn't really been fussed about getting to know anyone either, although that hadn't stopped people chatting to her. As she ambled along its streets, trying to get a sense of the place, men and women both old and young would ask her where she was from; it happened so often that she knew she must look like a stranger with her Western shirts and her heavy cowboy boots. Not that any of the locals minded that she wasn't from those parts: they'd have all chatted to her for hours if she'd let them.

Some of them pulled up a chair during her meals to tell her their stories of Cyclone Tracy, which had ravaged Darwin less than three years before, on Christmas Day in 1974, and she could certainly see signs of the new city that was rising in its wake. It had a hodge-podge of architectural styles – or no style. One man told her that Darwin was a wasteland of 'ruined houses and ruined bloody lives'. Some people had lost everything in that cyclone. Some people were missing friends who were evacuated and never came back. But amongst it all there was a sense that things had to get done. The city had to get back on its feet.

Darwin was the strangest place she'd ever been, she'd thought at the time: a city starting over in the tropics, surrounded by a sea shining with the colour of opals she'd admired in a shop in Sydney, and no one with any sense would go into the water because of crocodiles and what were known as 'stingers' – marine creatures that could be too small to see and too deadly to survive.

Darwin also had the strangest sunsets. That first afternoon one of the staff at the small hotel where she was staying recommended she go to the Ski Club – the waterski club, she'd been told when she asked where the snow was – at Fannie Bay to see the sunset, and she watched as the sun blazed deep orange then suddenly disappeared, as if it had never been in the sky at all. This Territory sunset seemed just right for a place that was so hot and so wild.

Except now that she lived five hours south of Darwin Della had come to know that not all Territory sunsets were like that. Here the sunsets lingered, casting long shadows over the rolling red-dirt hills, turning them the colour of Hershey's bars. She was still getting used to how one place could look so different depending on where the sun was in the sky.

In that one book club meeting she had learnt more about her new home than she had in all the months she'd spent on Ghost River Station, and when Sybil had asked her if she'd like to join them next time, Della hadn't hesitated to say yes. As she pressed her forehead against the window of the truck she found herself thinking about the book they'd discussed, about the tragedy at the centre of the story: an impossible love. She'd never felt as strongly about anybody as Meggie and Father Ralph. She wondered what it would be like, to love someone so much and know you could never even see them often. It must be painful – or so she imagined. If it was even real. Sometimes Della thought love affairs in books could never match anything that happened in real life.

She thought about Sallyanne and how she hadn't mentioned her husband once. She wondered what Sallyanne's children looked like, and tried to guess at the real reason Rita had moved to Alice Springs, because she didn't believe that she'd just wanted to 'try something new'. She liked Kate, too – they were both adjusting to this big new place they lived in, plus Kate seemed kind. And while she could see that Sybil was very much used to efficiently taking care of everyone and everything, there was a softness there too.

Della was also thinking about Stan as he sat beside her, driving her home. Thinking about him and trying not to look at him too much, because he was another attachment she felt forming. An attraction. When he'd arrived that morning to pick her up he'd smiled at her and she'd felt ... something. A tickle in her chest. A tug in her belly. It was the same something she'd felt once before when a ranch hand from a neighbouring property used to visit her at home. She hadn't acted on it then and she didn't intend to act on it now, but she couldn't deny it, especially when the tickle and tug were in her again now as she looked out the window.

'Isn't it going to be too dark for you to drive home tonight?' Della said as she watched the light continue to fade. 'Sybil said these roads shouldn't be driven at night.'

'It's fine,' he said, his voice calm, reassuring. 'My brother works at Ghost River, so I'll see him. Share his swag.'

She turned to look at him, his dark skin almost disappearing into the gloom. But she could see his smile and hear his laugh; she could make out his long, elegant fingers as they curled around the steering wheel.

'I'm joking,' he said. 'We haven't shared a swag since we were little fellas.'

'Who's your brother?'

'Bob. Bob Ridge.'

Of course he was. She knew Bob had a brother at Fairvale and she couldn't believe it hadn't occurred to her to ask him who it was before Stan had picked her up that morning.

'I know Bob,' she said.

'I know you do.' She could hear him smiling more than see it. 'He's mentioned you.'

'Really?'

'Sure. There aren't many women who get work with the cattle, y'know? He thinks you're good. You work hard.'

'He's been kind to me.'

Stan laughed and Della loved the sound of it. 'Kind? Bob? He's tough as nails. He must really think you're good if he's being kind.'

Della had never seen Bob be tough with anyone. Maybe he was only tough on his brother – or had been when they were growing up. She thought she should drop the topic, though, since she and Stan were unlikely to agree on it.

'Stan. Bob. They're kinda plain names,' she said.

'Not pretty like Della, eh?'

He said it so gently that she felt the tug grow stronger.

'They're not our real names,' he said.

She frowned. 'They're not?'

'I could tell you our real names but you'd never remember them. No one round here can.'

He was looking forward, at the road, so she couldn't read his expression, didn't know if his last sentence was a comment or a criticism.

'They're your . . . tribal names?' She didn't want to say the wrong thing. She wanted to be respectful of the people who belonged to the land here, who belonged to whatever Ghost River and Fairvale and all the other pastoral holdings had been before they had marked out their boundaries. That was something else she'd learnt today: the Territory was divided into large holdings, some bigger than European countries and none of them owned by Aboriginal people.

'Yeah,' he said. 'But Bob calls me Stan and I call him Bob.' He grinned. 'It's just easier.'

She peered out the window again, watching the shapes of the plants and trees and palms in the fading light.

'I never know what these trees and things are called,' she said, and she wasn't sure if he'd heard her over the rumble of the truck and gravel churning underneath it.

'I'll teach you, Della,' he said, his voice light, her name sounding soft, precious.

'Will you?' she said, daring to look at him. He kept his eyes on the road.

'Sure,' he said. 'I could come visit you.'

Now he turned his head to her, but his irises were hidden by the impending night.

'Would that be all right, Della girl?'

She felt thrilled, and ridiculous because of it. She wasn't a teenager anymore – she was twenty-three years old, and handsome men shouldn't make her giddy. Yet he did.

'Yes,' she said. 'That would be all right.'

Della smiled to herself and felt her heart beating faster all the way home to Ghost River.

CHAPTER NINE

The sun had not long set as Rita and Sybil settled into the worn cane chairs that resided in one part of the verandah that wrapped itself three-quarters of the way around the Fairvale 'big house', as everyone called it. To the workers it was the big house because the boss – Joe – lived in it and because it was larger than the cottages and other buildings that made up the small village that was Fairvale Station.

When Rita had first visited Sybil here, early in her marriage, the big house had been the only decent, habitable place on the property. In the years since, Joe and Sybil had built proper accommodation for their workers and in the Aboriginal camp. Ruby the cook had her own domain, near the big house yet still separate from it.

Rita had once joked that Joe could launch an invasion from Fairvale, so organised and complete did it seem; Joe's response was that he thought Sybil would make a better general than he. Joe's regard for his wife – his deep love for her – had allayed Rita's early fears that Sybil had made a mistake, not necessarily in marrying Joe but in moving to the Northern Territory, so far from what she knew and where her life had been. Sybil had had her reasons, though.

A horse whinnied somewhere in the dark and Sybil turned her head towards it. Rita followed her gaze, although she couldn't see anything of great interest. In the light of the half-moon she could make out cattle yards and, beyond them, stands of trees by the creek that would probably dry up before too long now that rain wouldn't fall for another few months.

The yards had been alive with workers just a few hours earlier – Sybil had long ago explained that once the dry season arrived they had to work hard to make the most of it, knowing that not much could be done during the wet. When the rains came some of the stockmen would go home – some as far away as Queensland and New South Wales – and return in the dry. Then they'd all go hell for leather again until the seasons changed and the population ebbed.

Now the yards were empty and the workers had all retired to their quarters; so had Joe, Ben and Kate, saying they'd leave Rita and Sybil alone to spend some time together.

Since she'd arrived two days ago Rita had barely had Sybil to herself. That first night everyone had been at dinner, Ben holding court as he told stories about feral cattle and spooked horses, then yesterday, after Sallyanne and Della had left, Joe decided to join them to discuss his take on *The Thorn Birds*. He had borrowed Sybil's copy without her knowledge, and had them laughing raucously at his commentary on how Mary Carson's property, Drogheda, should really have been run. 'No priests' was his first line of advice.

'They may know about keeping flocks obedient,' he'd said, 'but that's no use with a mob of cattle that are trying to outrun a branding iron.'

They'd all tumbled into bed late – so late that when Joe and Ben woke before dawn they could be heard uncharacteristically stomping around the house, as if in protest that the women could lie in, even if they weren't asleep.

The day had passed in its usual Fairvale flurry – Kate in the office keeping the accounts up to date, Sybil in what seemed to be ten places at once – as Rita observed it all in motion, grateful to not be needed for anything for once. When she was at work she could be needed for the worst reasons – for a sick child, a dying mother, a man stricken by snakebite. It was a relief to know that other people had those responsibilities here. As the boss's wife Sybil had to be nurse and housekeeper and hotel keeper – it was rare for there to be no visitors to Fairvale, whether it was stock inspectors, vets, government officials or friends, like her, from other parts of Australia. Sybil was on a constant cycle of changing and washing sheets, laying out towels and updating Ruby on who was coming and going, and when. Just watching her was enough to exhaust Rita.

At least Sybil didn't have to cook all the meals – although she would always cook on Ruby's days off. Tonight, however, Ruby was on duty and Sybil could relax for a bit. And now that dinner was over, Rita and Sybil could take an hour or so to talk in the way they so rarely did. Since Sybil's children were little, they'd had only an hour here and there whenever Rita was able to visit. Phone calls were measured in increments of three minutes and at the twelve-minute mark the operator would always come on the line to ask if the call was being extended. Rita was sure that the operators listened to the whole conversation, so she was loath to say anything too revealing.

'So how's the Alice?' Sybil said.

'Dry,' Rita said, chuckling. 'I still get surprised by how much.'

'You did move to the desert,' Sybil said, stifling a yawn. 'Mind you, it took me at least a year to get used to the weather here. It's not like Sydney.'

'It certainly is not.' Rita thought for a few moments. 'What are you going to do about Lachie? Or are you going to keep telling yourself that you can cope if he never comes back?'

Soon it would be too dark for Rita to see Sybil's face, but she could still detect the twist of anguish that vanished almost as quickly as it arrived. Sybil was an emotional person: Rita had always known this even if Sybil persisted in believing that she was in control of herself at all times. All she managed to control was the speed at which she covered her emotions. It was usually fast enough to escape detection by most other people, but not by Rita, who knew her far too well.

'Come on, Syb – don't you dare tell me a tall one,' Rita said.

Sybil sniffed. 'A fib isn't a lie.'

Rita laughed. 'I think it is.'

'Barney, what are you doing?' Sybil said.

Rita looked down to see Sybil's dog plonking himself onto his mistress's feet. He was a slightly fat blue heeler with a large black patch around one eye and a nose that was always running. Since Rita had arrived she'd noticed that he barely left Sybil alone, even though he had been out on musters for years and had only recently given up working.

'Obviously he likes being a house dog. Can't imagine why when he has such a taxing lifestyle,' Rita said as she heard the sound of ice moving in a glass – Sybil taking a sip of whisky. Rita drank some of her own.

'He should like it – he was a lousy cattle dog.' Sybil bent down and scratched him between the ears before sitting up again. 'He's been a good companion for me,' she said, her voice quavering just a little.

'Syb, you have other good companions here,' Rita said gently. She was angry at Lachie for hurting his mother but that didn't mean she should let Sybil hear it in her voice. 'And

I may not live close by but you know that I'll come running if you need me.'

Sybil sighed. 'I do,' she said, and again Rita heard the ice in her friend's glass.

'So . . .' Rita swallowed. 'We were talking about Lachie.' She didn't want to make Sybil upset but she couldn't ignore the subject when it would have to be on Sybil's mind. Sybil loved her sons far too much not to worry about them.

'Were we?'

Rita cleared her throat.

'All right.' Sybil paused. 'I don't know what to do,' she said, her voice quavering just a little. 'We've called everyone we know. They haven't seen him. I want Joe to jump on a plane to find him but I don't know where he should go.'

'Lachie would never go to friends of yours,' Rita said.

'What? Why not?'

'Syb, that boy has always fought against everything you've ever given him or offered him or made available to him. You know I love him because he's your son, but he's contrary. Always has been.'

Rita drank again, surprised at her own audacity, even if she'd rather have called him something a little worse than *contrary*. She'd thought these things about Lachlan before, of course – every time she saw him be mean to his mother, or Sybil told her about something diabolical he'd done.

'I know,' Sybil said softly, and Rita heard the catch in her voice.

'You know?'

A creak in Sybil's chair made Rita turn to look at her: she could see lines around her friend's eyes. Maybe the gloom was making them appear more deeply etched than usual.

'He's never belonged to us,' Sybil said. 'No matter what I tried. No matter how much he meant to me.'

Another creak, and Sybil's head turned away.

'I failed,' she said.

'Now you're being ridiculous,' Rita said. 'You and I have been around enough families to know that parents can do their very best to steer a child in the right direction and they can still take a wrong one. Remember that kid we treated whose parents had locked up his bicycle and he not only found some wire cutters to break it loose but took off in the middle of the night and wound up fracturing his femur in that ditch?'

'Is that really the same thing?' Sybil said, starting to laugh.

'Maybe not,' Rita conceded, pleased she'd at least shifted Sybil's mood. 'But sometimes it's hard to come up with a good example on short notice.'

Sybil inhaled loudly. 'Maybe it's not such a bad example after all. Lachie's been trying to cut himself loose forever. That doesn't mean I want to give up on him.'

'And how's Ben going with his new responsibilities? Those shoulders look broad enough to cope.'

'We're lucky to have Ben,' Sybil said quickly.

'And Kate?'

Silence.

'Oh yes,' Sybil said, almost whispering. 'She and I were a bit scratchy with each other at first, but it's working out now.'

Rita decided to change the subject – talking about Lachie was making them both maudlin. 'I've been reading Ruth Park again.'

'Which one?'

'*Harp in the South. Poor Man's Orange.*'

'A little light entertainment.'

Rita smiled wryly. 'Maybe our foreigners would like to read something of hers – it could be an education for them.'

'"Our foreigners"?' Sybil said, her laugh sounding weak. 'That's not a bad idea. But perhaps we should ease them in slowly. They've just had *The Thorn Birds*, after all.'

'So what do you have lined up?'

Sybil pressed her lips together and half closed her eyes.

'Nothing yet. I might ask Kate if she'd like to suggest something.'

'Good idea – the younger ones might have some interesting suggestions.'

'You're hardly old enough to talk about younger ones.'

Rita's smile was tight. 'I am.' She held up a hand. 'Don't start.'

'You have no idea what I was going to say,' Sybil said. Rita knew that look on her friend's face: Sybil was pretending to be offended.

'You were going to say that I'm not over the hill. As you've been saying to me for at least ten years now.'

'Because it's true.'

'I'm not concerned that I'm not married,' Rita said, the line well rehearsed.

'Who said anything about marriage? I keep hoping you'll take a lover and then tell me stories about him.'

Rita hooted. 'I am not likely to meet anyone in Alice Springs. The only single man in town is eighty-two and I've heard he has a different girlfriend for every night of the week.'

Sybil made a noise of exasperation. 'You and your exaggerating,' she said, then she folded her hands in her lap. 'We should be able to get in another meeting before the wet starts. How's September looking for you?'

'I'll ask my patients not to break any bones for a while, let me have a day off.'

'I think we'll do them twice a year,' Sybil said. 'May and September. Or October. Depending on when people are available. And I know it's the end of June now but I only had the idea when the wet was over, so I was a bit late starting.'

'So we'll meet in the dry season only?'

'It's easier for everyone to get around. I can't ask people to come here in the wet.' Sybil gestured in the direction of the creek. 'They'd drown trying to get in.'

'So we're the "dry season readers", then, are we?'

'We're the Fairvale Ladies Book Club,' Sybil said with what sounded like pride. 'And you can read whenever you like. But we'll meet in the dry. Use the wet to find good books.'

'That sounds like a solid plan.' Rita sighed contentedly.

A dog barked a few metres away, then another, causing Barney to lift his head momentarily. The sounds of Fairvale at night were not so different to those of Alice Springs. Rita turned to smile at Sybil but her face was now completely consumed by the dark.

For more than thirty years they'd known each other now, and they had both experienced sorrow and happiness in that time. They were both old enough – had lived enough – to be of the belief that no one else could alleviate your pain or give you joy. You had to do it for yourself, and if you were lucky there was someone to stand witness.

Rita and Sybil had been each other's witnesses all that time. She would stand with Sybil as the changes in her life continued to settle. Sybil would stand with her when the next good or bad thing arose, as it would. As it must. That was life, and nowhere was it more vivid – more extreme, she believed – than in this Northern Territory.

For now, she would cherish these few minutes to sit with her friend and know that she would see her again soon. It was a luxury she hadn't had for too many years.

CHAPTER TEN

A car drove past and honked. Sallyanne turned her head, but the honk didn't seem to be meant for her. She looked around for Tim and Billy, who were helping her carry the shopping to the car while Mick stayed home with Gretel. Hopefully not letting Gretel get into mischief; she was never entirely sure he paid attention. Not that she could be judgemental about that: she'd been thinking about romance novels instead of keeping an eye on her sons. Luckily, they were only a few steps behind her, busy whacking each other's arms and giggling each time someone yelled 'Ow!'

'Kids, stop that!' Sallyanne said wearily. They weren't really hurting each other but she knew it wasn't good to let them get away with hitting.

'Could you help me put these bags in the car?' she said, pushing the trolley towards the Kingswood.

At least it wasn't humid. Sallyanne always preferred the dry season. She had never liked humidity, even when she was a child. It made her feel as if the world was a prison and she wanted to break out of it; when she was young, before she learnt that young ladies should control their tempers, that feeling of being trapped inside the weather would make her cranky. Her mother would always laugh at her tantrums and say that she understood, because the humidity made her want to whack someone over the head. But her father would say that if she didn't learn to behave, no man would ever want her.

It hadn't been a message she'd understood at eight or nine or even twelve years of age. By her teenage years, though, she was practising counting to ten whenever she felt upset. She was rewarded with the attention of local boys who all mentioned her blonde hair and blue eyes, even though she knew that what they really liked was her figure. The curves that Sallyanne had cursed as soon as they appeared – because they made her 'fat', as one unkind skinny girl at school pointed out – were the most noticeable thing about her.

Mick had been one of those boys, although not one of the first. They were at school together and he had seemed shy, although she would learn later that he was, instead, almost too sure of himself. He let the other young men wear out their platitudes and fail to capture her attention, then he came in and told her that he liked her compositions in English class and needed her help understanding how World War I started.

She was so taken aback that he seemed to like her for something other than her looks that she helped him learn about the Great War. He was funny – a larrikin, her father would have called him if he'd met him at the time, which he didn't, because Sallyanne didn't tell her parents that she had a boyfriend.

She'd had plans for her life; for all the time she and Mick spent together, she wanted to do some things on her own. She told him that when school ended she wanted to move away for a while – to a city, maybe Melbourne, maybe Sydney – and see a bit more of Australia, if not the world. Then her mother had died when she was sixteen and Sallyanne's determination to leave Katherine had wavered. She wasn't close to her father but she didn't want to abandon him altogether. And Mick had seemed like something reliable in her life, something familiar, at a time when she'd needed that. She wasn't sure if she loved him but he seemed to love her – or care for her, at least.

After school he'd taken up an apprenticeship with a local plumber; Sallyanne had gone to work in the pub that her father had owned for twenty years. Initially he'd said it wasn't fitting for a 'young lady' to work in a hotel, but jobs for school leavers weren't abundant in Katherine and she didn't want to leave town and move to a cattle station to work, which was the only other option in these parts. She didn't ride, nor was she interested in cattle, so a station job would mean being someone's cook or cleaner. There was no question of her going to university – there wasn't one in the Northern Territory, and she had no burning desire to study elsewhere. There was no degree for what she wanted.

So the pub it had been, and she hadn't minded the work. She chatted to the customers and heard all sorts of stories. She read her romance novels – her Georgette Heyers with their enthralling tales of Regency life – when she wasn't seeing Mick, and she kept up with her friends, who were all starting to get engaged. Their lives seemed like something out of one of her books: their boyfriends all got down on one knee and proposed, and the girls all had shiny rings that probably weren't that expensive but looked impressive. Sallyanne hadn't been desperate for Mick to do the same but she did wonder why he hadn't. Wasn't that how their lives were meant to turn out?

Late one afternoon Mick had come in with one of his mates from work.

'Sal!' he'd yelled from across the bar and she was surprised to find that she felt wary at the sound of his voice. Usually he went to another pub to drink at the end of the day because she'd told him she couldn't talk to him while she was working.

She'd walked over to where he was leaning on a high bar table, his eyes glassy. So he'd been to the other pub already – she could see it and smell it.

'Hello,' she'd said, smiling tightly.

'This is Damo.' He'd jerked a thumb towards a young man who looked like he'd been dragged backwards through a pipe, because he probably had.

'Hello Damo,' she'd said, feeling shy. When she was behind the bar Sallyanne was never shy – she liked the way the job almost gave her permission to be someone else. But out here on the floor, meeting a friend of Mick's, she was just her.

Damo sniggered and she flinched.

'Yer not wrong, Micko,' Damo said, elbowing Mick in the ribs. 'She's a stunner. What are you doin' lettin' her work here?'

What she should have said was that he didn't make decisions for her. She didn't, though. Nice girls didn't make retorts. She'd learnt that by watching the women she grew up around, who always stayed quiet when their husbands made remarks about how they were too fat, or their cooking wasn't what it used to be, or they'd lost their looks and their husbands might trade them in for a new model.

'She won't be here forever,' Mick had said, giving her a look she couldn't quite read. 'Will you, sweetie?'

She hated being called 'sweetie' and he knew it, not that it stopped him. She wanted to be called 'darling' like the women in her books were. Someone's *sweetie* was a whim, a fling, a mere folly; to be a *darling* meant something. A darling was important.

'Oh, I don't know,' she said. 'Can I get you two a beer?'

He'd grabbed her wrist then and she'd pulled back involuntarily, shocked that he would do something like that. He could be belligerent when he was drunk but he'd never put a hand on her before.

Don't say anything, she could almost hear her mother telling her. *Don't embarrass him.*

'Mick,' she said quietly, because he was hurting her and she didn't know how else to say it.

'You won't be here forever,' he said, squeezing her once, hard, before he let her go, 'because you're gonna marry me.' He looked triumphant. 'Then you won't have to work.'

'That's the way, mate,' called a voice that Sallyanne knew belonged to George, one of the regular drinkers. 'Make an honest woman out of her.'

Sallyanne turned to see George raising his half-empty glass and all the things she wanted to say to him, too, fizzled inside her. *I'm not a* dishonest *woman*. But there was no one who cared to hear it, and alive in her was something she wanted yet feared at the same time: the relief of not having to work every day, the release of having someone to take care of her for a while. Her mother hadn't worked outside of home, and nor had her mother's friends. Not all of them had husbands who were mean, so maybe the trade-off wasn't too bad.

Eventually Mick proposed properly – on both knees and with his great-grandmother's ring – and they were married six months later, when she was twenty-three, waiting for the dry season so their wedding day wasn't a sodden mess. Mick then talked about babies incessantly – his mother wanted grandchildren, he'd say, as if that was meant to be motivation for his wife. Sallyanne wanted them too, although her friends who'd already had their first babies had told her terrible stories about how they'd been torn during the births, or said that the nurses weren't very sympathetic. She didn't know anything about how to stop herself getting pregnant, though, nor was she going to ask her doctor – he'd told her when she married that it was her job to have babies as quickly and often as possible. A year after the wedding she had given birth to Tim. Now he was ten and Billy was eight. At three years of age Gretel was the 'surprise' third child she hadn't wanted to have but now couldn't imagine living without.

'Mu-um, whyyy do we have to help?'

'Tim, stop whingeing.'

Sallyanne opened the boot.

'Here you go,' she said, gesturing to the bags. 'Help me lift them in.'

'Whyyy?'

Sallyanne sighed. 'To build strong muscles. Come on, Billy, you help too.'

Her middle child poked out his tongue at her but Sallyanne felt too weary to reprimand him. As Tim and Billy shoved the bags into the boot, she plucked their already melting ice-creams from one bag and handed them out.

'Are we going to the springs now, Mum?' Tim said as he ripped the paper off his pine-lime Splice.

She'd promised them a dip in the hot springs, which weren't all that hot on a day like today; instead they were mildly refreshing, but the kids liked the bubbles that fizzed against their skin in one section of the springs, and they liked to pretend that they were looking for crocodiles in the pristine waters of the little channels that ran between ancient trees. There might be crocodiles in those waters – there were crocodiles all around these parts – but Sallyanne had learnt that it didn't pay to worry about them too much. If a person worried about all the things that could maim or kill her in this country, she'd never get out of bed in the morning.

Sallyanne closed the boot. 'Sure,' she said. 'Let's just drop the shopping home first.'

'Mu-um!'

'Billy, get in the car!'

The boys resumed their hitting and giggling after they'd buckled themselves into the back seats. It wouldn't last for long; their house was only a three-minute drive away – too far to carry all that shopping, though, if they'd gone on foot. Heaven knew that it would be easier to do the whole thing without them. Except she liked having them along, even if they could be a handful.

As she pulled the Kingswood into the driveway Sallyanne hoped Mick would emerge from the house to help her take the bags in; the door stayed shut, and she could hear Gretel crying. She decided the shopping could wait.

Leaving the boys to get themselves out, she yanked open the front door and found her daughter sitting on the kitchen floor, one of her books open in front of her, toys scattered around, her face red, tears on her cheeks and gunk running from her nose.

'Darling,' she said, bending down to scoop her up and kissing her three times on the cheek. 'Where's Daddy?'

Gretel sniffed and hiccuped in reply.

Mick wasn't in the living room adjacent to the kitchen.

'Mick!' she called and was met with silence.

'Mick!'

She peered into the bathroom and their bedroom but he wasn't there. She pushed open the back screen door, Gretel's head now on her shoulder, and saw him: slumped in a chair, his head back and his mouth open, a can of beer on the grass beside him.

She should have known. He'd begged her to let him look after Gretel while she was at the shops. He had promised her – sworn to her – that he wouldn't take his eyes off her. Not like last time, he said. He'd do better. Last time their daughter had fallen over on the driveway and hit her head, and he hadn't thought to take her to the doctor or the hospital despite the blood that was running down her face. He'd been drunk then – so drunk that she knew he must have started drinking even before she'd left the house, because she was only gone for half an hour. She'd told him that she'd put up with his drinking when it was just her it affected, but she wasn't going to tolerate it now that he was hurting the kids.

He'd begged for another chance. Now here he was, passed out.

Sallyanne let her mind dart to the place it visited whenever he was like this. It was her refuge, even if it wasn't real and she knew she wasn't likely to make it real. She always calculated how long it would take to pack up the kids and leave him altogether. Leave the house, leave Katherine. Go to Darwin, where thousands of people were making their lives anew just as the city was being rebuilt. She could disappear there. Mick would probably be too lazy to look for her. Or maybe he wouldn't be – maybe he'd pursue her with everything he had, knowing he earned the money and she didn't, so he could afford a lawyer and she couldn't.

That was what kept her here – the uncertainty of not knowing what he'd do. Once Sallyanne thought she'd known him and he'd changed. After he started drinking ten tinnies a day he'd changed again. In fact, all she could rely on was the fact that he'd change. So next he might change into the responsible father who wanted to punish his runaway wife. And he'd win. He'd defeat her. The law was not on her side. She knew that from stories she'd heard – of women in town who'd tried to leave and been told they could go but they'd never see their children again. She'd heard all about this new Family Court but she didn't believe it was going to help her. Not right now.

'What's Dad doing?' Billy said, and Sallyanne looked down at him.

'Having a sleep,' Sallyanne said.

'Can he come to the hot springs?' said Tim, looking excited.

'No, love.' Sallyanne shifted Gretel to the other hip. 'Let's leave him to sleep. Come on – change into your cossie and we'll go.'

'Yeah! Hot springs!' Tim said as he raced to the bedroom he shared with his brother and Gretel grew heavier in her arms.

She couldn't help but smile when her children were like this. Their lives were simple, composed of things to do and places to go. She wanted to keep them like that for as long as possible.

'Have you got your towel, Billy?' she called to her second son as he skipped past her, heading for the car.

'Yeah, Mum!' he yelled, although she couldn't see it in his hand.

She should really go into his room and find it. Except she might not stop at the towel. She might pick up his clothes, and Tim's, and throw them in a bag. She might take one dress for Gretel and one for herself. She might get in that car and drive as far away as she could, and leave Mick where he was. Leave him to wake up and wonder where they'd gone.

If only she were brave enough to do it.

CHAPTER ELEVEN

There was flour all over her jeans, and at that point Kate realised she should have accepted Ruby's offer of an apron. She had to wear these jeans until wash day, and now she was going to look grubby.

When Sybil had suggested that Kate might like to spend some time in the station kitchen with Ruby, learning how to bake and perhaps cook some of the meals, Kate had been elated: finally, she would have a substantial job that could contribute to life on Fairvale. The station kitchen wasn't modern but with its two large ovens and long benches it could provide meals for everyone on Fairvale. The kitchen in the big house was Sybil's; here, with Ruby, Kate felt like she could have something of her own.

During the handful of years she was living and working in London she'd never cooked much, despite her mother's insistence that she would have trouble finding a husband if she didn't know how to cook for him. Kate knew her mother meant well, but she was far too busy enjoying her life to worry about that – and, as it turned out, it hadn't mattered. Out of all the men Kate had met in her relatively young life, Ben was the one with the least fixed ideas about what men and women should do and how they should behave. Ben took everyone as he found them and judged no one.

However, that didn't mean that Kate had no wish to learn a skill – especially one that would help her feed the station for years to come. She just wasn't particularly successful at it today: Ruby was teaching her how to make bread and Kate had managed to spread flour on the floor, across the entirety of the huge work bench and all over herself.

'Look at you!' Ruby said as she rubbed her hands on her apron. 'White Christmas!' She cackled and Kate tried not to blush.

'I'm sorry,' Kate muttered, looking around for a cloth to wipe up the mess.

'Don't be sorry, love,' Ruby said. 'Happens to everyone first time. You just have to get used to how the flour moves when you pour the water in. Here. Watch.'

Ruby walked to her work space – thankfully not so close to Kate's that Kate had ruined it – and shaped the flour into a well, keeping it away from the edge of the bench. As she poured water in slowly she used her other hand to work the flour into the middle of the well, pushing away from the edge. It didn't take long for her to create a ball of dough that she started to knead vigorously.

'Just takes practice,' Ruby said, keeping her eyes on the dough. 'You want to try again?'

Kate hesitated.

'You can't be scared of bread, love!' Ruby said, laughing. Kate loved that laugh: it started low and ended high, and Ruby's whole body shook with it.

'Plus I'm an old girl,' Ruby continued. 'I can't keep making bread for the rest of my life. Someone has to take over.' She grinned slyly in Kate's direction.

'You don't have a daughter who wants to do it?'

Ruby shook her head.

'She's gone to her husband. Over on Ghost River Station.'

So Della must know her, Kate thought. And maybe Stan too – Ben had told her that Stan's brother worked there.

'What's her name?'

'Rose.' In Ruby's smile there was a hint of sadness. 'My Rosie girl.'

'So you are Ruby and Rose?' Kate loved the poetry of it but she didn't want to make a fuss.

'We sure are. Pink twins!' Ruby cackled again and Kate's face split in a grin.

'Does Rose bake?'

'No, missus – she says that's my job. But her husband might make her start. He says she needs to learn how to cook like me!'

Kate smiled as she attempted to shape the flour once more.

'Would you mind calling me Kate?' she said, knowing it was an audacious request. All the Aboriginal workers called Sybil 'missus' and Joe 'mister'. No doubt there was a reason for it but Kate was uncomfortable being the second 'missus'. It made her feel old, for one thing.

She glanced at Ruby, who looked to be considering her request.

'How about Katie?' Ruby said. 'Kate is a grown-up lady's name.'

Kate snorted, wondering what her mother would think if she heard that. 'Sure.'

Ruby turned completely towards Kate.

'No babies for you, Katie?' she said.

Kate felt pain – simple and sharp. And so at odds with the kindness she saw in Ruby's face. She knew that the older woman didn't mean to hurt her.

'Not – not yet,' Kate managed to say, trying not to show that pain on her face.

'But you want them?' Ruby looked serious now.

'Of course,' Kate said quickly. 'It just . . . hasn't happened yet.'

Ruby put a hand on her arm. 'You love Mister Ben?'

'Yes.' She nodded, and smiled as she thought of her husband's cheeky grin. Oh yes, she loved him.

'And he loves you.' It wasn't a question. 'Then everything gonna be all right.' Ruby grinned. 'You just believe, Katie girl. Everything be all right.'

Kate didn't know if it was a prediction or a benediction. Ruby was the first person who had directly asked her about babies. Sybil and Joe no doubt thought about asking but never would – they'd feel as if they were intruding on their son's business. But in not being asked, Kate had felt as though her desire to have a child, her sadness that it hadn't happened yet, weren't real. She had felt alone, even when Ben was with her.

Standing with Ruby's hand on her arm, with Ruby's big, loving smile directed at her, Kate had the strangest sensation of feeling hollow, as if everything she was had been scooped out and all that was left was vulnerability. Except she didn't feel weak, as she'd always thought a vulnerable person must be. She felt hopeful – as if the removal of everything else had cleared a path for her.

'Thank you,' she said, and as she smiled she felt clearer and happier than she had for a while. 'Now – can you please watch me while I do this?' She pointed a flour-covered finger at her newly created well. 'I want to get it right.'

Ruby had a gleam in her eye as she stood, hands playing with her apron, watching as Kate picked up a jug of tepid water, already frothing with yeast and sugar.

'Slowly,' Ruby said, nodding her head like a metronome set to *largo*.

Taking a deep breath, Kate started to pour. She risked a glance at Ruby and that was enough to make some of the liquid start to run over the edge of the bench.

'Oh no!' she cried, putting the jug down and frantically trying to scoop everything together.

Ruby started her cackle again. 'Time for the next lesson,' she said. 'How to fix mistakes.'

Kate's first reaction was to feel embarrassed. Then she started laughing. If Ruby didn't mind about some spilled flour and water, she wasn't going to either.

After another attempt, and a successfully made ball of dough at the end of it, Kate realised she'd had more fun in the kitchen than anything else she'd done in a long while. And if she could actually learn enough to be of some use . . . she wanted that, more than anything. At the end of each day she wanted to feel within herself that she was achieving things.

CHAPTER TWELVE

Rita took a look around the sad-looking wheat farm that Darryl had flown her to, a few hundred kilometres south of Alice Springs, in South Australia. The Royal Flying Doctor Service for the Northern Territory also worked into the neighbouring state, so the little plane could take them between extremes: from arid country in the Territory to agricultural land in the south.

Growing up in Sydney, Rita hadn't really thought about the rest of Australia and had certainly never contemplated that it would be so diverse. She often marvelled that one continent could hold so much difference, and she was lucky to have the best bird's-eye view out the window of the plane. When her time in the Alice was done – not that she had plans to leave soon, but she couldn't, wouldn't, stay forever – the memories of the land below her were what she would cherish most. She could go back to a small house or an apartment in Sydney, stick closely to the places she knew and roads travelled hundreds of times before, yet the vastness of the Australian interior would live in her, too.

The wheat farm was home to a boy named Albert who had fallen off his horse and appeared to have broken his radius. Normally Rita would assist a doctor as he took care of the matter but the last doctor had left in a hurry, offered a more lucrative position in Adelaide that apparently had to be commenced straightaway. So Rita was making all the decisions and doing all the treatments alone. She was capable, and competent; she also knew that if the matter was truly serious the patient would go straight to a hospital. That didn't mean she didn't worry each time, though; she wanted to do everything correctly.

Luckily, this particular case was, medically speaking, straightforward. Rita chatted to Albie – as he was known, his mother said – to distract him as she palpated his forearm and tried to ascertain the severity of the injury. The child's parents stood by, the mother with her mouth twisting and her face pale, the father looking like he'd rather take a gun to Rita than let her touch his son – except he couldn't help Albie, so he had no choice but to watch.

'That hurts there, does it?' Rita said gently as she put a fingertip near Albie's elbow. He bit his lip and nodded.

'Don't be a sook, son,' his father barked and the boy flinched.

Rita didn't look at the man; he wasn't the first tough father she'd encountered and her tactic was always the same: don't acknowledge their behaviour. Her theory was that these men wanted to be recognised as tough – by their wives, children and anyone else they met. By not giving this man the acknowledgement he wanted, Rita knew, she was denying him the power he desperately needed. He had to be desperate for it, otherwise he wouldn't behave so badly – that was another theory she'd developed over years of seeing every kind of person under the sun pass through the hospitals she had worked in.

Rita saw Albie's mother look nervously at her husband, who was now grinding his jaw as he glared at Rita. She noticed that there was a faint shadow underneath one of the woman's eyes and to the side – the remnants of a black eye, perhaps. Maybe that's why Albie was being stoic: he'd been through worse than a broken bone.

'I'm going to put Albie in a sling,' Rita said, directing her remarks to the boy's mother. 'But he really needs to get to a hospital or a clinic so the bone can be set in a cast. Is there somewhere fairly close you could drive him?'

'Can't do it,' his father said.

'Why not?' Rita said as Albie's mother winced.

'Too much work here,' came the gruff response. 'No one can get away.'

'Couldn't your wife—'

'No.' He stepped closer to Rita and for a second she wondered if he was going to hit her. But she couldn't let him see hesitation in her. She glanced over to where Darryl was standing next to the plane, his feet planted, his arms folded, chin up and fairly substantial belly thrust forwards. He nodded at her once.

'Right.' Rita stood up and smiled down at Albie. 'Perhaps you'd like to come in the plane with us, then?'

'No,' his father said, almost snarling, and Rita knew that was the end of it. The child was going to have a wonky arm for the rest of his life because his father didn't want to let his son or his wife out of his sight.

Rita looked at Albie's mother. The woman wouldn't lift her head, wouldn't look her in the eye.

'If you won't take Albie to a doctor for follow-up care, I'll need to come back and check on him,' she said briskly. 'And in the meantime he needs to keep his arm in that sling, and as still as possible.'

'Are you done?' the father said.

Rita didn't want to leave Albie in this situation – she wanted to make sure he was properly looked after – but she would leave here with Darryl, leave this boy and his mother behind to deal with the brute they already dealt with every day. As she'd done so often in the past, she'd have to put Albie out of her mind and tell herself that he would be all right. She couldn't do her job otherwise. If she worried about all the patients she'd known, her brain would explode and her heart would collapse. She'd let him go, as she'd done with others.

'Yes, I'm done,' she said. 'Goodbye, Albie. I'll see you again soon.'

'No, you won't,' said his father.

'Yes, I will,' Rita said, staring at the man. 'We have a duty of care to your son and we'll fulfil it. And if you don't allow us to, I'll need to have a word to the appropriate authorities.'

The man's chin jutted forwards but he didn't reply. Rita took the small victory and picked up her medical bag, looking towards Darryl once again. He gave her a thumbs-up. She nodded to Albie's mother, smiled once more at the boy and walked the few paces to the plane.

'Bit of a dickhead, was he?' Darryl muttered as he held out his hand for her bag.

'You might say that,' Rita said, climbing into the plane. 'Just get me home.'

'Yes, boss.'

She saw his eyes crinkling behind his dark aviator sunglasses and felt herself relax for the first time since they'd arrived.

During the flight back she closed her eyes, feeling weary and not wanting to look out at the landscape for once. Before she knew it they'd arrived at Alice Springs airport – or 'air paddock', as Darryl liked to call it.

The Flying Doctor had its own little home on the paddock. From there the staff would wait for the calls for help to come over the radio. Sometimes the days would be long and filled with nothing but waiting; the adrenaline that Rita always felt at the start of a shift would dissipate within an hour or so and then she'd sit around wondering if she should pick up her book or listen to the local radio station.

It was a weird kind of job: when they weren't out on their occasional clinic days they were waiting on something bad to happen, which then precipitated a flight and even more waiting as the plane flew to somewhere far away. She'd learnt to manage her energy levels and her sense of expectation – being on high alert at all times had worn her out at the start. Once a call came through she'd feel a spike of stress as they got onto the plane, then she'd try to make herself relax on the flight. She needed to be calm and focused when they arrived.

The last few days, because she'd been working on her own while they waited for a new doctor, she'd crossed all her fingers and toes that the calls weren't going to be too serious.

'Lightweight,' Darryl had said of the departed doctor, wrinkling his nose as if at a bad smell. 'That bloke couldn't have handled another day out here if he'd had a personal fan carrier, a dedicated grape peeler and a maiden to run ice down his delicate little city spine.'

'Hey,' Rita had protested gently.

'What?'

'I have a delicate little city spine.'

Darryl had laughed heartily.

'You?' he'd said. 'You might be from the city, darl, but the only time you'd have been delicate was when you were a bloody little baby. And even then I bet you went ten rounds with your mum each time she tried to feed ya.' He had laughed some more and taken a drag on his umpteenth cigarette.

Rita had felt strangely flattered and then wondered if she shouldn't feel that way – was she really so unladylike? Her mother would be horrified. She couldn't help being herself, though, and she was too old to stop trying. She shrugged. If she wasn't a lady now, she was never going to be. Although she was lady enough to be pleased that Darryl always picked up her bag when they alighted the plane.

He grunted as he put it on his shoulder, then he gestured for her to go ahead of him.

'Your Majesty,' he said, genuflecting.

Rita waved her hand as she'd seen the Queen do and walked ahead of him.

In the doorway of the Flying Doctor office she saw an unfamiliar figure leaning against the frame, holding the flyscreen door open with one hand. He was handsome – that was immediately clear; his golden-brown hair was neatly cut and she could see that he had a well-established tan. On his long, lean torso he wore a pale blue cotton shirt with the sleeves rolled up, his legs encased in tan moleskin trousers and brown R.M. Williams boots. Rita had been in the bush long enough to recognise the shape of those boots from several metres away, and she'd only once made the mistake of asking someone what make of boot he wore before being laughed at heartily. 'Only two kinds of boot out here, darl,' the cocky had said. 'R.M.s or nothin'.' So either this handsome fellow leaning in the doorway was from the bush or he was a quick study.

'Hello,' the stranger called as Rita neared the shed. 'Are you Rita?'

'I am,' she said, coming closer and seeing just how hand-some he was. 'And this is Darryl.' She nodded her head backwards. 'He's my porter.'

She heard Darryl make a noise as he approached. 'I'm the bloody pilot,' he said, indelicately dropping her bag on the ground.

The stranger laughed. 'I'm Hamish,' he said, shaking first Rita's hand then Darryl's. 'I'm the new doctor.'

Rita appraised him and hoped he wouldn't notice. He looked to be younger than her, but not by much – which meant he had enough experience that she wouldn't have to hold his hand. That was a relief, given that the previous incumbent of the role had had far too regular gaps in his knowledge.

'Where ya from, doc?' Darryl said, pulling his packet of Benson & Hedges from his shirt pocket, opening it and peering inside.

'Brisbane,' Hamish said. 'And you?'

Darryl looked surprised. 'Here,' he said. He nodded at Rita. 'She's from Sydney.'

'And *she* needs a cup of tea,' Rita said.

'I need something stronger,' said Darryl as Hamish stood back to let them walk through. 'Doc?'

Darryl yanked open the door of the small fridge that barely kept anything cold in this shed with its corrugated-iron roof and intermittently working fan. He pulled out a can of KB Gold and offered it to the newcomer, who shook his head.

'No, thanks,' said Hamish. 'I've found that alcohol and heat aren't a good mix for me.'

As Darryl opened the can, he waggled his eyebrows. 'Going to be a long summer for you, then, isn't it?'

'So were you in a hospital or private practice?' Rita said, flicking the switch on the kettle.

'Hospital,' Hamish said, walking over to stand next to her. 'I've been at the Mater.'

Rita nodded. 'Tea?' she said.

'Thank you.' He smiled at her and Rita looked away. He really was too striking for his own good, and she wasn't meant to be noticing handsome men. It was part of the deal she'd made with herself several years ago: she wasn't going to look, she wasn't going to daydream, she was just going to focus on work.

'Have you been working here long?' he said.

'A year or so. Milk?'

He shook his head. 'Do you like it?'

Rita glanced at Darryl, who was draining the can.

'I do,' she said. 'It takes some getting used to, and sometimes you see some dreadful things. But I suppose you see them in cities too.' She put teabags into the mugs. 'The people you meet make it worthwhile.' She looked at him pointedly. 'The people we treat, I mean. Not Darryl.'

'Oi,' the pilot said.

'Oh, are you still here?' Rita said airily. 'Shouldn't you be heading home to your long-suffering wife?'

Darryl sighed heavily. 'I should.' He held out his can to Rita. 'Put that in the garbage, would you, darl?'

'Put it in the garbage yourself,' Rita said. 'That might work at home but it doesn't work here.'

'Doesn't work there either,' Darryl said with another sigh. 'Just thought I'd try it on. A man needs to be the king of the castle every once in a while – isn't that right, Hamish?'

Hamish looked uncertain. 'I, um . . .'

'Off you go, Daz,' Rita ordered. 'See you tomorrow.'

'Rightio.' He waved as he walked towards the front door of the office. 'Adios, comrades.'

'He's a bit of a character,' Hamish said, smiling.

'It comes in handy on long flights,' Rita said. 'Never a dull moment.'

She handed her new colleague his mug of tea.

'Let's take a seat,' she said, 'and I'll fill you in on our little operation.'

'Thank you,' Hamish said warmly as Rita sat.

They talked for several minutes as the next shift arrived: Michelle, the other nurse, and a pilot called Kevin who alternated shifts with Darryl. The rumour – from Darryl – was that Kevin had flown helicopters during the Vietnam War and it wasn't wise to upset him because he had 'shell shock', as Darryl would say, nodding gravely.

Nothing Darryl told her about Kevin tallied with the cheery man wearing too-tight shorts and too-long socks who always greeted her with a big smile and a wave. Darryl's other Kevin rumour was that he and Michelle were an item – 'I swear, Rita, I saw them pashing out the back!' Darryl had told her once, although Rita recognised that twinkle in his eye.

She had decided that Darryl was either teasing her or outright lying to her most of the time, but instead of being annoyed about it she took it as a sign of him trying to help her fit in. He told stories and he made her laugh. Not that she would share any of this with Hamish. He'd have his own experiences of Darryl soon enough.

'Well, the cavalry's here,' Rita said, pushing back her chair and standing up, 'so I'll leave you to it.'

'Thank you,' Hamish said, his eyes crinkling as he smiled. There was something in his smile she couldn't place: weariness, perhaps. 'I hope we get to work together soon.'

'I'm sure we will.' She wanted to say something meaningful, to mark his first day. Instead she stared at him too long and watched his expression change to one of mild confusion.

'All right, I'm off.' She spun quickly and marched away, turning her head briefly to see if Michelle or Kevin were going to talk to the newcomer. All she saw was Hamish looking at her with a faint smile.

CHAPTER THIRTEEN

Sybil's morning had almost overtaken her. She'd been up since before dawn – the usual time, because she liked to be up whenever Joe was. Since then she had gone to check on two of the children in the camp, one of whom had sliced his leg open on a nail and the wound wasn't healing the way Sybil would like; the other had a cold that had lingered too long and he'd been wheezing over the past couple of days. She was yet to decide if she'd drive them to the hospital in town after lunch; she still had her nursing skills but she didn't presume to know everything.

Then she had changed the sheets in the guest cottage and made it ready for the stock inspector who was due to arrive this afternoon. She'd written some letters: to Rita, to an old nursing friend now living in Perth and to her brother, Geoffrey, in Sydney. She'd also written to Kate's parents. She sent them a letter every two or three months, wanting to have some connection to these people who were now members of her family, even if they were on the other side of the world.

Now she was making Joe lunch at home, as she did on the days he was working close to the house, although today she was preparing something different for him, after going to town the day before and returning with fruit. It was such a rarity that she knew he'd appreciate a fresh fruit salad, and a sandwich made with cheese and onion. They were all so used to eating the same thing – beef, mainly – that anything else was exotic.

'Hello, my love,' he said as he came in through the kitchen door, kissing her on the cheek before hanging up his hat.

'Hello.' She ran her fingers through his hair, which was flat against his skull after a morning in the heat, then she patted his cheek. He was looking tired, she thought, his intensely blue eyes a little duller than they used to be. Since Lachie had left he'd looked a little defeated, too, which wasn't like him. He was always the man who had a plan to manage everything, who wouldn't be cowed by any circumstance.

'I have a surprise for you,' she said.

'Oh?' he said, sitting down slowly.

When Sybil had met Joe at the age of twenty-five, he was eight years older. She was fifty-one, but she'd never thought of the age difference as being so great – until now. He was starting to look and act like an old man. Had it come on gradually – had she not noticed? Or had he been wearing out over time?

'I don't want to blow your socks off,' she said, winking, 'but I have fruit.'

His face brightened.

'Don't tell me,' he said. 'Apples?'

'And oranges.' She laughed. 'It's been a year since we've had those, I think.'

He smiled. 'That sounds wonderful, love. A real treat.'

'Tell me about your morning,' she said as she went to the bench and started peeling and cutting.

Joe began telling her a story about a lame bull and Stan running around trying to catch it while Ben tripped over his own feet, and she thought about the first time he'd told her a story, the first time they'd met.

She was enjoying her work then, having risen faster in the hospital hierarchy than she had anticipated. Still doing some nursing and managing junior nurses too – although sometimes she found it hard to pull rank. It was just as well she liked the job, because outside of work her life felt at a standstill.

Sybil had always thought she'd be married by the age of twenty-five with at least one child. Everything in her life had been geared towards that, and she had been on track when she became engaged to her school sweetheart, Ray, at the age of nineteen, amid pledges that she would give up nursing as soon as they married. He wanted to earn some money first, however – she had his promise, she could count on that, but he wanted to make sure he could buy her a house when the time came. So they had waited.

One day in January 1950 Ray had asked her to go to the beach with him and some friends. Queenscliff Beach, he'd said, and Sybil had said no. She had learnt to swim at the adjacent Manly Beach in Sydney's north, her father teaching her and her brother how to read rips, how to avoid dumping waves, and when not to go in at all. She'd slipped up once as a teenager and been caught in a dumper at Queenscliff and she'd vowed she would never go back, the memory of being tossed and turned, water rushing into her nose and sand into her mouth too vivid.

For Sybil, Queenscliff should be avoided altogether, that day as much as any day. Moreover, another nurse had asked her to swap a shift so she could go to lunch with a young man she'd met at a dance the week before. Sybil had taken the shift and kissed Ray goodbye.

He was a strong swimmer, mildly boastful about his ability to handle any conditions. Like Sybil, he'd grown up amongst waves – but unlike her he hadn't been taught how to read the beach. Maybe that was why he'd caught the wave that dumped him, hard, onto the sand, breaking his neck. He'd drowned before his friends realised he hadn't emerged in the churn of white water.

For years afterwards – even once she had moved to Fairvale and become a mother – she would close her eyes and see her father standing in the doorway of her apartment in Elizabeth Bay. She'd been so proud of that place – and barely able to afford it, so she'd asked Rita if she could take the other bedroom. They'd been happy there.

Her father had silently passed his hat from hand to hand, his eyes serious, just as Rita had emerged from her bedroom.

'Sybil, love . . . ?' her father had said quietly, his voice catching, and Sybil's first thought was that her mother had died.

'Y-yes?' she'd said, feeling her shoulders shaking. It was so strange, that response, and she felt so detached from it, in that moment, that she wondered how one thought in her brain could have that particular effect on her body.

'Love,' he'd said, closing the door behind him. Rita had stood with her arms folded across her chest, her lips pale and pressed together, her face rigid.

'It's Mum, isn't it,' Sybil had blurted, moving to put her hand on her father's arm.

'No, love.' He'd closed his eyes and shaken his head slowly. 'It's Ray.'

It's Ray.

She knew. She knew because she had seen doctors deliver bad news as simply as that. *She's gone. It's over. We're sorry but . . .*

She wanted to say something. She tried. Then Rita's arms were around her and she was holding her so tightly, like she was holding her up, and that's when Sybil realised she was doubled over. She felt a warm hand on her back – her father's, it had to be – and she heard a noise. A ragged, almost guttural noise.

'Syb,' Rita was whispering. 'Syb, Syb.'

There was that noise again. It was so odd. It sounded like it was in her head but also coming from outside the room.

She took a breath. She had to think about it because she wasn't sure if she was breathing. Then that noise again. That noise was her, wasn't it? She could feel it pulling itself up from her gut. It wasn't a cry. It wasn't a howl. It was a protest.

This is not real. I refuse to believe it.

Such rational words and she wanted to say them. But all she had was this noise, and Rita's arms holding her tight, and her father's hand now on her head, as if he was trying to keep her in. As if he knew she wanted to run out that door and away from the fact that Ray was gone and so was the life they had planned together, and each day from today would be an effort to wake up and stand up and wash and eat and just be human.

But Sybil had made that effort. With Rita's help, she had found a way to exist, even if she felt like she was moving through sludge most of the time. She couldn't say that she felt a little better each day. She marked time differently after that: in increments of years. One year after Ray's death she was somewhat improved; at the two-year mark she felt like she was sliding backwards into the morass of hopelessness that she'd almost wanted to drown in during the weeks immediately after his death. Then something shifted; the sludge thinned and she felt more free. She missed him – every day she missed him – but she felt she was coming back to herself again.

Three years after Ray's death, she was sitting with friends in a café in Double Bay; Joe was staying in a hotel nearby. He knew one of her friends and called out hello from across the road. Sybil admired how capable and strong he looked as he came bounding over, shaking hands with the men, tipping his worn-in Akubra to the women. His face was open; it made him look honest. His eyes held curiosity. He was articulate and intelligent; she found out in those first few minutes that he was visiting Sydney for a few days then returning to work on the property in the Northern Territory that was his birthright. He told her about Fairvale, about how much he loved it.

Joe's life in the Territory made him exotic, and after meeting him again – upon his request – Sybil could tell that he was kind and thoughtful. Within the week he was unafraid to tell Sybil that he had fallen in love with her and that he wanted to marry her and take her home with him. Sybil told Rita years later that she didn't love Joe then, because her heart was still broken over Ray; she wondered if she'd ever love anyone again. But Joe was offering her something she couldn't offer herself: hope that life would be different, that she'd have a purpose. Joe had purpose, and vigour. He had plans for the future and he was so *alive*. So she agreed to marry him and move to the land that had always been his home, despite her parents' protests that she had made a decision she would regret.

She had missed home – powerfully, at first, while also telling herself that she had to stick with the life and the man she had chosen, because it would be ill-mannered to do otherwise – and over time she had come to love Joe. It wasn't the same as loving Ray – it was better, because she appreciated it more. She could never tell him that, but she found ways to show him.

As Sybil set the fruit salad in front of him, Joe put his hand on her wrist.

'You take good care of me,' he murmured.

'You take good care of me too,' she said softly, kissing his cheek.

'You deserve it.' He picked up half of the sandwich. 'You're not having any?'

'In a bit.'

'I haven't seen you eat much since Lachie . . .' He grimaced.

'I know. I'm still worrying about him, I guess.'

It was the simplest truth, because what else could she say to her husband: *I think I let him get away with things because you used to be too tough on him as a kid, and now he's getting away with leaving us altogether.*

So many times she had replayed her last conversation with her eldest son; she would lie awake as Joe slept, straight as a board, beside her, letting it loop around. She didn't know if she was hoping it would be different the next time it played or if she wanted to cling onto the sound of Lachie's voice, trying to hear any skerrick of love in it.

The radiotelephone had rung in the office that day last August and Joe had been next to it. She didn't know what was said in the first few seconds but Joe had stepped into the hallway and hollered into the kitchen, telling her to hurry.

Lachie, he'd mouthed as he handed her the phone. She put her ear to the line and heard the other people on it. She regularly wished that the party line didn't have so many witnesses to her conversations, and never more so than today.

'Lachie?' she said into the phone. She had felt almost lightheaded with relief that he had contacted them.

'Yeah. Hi, Mum.' He sounded distant. Distracted.

'Where are you, darling?'

'Um . . .' She heard a sharp sigh. 'Doesn't really matter, does it?'

'It does to me.' She felt fear pushing into her. Why didn't he want her to know where he was?

'How will I know where to find you if I don't know where you are?' she said.

'I don't want you to find me, Mum,' he said and there was the brittleness he'd always had, as if he wanted to cut her with his words. He had tried often enough over the years and she hadn't developed armour against it so much as learnt to heal quickly.

'But darling—'

'I'm not coming back,' he said fiercely. 'I don't want anything to do with the place. Let precious bloody Ben have the run of it.'

'Lachlan, that's not fair. Whatever you're up to has nothing to do with Ben.'

There was silence and she worried that he'd simply dropped the phone and run away.

'Three minutes,' came the operator's voice on the line. 'Do you wish to extend?"

'Yes!' Sybil said before Lachie could reply.

'Course it does,' Lachie said, and she thought she heard him laugh. 'He's always been the one. Couldn't do any wrong. Everything I did wasn't good enough, was it? I wasn't smart enough to run the place – isn't that what Dad said?'

Sybil gasped. Once, in anger at Lachie's refusal to do his schoolwork when the boys were still being educated at home, Joe had made that remark. Just once. He'd never said anything like it again.

'That's what you're upset about?' Sybil said. 'That can't be the reason you don't want to come home – not after all these years?'

Lachie was silent but at least she could hear him breathing. 'It was the start of the reasons,' he said after a few seconds had passed.

'We love you and Ben the same,' Sybil said, but she was sure it sounded like a feeble rationale to a man who had probably made up his mind differently.

'Sure,' he said. 'You tell yourself that.'

'Lachie—'

'Mum, don't try to talk me out of it. I don't want to be there. I hate it.'

She felt the shock of his words; perhaps he intended it. And she was glad Joe hadn't heard them.

'Why?' she said, almost whispering.

He laughed, a sharp sound without any humour in it. 'I just do. I don't want to work with Dad. I don't want to run the place. I don't care what you both planned for me. I'm not doing it. I'm not going to spend my life working seven days a week for no bloody fun and no bloody money. I deserve better than that.' He paused. 'Don't you reckon?' he said, sounding almost triumphant.

She remembered all the times she'd told him he was special because she had believed it. She also remembered how much he had shown his dislike of Fairvale after he had started going to boarding school in Sydney. He had complained that he wasn't going on overseas holidays like his friends did; he had asked why they didn't go skiing in winter, why they didn't have a house at the beach. He had started criticising her for not wearing more fashionable clothes, and his father for wearing old boots. And they'd let him get away with it, too afraid that he might reject them altogether. Their plans had always been predicated on Lachie taking over just as Joe had taken over. He'd had a younger brother who had stood aside, just as Ben would have to do.

Now their fears were their reality and Sybil could see how foolish they had been: Fairvale would carry on without Lachie but Sybil hadn't seen her son for months. She wanted to go back in time and tell him that it didn't matter what he did – that he didn't have to stay on Fairvale – if only he would stay in their family.

She couldn't argue with him, though; he wasn't giving her any openings to do so. His mind was made up. 'I miss you,' she said.

'Right,' he said.

'Will you stay in touch? If you won't tell me where you are?' Her arms and legs felt heavy and she recognised the sensation: grief, pulling her down, towards the earth. She so wanted to yield to it.

'No,' he said.

'Please tell me where,' she whispered.

'Bye, Mum.'

There was silence on the line; the other people on it must have been listening to their conversation. Before long everyone in the area would know that Lachlan Baxter wasn't coming home.

Squeezing her eyes shut briefly – hoping the memory would be squeezed out too – Sybil reached towards the other half of the sandwich on Joe's plate.

'I guess I should eat,' she said.

'That's my girl,' Joe said, smiling briefly. 'Starving isn't going to bring him back.'

'No.' She took a bite and tried not to gag on it.

'Things will work out,' Joe said in a more gruff tone than usual. 'We've got Ben. We're probably lucky that at least one of them's interested in staying.'

'But Ben doesn't know—'

'He knows enough,' Joe said, putting his sandwich down. 'And he'll learn what he doesn't know. Maybe . . .' He picked up the food again.

'Maybe what?'

'Maybe it's better this way,' Joe said. 'Maybe it's how it was meant to be all along.'

'But Lachie's our son,' Sybil said.

'He caused a lot of damage.' Joe's voice had an edge to it of a kind Sybil had never heard before, and his eyes warned her not to retort that maybe they'd damaged Lachie first. Joe had raised his sons the way he'd been raised, and he'd left behind the parts that didn't work, even if he'd realised it too late. They'd talked about this, the two of them. Over and over, as the boys grew up, they'd discussed all the things they were doing wrong and right.

'That's hard to accept,' Sybil said, swallowing.

'Yes, but it's true.' Joe sighed, the noise loud in their large kitchen. 'We have to keep living, love. If Lachie wants to see us again, he will. We can't force him.'

'I don't want to give up on him,' Sybil said quietly.

'Then don't. But don't give up on yourself either.' His smile was faint and kind. 'Now tell me what you're reading for this book club,' he said as she took another tentative bite.

She chewed and swallowed.

'It may not end up being right for the book club,' she said. 'I'm reading it to find out.'

She looked at him and he lifted his eyebrows and nodded once.

'It's called *The Group*. It's an American novel,' she went on.

'Never heard of it,' he said, and smiled. 'Although that's probably not a surprise. You know I'm not that keen on novels.'

'I do.'

Joe liked facts: history, science, current affairs. He'd made an exception when he'd read *The Thorn Birds*; she knew he'd made it for her, and it was only one of the countless reasons she loved him.

'It was published a while ago,' she continued. She tried to remember if she'd seen a year on it anywhere. 'Maybe in the early sixties.'

'You haven't read it before?'

'No. Rita told me about it recently. She has some American friend – I think there was a recommendation. Anyway . . .'

'Don't stop,' he said, picking up his cup of tea and taking a loud, slurping gulp. 'Tell me what it's about.'

'It's about a group of friends. Women.'

'Sounds appropriate,' he said. 'Why do you keep stopping?'

She sighed loudly. 'Because . . . I like it. A great deal. But I'm not sure if it's appropriate for the book club. It's a bit . . .' She searched for the right word. 'Racy.'

'Racy!' Joe hit the table with one hand. 'Stone the bloody crows! I can't have my innocent little wife talking about a racy book.' His eyes were teasing her and she started to laugh.

'We're sheltered out here.' She smiled at him as he took another sip of tea.

'Too right. Everyone here is as pure as the driven snow. It's not like you've ever met a drunk or hidden that girl who got herself pregnant to a married man. I think you can handle racy.'

'It's not me I'm worried about,' Sybil said, fidgeting with her own cup and saucer.

'Who, then?'

'Kate,' Sybil said. 'I don't know if it's a book she'd like. She's English. They're . . . polite.'

'I think Kate can handle herself. She took off on that horse this morning like she was ready to outrun Ben,' Joe said, then he looked at his watch. 'But if you'd like to explore what "racy" means, I can take a bit longer for lunch.' He cocked his head towards her and smiled slowly.

Every now and again they would do this: when the house was empty and they knew it was unlikely anyone would return soon. It was the only time they had to themselves; the only space they could create that was just the two of them. After so many years of marriage Sybil was surprised that he still found her attractive, although she had no doubt about his charms for her. He was still tall and strong and handsome, even if his face was more weathered and his hair was greying. His eyes were still bright, his smile was still magic and she loved him more than she ever had.

Joe stood. 'My lovely wife,' he murmured, extending his hand.

'My darling husband,' she said, taking it.

She led him down the hallway, towards their bedroom, and as she felt his lips on the back of her neck, she sighed, and smiled, then closed the door on the world.

CHAPTER FOURTEEN

The knock on her door woke Della from the nap she hadn't meant to take. She'd been daydreaming about Stan. He'd visited that morning and she was still trying to work out why she liked him as much as she did. She barely knew him. He barely knew her. They hadn't spent so much time together that she could say she knew much about his life. There was something about him, though, that made her feel light.

'So you've come back to see Bob?' she had asked him after she'd watched him stroll up to the stables, her heart hammering in her chest as he smiled when he saw her.

'Now, why would I want to do that, Della girl?' he'd said. 'I saw him all my life.' His smile was natural, open. She couldn't help smiling back.

'I'm here to see you,' he'd said, his smile relaxing as his gaze became more intense.

Then he'd turned to Arthur, who had given her all sorts of trouble when she'd put his saddle on. She was dismayed to watch her horse whickering into Stan's chest, giving him a gentle nudge as Stan scratched under his chin.

'I can't believe it,' she'd breathed and Stan's head had whipped up.

'Why wouldn't I be here to see you?' he'd said, lines forming on his brow.

'Oh – no!' she'd gasped. 'I meant – I can't believe Arthur likes you. He's difficult with most everyone.'

Stan had nodded slowly. 'Just gotta be kind to 'em, eh?' he'd said, putting his nose to Arthur's cheek before looking at her again. 'They're like people that way.'

They had gone for a walk together, out of sight along the riverbank. It wasn't that she didn't want to be seen with him – she just didn't want gossip. She'd grown up near a small town and was all too aware of what they could be like; Ghost River was the smallest of small towns.

Another knock – firmer this time – got her standing and walking swiftly to the door, which she yanked open to reveal the bulk of Ross Watson.

'G'day,' he said, leaning towards her. She took a step back.

'Hello,' she said, trying not to feel nervous. It was still light out – there would be people around. It was Sunday afternoon so there wasn't the usual bustle but she could hear someone calling in the distance and someone else responding.

'What're ya doin' here on your own?' Ross said, and Della realised that stepping back to get away from him wasn't going to work because he'd end up in her room. Instead she stepped to the side of him, hoping to draw him out.

'Reading,' she said, fibbing because she didn't want to engage him in any kind of conversation and she knew he didn't even read the newspaper.

He looked around the room. 'That fella isn't here?'

Della felt her stomach tighten. So they had been seen; she shouldn't have hoped they wouldn't be.

'No,' she said.

'Reckon you should stay away from him.' Ross's jaw went hard and his eyes were empty. Della tasted something foul in her mouth. Something metallic. Adrenaline. She hadn't realised she was scared of him but now she knew.

'Why is that?' She probably shouldn't ask – she didn't want to know his answer – but she couldn't think of another way to keep him at a distance.

'I think you know why. You'll end up like that Amelia.' He sounded light, almost as if he was giving her a friendly warning. 'Got knocked up, didn't she?' he said. 'Heard it was Lachie Baxter.'

He laughed cruelly and Della's fear increased. 'Well, he shot through. So she had to take off too.' He poked a finger at Della's chest and she recoiled.

'Can I help you with something?' she said, putting her shoulders back, trying to look tough.

'I reckon you could help me with a lot of things.' He stepped one foot towards her, smiling at her in a way she definitely did not like. 'You looking for someone to keep you warm?' he said.

'No.'

'You must be. Girl like you, ya shouldn't be alone.'

She took a big step out of her door, so he had to turn away from her room to face her.

'That's not really your decision,' she said, dropping her voice, hoping she sounded strong.

He shrugged, looking completely unworried. 'I reckon it is.' His eyes narrowed so she couldn't read them anymore. 'All the sheilas pretend they don't want it. But they always do.'

She tried to breathe slowly but it was impossible. A ball of fear, mixed with anger and dismay, was now lodged firmly in her chest.

Ross put his hands on her shoulders and Della made herself as stiff as she could, not wanting him to perceive any kind of invitation in her body.

'Take your hands off me,' she said.

'Or what?' he snarled.

She shoved his chest but he held onto her. Now the taste in her mouth was of bile.

'Della!' The rasping tone sounded blessedly familiar and Felicity appeared at the corner of the big house, in sight of Della's door. Della felt her knees start to wobble.

'Yes?' She wanted to cry with surprise and relief.

'I can't find those biscuits you made,' Felicity said as she drew near. She stopped as she saw Ross.

'What the hell are you doing here?' she said. She turned her glowering face towards Della, and Della knew what she was thinking.

'I'd like to know the same thing,' Della said loudly.

Ross dropped his hands, stepping back from her.

Felicity put her hands on her hips. In the fading light of the day, Della could see her employer's eyes narrow.

'Ross Watson, I told you what would happen if I caught you doing this again.'

'It isn't my fault,' he said petulantly.

'Isn't it? You are at Della's door, not the other way around. So I would suggest this is very much your fault.' Her mouth set in a line. 'Aug will run you into town tomorrow. And don't go looking for a job anywhere in the Katherine region because you won't get one.'

'I didn't do anything,' he said, sounding angrier.

'You were about to,' Felicity said curtly. 'And you have in the past. Leave Della alone.' Felicity tossed her head in the direction of the men's quarters. Ross glared at her; he looked like he was grinding his teeth.

'Some sheila won't open her legs and you're telling *me* to shove off?' he ranted. 'She's the one who should go. She led me on. It's not my bloody fault she changed her mind.'

Felicity looked amused. 'And how, exactly, did she lead you on, Ross Watson? Like the last one did, is that it? Smiling at you when she served you dinner? Smiling at you the way she smiled at everyone?'

'She wanted it,' he muttered. 'She just pretended she didn't.'

'I'm sure,' Felicity said loudly, 'that there are young women in whatever part of Australia you are from who will be delighted to meet you. Who will even open their legs for you, as you so charmingly put it. But there are none here.'

Ross frowned and his mouth dropped open. Della dug her fingernails into her palms and wished he was already gone.

'Can I get my pay?' Ross said, his shoulders sagging a little.

Felicity's chin lifted and she moved her feet slightly apart. 'I'll wire it to you,' she said.

His jaw went hard once more but he turned away and heavily put one foot in front of the other as he walked off.

Della looked back to Felicity, who was staring at her.

'You can't encourage them,' Felicity said, folding her arms across her chest, her bosom pushed so high that it was almost at her collarbones. 'Men don't know when to stop.'

'I didn't encourage him,' Della said, squaring her shoulders towards the older woman. 'I have never once said anything to give him the idea that he could do that.'

They glared at each other and then Felicity nodded slowly. 'All right,' she said. 'But I don't want to see any other young men round here. You're too good a worker to lose.'

Della bit her bottom lip to stop herself responding.

For the first time since she'd left home, Della wished she had her brothers around to protect her. She hated that she thought like that – she didn't want to have to rely on anyone for anything – but, growing up, they'd always looked out for her, always kept away anyone whose attention she didn't want. There had been a few of those anyones: because she was small, boys at school seemed to think she was some kind of mascot. They'd tease her and try to pick her up. One or more of her brothers would appear, almost as if they sensed what was happening, and Della would be left alone.

She'd never felt unsafe on Ghost River – before now.

Shutting the door behind her, Della sat on the edge of her bed. The ball in her chest had gone but adrenaline had churned her stomach and she felt like she might vomit. She looked around for any kind of receptacle and saw nothing apart from a water glass. She wasn't going to vomit into that. And she wasn't going outside to the lavatory, either.

She swallowed down the metallic tide and tried again to slow her breathing.

For the first time since she'd arrived in Australia, homesickness moved through her body. It started in her gut and coursed to her fingers and toes. It made her belly feel hard, and her ribs got tight. She squeezed her eyes shut as memories of all she'd left behind appeared on the backs of her eyelids. And she wept. For everyone she missed, for all the uncertainty of her future. There was anger in it: at Ross, for making her feel so vulnerable; at herself, for not being more on guard. In her desire to be free, to have adventures, to cut herself loose from what she knew, was she a fool?

Knowing that no one would hear her, Della let herself cry for as long as it took. When it was over, in the last light of the day, she marched to the stables and lay her head against one of the horses, soothing herself the way she always had, thousands of miles away, back home.

CHAPTER FIFTEEN

Kate put down her pen and gazed out the window of the office, listening to the sounds of the house. To the absence of sounds in the house. In the mornings she often had the place to herself.

She looked down at the letter she was halfway through writing to her parents. Whenever she finished her work, either in the station kitchen or in the office keeping the accounts, she would write: to her parents, her friends. She filled the letters with details about Fairvale and the people on it: Ruby; Stan, who always tipped his hat to her; Stan's cousin, Harry, one of the stockmen who'd come with the dry and leave with the wet, whereas Stan stayed put year round; Harry's wife, Barbara, and their two young children. There were others – lots of others, including visitors from town who would bring newspapers that she would seize upon and scour for news of home. She still felt English; she didn't think that would stop, even if now her skin was a permanent shade of brown and her dark hair had turned chestnut under the Territory sun.

Her mother wouldn't recognise her: wouldn't know her neatly groomed daughter if she saw Kate with her hair wild and longer than it had ever been, with her best white shirt stained by red dust. Still she continued to wear it, not applying any lipstick or keeping her nails filed, because those things didn't matter out here where each day was alive with sunshine and animals and dirt and trees, with people calling to each other, laughing across the cattle yards, horses protesting the tightening of saddles . . . and Ben, always Ben, leading his men with a laugh and finding time for a quiet word with the station children who would cluster after school at the yards, watching with big eyes as 'Mister Ben' and the others went about their work. Today he was castrating bulls, he'd told her. She hadn't cared to ask for more detail.

Her husband started each day with so much enthusiasm that it always rubbed off on Kate, even when she was having a melancholy day. A day when she was prone to dwell on the fact that she was showing no signs of being pregnant. She was getting better at not letting herself become morose on those days; Ben's relentless optimism about life in general helped.

Joe had remarked to her once that Ben had 'come into his own' since Lachie had left. It had been said approvingly; Joe had looked pleased. Kate had almost taken the opportunity to ask Joe about his absent eldest son but then the conversation had moved on and Joe had told her that they'd better start planning for the Katherine Show, which was coming up in July. Almost everyone on Fairvale would go to the show – and everyone they knew would be there – so they had to make sure all tasks, big and small, were taken care of by then. And Joe had told her that Sybil usually bought some new clothes just to wear to the show, 'so don't you feel you can't do the same', he'd said with a nod and a serious expression on his face.

'Oh, you *are* in here,' came Sybil's voice from the doorway and Kate jumped.

'Sorry – I scared you.' Sybil stepped into the office.

'It's fine,' Kate said. 'I was daydreaming.'

'It happens around here.' Sybil's gaze shifted to the window then her eyes met Kate's. 'Della's arrived.'

'I didn't hear the truck,' Kate said, getting to her feet.

Sybil's smile flickered. 'Stan can be stealthy when he wants to be.'

'I guess so. I'd better pull on my boots.'

Kate and Della had originally planned to ride at Ghost River but Della had written a brief letter saying she'd rather come to Fairvale, with no reason provided. When Kate had told Sybil about the change, Sybil had given her a look that seemed to mean something – except Kate didn't know what.

'Have you decided which direction you're heading in?' said Sybil, stepping into the hallway to let her pass.

'Not yet. Do you have any recommendations?'

Sybil laughed. 'Hardly. I haven't ridden in years. It's more so we know where to look for you if you're not back by sundown.'

'Oh, we'll be back,' Kate said lightly, although she noticed that Sybil looked serious.

'Just in case,' Sybil said.

Kate stopped and her eyes met her mother-in-law's. At the start of her marriage, as she was adjusting to living with strangers at the same time as learning the extremes of the Northern Territory climate, Kate would have found Sybil's solicitousness irritating and, perhaps, an implicit judgement on her ability to cope with her new home. These days she understood it was simply part of Sybil's fabric. Now, Kate felt reassured by it; Ben didn't even notice it because it had been going on for his entire life.

'We'll head east,' Kate said. 'Out the back of the stables and over the creek. It's just for a walk.' She grinned. 'No wild galloping.'

Sybil's face relaxed. 'That's good. All right – have fun. I've made up a couple of canteens of water for you. They're in the kitchen.'

'Thank you.' Kate held her smile. 'I'll see you later.'

'Please bring Della in for a bite to eat when you're back,' Sybil called after her as Kate picked up the canteens, then opened the back door and checked her boots for snakes.

'I will!' Kate closed the door and glanced over at the garden gate, where Della was standing looking up at Stan, who had a bigger grin on his face than Kate had ever seen. He was a giant next to tiny Della, and Kate watched them flirting for a few more seconds before she started to feel like a voyeur. Now, perhaps, she knew what Sybil's look had meant.

'Hello!' she called as she walked over to them.

Stan's head turned towards her and he nodded once, although Della looked as if she'd been caught stealing coins from a collection plate.

'Hi, Kate,' Della said as Kate opened the garden gate. Kate went to kiss her on each cheek then remembered that at the book club Della had seemed more comfortable with a hug, explaining quickly that 'my people don't kiss hello and goodbye'. So Kate attempted an awkward hug and Della patted her shoulder in return.

'So you two are riding, eh?' Stan looked from one to the other.

'I'll bring her back safely, I promise,' Kate said, raising an eyebrow at him so he would be aware that she knew what he was up to: he liked Della. *Liked* liked Della.

'Oh,' Della said, then she coughed once. 'I don't think he's worried.'

Kate met Stan's gaze and saw the truth. 'I think he might be,' she said. 'But he's not coming with us, so there's not much he can do. Can you, Stan?' She winked at him and took hold of Della's elbow.

'The horses are this way,' Kate said, tugging her in the direction of the stables. 'And Stan will be here when we get back.'

Della swivelled her head to look back at him and Kate saw him tip his hat to them.

The two women walked in silence until they were out of earshot of the house.

'My, my,' Kate said.

'What?' Della asked, her voice high.

'If I was speaking Australian I believe I'd say that Stan is sweet on you.'

Della made a noise in her throat and looked away. 'I don't know about that,' she said, her Texan drawl taking its time.

Kate snorted. 'Honestly, Della, I think you do. But we don't have to talk about it if you don't want to.'

They reached the stables and Kate let go of Della's elbow. 'The horses are saddled.' She gestured towards Joe's favourite gelding, which he'd offered for their guest. 'That's Sonny. He's spirited but he always sticks to the rules, so I think you'll be fine on him.'

'I'm sure I can handle him,' Della said, walking over and stroking the horse's neck. 'And I don't mean anything else by that. I'm talking about the horse *only*.' She gave Kate a pointed look.

Kate laughed. 'I'm sure you don't.' She swung herself up onto her mount. 'This ride will take a couple of hours. Plenty of time for you to tell me about Stan.' She winked. 'Because I really do want you to tell me.'

Della widened her eyes at her. 'I will not.'

'You will too.' She nodded at the horse. 'Come on. You tell me about Stan and I'll tell you how Ben swept me off my feet and all the way to Australia.'

'Deal.' Della's face relaxed as she put her left foot in the stirrup and then she was in the saddle so quickly that Kate could tell she'd done it hundreds of times before.

'After you.' Della gestured to the stable door.

'No, after you – please.' Kate smiled as Della led her out of the stables, towards the creek.

They rode in silence until they reached the creek bed, Kate nodding to indicate that Della should ride down into it as Kate followed. They drew level and headed into what would have been upstream if there was any water.

'So,' Kate said, her ingrained social skills prodding her to speak, 'you mentioned at the book club that you have brothers.'

'Uh-huh,' Della said, squinting as she looked up at the cockatoos flying overhead. 'Huh.'

'What?' Kate glanced up at the birds that were rapidly moving away from them.

'We haven't seen those for a while.' She shrugged. 'Yeah. Brothers,' she said.

Kate wondered if Della would prefer not to discuss the topic – except she'd raised it once before, so Kate took that as an invitation.

'How many?' she ventured.

'Four,' Della said, and Kate was sure she heard a sigh.

'*Four?*'

Della shrugged again. 'Momma wanted another girl. She thought I could use the company. She gave up after four tries.'

'How . . . noble of her,' Kate said. 'I don't even have one brother. I can't imagine what four would be like.'

'You don't want to,' Della said quickly, then cleared her throat. 'I mean, they're all right – they're just a lot of *boy*, if you know what I mean.'

Kate laughed. 'I think I might.'

'Do you have sisters?'

'Mm-hm. Actually, just the one.' She tried to smile as she thought about her sister. Sometimes it was too difficult. 'We don't always get along,' Kate continued. 'I suspect she's glad I'm all the way over here.'

Della lowered her heels and her horse stopped. 'Oh?' she said, turning her head to look at Kate, who pulled up her own horse.

Kate shook her head, trying to indicate that the subject wasn't serious, suspecting that she was actually telegraphing the opposite.

'I was the popular one at school,' she said. 'My sister – Abigail – she . . . was less so.'

'I get it,' Della said, nudging her horse to walk on.

Kate felt relieved: she didn't really want to explain her relationship with Abigail. It was almost as fraught as Ben's with Lachlan – a point of commonality in their marriage that had become a deep, shared understanding.

'Would you like to trot?' Kate said, smiling brightly enough to eclipse the thought of her sister.

'Sure,' Della said, giving her horse a kick and pulling metres ahead before Kate realised what was happening,

CHAPTER SIXTEEN

The Kingswood felt as heavy as a tank as Sallyanne manoeuvred it out of Tindal and onto the Stuart Highway. Sybil had called her early that morning and asked if she could pick up Rita, because Rita's plane would be arriving later than planned and Sybil wouldn't be able to come into town and get back in time to have everything ready for the book club.

Sallyanne hadn't minded; she wasn't bothered by early: the children were always out of bed at first light and they had to be supervised. She'd had time to take them to her father's and give them the usual instruction not to bother Grandpa if they could avoid it. Her father didn't mind looking after the kids so long as they didn't talk to him when the radio was on.

'It's good of you to come,' Rita said and Sallyanne smiled at her quickly before shifting her eyes back to the road.

'I'm happy to do it,' she said. 'It's not far out of town.'

'No,' Rita said with a laugh, 'twenty-five kilometres is nothing out here, is it?'

'Not really.'

'So what's Mick doing with the children today – something fun?' Rita said.

Sallyanne felt like laughing out loud, not just at the idea that Mick might actually look after his own children but that Rita would presume that such a thing was normal. She thought about how she'd usually frame the answer to a question like Rita's. How she'd usually lie and say that Mick was busy today or working today or had something planned today so that he couldn't be with his own children. But who was she protecting with this lie?

'The children aren't with Mick,' Sallyanne said, and she could hear resolve in her voice.

'Oh?' Rita sounded curious instead of judgemental. That lack of judgement emboldened Sallyanne.

She exhaled.

'My husband has a drinking problem,' she said as they reached the outskirts of Katherine. 'I can't trust him with the children.'

Rita didn't respond and Sallyanne didn't dare to look at her. Perhaps this was when the judgement would come.

'That makes life hard for you,' Rita said finally.

Sallyanne took one breath. And another.

'Yes, it does,' she almost whispered. She gripped the steering wheel tightly.

'How long has it been going on?'

Forever, Sallyanne wanted to say, because that's what it felt like.

'A while,' she said instead. 'It happened gradually, you know? All the men drink here. It took me a while to notice that he was drinking more than he used to.'

'So who has the kids today?'

'My father.'

'Does Mick . . . hurt you?'

Sallyanne glanced to her left and saw that Rita was staring ahead of them. It made her feel more brave about answering the question.

'Not physically,' she said as she turned onto the Victoria Highway bound for Fairvale. 'But I always think he might. He gets . . .' An image of him standing over her was right there in the front of her brain, and she felt the way she always did when he intimidated her like that: she wanted to run.

She cleared her throat. 'He hasn't hit me,' she said. 'Or the children. But sometimes he hurts them just by forgetting to take care of them. And when I try to talk to him about it, he . . . he gets angry.' She swallowed, willing herself to keep her hands steady on the wheel. 'He's a lot bigger than me. It wouldn't take much . . . you know.'

The air in the car felt thick. She wanted to wind down the window but she didn't think there'd be any relief by letting the dry heat in.

'Is that the first time you've ever admitted that to someone?' Rita said, and all Sallyanne could hear in her voice was concern.

'It's the first time anyone has asked me.' Sallyanne felt the crush of the last few years with Mick; if she heard her ribs shattering with the pressure of it, she wouldn't be surprised. All that time, carrying that weight, and no one else had even noticed her bowed down by it. Until now.

She counted her breathing. One-two in. One-two out. Just the way her mother had taught her when she'd been nervous about an exam or worried about something at school.

'I'm sorry to hear that,' Rita said, her voice quiet next to the din of the car. 'I'm sorry you're living with all of this.'

Sallyanne stared ahead. She knew this road well – even before she'd been invited to Fairvale she'd travelled it many times. That didn't mean she could afford to let her attention slip. There could be a dead animal lying across a lane or a car coming towards her that might suddenly veer the wrong way. Yet she felt relieved – not just that Rita had asked her about the thing she'd spent so long hiding but also that they were heading to Fairvale, to Sybil's house.

'You don't have to put up with it, you know,' said Rita. 'If you're scared of him, you could go to the police. Ask them for help.'

'They wouldn't care,' Sallyanne said.

'Why not? It's their job to protect people.'

Sallyanne wished she lived in a place where that was how the world worked. Maybe cities were like that – but not here.

'Mick went to school with one of the local cops,' she said. 'And he knows the others because he grew up here.'

'Didn't you grow up here too? I'm sure Sybil told me that.'

'Doesn't matter,' Sallyanne said sadly. 'Why would they listen to me? Who am I, after all?'

'You're Sallyanne,' Rita said, sounding almost indignant. 'I haven't known you very long and I can already tell you're a terrific person. I want you to call me the next time you're scared. Or even if you're not. Or call someone else, if you wish. But you can't carry this alone and you don't have to. If Sybil found out about this I know she'd rather you pack up your kids and pitch a tent on Fairvale than put up with it. Living like that – my dear, you shouldn't have to.'

Sallyanne felt tears prickle her eyes. She barely knew Rita and she was already being kinder than Sallyanne knew people in Katherine would be to her. Mick and his family were a fixture in the town.

'Thank you,' she said.

'No thanks required. And I won't say anything to Sybil unless you want me to. It's no one else's business until you make it so.'

Nodding, Sallyanne tried not to let tears spill out of her eyes. She needed to concentrate on her driving, keep her vision clear.

'Will you tell me something about your life?' she said, wanting to change the topic of their conversation before she became more upset, and also genuinely wanting to know. She had been mildly envious of the ease of Sybil and Rita's friendship when she'd seen it at close hand, at Fairvale. She had never had a friend like that, apart from her mother – and she certainly didn't expect that Rita would become that sort of friend for her. Yet she was curious about her; she was curious about them all.

'Why did you move to Alice Springs?' she continued, tasting salt on her lips, hoping Rita hadn't seen the few tears that had fallen.

'Ah, yes,' Rita said, her voice tight. 'Why indeed.'

Sallyanne glanced over and saw Rita looking out the window, one hand repeatedly tucking her hair behind her ear. Sallyanne wished she had hair like that: thick and dark; almost like a helmet. Her pale wisps could make her look like a newborn chick.

'I could say,' Rita went on, her voice soft, 'that it was because I wanted an adventure. And partly that's true.'

Out of the corner of her eye Sallyanne detected Rita's head turning away from the window.

'But, really, it was because I didn't have any reasons to stay in Sydney,' Rita went on. 'None that were worthwhile.'

Sallyanne wanted to say something – to let Rita know she was listening sympathetically – but any interjection now would be a token, so she decided to stay quiet.

'I'm not married,' Rita said matter-of-factly. 'I don't have children. My only family was my parents and my brother. And he moved to London twenty years ago and has barely been home.' She paused. 'So I spent a lot of time with my parents. And I was happy to do so. We were friends.'

Sallyanne glanced at her quickly. Rita was looking at the road ahead of them with a faraway expression.

'Anyway, a couple of years ago Mum died of cancer.'

'No,' Sallyanne said, an ache of recognition manifesting inside her. That was how her mother had died: undiagnosed for too long, told she had 'women's problems', then a tumour was found in her ovary and she was dead eight weeks later.

'Dad was lonely,' Rita went on. 'I tried to help him through it but I couldn't be there all the time. He had a heart attack six months later.' She was silent for several seconds. 'So that was that. My family was gone. Then I heard about the Flying Doctor and it seemed like a good idea.'

'And has it been?' Sallyanne said hurriedly, feeling bad that she'd introduced a subject that had made Rita sad.

A vague smile formed on Rita's lips. 'It has, actually. The Alice is an interesting place. No one puts on airs and graces. That's probably true of the whole Territory.'

Sallyanne nodded vigorously. 'Sometimes I think we could use a few of them.'

'I like it,' Rita said, her voice lighter. 'There's no waffling. People say what they mean. And I get to visit some interesting places in this job. There's so much extraordinary country. Places I'd never dreamt of.'

'So you're going to stay for a while?' Sallyanne hoped she would: she liked Rita. She hoped that Rita liked her and didn't just feel sorry for her.

'I reckon so. Yes.' Rita nodded once, decisively. 'Now, why don't you tell me about growing up in Katherine? I know nothing about the place. You'll have to teach me.'

Sallyanne kept her eyes on the road ahead as she talked. She hadn't talked like this to anyone since her mother had died. She hoped Rita meant what she said and didn't leave Alice Springs anytime soon – Sallyanne already knew she would miss her.

CHAPTER SEVENTEEN

Wiping the back of her hand across her forehead, Sybil pulled open the oven door to check on the biscuits that had started to cook fifteen minutes before, wondering why she would bake anything on a day like this, at this time of year, in this part of Australia. Ovens were meant for cold places, where they could heat the house while they did the work of cooking food. Yet no one she knew would dream of doing without one. They wouldn't question the wisdom of using technology meant for English winters that had been imported into a place where winter never came. Not winter as the English knew it – as Kate knew it.

'They smell delicious,' her daughter-in-law said as she leant in the doorway. 'Are they for us?'

'They are,' Sybil said, grabbing a tea towel and pulling out the top tray, inspecting it before she put it on the bench top. 'They're Rita's favourite. She's coming all this way so I thought at least she deserved a biscuit.'

Kate nodded, looking pale for someone who was spending increasing amounts of time in the sun. Sybil could tell that her daughter-in-law was suffering through this build-up; she was limp and tired a lot of the time.

'Would you like to try one?' Sybil said.

Kate shook her head quickly. 'That's all right. I'll wait until the others arrive.' She looked at the clock on the kitchen wall. 'I thought Rita would be here by now.'

'The plane took off late,' Sybil said, turning off the oven and shutting the door. 'Sallyanne's bringing her.'

'Oh.' Kate nodded slowly. 'You've never mentioned Rita having a . . .' She frowned briefly. 'Friend.'

Sybil arched an eyebrow. 'A man friend?'

'Yes,' Kate said, then looked almost embarrassed.

'That's because she doesn't have one,' Sybil said, wondering why Kate was so interested in Rita's lack of a love life.

'So Rita has never married?'

'No. She's never met the right man.'

'She wants to, though? She wants to be married?'

Sybil looked at her curiously.

'I don't think so,' she said. 'She enjoys her life far too much.'

Kate looked startled. 'Really?'

'Marriage isn't for everyone,' Sybil said, putting the tea towel on the back of a chair. 'I hear a car.'

⌣

Sybil looked on with amusement as Sallyanne held her copy of *Love in a Cold Climate* to her chest.

'I just loved it,' Sallyanne said.

'Really?' Kate looked bemused. 'Didn't you think they were all a bit boring? They just sat around in drawing rooms talking about other people and doing not much themselves. That's the women. The men were all standing by fireplaces gossiping.'

'But it was such a scandal, don't you think?' said Sallyanne passionately. 'That old man marrying that young girl?'

'And all their friends and relatives making out that despite his age he had no control over the situation – that he was somehow forced into it.' Kate looked almost grumpy. 'He was just an old sleaze interested in a very young woman for her money.'

'Sybil, do you only choose books about dirty old men?' Rita said, raising an eyebrow.

'Father Ralph wasn't a dirty old man!' Sallyanne cried.

'Of course, it was true love,' Rita said, amusement showing in her eyes. 'I do think Sybil has a bit of a taste for this subject matter, though.'

Sybil wrinkled her nose. 'If you're going to tar me with that brush you'll need to include my daughter-in-law.' She flashed a smile at Kate. 'It was her suggestion.'

'Well, well, Kate, clearly all this time spent around Sybil has taken a toll.' Rita glanced at the plate of biscuits. 'Oh, you made ginger nuts! How did you manage to get the right ingredients?'

'I traded in a steer for ground ginger,' Sybil said seriously and was rewarded with a look of astonishment on Rita's face.

'You didn't!' Rita said.

'She did,' Kate said firmly, and Sybil was surprised: Kate wasn't known for encouraging jokes played on others.

Rita looked from one to the other. 'Is ginger that hard to come by here?'

Sybil started to laugh. '*Rita*, I bought it in town. The steers are all intact. Until we take them to the abattoir, that is.'

'Oh.' Rita took a bite and made a rapturous expression. 'I haven't had these in so long – thank you. And give my best to your steer.'

'Della, you're being quiet,' Sybil said, pivoting her body towards the slight young woman who had curled herself into a corner of the couch. 'What have you been up to on Ghost River?'

Della looked quickly at each of them. 'Nothing much,' she said. 'Just doing my job.'

'Stan didn't try anything on the way over here, did he?' Sybil smiled, and in return Della blushed. So her suspicions were right.

'I . . .' Della blinked and looked down.

'That was my way of asking if he'd driven you safely,' Sybil said.

'Yes,' Della said quickly. 'It was fine.'

'Good.' Sybil pushed herself off her chair. 'I'm going to make some more tea.'

'I'll help.' Della jumped to her feet and trotted after Sybil to the kitchen.

'I didn't mean to embarrass you,' Sybil said when they were out of earshot of the sitting room.

'You didn't.'

Sybil could see that Della was agitated and she hoped that she hadn't said too much after all. 'Is something the matter?'

'I . . .' Della sniffed and folded her arms over her chest. She looked so small – like a little girl, yet tougher than any girl could look. 'I heard something. And I didn't know if I should tell you. But I thought you'd want to know.'

It came out in such a rush that Sybil was momentarily perplexed. 'Something about what?' she pressed.

Della's eyes held hers. 'Your son,' she said quietly.

'Ben?'

Della shook her head.

'What do you know about Lachlan?' Sybil said, trying to keep her voice from shaking.

'We had a cook – she left around the time I started.'

'Amelia, yes,' Sybil said impatiently. She remembered Felicity complaining about how Amelia had left without warning and how difficult it would be for them to find a new cook with the wet season coming on.

'I heard she left with – with him.'

Sybil hadn't heard a word, yet somehow all the way over on Ghost River Della had. She felt betrayed, but she didn't know whose fault it was.

Sybil thought back to Lachie's unexplained absences – all the times she thought he'd been in Katherine. Had he been at Ghost River instead? The idea had never occurred to her. He never visited other stations – he was barely interested in Fairvale, so he had no reason to go elsewhere.

'All right,' Sybil said. It was a clue, but not an answer. Lachie had had plenty of girlfriends – for a few years the Katherine Show had been an opportunity for angry fathers to confront Joe about his son's penchant for 'ruining' their daughters – so she wasn't convinced that Amelia was enough of a motive for Lachie to upend his life.

Della swallowed. 'There was a baby.'

Sybil could hear a noise: a roar of confusion mixed with a cry of anguish. Was it outside her head or inside? She couldn't tell. She could only feel her hands going cold and her throat tightening.

'Sybil?' Della's hand was on her arm.

'Yes?' She was staring at Della but not seeing her. 'What do you mean – a baby?' she said. But she knew.

'Amelia had a baby. The story – what I was told – it's your son's.'

Now Sybil felt angry: people had been gossiping about Lachie – about her family – and it had taken this long to reach her. It wasn't as if there weren't stock inspectors and vets and drovers and various other people travelling from station to station. They'd hear news like that. Which meant they had come here, looked her in the eye, talked to her, eaten with her, stayed the night in her house and said nothing.

'Do you know anything else?' Sybil said, trying to keep her voice calm. None of this was Della's responsibility, after all, and no doubt Della had conjured some bravery to tell her.

Della shook her head.

'Thank you,' Sybil said. 'I appreciate you telling me.'

Della nodded soberly. 'I thought you should know.'

'Yes, I should.' She needed to take a breath. Two. Ten. But she had guests. She would deal with the news later, with Joe and Ben. And Kate.

'Let's refresh this tea, shall we?' she said, handing the pot to Della.

1979

7 January   The brutal regime of dictator Pol Pot collapses in Cambodia

1 February   Religious leader Ayatollah Khomeini returns to Iran after fifteen years of exile.

8 March   The compact disc is demonstrated in public for the first time by electronics firm Phillips

28 March   The USA's most serious nuclear accident occurs at Three Mile Island in Pennsylvania

4 May   Margaret Thatcher becomes Britain's first female prime minister

11 July   NASA's *Skylab* space station crashes back to earth after an orbit of six years and two months

27 August   Lord Louis Mountbatten is assassinated by the IRA

9 October   Legendary Australian racing driver Peter Brock wins the Bathurst 1000 by a record-breaking six laps

4 November   The Iran hostage crisis begins with the siege of the US embassy in Tehran

9 December   The World Health Organisation declares the smallpox virus eradicated

CHAPTER EIGHTEEN

The wet season was dumping more rain on Fairvale than Sybil had ever seen. On the first day of the year she looked out of her kitchen window at her garden, which had bloomed after the wet began. She had watched with excitement as the plants and trees embraced the rain by deepening in colour, lifting their leaves and fronds to the skies; now her garden was heavy with moisture, branches dropping towards the ground, and the grass had furrows where the earth was moving with the rain. She'd be lucky if the whole thing wasn't a limp, ruined mess by the time the season was over.

She was alarmed to see Ben stomping across it, his boots sinking into the ground, leaving exactly the sorts of holes that would take an age to fix.

Pulling open the kitchen door, she poked her head out, a large drop of water falling right in the middle of her forehead.

'Ben!' she cried.

'Yeah, Mum?' He appeared in front of her with his usual grin, his hat laden with water, his clothes soaked.

'Couldn't you use the path? My lawn will be ruined.'

He squinted as he looked at the lawn. 'Got news for you, Mum – it *is* ruined.' He leant forwards and kissed her quickly on the cheek.

She sighed. 'Are you coming inside?' she said.

'Nah – I was just checking to see if Dad wants to come to the camp with me. I need to fix a few things.'

'We're about to have tea.'

'Ooh – tea.' He winked. 'Can't interrupt that little ritual then, can I?'

Sybil smiled, never able to resist her son's teasing. 'You could join us.'

'Thanks, but I'd better get on with it. Dad can find me later if he wants.'

'All right, darling.'

Ben tipped the brim of his hat to her. 'See you later.'

She gave him half a wave and closed the door behind him, trapping in the humidity but closing out the rain.

As Sybil turned towards the stove she saw the letter on the kitchen table that didn't hold any news she wanted to learn. She'd read it twice and the contents didn't change: it was her brother, Geoffrey, telling her that he'd made enquiries about Lachie but had discovered nothing. Sybil didn't really know why she'd asked Geoffrey to help, except it had been her instinctual response. He was a lawyer, so she thought he might have ways of finding people that she did not. He'd been trying for weeks now and had turned up no trace of Lachlan Baxter. Geoffrey confirmed what she'd already suspected: Lachie wasn't in Melbourne, where he'd told them he was – and Sybil was now convinced he'd been lying about that. He wasn't in Brisbane, or Adelaide or Perth. Geoffrey had decided that Hobart was unlikely – a man used to the climate of the north would hardly choose to move to the icy southernmost part of Australia. And Canberra – Geoffrey was of the opinion that no one moved to Canberra voluntarily and Lachie was someone who only did what he wanted.

Sydney had taken the longest to scour and there was no Lachlan Baxter there either, except Sydney was so vast that it was plausible he was there but impossible to find. Sybil thought that if *she* wanted to disappear she'd probably do it there.

Given how easily he seemed to have turned his back on his family, she thought it most likely that he hadn't actually left with Amelia but had abandoned her, and therefore Amelia had been forced to find her own way to manage her circumstances. He wouldn't have wanted the baby – he didn't want the family he had, so he was unlikely to want to create another – and that would have been a powerful enough reason for him to disappear. He was avoiding his responsibilities, as he had done for so much of his life.

That meant Amelia and Sybil's grandchild were out there somewhere, possibly needing help. They were *her* responsibility now. Hers and Joe's. If Lachie wouldn't – or couldn't – take care of this young woman and her child, it was up to them to do so.

'Sybil, love?'

It was Joe, calling from the front of the house. He must have come in the other door, which was unusual for him – he tended to enter via the back door, just as Ben did.

'In the kitchen,' she replied, then she put the kettle on the stove.

'Would you mind asking Kate if she'd like tea?' she called.

Sybil heard his footsteps stop, presumably at the office where Kate was working. 'Kate?'

Sybil lifted her head as she heard the concern in Joe's voice. She took the kettle off the stove; she had been trained by her mother never to leave things alone on stoves, even for a second. It was automatic now.

She hurried down the hall.

'What is it?' she whispered to her husband, who was leaning in the office doorway. His eyes held confusion and worry.

Looking into the room, Sybil saw a pale Kate sitting, one hand on her abdomen, her eyes closed.

'Kate?' she said gently, but she didn't need her daughter-in-law to respond for Sybil to know that she was in pain.

'Give us a minute, will you, darling?' she said to Joe, hoping he read what was in her eyes: that Kate wouldn't want a father-in-law – any man – to hear the conversation that could come next.

After he'd left, Sybil crouched down next to Kate's chair. Kate was wincing, gasping, both hands now on her belly.

'Cramps?' Sybil said.

Kate's eyes opened and Sybil saw fear.

'I'm pregnant,' Kate whispered, her eyes closing again.

Sybil couldn't help the flash of surprise before she gathered herself.

'How many weeks?' she said softly.

'I think . . .' Kate winced again. 'About ten.'

Ten? And she and Ben hadn't said anything? Moreover, Sybil hadn't noticed. She prided herself on detecting pregnancy early, having seen it so often in her career.

'Ben doesn't know,' Kate said quickly and her eyes filled with tears. 'I didn't want to get his hopes up.' She smiled wanly, then her mouth turned down. 'Too late now.'

'What do you mean?' Sybil put a hand over one of Kate's.

'I think I'm bleeding,' Kate whispered hoarsely, a tear dropping onto her cheek.

Sybil didn't need to ask for details. When women said they thought they were bleeding, it meant they were, no thinking required. She'd heard it so often, that qualifier: 'I think'. She'd long ago decided that it was meant as a talisman or incantation, the woman in question hoping it would ward off what was really happening.

A bleed didn't necessarily mean the baby was lost but they had to get her to a doctor – to hospital, preferably. They had to take her to Katherine. Even if the creek hadn't cut their access it would have been a two-hour drive to town over mostly unpaved road. It seemed almost like luck that they couldn't take her that way.

'We have to get you out of here,' Sybil said.

'*No.*'

'Kate,' Sybil said, deploying the stern tone she'd used on reluctant patients so many times, 'that wasn't a suggestion.'

'I don't want Ben to find out,' Kate said, more tears falling from her eyes, dropping onto Sybil's hand.

'My dear,' Sybil said, standing up, 'he will be far more upset if he finds out later that he wasn't told.'

Kate looked up, her eyes bright.

'He wants what's best for you,' Sybil continued. 'And that's getting you to town.'

She put her hand on Kate's shoulder; it might not give much reassurance to the young woman but it was better than nothing.

Sybil knew she didn't have time to dither – no time even to catch Ben – but she had to think carefully about how to take Kate into town.

No truck could get through that water and she wouldn't risk it even if the creek was half as high – a big truck could be swept off the road in a strong current. She could call the Flying Doctor but with the ground so sodden it would be difficult for the plane to take off.

Her brain calculated the possibilities: who was close by and what transportation did they have?

Then she remembered: Ghost River Station had a helicopter. They'd started using one to muster their cattle a couple of years before. Everyone had laughed at Felicity and Aug, said that horses were better than anything, but on a station the size of Ghost River horses – and men – wore out after a few days and the helicopter had proved a boon.

No one was mustering at the moment – not in the wet. That meant the helicopter would be sitting idle near the homestead and she hoped someone would be around to fly it.

She picked up the radiotelephone that lived on the desk in the office and heard voices on the line. She didn't have the luxury of a line to herself, but she didn't want everyone on the party line knowing her business either. She'd have to keep the conversation short and avoid detail.

'Val, I need Ghost River,' she instructed the operator. She should ask for the number not the name, but she couldn't remember it. Strange that she couldn't – her memory was always so good. Strange, too, the feeling in her legs, like they were shaking.

'Hello to you too, Sybil,' Val cracked.

'Val, I'm in a hurry,' she said, trying not to sound irritated lest Val decide not to put her through at all, as she'd been known to do when the mood struck her.

'Yeah, yeah, keep your shirt on.'

Sybil listened as Val connected the call.

'Felicity,' Sybil said, almost stuttering in her relief.

'Hello, Sybil,' Felicity trilled. 'Funny you should call, I—'

'We need your helicopter,' Sybil said and the other voices on the line went quiet. There was no time for niceties, and Felicity would make her pay for that later. For the next year, at least, Felicity would remind her that she had been *so rude on the telephone that day.*

Kate gasped and Sybil looked down at her, seeing her tilt completely forwards, hearing her cry. No, there was no time.

'We're not mustering,' Felicity said. 'The rain—'

'It's a bit of an emergency. We need someone to get us into Katherine.'

'Us?'

'*Felicity.*'

As she kept watching Kate, Sybil heard a noise of exasperation, then the sound of Felicity calling to someone and the other people on the line recommencing their chatter. They'd have something to gossip about once she was off the line: *Sybil Baxter needed a helicopter for something – what could it be? And didn't you know Felicity used to tell people that she was meant to marry Joe but Sybil swooped in and took him? Poor Felicity got stuck with that useless Aug. Ghost River is hers, though, not his – didn't you know? She's an only child, and her father had to leave it to someone.*

On it would go, and Sybil had heard it all before. It was a way of passing time, she supposed, but why did time always move so slowly when it needed to accelerate? She needed Kate to be in that helicopter already; she needed her to be with a doctor, being told she was all right, that the baby was fine.

'Aug can take you,' Felicity said as she came back on the line.

'How many people can it fit?' Sybil said.

'Two. Him and one other.'

Sybil exhaled. Kate would have to go alone and she'd have to rely on Aug to come back for her. It wasn't the best option but it was the only one.

'That would be wonderful,' she said. 'Thank you.'

'Fifteen minutes,' Felicity said. 'And I'm never letting you win at bridge again.'

Sybil couldn't help smiling – if that was the price, she'd pay it and never think twice.

'Thank you, Felicity. He can put down next to the yards.'

She ended the call and crouched beside Kate again, taking both her hands. She could see the effort on Kate's face as she tried not to cry. She knew that in marrying Ben and coming to such a strange place, Kate was brave. Sybil hadn't acknowledged it at the time, perhaps because she'd done it herself and to think of it as bravery seemed so grandiose, but bravery it was. This was a different kind of bravery, though – this time Kate wasn't willing to go where life was taking her.

'Aug's coming to fly you into town,' Sybil told her. 'I'll radio the hospital and see if they can meet you at the airstrip.'

'Helicopter?' Kate said, gasping again.

'It's the only way. And I'll be on the next one into town, okay? Aug can only take one of us at a time and I want to make sure the hospital looks after you.'

'Ben?' Kate said, shaking her head, and Sybil guessed at the reason for it.

'Ben would want to know,' she said as kindly as she could. 'Kate, love, he would just die if he found out you were in trouble and he hadn't been told.'

'Do you think it's trouble?' Kate said, and her shoulders shook.

'I don't know,' Sybil said truthfully.

She wished she could hear the chopper's rotor blades already. Wished that Kate wasn't bleeding, that this day would start again, that hard decisions and unpleasantness would never visit this house the way they had when she had bled just as Kate was bleeding now – once, twice, and neither instance ending with a baby. That wasn't for Kate to know today, though. Today they had to get her daughter-in-law to a hospital and the story would unfold from there, out of anyone's control.

CHAPTER NINETEEN

Kate could feel the horse's mane wrapped around her fingers, the coarseness of the hair at odds with the animal's sleek coat. She held the reins in one hand and dug her fingers deeper into the mane as she and the horse moved as one. It was her way of telling the horse that she was there with it – they were together on this adventure.

That was strange: there was a person in the distance, waving. Was it her mother? What was her mother doing here?

She looked around. Where was this place? These trees lining the path – they were oaks and elms. Trees she hadn't seen for more than a year now. She looked down and there was lush emerald grass beside the path. She hadn't seen grass like that since she'd left England.

She looked at the mane wrapped around her fingers: it was black. This horse wasn't Mrs Simpson. Mrs Simpson was chestnut. Whose horse was this? And how did she get on it?

As she gazed ahead she saw the path changing – no, it was disappearing. Was her mother calling to her now? She heard something behind her. Was it her mother? Was it Sybil? Someone was saying, 'You're all right.' But as she looked at what was ahead – an open plain, hardly any trees, dark clouds in the distance and a mob of cattle – she wasn't sure.

'You're all right.'

There was that voice again. Was it over her shoulder? She turned around to look but there was no one there. Even the oaks and elms were gone. Behind her was a black-soil plain; beneath the black horse's hooves there was red dirt.

That's when she saw the snake slithering beside them. It was coppery brown. Sybil had warned her about brown snakes. The snake started to wind towards the horse's legs. Kate dropped her heels and her seat and yanked on the reins but the horse wouldn't stop. The snake was getting closer – should she try to kick the horse into a gallop and outrun the snake? Was there time? It was so close now, she was sure it was going to bite the horse. Then the horse would fall and she'd be on the ground and perhaps it would bite her too. She was so far from help out here – she couldn't see the big house, she couldn't see any other people. What could she do? Who was going to help her? Was she going to—

'No!' she cried.

'Kate.' It was Sybil's voice this time, she was sure of it. Except Sybil never sounded that gentle.

She could feel a hand on her cheek. It was warm. It felt soft.

She opened her eyes and tried to comprehend what she was seeing. There was red dirt, but it was outside a window, and there was rain falling on it. There were two trees outside that window. Not oaks. Not elms. They had bark that was shredding. Gum trees. She wasn't in England. Nor was she out on Fairvale's plains. There was no horse here.

She was in a bed. It didn't feel very comfortable and it had metal railings around it.

The room was sparse. White. There was a saggy chair in the corner and not much else.

She looked up to see Sybil frowning at her. Not Sybil's usual frown, which when Kate had first arrived at Fairvale she'd thought was one of disapproval. There was concern there instead and Sybil was stroking her head. It felt nice. Comforting. Like something her mother would do, except her mother wasn't here either.

'You're in hospital, love,' Sybil said.

Now she remembered: that tiny helicopter, and Aug chattering away to her about how hard it was to find stockmen who wouldn't try to race off with other staff members, and all the while she felt something warm and wet between her legs and knew what it was, what it meant, but she kept silent and let him talk, let it become a distraction. She had a vague memory of a car at the airstrip and a doctor with a kind face, and a nurse who held her hand. Sybil appeared at some stage, just before she closed her eyes, just before they told her to count back from ten. She had made it to eight.

She gasped, and it felt like a punch to her chest.

'The baby,' she said, knowing the answer but wanting to hear someone else say it, wanting it to be confirmed as real so she knew she wasn't going mad, so she hadn't just imagined everything.

Sybil kept stroking her head.

'Kate, it's lost,' she said quietly.

Another punch.

Her first pregnancy and it was over. After so many months of failing even to get pregnant, she'd now failed to hold on to their baby. She'd failed to give Ben a child. She was useless. He needed to find another wife. Someone who was stronger, healthier, more cut out for this hard life on the land, someone who could take it all and still have babies.

'I'm going to tell you something,' Sybil said, 'because what you're thinking is clear from the look on your face and you need to stop thinking it.'

Kate glanced up, then away to the window and nodded slowly.

Sybil pulled a chair next to the bed and took her hand.

'I've had miscarriages,' she said. 'I've also had babies. They go together, Kate. Not every pregnancy is meant to hold, and a lot of women who have babies have also had miscarriages. It's tough when it's your first.' She squeezed Kate's hand. 'But it won't be your last pregnancy. You can get pregnant, that's the important thing. I know it doesn't seem like it now. But you'll be all right.'

As Sybil placed one hand on her hair and gently stroked, Kate closed her eyes.

'I don't think . . .' She licked her lips. They felt dry. Everything about her felt worn out and used up and weathered. 'I don't think I believe you,' she whispered, squeezing her eyes shut.

'No,' Sybil said. 'I don't imagine you do.'

'I did something wrong, didn't I?' Kate said, keeping her eyes shut.

'No, love. They just happen. Believe me – I've nursed women through this apart from going through it myself. I didn't do anything wrong. Nor did they. Nor did you. It's nature and we can't control it. Or understand it, most of the time.'

Kate wanted so much to believe her, yet that didn't stop her raking over her memories of the past few weeks, trying to identify a clue. A reason.

Sybil kept stroking her head. 'You poor thing,' she said, her voice sounding like a lullaby. 'I know you're going to blame yourself but I promise you, Kate, you're not at fault.'

No matter what Sybil said, though, Kate knew she should have done something differently – if only she knew what that was meant to be. It wouldn't do her any good, though, to keep mulling it over now. There would be time, later, after Sybil had gone and the sun had set.

'Where's Ben?' she said. 'Can he get in?'

'No,' Sybil said. 'The road's still closed, and Aug's patience with us only extended so far. He'll be here as soon as he can.'

Kate might be home before that happened – although how she'd get back to Fairvale she didn't know. And as much as she loved Ben, there was a tiny part of her that was glad she wasn't seeing him now. The sadness – the anger, for that's what it really was – that she was managing to keep on a simmer below the surface would erupt if she saw him, because he would feel it too. While sharing it might, to one way of thinking, lessen the burden, Kate suspected that it would instead intensify what she was already feeling, and she wanted to be stronger when that happened. She wanted to have a plan for the future, for what they would do if there was another miscarriage, or if there wasn't a baby at all.

'In the meantime,' Sybil said, cutting into her thoughts, 'we need to think about the next few days. They'll discharge you soon, but ideally you'll stay close to the hospital for a little while. I have an idea.'

After a minute or so Kate felt herself waning, and a few seconds after that she heard Sybil saying that she'd let her rest and come back later. She felt Sybil's lips on her forehead; then sleep, or unconsciousness, overtook her and she slid into a place without dreams.

CHAPTER TWENTY

The slam of the truck door in the driveway made Sallyanne jump. She knew it was Mick and she knew he was angry. Carefully, she put the knife she was using into the sink; the cucumber would have to stay, half chopped, on the cutting board. She felt her heart beating – a little faster, then a little faster still – and tried not to give into her fear. He'd been like this so often lately, and sometimes not even when he was drunk.

'Sallyanne!'

She wiped her hands on her apron before pushing open the kitchen's screen door. 'Mick, please keep your voice down,' she said as she walked towards him, trying to sound firm. Like someone he couldn't boss around. 'I thought you were going straight to Dad's after work.'

His hair was sticking up and his eyes looked unfocused as he glared at her.

'You forgot to put my fucking bag in the truck,' he said, stepping closer to her as her inhalation stopped in her chest.

She could smell beer on his breath and wondered if she should let him drive away again. Not that she wanted him to stay, and she felt like a terrible person for wishing, just for an instant, that he might have an accident and have to go to hospital for a few weeks. Or, maybe, never come back at all. That made her horrible, didn't it? She shouldn't think that way. She wasn't a good person, and she'd always tried to be one.

'I didn't know I was meant to,' she said, willing herself not to sound meek. She'd been working on that: *calm, steady voice; look him in the eye even if you're scared*. Rita had given her some tips the last time she'd called. 'I left it by the door. I thought you'd see it.'

'Yeah, well, how was I meant to know that?'

She had to consider her answer carefully: if she apologised for not putting the bag in the truck or for leaving it by the door, he would tell her she was stupid and worthless, and he'd remind her of it for weeks. And if she retrieved the bag from the house and put it in the truck herself, she would be weak and he would know it, and that, too, would be an opportunity for him to castigate her. So she was trapped. If only she'd thought about these possibilities beforehand – she should have guessed how he'd react and just put the bag in the truck, then she wouldn't have to stand out here with the neighbours listening, her daughter having a nap that she could wake up from at any time, and Sybil about to arrive with Kate, straight from the hospital.

'I'll get the bag,' she said, deciding on the middle way: no apology but an action of appeasement.

Before he could say anything she almost skipped the few steps back to the kitchen, picked up his bag and brought it to him, holding it out with a straight arm.

'So how long am I not allowed in my own home?' Mick said as he took the bag, sounding slightly mollified.

'It depends,' Sallyanne said, then she coughed once. It was so hard for her not to sound small when she spoke to him. He'd been making her feel small, and she'd started speaking that way. She had to practise, like Rita said, speaking as if she took up a whole room.

'Kate needs to rest some more and they can't get her home until there's less rain.' She glanced up at the sky, which looked menacing but would probably hold for the rest of the day. The wet-season rain tended to fall in the morning and leave them alone in the afternoon.

'What's wrong with her, anyway?' Mick said, looking at her closely. Probably trying to catch her in a lie, as he kept saying she lied to him – and in this case he was right.

'She had her appendix out.' It was the excuse Sybil had suggested, because it wasn't as if anyone would go poking around Kate's abdomen looking for the surgical wound.

'Hm,' he said. 'So what am I meant to do – stay with your father until you tell me to come home? It's my bloody house. I have a right—'

'I know you do, Mick,' Sallyanne said firmly. 'But Kate has nowhere else to stay. I'm asking you to do this favour. For me. For my friends.' She scanned her brain to see if she could offer him something more to his liking. 'And you know Dad likes a beer – he'll be glad of some company while he has a few drinks each night.'

Mick grunted.

'Anyway, he's expecting you,' she said breezily. She stepped forwards and pecked his cheek. 'I'll call you tomorrow.'

His lips disappeared into a thin line and she had no way of telling if he was about to yell at her again or go on his way.

'Yeah, right,' he said. He yanked at the driver's-side door and got into the seat, pulling the door towards him so forcefully that the truck rocked.

She opened her mouth to say goodbye but he wasn't looking at her, so she didn't bother.

The truck's tyres squealed as Mick reversed it onto the road. He hadn't asked about the children. She wished she was surprised. She wished she wasn't upset. But for them – for three little people who needed a father who was consistent and caring – she was.

Sallyanne waited until she couldn't hear his engine anymore before she went inside, picked up the knife and resumed slicing the cucumber.

＿

Sallyanne knew she had been lucky to have three babies and no mishaps at all with the births. She had heard stories of D&Cs in a fourth month of pregnancy, or miscarriage after miscarriage before a baby finally arrived, or a longed-for baby stillborn, or something else going horribly wrong. It didn't take much for her to remember that it wasn't so long ago that a lot of women died in childbirth. Some still did, of course – Lynette from school, for example. Massive haemorrhage and gone a few minutes after the birth. Her husband left with a toddler and a baby he later said had been Lynette's idea: he'd only wanted one child.

Any pregnancy was a roll of the dice, Sallyanne reckoned. She'd had easy babies, but now she had a difficult husband, so maybe everyone got their share of burden to deal with. Make that every *woman*: the men she knew didn't let much touch them. Lynette's husband had found himself a girl not long out of her teens who was prepared to take on someone else's kids, and now she was his second wife.

That didn't mean Sallyanne was going to make Kate listen to her concerns about Mick. The poor girl had enough to deal with. Not long after she'd arrived the children had tried to climb all over her and bother her with questions about

England. Tim and Billy tried to mimic her accent and then asked her if she'd met the Queen and Prince Philip. Sallyanne had been appalled at their behaviour; Kate had laughed weakly and told them about Buckingham Palace.

During the night Sallyanne had heard Kate softly crying. She'd wanted to go to her but didn't want to intrude on what must be grief.

This morning she'd waited until she heard noises from Kate's room before she put on the kettle and made some toast and a soft-boiled egg to take in for Kate's breakfast.

Holding the tray in one hand, she knocked gently on the door of the spare bedroom.

'Yes?' she heard.

'It's just me. I have some breakfast.'

'Oh.'

Sallyanne heard movement, as if Kate was sitting up.

'Thank you,' Kate called. 'Please come in.' Her voice sounded strained and Sallyanne realised that she was likely to be making an effort to put on a brave front.

As the door opened Sallyanne saw Kate propped awkwardly on the pillows. She was wan and there was a hint of darkness beneath her eyes.

'Did you get any sleep?' Sallyanne said, putting the tray on the bedside table.

'A little.' Kate's smile was brief and joyless. 'I've been reading your book.' She pointed to Sallyanne's worn copy of *Snugglepot and Cuddlepie* by May Gibbs. 'I wish I'd been given it when I first arrived here. It would have explained a few things.' She smiled awkwardly as she shifted herself to reach over for the teapot.

'I'll pour,' Sallyanne said, turning the pot once clockwise, as her mother had taught her to do. 'I'm glad you like it.

I know it's a children's book but I still read it sometimes . . . Tim and Billy love it, but Gretel is scared of the Banksia Men.'

'So am I!' Kate said. Then she laughed – the first laugh Sallyanne had heard since her arrival. Sallyanne grinned, pleased beyond any measure she knew that she'd helped Kate feel better.

Sallyanne handed Kate the plate of toast and received a smile in return.

'It must have been strange,' Sallyanne said, closing her eyes and trying to imagine Kate as she arrived in the Territory for the first time, 'to see Fairvale when you got there. The Territory is so different. To England. To anywhere.'

Kate nodded as she swallowed some of her breakfast. 'Honestly, I thought I was in a movie for a while. I kept expecting someone to dismantle the set. It's . . . improbable here, don't you think?'

Her eyes were bright, the tone of her skin better than it had been even a few minutes before.

'The colours don't seem natural,' Kate went on. 'The sky is so big – bigger than anything I've ever seen. But I suppose you're used to it.'

Sallyanne considered the statement, a tumult of feelings and thoughts about her home inside her.

'I don't think you ever get used to it,' she said softly, thinking of the waterfalls in Katherine Gorge during the wet season, of the torpor of the build-up, of the dirt that tried, always, to reclaim the town. 'It doesn't really feel like it belongs to us. It's . . .' She sighed. 'Or maybe we don't belong here.'

Kate's gaze shifted to the window; outside the rain was falling, making the leaves of next door's trees heavy.

'I know what you mean,' she said, catching Sallyanne's eye. 'But I want to belong.'

Sallyanne laughed nervously. 'Maybe I just don't belong in my own life. Maybe that's my problem.'

'You have a problem?' Kate said, frowning.

'Don't I?' Sallyanne said. 'I don't do anything but raise my children. I'm stuck here in this house.' She gestured to the ceiling. 'In town. Where you live – it's so much more exciting.'

Kate made a noise of disbelief. 'I'd hardly call cattle "exciting". And you say that raising the children is all you do – it's such an important job. The most important job.' Her voice trailed off and Sallyanne immediately realised how insensitive she had been, dismissing motherhood as inconsequential when Kate had just lost a baby.

'I'm an awful person,' she blurted.

'What? Why?' Kate was still frowning.

'You've been – you've had—' She didn't even want to say it. 'I'm saying motherhood isn't worth much when you—' She shook her head. 'I'm sorry.'

Sallyanne wanted to cry with the horribleness of it all but that would be rude: she would be getting upset because she'd behaved badly and that would make her guest uncomfortable. Some days, she thought, she just didn't fit anywhere.

As she pressed her teeth together, trying not to cry, Kate took her hand.

'You are far too hard on yourself,' Kate whispered. 'You are such a kind person. Look – you've taken me in and you barely know me.'

Sallyanne's bottom lip trembled as she looked into Kate's big eyes, so frank in their expression of understanding.

'And you are doing a wonderful job as a mother,' Kate carried on. 'Your children are lovely. They're so full of life, Sallyanne – were you like that as a child?'

Sallyanne had to think about it. What *had* she been like as a child? Bookish – she was sure about that. But she could remember squealing with joy as she rode her bicycle down the middle of Third Street and as she floated in the hot springs and felt the fizz of the water in one little part. She always wanted to go to the hot springs – she didn't know why she hadn't remembered that when her own children started begging to do it. The hot springs, so the story of the local tribe went, were the urine of the Rainbow Serpent. As a child she'd loved the ickyness of that idea – that she was swimming in wee, even if the water was really so clean and clear that it was obviously not wee.

'Yes,' Sallyanne said after a few moments, 'I think I was.'

Kate looked at her as if she was studying her face. 'I bet you were,' she said. 'You're just like that now.'

Sallyanne's mother had once told her that she would never see herself the way other people saw her, so she shouldn't be so hard on herself. 'You don't see how lovely you are,' she would say. 'You don't see how your smile lights you up.'

Sallyanne didn't know how to react. She put her hands on her cheeks, which felt hot, and let her gaze drop to the floor.

She should say thank you – that was the polite thing to do. But she just couldn't.

'Della called,' she said instead.

'Oh?' Kate pushed herself further upright, the book sliding off her lap onto the bed.

'She wanted to know how you are and, um, she asked me to tell you that she'd come to visit if she could but she can't get across the creek.'

Kate half smiled and nodded. 'Of course,' she said. 'Sybil had to get the Ghost River helicopter to take her home, but I don't think Aug would bring Della in just for a visit.'

'I'd love to have a ride in a helicopter,' Sallyanne said, starting to envisage what it would be like to do something so exciting. What she would see if she was up there above the earth, looking down at the trees and the river and the whole majestic sweep of this countryside that she belonged to – that she now knew *was* where she belonged, even if she occasionally had a flicker of wanting to be somewhere else.

Sallyanne realised her mind had drifted again and when she looked at Kate, wondering if her guest would think her strange, she saw only a funny little smile.

'Where did your brain go just then?' Kate said, still smiling.

'I'm sorry,' Sallyanne said quickly, feeling her cheeks going warm again.

'Why? I wish I could dream so easily.' Kate's eyes dropped. 'It might make life easier to put up with.'

'Oh, Rita's coming to visit,' Sallyanne said, remembering the other piece of news she had to share.

'Rita?' Kate frowned.

'She said it's a house call.'

'She's flying from Alice Springs to make a house call?'

'She said since Sybil can't be here she's going to check up on you instead.'

Kate exhaled loudly. 'I had no idea you were all so worried about me.'

'Why wouldn't we be?' Sallyanne said.

Kate's eyes looked so bright then – shiny. Like she was . . .

Sallyanne realised that Kate, who had displayed so little emotion those first couple of times she'd seen her at Fairvale, was crying.

'Thank you,' Kate whispered.

'Don't thank me,' Sallyanne said. 'It's what friends do.' She attempted a smile. 'Like friends sometimes read May Gibbs books to other friends' children.'

Kate laughed and sniffed, then lifted her knuckles to her cheeks, wiping away her tears. 'Send them in,' she said.

CHAPTER TWENTY-ONE

The vista was vividly green as Della let her horse walk slowly across the rain-flattened tussocks on the sweeping plain of Ghost River, following the stock trail. The scrubby trees that looked so sparse in the dry season now had leaves alive with water. She'd worked the morning in the big house, helping Felicity, and as the rain had cleared in the afternoon she'd decided to go for a ride. But she hadn't counted on having Stan as company.

Over the past few months Della and Stan had seen each other when he drove her to Fairvale for the second book club meeting, and when she'd gone to Fairvale a fortnight ago to see Kate after she'd returned home from hospital and her stay at Sallyanne's. And now he was here at Ghost River, riding beside her.

'I can never believe how different this place looks in the wet,' Della said. 'I know it changes. It's just . . .' Ahead of her, the trail was straight, marking a black-soil plain that stretched so far on each side and behind her that it seemed to cover the whole world. In the dry they would be stirring up dust, riding along here. In the wet the dirt stayed put.

She turned to look at Stan, sitting straight in the saddle, one hand relaxed as it held the reins near the horse's neck, the other by his side. Western style, that's how he was riding. American style. Just like her.

'It's good country,' he said, his voice sounding distant, his face tense for an instant before it relaxed.

'Is it your country?' she said. She hadn't asked him, or Bob, before.

He looked at her as their horses walked on.

'No,' he said. 'This is Wardaman country. Our country is Jawoyn.'

'And is Fairvale on Jawoyn land?'

He shook his head. 'That's Wardaman too.'

'I don't . . .' She paused, not knowing how best to say what she wanted to. 'I don't know how it works but . . . don't you want to be in your own country?'

He smiled. 'Course I do, Della girl. But the work isn't there for me. It's in this country.' His smiled disappeared and his expression turned serious. 'And you're in this country too. That's plenty good reason for me to stay here.'

She held his gaze for a second or two then looked away, feeling shy. She didn't know why she couldn't look at him. Maybe she was embarrassed about liking him so much.

'Why are you here?' Stan said, his voice gentle. 'It's not your country either.'

Della looked around her once more and felt the undulations of Arthur's gait beneath her. They'd been getting along better. She had learnt to read Arthur better and he seemed less grumpy about having her on his back. She looked up at the sky, which held heaviness, the promise of more rain. Even when the clouds closed in, it was still the biggest sky she'd ever seen. Bigger than Texas.

'I wanted an adventure,' she said after several moments

had passed. 'I wanted . . . more. My town is small. I had a feeling I'd get stuck there if I stayed any longer.'

She risked glancing at him and was rewarded with a grin. 'You didn't want to be stuck?'

'No.' She took a deep breath in. 'I want to be free. I want life. You know what I mean?'

She was surprised as Stan pulled up his horse. 'Yeah, Della girl, I reckon I do.'

She turned Arthur around so she could face him, then moved up next to his horse. 'Why are we stopped?'

He lifted his face to the sky. 'It's gonna rain again soon. I reckon we should turn back.'

She looked up too but couldn't see what he saw. For all the time she'd spent outdoors she hadn't learnt to read the weather the way so many people did here. She could recognise that rain was coming but she couldn't predict when.

'Okay,' she said, about to nudge Arthur's flanks.

Stan put out his hand and stopped her. 'Let's just wait a little while,' he said. 'That rain's a few minutes away.'

She looked back down the trail to the house in the distance. 'It'll take us an hour, at least, to get back.'

He grinned again and she felt her heart tug, the way it always did when he smiled at her. 'Not if we gallop,' he said.

She felt she should ask him why they were waiting, but something told her that she knew, really, why it was. As he reached over to cover her hand with his, there was no reason to ask anything. As his lips met hers, she fancied that she would never talk again if it meant she could have this – have him – every day of her life.

She felt him grab Arthur's reins, pulling her horse closer, pulling her closer. Della took her free hand to his shoulder, to steady herself so she didn't fall off. Because she felt the danger of that, with this kiss different – better – than any kiss she'd had before, with her insides turning to mush and her brain melting.

When he pulled back from her she stayed where she was, her lips parted, looking into his dark eyes and wondering what he saw in hers.

'Do you feel free, Della girl?' he murmured and she nodded.

'Do you?' she whispered.

He breathed, in and out, slowly. 'Out here I do,' he said, and his fingers played on her cheekbone.

Then he looked over his shoulder, in the direction of the house.

'Back there,' he said, 'I'm not so free.' He turned to her. 'You and me, we can't be together back there.'

Her chest felt heavy. 'So this . . .' She panted her breath out.

'I had to kiss you,' he said, smiling sadly. 'I've been thinking about it since I met you.'

'You – you have?'

'Yeah.' He laughed. 'And you've been thinking about kissing me too.'

She blushed, because he was right.

'But we can't kiss again?' she said.

'I reckon we can,' he said. 'But not at Ghost River. Your boss lady – she won't like it.'

Della almost gulped with relief. She'd thought 'back there' meant anywhere there were other people.

'So Fairvale is okay?' she said, feeling like a schoolgirl planning when she could sneak out of her parents' house.

'Sure it is. Mister and Missus Baxter, their only rule is that people are kind to each other. We just have to get you there, don't we? That's what we have to work out.'

'I'm going to see you again.' In her head it had been a question, yet it hadn't emerged that way aloud.

'If you want to,' he said, looking suddenly nervous.

She'd never had someone ask her so plainly. Courtship rituals of young Texan men had mainly involved them telling her what they wanted, not asking her what she wanted. Now she was being asked Della wasn't sure of the answer. But she needed to have an answer because Stan was asking her to choose. It was the clearest indication she knew of his regard for her.

'Of course I do,' she said, her smile as wide as she could make it.

He was visibly relieved. 'Then we'd better find reasons for you to visit,' he said, just as a splodge of rain dropped onto Della's hand.

Stan squinted at the sky. 'Time to go,' he said. 'How about we race back?'

Before she had time to answer he'd turned his horse and kicked it into a gallop. She urged Arthur to pick up his pace but she was still behind Stan, watching as he rose from the saddle, bending forwards over his horse's neck, one hand holding the reins and the other in the air, as if he was cheering their journey home.

Della was happy not to catch up. Happy to watch him ride. She knew he wasn't leaving her behind so much as racing ahead to whatever awaited them – together.

CHAPTER TWENTY-TWO

Rita had seen many dead bodies in her years of work and she'd learnt that there were no rules to dying: people went old, they went young; they went suddenly and they went after long suffering. There was nothing to say that you only died once you'd achieved a certain amount of things or seen enough of the world, or if you'd loved well and could be surrounded by those close to you as you left this plane of existence and moved to another.

She'd also seen enough bodies to know that dead was dead. Once the heart stopped beating and the lungs stopped moving, once the brain no longer sent its messages speeding out to fingers and toes and tongue, there was nothing left. There was no essence of the person who had once inhabited that body. What remained was a shell that looked like the person whose family now mourned, whose friends would miss them.

Rita had tried to develop a personal theology out of this, wanting to believe that there was a soul that floated off somewhere to be held in a special place in the universe. She'd never seen it, though. For a while she'd looked – as a patient died she would watch them for a few minutes, just to see if she could capture something that no one else had ever seen.

Of course, she wasn't the special one who was going to figure out the mystery of death just by watching. Dead was dead.

The eyes of the girl who lay on the bed before her were closed; her white-blonde hair was splayed on the pillow.

'It's all right, mate,' the girl's father was saying to her brother, who was sniffling into his mother's waist, his face streaked with tears. His mother had her hand on the side of his head, her own face blotchy with crying.

'It's not your fault,' the man said gently, awkwardly patting his son's shoulder.

'I—' the boy hiccuped, 'I should have told her – her – to run away.'

'No, son. It's not your fault. You can't control snakes,' he said. Rita couldn't believe how composed Mr Stephens was.

The boy started to whimper then and his mother bent down to kiss the top of his head. One child left. Rita knew why they would never be angry with him, regardless of how the scenario had played out.

The parents had put a tourniquet on her, once their son's shouts had brought his mother from the house. She'd fumbled; in the panic of seeing her youngest child frantic and weeping, the bite marks clear on her ankle, she had forgotten everything she'd ever known about treating snakebite. She had shrieked for her husband, who had pounded his way over from the horse he was saddling. He'd been calmer, more used to dealing with the consequences of their life way out here, so far from help.

The tourniquet had been applied correctly, Rita could see. The father had radioed the Flying Doctor straight afterwards. But by the time the plane had landed the girl was gone. She was so little; the venom hadn't had to travel far to kill her.

'We need to take her,' Rita said as gently as she could.

Mrs Stephens looked around, her confusion clear.

'Why?' she said. 'Can't she stay with us?'

Hamish put a hand on Mrs Stephens's shoulder. He was good at this; Rita had seen it a few times now. People in shock couldn't understand a rational explanation so Hamish would use his calm, deep voice, knowing that the tone alone would reassure them.

'There are some things we need to do for her, Mrs Stephens,' he said, his hand still on her shoulder.

'But you'll bring her back?' Mr Stephens said, looking from Rita to Hamish. 'We need to . . . we want to have her back here.'

'We will,' he promised, withdrawing his hand and nodding once to Rita, who followed him to the next room.

'Do you need Darryl to carry her to the plane?' Rita said, keeping her voice quiet so the Stephenses couldn't hear her.

Hamish shook his head. 'I'd like to do it.'

He looked tired – he'd been looking tired ever since he arrived, the bright-eyed optimism of his first day replaced by the rigours of shift work, long hours in the plane, unpredictable cases and violent, unusual deaths.

'I'll go and tell Darryl we're ready.' Rita picked up her bag – which had been useless in this instance – and started for the plane. She didn't say goodbye to the family – they wouldn't know she was there, would barely remember anything that happened after their girl died. In years to come their recounting of this day would likely not include the Flying Doctor at all. She'd seen it before: stories of sudden deaths were malleable depending on who was telling them and when.

It didn't matter how many times she'd seen it, though: losing the little ones was always terrible. Early in her career

Rita had learnt how to control her facial expressions so she didn't betray her emotions in front of patients and their families, and that had led to her being able to control the emotions themselves. Once she left their side, though, she stopped trying to control anything. As she walked to the plane, walked towards Darryl who was leaning against the fuselage, smoking, she let herself cry. She would never get used to the deaths of children, and she hoped she never did.

~

'This salad's a bit pathetic,' Rita said, putting a plate in front of Hamish. 'Sorry.'

He smiled weakly. 'Please don't apologise. You've made me dinner – it's a lovely gift.'

Rita made a face. 'Wilted lettuce and a steak that I hope I haven't overcooked. I'm not that good in the kitchen.'

'Rita,' he said with a note of warning.

'Yes?'

'Stop apologising for doing a nice thing.'

She made another face. She found herself doing that around Hamish quite regularly. Over the last few weeks of their friendship she'd become insecure about things that she'd never even bothered to contemplate before, like her cooking skills. She wanted to impress him: that was the reason.

'All right,' she said, sitting down. 'I'll stop.'

He smiled tightly and picked up his cutlery.

'Would you believe that's the first snakebite I've attended?' he said, cutting into his steak.

'I would,' she said. 'I only saw a couple before I came here, and that was when I was training, working at a hospital near the bush in Sydney.'

He nodded, chewing, his face serious. 'I saw a few when I was a child,' he said. 'Just not as a doctor.'

'Where did you grow up?'

'Young,' he said. 'Do you know it?'

'I know vaguely where it is. Close to Canberra?'

He smiled wryly. 'Close in bush terms, yes. My family had a small holding. Dad worked as a solicitor in town. Conveyancing, that kind of thing.'

'So he wasn't a farmer?'

'No, he just liked the idea of having property.'

This was the first time he'd told her anything of his younger life. They'd discussed his university years in Brisbane, where he'd moved to study because his maternal grandparents were there and he could live with them, whereas there was nowhere in Sydney for him to stay if he'd studied there. Those sorts of calculations were foreign to Rita: she knew so many people in Sydney that she could do a tour of homes for several months and not run out of places to stay.

While Hamish hadn't said much about the years before he moved to Queensland, he'd told her a lot about the time since: that he had married young and now had two children in their early twenties; that their mother had died two years ago, felled by a cerebral haemorrhage.

'Quick as anything,' he'd said. 'I was home and I . . .' A shadow had passed across his face. 'I couldn't do anything. She was gone by the time she hit the floor.'

He'd looked almost embarrassed, and Rita knew why: they were medical professionals and things like that weren't meant to happen to them. Their loved ones were meant to have an advantage because they, the doctors and nurses, should be alert to symptoms and highly reactive to them. In reality, doctors and nurses could be tougher on their relatives than on anyone else. Rita knew former colleagues whose children had to be vomiting in the school playground before their mothers would believe that they were sick.

'That must have been awful,' Rita had said. 'And "awful" is really such an inadequate word.'

'It was,' he'd said. 'And it's a pretty good word for it.' His eyes had half closed. 'My wife – Rachel – she'd done everything for the children.'

He opened his eyes fully now and looked at her. 'I found out how bad a parent I'd been,' he continued.

'I'm sure that's not true,' Rita said quickly.

'Oh, it is.' He smiled ruefully. 'I knew the details of their lives – what they'd studied at school, what sports they'd played – but I didn't really know what they were like. I was home so rarely when they were awake that they were always on their best behaviour.' He looked briefly pained. 'Like they were scared of me.'

His eyes had closed briefly once more.

'So in the last couple of years I've had to learn how to be a father, properly. If any good has come out of Rachel's death, it's that.'

He was close to his children now, but they had their own lives – his daughter working as a paralegal, his son following him into medicine – and Hamish had become lonely living by himself in the house in which they'd grown up. He needed distraction from his memories and his feelings of guilt – he would always have them, he said, because he hadn't been able to save his wife – and he started to think that Brisbane was the problem. He needed to go somewhere he'd never been, somewhere with no memories. So he took up the job with the Flying Doctor and moved to Alice Springs.

Rita had been wrong when she thought he was younger than her: he was the same age, forty-eight. He looked younger, the shape of his face retaining a youthfulness that she wished she still possessed. But he was a 'proper grown-up', as she liked to say.

They had talked a lot since they'd met. She felt comfortable with him, and he seemed to feel the same with her. Since she was past the stage in her life when she might look for a husband, she took him as she found him: a dear companion. He gave her no indication that she was anything else to him.

'You didn't want to stay in Young?' Rita said.

'I love the bush but Dad was disappointed that I didn't want to take over his practice. I wouldn't have made a good lawyer.' He laughed. 'I don't know why he thought I would.' He shrugged. 'I would have had to leave even if I was to become a lawyer. There's no university in Young.'

'Maybe he just wanted you to stay close to home – that's why he wanted you to work in his practice.'

Hamish raised his eyebrows. 'Maybe. I visit when I can, but . . .' He sighed and looked out the window. Rita's house was on the edge of town and in the wet season she was surrounded by greenery, so bright against the red dirt and the red rocks in the distance. Before she'd arrived in the Alice she'd envisaged a giant patch of dirt with a few buildings on it; the vibrancy, the pulse of energy in the place, had been a surprise. Some days she thought she could feel it, coming up through the earth. It wasn't like anything else she'd experienced in her life and she didn't have the right words for it – wouldn't say anything about it to another person, even if she did. Because it felt almost spiritual, somehow, and she was not a spiritual person.

'It's not like here,' Hamish continued. 'It can get so dry and brown down there. In a drought . . . it's a miserable place to be. It's so much more alive here. Even in the dry season, it's so alive.'

He looked back at her and as their eyes met she felt something flutter in her belly.

She recognised that flutter. It didn't lead to anything good. It just caused her to daydream and those dreams amounted to nothing.

'So what do you think of our prime minister?' she said, grasping at a subject that was guaranteed to deaden whatever she was feeling.

Hamish regarded her with a quizzical air, then he laughed, short and sharp.

'Fraser?' he said. 'He's all right for a Victorian sheep farmer. I'm more interested in the mob up here, actually.'

'The Territory government?'

'The Territory self-government, yes.' He ate another mouthful of steak. 'This is delicious, thank you – I appreciate you cooking for me.'

Rita felt her cheeks burn.

'You're welcome,' she said. 'Self-government was necessary, wasn't it?'

'Yes.' He nodded vigorously. 'But it's so new – they'll take a while to work out what they're doing. Decades, perhaps. No one has any experience in running the place.' He smiled at her. 'I love the fact that I can talk about politics and things like this with you. It's hard to find friends who are . . . sympathetic, shall we say. A lot of people think I'm a bore.'

'You're not,' Rita said. 'And I'm happy to discuss it.' Happy to talk about anything other than his life, her life, his past, her past. Their futures. She would keep the conversation on other subjects for as long as it took for that flutter to dissolve. She could be disciplined in the meantime. It was her specialty.

Rita ate one mouthful, then another. Concentrating on her food, not looking up often, she let Hamish talk for the rest of the meal.

CHAPTER TWENTY-THREE

The newspaper lay on Sallyanne's kitchen bench, teasing Sybil to pick it up. She hadn't seen a paper for weeks and this one was worth reading – announcing, as it did, that Great Britain had its first female prime minister, a grocer's daughter named Margaret Thatcher. It would have felt too impolite to start reading it, though, when Sallyanne was pottering around her kitchen making tea for everyone and Rita, Della and Kate were in the sitting room talking about a tornado that had killed forty-two people in Texas a month before.

'Who knew Texas was so dangerous?' she could hear Rita saying.

'I did,' Della said. 'Why do you think I left?'

'Isn't it terrible?' Sallyanne said, breaking Sybil's concentration.

'The tornado?' Sybil said.

'No.' Sallyanne pointed to the newspaper. 'That woman becoming prime minister.'

Sybil was surprised: Sallyanne liked traditional things, certainly – her declared fondness for Georgette Heyer alone suggested that – but surely she couldn't object to a woman leading a country?

'You don't think women should be prime ministers?' Sybil said.

'Of course I do! But she's awful – that hair. That voice!' Sallyanne huffed, then looked hurt as Sybil started to laugh.

'You can't judge a leader on those sorts of things,' Sybil said. 'Have you ever judged Malcolm Fraser on his hair and voice?'

Sallyanne stopped moving. 'No,' she said. 'Should I?'

'What's good for the goose is good for the gander, no?' Sybil patted Sallyanne's arm. 'As long as you're applying equal standards of judgement to men as well as women, you can say what you like.'

Sallyanne's face, always so lively, ranged in expression from crestfallen to hurt to determined.

'All right,' she said. 'I didn't like Gough Whitlam's voice.'

Sybil couldn't help laughing louder at the unexpected turn of conversation.

'I think he sounded pompous,' Sallyanne said with a definitive jut of her chin.

'I think you're right. Now, how's that tea coming along? I fear Rita is going to start telling Della why Texans should be ashamed of themselves for the death of Jack Kennedy, so we need to get in there.'

'Oh.' Now Sallyanne looked sad. 'That was awful, wasn't it?' She sighed and started scooping tea into the pot so vigorously that Sybil feared they'd all have a brew that looked more like coffee. 'Imagine losing your husband like that.'

The tea scooping stopped suddenly and Sallyanne looked through the door, to where the other three were sitting. Sallyanne's house was small, which made it cosy to have the five of them there. When she'd called Sybil to say that neither Mick nor her father were available to look after the children so she couldn't come to Fairvale but she'd be happy to have them all to her house in Katherine, Sybil had agreed instantly: it was time that the location of their book club meetings was convenient for someone other than her and Kate.

'Just as well Mick isn't in politics, isn't it?' Sybil said, pulling the pot away while Sallyanne remained distracted. She poured water into it and turned it anticlockwise twice – her mother's instruction – while Sallyanne stayed still, her head turning to watch her.

'What's the matter?' Sybil said.

'I was thinking about our book.'

'*Picnic at Hanging Rock*?'

'Yes.' Sallyanne gazed away again. 'Don't you wonder . . .'

After several seconds passed in silence Sybil was tempted to prompt her but decided to wait. Sallyanne's attention could wander sometimes; she always returned to the group, though, and Sybil had deduced that it was part of her personality and not to be tampered with.

'What if you could just disappear, like those girls?' Sallyanne said, her eyes meeting Sybil's and darting away.

'But they didn't disappear. They died.'

'Yes, I suppose they did.' It was almost a whisper and Sybil could only guess at what Sallyanne was really thinking.

'Sallyanne,' she began, 'do you—'

'I'm fine.' Sallyanne smiled – and she had such a lovely smile that it could obliterate anyone's concerns about anything. Not that Sybil was fooled.

'I'll take your word on that,' Sybil said. 'But you know where I live. Don't use the telephone if you need anything – I'm on a party line and people will hear. Just turn up. Even if it takes you two hours to get there. And the children are welcome too.'

Sallyanne's mouth half opened and she blinked.

'Really?' she said, disbelief in her voice.

'Of course.' Sybil nodded towards the sitting room. 'Now let's go. I could swear Rita just said something about Dealey Plaza.'

Sybil picked up the tray holding the teapot and cups and stood back for Sallyanne to go ahead of her.

'Rita, what did I say about the subject of Jack Kennedy?' Sybil said as she put the tray down with a clattering of cups.

'All we were talking about is how interesting it must be to live in a state where something so ... *significant* happened,' Rita said.

'Is that true?' Sybil said, peering at Della, who half smiled.

'Well ...' she said, glancing at Rita, who widened her eyes. 'Sure.'

'Hm.' Sybil sat down next to Kate. 'Would you like milk?' she said.

Kate nodded quickly. Sybil saw an attempt at a smile, although Kate's eyes were sad. They'd been sad for months and Sybil didn't know what could be done to change them. She didn't believe in forced jollity, nor did she think Kate would respond to it, but she felt that *something* should be done. Maybe Kate needed a holiday – away from Fairvale, away from them.

'How are you, Kate?' Rita said.

'I'm ...' Kate glanced at Sybil, who smiled encouragingly. 'I'm all right. Getting better.'

'You've had a hell of a knock,' Rita said, stirring sugar into her tea. 'It'll take some time. But at least you have a world-class nurse living in the same house. If I were recuperating, I'd want Syb looking after me.'

'I don't know that I've been much help,' Sybil said.

'Oh, you have been,' Kate said matter-of-factly, leaning forward to pick up her cup.

Sybil was startled to the point that tears pricked the corners of her eyes. She and Rita shared a look.

As Kate turned to her, she smiled and patted Sybil's hand. Yet another surprise. 'I notice all the little things you do.'

Sybil blinked quickly and glanced into her lap. There was nothing interesting there but she didn't feel she could look at Kate, or at anyone else.

'So when can we go riding again?' Della said, and Sybil took her chance to sip her tea and take a bite of cake.

Kate breathed in audibly. 'Soon,' she said firmly. 'I'll be ready soon.'

'Great news,' Rita said, winking. 'Sal, should you learn to ride, do you think? Because if you ride, maybe I can convince Syb to get back on a horse. It's been a while, hasn't it, Syb?' She grinned wickedly.

'Never,' Sybil said sharply. 'And you can't talk – you haven't been on a horse since you were in primary school. Don't let that stop you, though, Sallyanne.'

'I think I'd like that,' Sallyanne said, nodding. 'I think I'd like that a lot.'

'Great,' said Della. 'Then you can come out with Kate and me.'

'Oh, I won't be ready that quickly,' Sallyanne said, shaking her head.

'Sure you will.' Della smiled reassuringly. 'That could be how we teach you.'

'Oh, I—'

'There's no rush, Sallyanne,' Kate said soothingly.

Sallyanne looked quite pleased with herself. 'I've always wanted to ride,' she said.

From the garden came the sound of a child shrieking and Sallyanne got to her feet.

'Excuse me,' she said, sighing loudly. 'I have to go and see if my boys have killed each other.'

'Mummy!' came a cry from down the hallway.

Sallyanne sighed again. 'And now they've woken Gretel.' Her brow wrinkled. 'How will I ever be able to go riding?'

'I'll look after them,' Sybil said. 'When you come back we'll work out a day.'

With a grateful expression, Sallyanne left the room.

'That woman needs a break,' Rita muttered.

'And it's up to us to give her one,' Sybil replied. Kate and Della nodded in response.

'We have a plan, ladies,' she said.

CHAPTER TWENTY-FOUR

Ten loaves of bread were sitting on the station kitchen's bench, rising; the oven was on, ready; cake batter was sitting in a bowl, and all Kate wanted to do was go back to bed. When she'd agreed to take over kitchen duties so Ruby could visit her daughter at Ghost River Station – driven by Stan, who was only too eager for an opportunity to see Della – Kate knew she was capable of doing the work. She'd been by Ruby's side in the kitchen for months now; she'd taken notes on everything and Ruby had given her specific jobs to do. She just hadn't counted on not feeling up to the task.

Kate hadn't really been feeling up to any tasks since she'd returned to Fairvale from Sallyanne's house. Each day dragged, despite Ben's efforts to get her out of bed early, to jolly her along.

'Darling?'

Kate jerked her head up. There was Ben, standing in the doorway, looking at her with concern, as he'd been doing quite regularly of late.

'What are you doing here?' she said, more harshly than she'd meant. She could see it in his face, too – the surprise in his eyes.

'I came to see you.' He stepped one foot inside, then another, and went no further. 'How are you going on your own?'

'Fine,' she said quickly. 'Just about to put the bread in.'

'We really appreciate it,' he said, taking two more steps towards her.

She smiled weakly, hoping to recover some ground. 'I'm happy to be of use.'

She wondered if he thought of her as a horse that needed to be broken in all over again, hence the way he was approaching her, almost with his hand outstretched to calm her. Or maybe he was worried she'd be like one of those bulls he caught, ready to charge around and damage things. She didn't know which she'd rather be. She didn't know which she felt like.

'I thought we could go for a ride – later,' he said tentatively. 'I can knock off a bit early.'

A ride. Outdoors. She hadn't been on a horse since . . . Since before. She'd stopped riding when she realised she was pregnant. She'd missed it. She'd missed her horse. Mrs Simpson.

She had laughed out loud when she'd been told she'd be riding a gelding called Mrs Simpson. Joe had explained that since the horse had had his 'crown jewels' taken away, it seemed only reasonable. He'd laughed as Kate's cheeks turned red.

'I tossed up whether The Duchess of Windsor would be catchier,' he said, 'but it was too long. So Mrs Simpson he is.'

She'd spent a bit of time with Joe over the past few weeks. Increasingly he was staying behind while Ben led the stock camp out to muster, often away for days at a time while they moved the cattle from one area of Fairvale to another. Joe no longer needed to go out with the cattle but he had been slow to let that part of his life go. He missed the land, he'd told her; missed the sense of limitless possibilities that came with a property that stretched as far as he could see; missed the colours of the black-soil plains and the life they supported. He had favourite hills, he'd said. Some of them had caves with Aboriginal drawings on their walls. He knew where they all were – he didn't need a map. He'd shown Ben, he said. Ben should take her one day.

Ben never spoke about Fairvale the way Joe did, but Kate knew that he loved it all the same. Joe had sparked a curiosity in her, though, the more he told her about what was out there, beyond what she could see from the big house. It was the one thing that had been motivating her. Kate had the sense that if she could have the courage to go out there, out on Fairvale's plains, she would realise that the world was a lot bigger than her problems. But she'd been sad for so long she didn't know who she was if she let that sadness go.

'That would be nice,' she said, regretting the word as she said it. 'Actually, Ben,' she said, trying again, 'it would be lovely.'

She was rewarded with one of her husband's blinding smiles. 'I'll come and get you after lunch,' he said.

He walked all the way over to her and enfolded her in his arms. He hadn't hugged her like that in a long time. She slid her hands up his back.

'I've missed you,' he said into her hair.

Feeling her breath catch in her throat, Kate knew she'd missed him too.

'I want to come back,' she said, 'but I don't know how.'

He kissed her temple and squeezed her against his chest. 'We'll work it out.'

She wanted to believe him so she nodded, and hoped that he couldn't feel the tears she was crying onto his shirt.

~

The horses left at a walking pace, heading south alongside the creek. Kate felt like she was riding for the first time – and Mrs Simpson had certainly acted as if he was meeting her for the first time. He hadn't been kind when she'd saddled him up and he'd tossed his head when she tried to put the bit in his mouth. He'd calmed down after Ben had given him a scratch behind the ears. Kate had forgotten that's what he liked.

'I don't come this way much,' Ben said after a few minutes had passed. 'We're always riding out there.' He nodded to the east. 'It's pretty here. I'd forgotten.'

Kate looked around at the cycad palms dotting the ground, their deep-green fronds resembling a porcupine's quills. They could seem fierce but they were so beautiful, providing contrast to the thinner, paler gums.

'Lachie and I used to go out overnight,' Ben said, squinting up into the sky. 'Mum would make us cakes and biscuits. We'd take some corned beef.'

He went quiet and Kate glanced over to see him looking wistful.

'They were good days,' he said, then cleared his throat.

'You were close, then? As boys?'

'We got on,' Ben said. 'Now I think about it, we got on best when we were out here.' His laugh sounded hollow. 'He didn't like me much when we were at home.'

'Was he . . . mean to you?' Kate said as Mrs Simpson stepped smoothly over a fallen log.

'Yeah, I guess you could say he was mean. "Violent" might be another word.'

Kate glanced over again and this time Ben's face had a pinched expression.

'What did he do to you?'

Ben shook his head. 'Lachie didn't like anyone or anything, and I'll be blowed if I know why. He got everything he wanted. Any girl he met thought he was the best thing since sliced bread. Mum and Dad thought he was the centre of the bloody universe.'

'And you?' Kate kept looking at her husband, trusting Mrs Simpson to know what to do as they walked along.

Ben sighed heavily. 'I loved him, y'know – like a brother should. But he didn't love me. Things are better with him gone. Calmer. Mum's sad about it but even she would have to admit that life is easier now we don't have to tiptoe around precious Lachie.'

'Do you think he'll come back?'

'Anything's possible. But I'd say he wants to stay gone. He's probably got some scheme going. He could end up on the other side of the world. Or in jail.'

'Really?'

'Like I said, he can be violent.' Ben frowned. 'Stan told me once that he wouldn't be surprised if Lachie killed someone.'

'That sounds a bit . . . extreme,' Kate said. 'Especially from Stan.'

Ben's eyes turned to slits before he opened them wide again. 'He saw Lachie kicking one of the dogs once.' Ben winced. 'Kicking him for no reason. By the time Stan pulled him off, the dog was so bad he had to . . .' He swallowed. 'They had to shoot it.'

'Why did Lachie do that?' Kate said, almost whispering.

'Who knows?' Ben shot her a glance. 'He didn't explain it. But Stan was convinced he was just warming up. To something worse.' He swallowed again, slowly, as if he was swallowing a stone. 'I don't know if I'd go that far. But . . .' He looked away and Kate decided to leave the subject alone.

They rode in silence, Kate thinking about this ghost in their family. She'd tried not to think of her lost baby as a ghost but she couldn't help it – yet here was Lachlan, haunting them even while he was very much alive.

'Sometimes I wonder,' Ben said. 'If our kid – one of our kids . . .' He sighed. 'What if he turned out like Lachie? What if it's something Lachie inherited from some relative we don't even know?'

Kate couldn't look at him.

'There's no point wondering that,' she said.

'Why not?'

She tried to keep her breathing calm.

'You know why,' she said tightly.

'I don't,' Ben said. 'I really don't.'

'I can't hold a pregnancy.' Kate tried to stop her voice from trembling. 'What if it happens again?'

'It happened once, Kate. There is no way that means it will happen again,' he said, and he sounded so rational, so calm, so steady. He hadn't once blamed her, he hadn't once become upset. He'd just told her they would be fine. Whatever happened, they would be fine. But she didn't believe it.

Kate pressed her knees into Mrs Simpson's flanks so he picked up pace, edging ahead of Ben's horse. It was better to ride in front of him while she composed herself.

'Kate,' he called when she was a few metres ahead of him.

She knew he'd follow but she needed more time so she kicked Mrs Simpson into a canter, tempted to let him go faster, to gallop past the skinny, spindly trees with their bright-green leaves, over the black soil of the plain and the almost-white bush grass that sprang from it, past the occasional cow carcass or sun-bleached skeleton, around metre-high termite mounds and burnt stumps that reminded them all of the last time a fire came through, and past the flash of the creek as it weaved in and out of the landscape. All the parts of this countryside that she had come to know – and love, she realised, as she felt Mrs Simpson's haunches rolling beneath her, squeezing her thighs into his sides to keep herself stable.

It would be so easy to urge him to go to his limit. They'd trusted each other once, when she'd ridden him regularly; she believed he would do what she asked of him and she'd let herself be taken. They could run to the horizon. Away from Fairvale. Away from everything her life hadn't become.

Kate could hear Mrs Simpson breathing heavily; the sound was matched by that of her own ragged breaths. As tears fell from her eyes they were whipped away in the speed of the ride. It was the best way to cry: no evidence.

The ground started to change – the creek was widening and there was bracken alongside it. She hadn't been here before. She didn't know this country the way Ben knew it. Now fear gripped her: she wouldn't be able to predict when Mrs Simpson might come to a thick fallen tree that he would try to jump, and she'd have only a second's warning to shorten the reins and lean into his neck, to squeeze her legs as tightly as she could to keep herself steady and mutter a prayer or a curse, whatever came first to her mind, and if she missed that cue she'd fall off. She might break a leg. Or her neck.

She slowed to a trot, Mrs Simpson tossing his head. Looking up to the sky, she remembered the first time she'd seen that Territory blue. It wasn't like any other sky. She looked around her, at the different hues of this place. She felt the sun on her back and smelled the earth beneath her. She felt her heart pounding, her hands starting to shake with adrenaline, her fear of falling dissipating.

She knew what the fear meant: she was alive. She *felt* alive. For the first time in months she didn't have to coax herself into believing it. And she wanted to stay alive. As much misery as she'd had, that, too, had been evidence that she was still here. That she wanted to be here.

Within a minute Ben appeared beside her, his horse clearly not used to the exertion. On a muster, he'd told her once, they barely broke into a trot.

'What the hell was that?' he said, and she could tell he was trying not to appear too agitated.

She gasped for breath. 'I felt like a run.'

'Don't do it again,' he ordered, his voice deep, his eyes boring into her. 'I can't lose you. Not out here. Not anywhere. Do you understand me?'

She nodded.

'What was that really about?' he said, his voice softer now.

She turned her head away from him, squinting into the sun. It was a good question – what *was* it about? Because it hadn't just been about leaving him behind. Perhaps she'd wanted to prove that she could do something herself. She could ride. She could gallop. She could make decisions.

'Katie?'

She blinked, feeling tears on her cheeks. They were cool, and calming.

'Katie,' he said again, and there was something querulous in his voice.

'It doesn't matter,' she said. 'It's over now.'

His eyes held hers and she saw what was always there: the kindness in him; the boundlessness of his heart. She breathed in sharply.

'Let's go a bit further,' he said, nodding in front of them, 'then turn back.'

She nodded in answer and let him walk slightly ahead of her as she took in the sight of his long back and neck, his strong shoulders, the vastness of Fairvale around them, the arc of her past and her unknowable future. She had to find a way to be happy here that didn't depend on having a baby. If that baby never came she would still be Ben's wife, and he would still be her husband. He had made it clear that he thought everything would be all right regardless of whether or not they had children, and she owed him the same belief. He was a good man, her Ben. Good and true.

Kate nudged Mrs Simpson to catch up to Ben's horse and they walked on side by side.

CHAPTER TWENTY-FIVE

The day was almost too hot to be believed as Della sat with Kate on the verandah of Fairvale's big house. They were well covered by the awning but the heat seemed to swirl up from the ground, wrapping itself around them and staying trapped.

Della picked up the glass of water that had only been sitting next to her for five minutes, and made a face as she discovered that the water was warm. Too warm to be enjoyable.

'Is there nothing cool here?' she said, putting the glass down and blowing air up towards her fringe, which insisted on sticking to her forehead.

'Sadly, we've run out of blocks of ice,' Kate said, starting to laugh.

'Oh, those blocks of ice that you've been keeping secret all this time?' Della laughed too, looking over at her friend.

Bob had given Della the day off – they needed to rest the horses, he said, although she wasn't convinced that was the real reason. She knew he was in favour of her relationship with Stan, and that he'd kept news of it from reaching the rest of Ghost River. She appreciated that.

'You know, I've always wondered why people drink tea in

hot climates,' Kate said. 'I know why we drink it in England – but India, for example. Who could bear tea there?'

'I really don't know. We don't drink tea where I come from.' Della thought about her mother's coffee pot, always on the stove, her brothers draining it every time.

'Really?' Kate looked thoughtful. 'I'm trying to imagine a life without tea.'

'I can tell you all about it if you really want.'

The sound of a man shouting made them both turn towards the cattle yards.

'Is that your boyfriend yelling?' Kate said.

Della couldn't help looking surprised: she had never used that word about Stan to Kate – to anyone – skirting around it each time they discussed him. Not that she talked about Stan that often. Or maybe she talked about him more than she thought.

'Don't make that face,' Kate said with a cheeky tone. 'You know that's what he is.'

'I don't,' Della said with some force.

'Della, he adores you. And I believe you feel the same way about him.' She reached over and squeezed Della's hand. 'It's so lovely. Such a good story. We're all happy for you.'

'You all?' Now Della wondered what was being said about her at Fairvale – or maybe by 'we're all' Kate meant the book club. Was she talking about Stan to Sallyanne? Rita? Della knew what it was like to be talked about: back home a girl had only to smile at a boy and half the town started saying she was fast. But she thought she'd escaped that here.

'Look at you!' Kate said, laughing. 'The way you're staring at me you'd think I'd said I was leaving Ben to marry Prince Charles.'

Della blinked, trying to shake whatever it was her face was showing. 'He does need to get married,' she said.

'Yes, he does. At the rate he's going he'll run out of eligible aristocrats and he'll end up with Caroline of Monaco after she leaves that sunbaked husband. And you can *imagine* what the English press will say about that. They're already hunting any woman he blinks twice at.'

Kate sniffed and brushed her jeans, which were marked with red dust.

'Bloody dust,' she muttered. 'It gets in everything.'

Della laughed as heartily as she ever had in her life.

'What's so funny?' Kate said.

'You are,' Della said, still laughing. 'You hardly said two words to anyone when I met you. Now you talk about anything. And you *swore*.'

'That's rich, coming from you! You were like a little mouse at that first book club. And everyone says "bloody" around here.' Kate smiled at her friend.

'I was shy,' Della said.

'We both were.' Kate raised her eyebrows. 'Not anymore. The Northern Territory has a way of beating that out of you, doesn't it?'

'Maybe I've just loosened up.'

'Or maybe *someone* has loosened you up?' Kate gave her a light pinch.

'Kate!' Della gasped. She was rewarded with Kate's pealing laugh. It was such a contrast to the Kate seen at Sallyanne's house; Della was relieved Kate seemed to be enjoying life again.

'I know – I'm naughty,' Kate said, sighing contentedly. 'Now, isn't it time you suggested a book for us all to read?'

'Isn't that Sybil's job?'

Kate shook her head. 'I know she would love a recommendation from you. She wants to make sure we have – how did she put it? – "American stories". She is sure you'll know some good books. So, Miss Della from Texas, what American stories do you suggest?'

As Kate looked at her expectantly, Della felt her brain stall. This happened any time someone asked her to recommend a book. She had read so many that they all swirled together sometimes. One name, though, pricked its way through the morass.

'Flannery O'Connor,' she said.

'Who?'

'She's a writer from Georgia. Actually, she's dead now. She wrote short stories. There's one – "A Good Man Is Hard to Find".' Della shuddered. 'It's so good but it's kinda scary too. In the way that stays with you, you know?'

'I do. Do you have a copy of it?'

'Nuh-uh – but I could write my momma and ask her to send my book. It's still at home.' She could picture it on the single shelf in her old bedroom, next to her daddy's Damon Runyons and her own Ernest Hemingways, and the copy of the Bible that her grandmother had given her when she turned twelve, urging her to read every page of the New Testament, in particular, so she could learn how to 'stay away from sin'.

When Kate smiled, Della noticed dimples she'd never seen before. 'That would be lovely,' Kate said.

'Ladies.' It was Ben, stepping up onto the verandah. Della hadn't even heard him approaching and wondered how much of the conversation he'd taken in.

'Hello, darling,' Kate said, standing up and hugging him.

They kissed quickly on the lips and Della looked away, feeling like an intruder.

'Stan!' Ben called. 'Get over here.'

Della stood up, feeling nervous – the way she always felt when Stan was nearby. They were good nerves, excited nerves. She never got sick of feeling them.

'Have you finished your work?' Kate said, her arms still looped around Ben's neck.

'Nah – just come in for lunch.'

Then Stan was behind him, smiling at Della, and her nerves vanished. They did that every time, too. Just seeing him made her feel calm.

'Stan, your missus and mine have been talking about us,' Ben said, and he winked at Della as her mouth fell open.

'Is that right?' Stan's smile was enormous as he looked at her, his eyes liquid, sweat causing his clothes to cling to him. Della used to glance away when she saw him like that. She used to think she should be embarrassed to want him so much.

'What have you been saying, Del?' Stan stepped closer to her.

'She says you're a lovely man,' Kate said. 'And I agree with her.'

'Mum said you made lunch for us,' Ben said to his wife.

'I did.' Kate nodded, then she turned to look at Della. 'Part of my ongoing culinary training with Ruby. It's in the house kitchen.'

She unhooked her arms and stepped off the verandah into the garden, Ben close at her heels.

'It's good to see you, Della girl,' Stan said, smiling at her with that way he had, tenderness mixed with fire.

She nodded. 'It's—' She swallowed, not sure if she could speak properly. He did this to her. And she didn't mind. 'It's good to see you too.'

Stan picked up her hand and kissed the back of it, then he interlocked his fingers with hers as they started to head towards the kitchen.

'How – how have you been?' she said, squeezing his hand.

'Better now I'm seeing you,' he said, squeezing back.

Della stopped and turned to face him. 'What's wrong?'

She caught a flicker of concern on Stan's face, then he smiled broadly. 'Nothing,' he said.

'I saw that, Stanley,' she said, frowning at him.

'Saw what?' He kept smiling but it looked forced now.

'That face you made.'

'No face, Del,' he said. 'You're dreaming.'

'I am not.' She let go of his hand and folded her arms across her chest. It was the best she could do to feel like she was standing up to him, considering he was so much bigger than her.

He exhaled through his mouth and folded his own arms. 'You wouldn't understand,' he said.

'I might,' she said, trying to sound confident.

'My family . . .' He pressed his eyes shut and when he opened them it looked like shutters had come down over them. 'They've been living on this place. Our country.' He sighed. 'But it's a station now. Like this one.' He nodded his head towards the cattle yards. 'Hasn't been our country for a long time.' He grimaced.

'Okay,' Della said, feeling she should say something to encourage him to continue.

'There are new owners. They want my people to leave.' He laughed bitterly. 'I mean, they are going to force my people to leave.'

'They can do that?' Della said. She knew that Fairvale had an Aboriginal camp and Ghost River didn't, although she had never questioned why it didn't. The only clue she'd had about it was once hearing Aug rant about 'those damned blacks', which she'd found strange, given that there were a few of 'those blacks' working on the station.

'Course they can,' he said and his face filled with an emotion she'd never seen on it: rage. 'They can do whatever they bloody well want. Our country isn't ours anymore.' His eyes were glittering and hard.

'I'm sorry,' she said, and she hoped he could tell how much she meant it.

'Yeah, well – I might have to go and help them,' he said more softly, reaching for one of her hands.

'What do you mean?' She clutched his fingers but kept her hand against her chest.

'I mean I might be gone for a while.' He pulled her gently towards him.

'For how long?'

'As long as it takes,' he said and Della felt a thudding in her chest. Not the good kind – the kind that happened when Stan kissed her. It was a thud of warning. She'd let herself fall in love with this man and now he might disappear. She'd daydream about him when they were separated but she didn't want to have to daydream forever.

'Stan! What are you doing?' It was Ben, yelling from the kitchen window.

'Coming, boss!' Stan called back.

'Don't call me that!' Ben admonished and a small smile appeared on Stan's face.

'When are you leaving?' Della said, needing certainty now: if he was going, she wanted to prepare herself.

Stan ran a fingertip down her nose and touched it lightly to her lips. 'When they call for me,' he said.

He bent down and kissed her – urgently, his lips hot against hers – and Della wanted to push him away. If she didn't know when she was going to see him again, she didn't want to have the memory of this kiss taunting her. She didn't want it to keep her awake at night as she missed him, wondering where he was.

Maybe it was the last one, though – their last kiss. So she should let every second of it imprint itself on her brain. She should wrap her arms around him and make it continue for as long as possible, trying to show him how much she loved him, how much she didn't want him to go. And how much she was prepared to wait for him.

CHAPTER TWENTY-SIX

Sallyanne kissed Gretel's forehead and her daughter snuffled in her sleep. Gretel had been having nightmares over the past week – ever since Mick had come home drunk one night and driven his car into the gate across the driveway. He hadn't bothered trying to open it the usual way and the noise of the crash had startled most of the street – once Sallyanne had run outside she saw several of her neighbours heading in the direction of Mick's now less-than-intact ute.

Gretel had followed her, barefoot, her nightie flying, even though Sallyanne had asked the boys to make sure she stayed in the house. So Gretel had seen Mick slumped sideways in his seat: not injured, just drunk. Not even unconscious, actually – instead he was in a stupor that Sallyanne recognised. A child Gretel's age couldn't tell the difference, though, and Gretel had thought her daddy was hurt. She had started wailing, loudly enough that yet more neighbours appeared.

The miracle of it all was that none of those neighbours had called the police. Sallyanne didn't want the shame of that, although she did wonder if having the police turn up might not jolt Mick into some kind of recognition of his behaviour. Not that they'd arrest him or even caution him – everyone knew that they turned a blind eye to the drunks in this town unless they were Aboriginal, and especially if they were men they'd gone to school with. No, the most she could hope for would be for them to ask him what the bloody hell he was doing driving his ute into the gate and scaring his kids.

After Sallyanne had calmed down her children and, with the help of two of the men in the street, had Mick brought inside and his ute parked in the driveway, she'd put Gretel to bed. An hour later the nightmares had started and they'd appeared almost nightly since.

'Night, bubba. Everything's going to be all right,' Sallyanne whispered as she stood up, even though Gretel couldn't hear her. It was ridiculous, really, the things mothers said to their children that those children either never heard or didn't understand. But they had to be said – they were a protection spell. Sallyanne always checked in on her children before she went to sleep, usually several hours after she'd put them to bed, just to make sure they hadn't evaporated in the night.

After looking in on Tim and Billy, Sallyanne leant against a wall in the hallway and closed her eyes, taking these few moments for herself before she rejoined Mick in the living room. He was watching television with the volume turned up so loud she was surprised that the children hadn't been woken by it. Except, she supposed, they were used to it.

Sallyanne ran through her list of tasks and errands for tomorrow. All things to do with the kids.

Surrounded by boys in a house that was filled with dirt and old shoes and general disregard for order, Gretel had appeared like an angel who returned Sallyanne to herself. Finally she had a daughter she could whisper to, read sweet stories to, who wouldn't kick her in the shins if she didn't like something Sallyanne did. Billy and Tim were good kids but they were a handful – Gretel, in contrast, was a relief. And a precious gift.

'Kids asleep?'

Mick's voice startled her.

'Yes,' she said softly, gesturing to the living room. 'I'll come in.'

'You avoiding me?' he said, blocking the doorway – filling it, really. He was well over six feet tall, and his wild curly hair stood up, adding even more height. His shoulders and chest – broad from years of physical labour – were impassable even if she wanted to try.

'No,' she half whispered, looking into his eyes, wishing they weren't going to have this conversation again. He was looking back at her but, not for the first time, she wasn't convinced he was seeing her.

'Then why are you hiding out in here?' he said. She couldn't hear menace in his tone; for once, he sounded genuinely curious. But she had to be on her guard – he'd been drinking since he'd arrived home from work.

'I wasn't hiding,' she said. 'I was just taking a few moments for myself. I don't get that many.'

He gave her a curious look.

'You spend all bloody day by yourself,' he said, and in the half-light she saw his lip curl. 'Doing whatever you bloody well want. Listening to stories on the radio. Reading those stupid books.' He sneered. '*Romance* novels.'

'At least I read something,' she said, mustering strength in her voice. She wasn't going to counter his argument that she did nothing – it was one of his favourites.

'That's because you've got time to read, haven't you?' He leant towards her and she could smell beer fumes, covering him like a cloud. 'You even read at nights when you could be . . .'

He placed a hand on her chest, just below her neck, his fingers splayed. His touch was warm and almost gentle. If she subtracted ten years from her life she would have welcomed his approach; she would have been eager for it. Now it felt like he was claiming her, stilling her and threatening her all at once.

Sallyanne swallowed and cast her eyes down, not wanting him to see her deepest desire: that he would take his hand off her immediately.

'Why don't you want to spend time with me?' he breathed. She tried not to recoil from the smell of his breath.

Sallyanne considered her answer. She never picked fights with Mick – she didn't want the children to hear. That didn't mean that she didn't want to pick fights – that there weren't times when she wanted to rail at him for how useless and hopeless and mean he had become. When he was sober, he was decent, even loving; when he was drunk he was belligerent and argumentative, and too many times he had shoved furniture or shouted at her with a raised fist to the point where she wondered which persona was really him. Perhaps when he was drunk she was seeing who he really was; when he wasn't, she saw only the mask he wanted her to see. But she preferred that mask; she and the children were safer with that mask.

'I do want to spend time with you,' she said lightly, simpering. 'I'll just put away the dishes and tidy up, then I'll be in.'

He watched her for several seconds then stepped back to let her through into the kitchen. As she passed she felt his hand squeezing her bottom. Revulsion made her toes curl and her hands clench.

'Don't be too long,' he said in her ear, his hand still on her, his breath stinking of hops.

She nodded, relaxed as he walked away, and wondered how long she could take to rearrange the cutlery drawer.

CHAPTER TWENTY-SEVEN

Sybil didn't know whether she should be comforting Kate or herself. Ben's announcement that he was going to take a job in Tamworth over the wet season had been a surprise. They were gathered after dinner, as they were every night, reading and talking in the sitting room until the day's work caught up with them and they went to bed.

'Are we in trouble?' Sybil asked after the silence had yawned too long.

'What do you mean?' Ben said, looking uncharacteristically sullen.

'Financially,' Sybil said. 'Do we need extra money? Is that why you're going?'

Ben's eyes flitted to Joe's and Sybil wondered what the pair of them had been keeping from her.

'No,' Ben said slowly. 'But a little extra wouldn't hurt.'

'The BTEC has taken a bit out of us, love,' Joe said, his mouth pressing into a line. The BTEC – the federal government's long-lasting, far-reaching scheme to eradicate brucellosis and tuberculosis from Territory cattle, either by breeding it out or shooting it out. Joe'd had to kill a lot of head these past few years, and even though they'd bought some new cattle – mainly to breed in a different strain and improve the quality of the beef – they were still several thousand down. It would have made things difficult financially but Joe had kept insisting that they were all right.

'You haven't said anything,' Sybil said, looking at Kate, whose face had gone tight, her shoulders up around her ears and her hands clenched together.

'We were trying to work our way through it,' Ben said, sounding annoyed – again, not like him. Sybil wondered how willing Ben really was to leave.

'I'm about as useful as udders on a bull during the wet,' Ben continued. 'Might as well go somewhere else and earn a bit of money. There's a cattle place near Tamworth – a bloke I went to school with runs it. He asked if I could help out.'

'No wet season in Tamworth?' Sybil said, although she knew the answer.

Ben shook his head slowly. He looked cowed, she thought. As if circumstances were on top of him. For the first time she could remember, she felt angry at her husband, sure that he had put pressure on Ben. She didn't believe her son would willingly leave Fairvale, even for a few months.

'Kate?' Sybil prompted. 'Are you all right?'

Kate's response was to close her eyes briefly. 'I'll have to be,' she said, almost whispering, 'as it seems I'm not going with him.'

'You could,' Ben said, although he sounded unconvincing. 'But I'll be working flat out. You wouldn't see much of me. It's just for the wet. I'll be back in April. You're, uh . . .' He cleared his throat. 'You'll have a better time staying here with Mum.'

Kate swallowed and looked at the wall.

'I don't really want to lose another son, Ben,' Sybil said, trying to keep her voice strong.

'You're not losing me, Mum,' Ben said impatiently. 'I'll be back. And I'll send the money home. It's good for us, Mum. It's what we have to do sometimes. Dad did it.' He glanced at his father, whose arms were folded across his chest, his face pale beneath his rusted-on suntan.

Sybil had forgotten that year when Joe had left her alone with two small children and his parents. The reason had been the same: to shore up the family finances. It had been the longest wet season of her life and she'd made him promise never to leave her for that long again.

'So you want to go?' she said.

'It's not a question of wanting, Mum. We have to do it. Dad and I discussed it. He obviously can't go – he has to run the place. It has to be me. Stan will be here to help out with the things I'd usually do. But you know that we're quieter in the wet. It's the logical time to go.'

Kate still looked pained and Sybil couldn't blame her: she hadn't moved across half the world to be left alone with her parents-in-law for months.

'I guess there's no point discussing this further,' Sybil said. 'It sounds like the matter is decided.'

'It is,' Ben said. 'I'll leave in October.'

And if Kate fell pregnant in the meantime she'd have most of the pregnancy – possibly the birth – without him. Already Sybil wasn't looking forward to the end of the year, to the months without him, to Christmas, wondering who he was with and if they were taking care of him. She didn't stop worrying about him just because he was grown up. It was the secret of parenthood no one had ever warned her about: that it could make a person simultaneously the happiest they'd ever been and the most concerned. She was managing her concern about Lachie – still asking Geoffrey to try to find him every now and again, still hoping that the post would bring her news or that the phone would ring and it would be him – but it was wearing her out. With Ben gone, too, she was unsure where her strength would hold.

'I think I'll go to bed,' Kate said, standing. She looked so vulnerable, and Sybil could tell – hadn't noticed before, in the way that things a person sees every day aren't automatically noticeable – that she'd become thinner. Kate had been riding a lot and Sybil had assumed it was her way of coping with grief over her lost baby and disappointment that another hadn't arrived. She could see now that the riding had made her daughter-in-law lean, almost hard, whereas before she'd looked soft. Strangely, though, she looked to have no armour, nothing protecting her against what life was now presenting to her.

Sybil knew that feeling: how love could first make you feel invincible and then exposed. There was so much potential for pain when you loved someone so much. Sybil had felt that pain when Ray had died, when Joe was away from her for stretches of time.

'I'll come with you,' Sybil said. 'I don't think I can concentrate on this book any longer.'

'Mum,' Ben said, starting to stand as Kate walked from the room.

'I'll look after her,' Sybil said. 'You just keep yourself in one piece and get back as fast as you can.'

She wanted to be cross at him – except if Fairvale failed, their whole lives would change so dramatically that they wouldn't know which end was up. Sybil had never seriously contemplated leaving the place and she didn't want to. Ben was making the sacrifice so she didn't have to think about it for a while longer. So she couldn't be mad.

Instead she kissed him on the cheek. 'I'll miss you,' she said, 'but I understand.'

She kissed Joe's cheek too. 'Goodnight, darling.'

Joe sat up straighter. 'Night, love.'

It wasn't until she was in her bedroom that Sybil allowed herself the comfort of a tear. Another son going away. She would just have to focus on the people who remained and count down the days until he returned.

CHAPTER TWENTY-EIGHT

While she waited for the kettle to boil, Rita pushed open the screen door that separated her house from the back garden. Not that it was much of a garden. She'd tried to make something of it – to give it something of the design and beauty of Sybil's garden – and eventually decided that here in the Alice nature was always going to be stronger than any ideas she might have about it. Especially her ideas about planting bushes and trees she had grown up with in Sydney, which were completely inappropriate here.

The sun was barely up but it already had some heat. It wouldn't be long, though, before they had cold nights – she hadn't known a desert could get so cold. Two Major Mitchell's cockatoos squawked from the tallest tree in her garden – they probably didn't like the cold either, but she admired the way the early light gave their pale pink feathers a different hue.

Rita turned her face towards the sun, something she had loved to do since she was a child growing up in a more temperate climate. She missed that climate, and she missed the lifestyle that came with it: bushwalks in the relatively mild winters, lazy days on the beach in the relatively mild summers.

She thought of precious days spent stretched out on Balmoral Beach beneath a tree right next to the baths; it was a coveted spot on a hot day and she'd always get down there early and spread out two towels. One for her and one for Charles. He would arrive later, once the sun had started to burn. Once he'd been able to leave his wife with a convenient excuse about being on call and the hospital needing him.

Rita hadn't meant to fall in love with him. She had previously abhorred women who became involved with married men, never finding plausible the reasoning that they 'couldn't help it'. Before Charles she had firmly believed that everyone could help it. Then she found that she, too, couldn't, and she became one of those women – it had seemed like a form of justice for being so judgemental about people she didn't know. Now she was the one who should be judged and, for all she knew, someone *was* judging her. Rita didn't like the idea – but she didn't give him up, either.

Those days on the beach, that one summer, were all they'd had apart from their time together at work. She closed her eyes and saw his straw-blond hair cut short at the back and sides and long on top; he would sweep it behind one ear if it fell in his eyes. She remembered how unimpressed she had been with him the day they had met.

'Sister Hammond,' he'd said as he swept up to her while she was writing notes on a chart, 'I've been sent to check on this boy.'

He'd gestured to the ten-year-old lying in the bed with a drip in his arm, a dressed wound on his abdomen and a pale face.

'And you are?' Rita had said, appraising him and instantly deciding that he was pompous just from the way he slid one hand into his jacket pocket.

'Mr Pierce,' he'd said, extending his other hand.

'You weren't the surgeon who operated on this patient,' she'd said, wondering why he was here.

'No, but as it's my first day they've asked me to take a look at all the patients so that I'm up to date.'

She'd narrowed her eyes at him, wondering if he was an impostor. No one had told her that a new surgeon was doing rounds today.

He leant in closer to her. 'Would you like to see my university records?' he'd said quietly in her ear.

Startled that she'd been caught out, she'd blinked rapidly and he had laughed.

After that day she had come to respect his skills and he hers; they had become friends, then close friends, but always within the confines of work. One day he had asked her to join him for dinner that night.

'Won't your wife mind,' she'd said, 'that you're not going home for dinner?'

'Perhaps,' he'd said, smiling easily, his grey eyes holding hers, 'but I don't plan to tell her.'

Later she would know that was the moment when she'd had a choice: if she had said 'no' to dinner they would have carried on as friends and her life would have been much the same and she couldn't say she'd have been worse off. She'd had a choice, except she was sure there was only one possible answer: *yes*. That was also the moment when Rita knew she was in love with him, and that he likely knew it too.

She never found out if he loved her in return. She hated that she had to use the term 'affair' for what they'd had; it had felt more substantial than that. Yet that's the word he had used when he'd broken it off.

They were lying in bed, their skin covered in salt, sand all over her carpet. It was always this way: a couple of hours on the beach, then they'd go to her apartment nearby and make love. He would be home in time for dinner, just as he'd promised his wife.

He'd kissed her eyelids, her cheeks and her chin.

'Listen, sweetheart, there's something I have to tell you,' he said, gazing at her with an expression that might have been love but that she was later sure was not.

'What?' she'd said, lightly scratching his chest with her fingernails.

'This affair . . .' He'd sighed – a touch dramatically, she'd thought, but he could be dramatic. It made him a good lover: he was fond of extravagant displays and great effort. Then she pushed past the sound of the sigh and thought about that word: *affair*. He hadn't used it before.

'We have to end it.' Now his eyes were full of pity. 'My wife's pregnant,' he'd said, and she'd wanted to vomit.

She shouldn't have been shocked, or even surprised: he had never told her that he would leave his wife for her. Yet she couldn't help her feeling of betrayal, nor could she help feeling angry – how could he sleep with two women at the same time? Wasn't she enough for him? She was disgusted with herself for becoming involved with him and mortified that she could have assumed she meant so much to him that he would no longer be interested in his wife. She hadn't been brought up to sleep with other women's husbands; she hadn't been brought up to forget who she was.

That had been five years ago, and since then she hadn't so much as considered another man as a romantic prospect. She hadn't trusted herself. One bad decision had broken her heart and left Charles to continue his marriage and become a father without consequence.

'Was that a kettle I heard?'

Rita jumped and turned around to see Hamish leaning in the doorway with a sleepy smile, his normally neat hair sticking up in places, his old T-shirt and shorts hanging loosely on his frame.

'It was,' Rita said. She wanted to shake her head like a wet dog might, to get rid of what was unwanted: her past. It was always with her, though, and while she'd never forgiven herself for becoming involved with Charles, she was glad that her need to leave him behind was one of the things that had brought her to Alice Springs. To Hamish.

She walked over to give Hamish a kiss, her hand on his waist, pulling him towards her.

The development of their relationship had occurred naturally. After weeks of friendship, one night after dinner Hamish had asked if he could stay and Rita could identify no reason why he couldn't. Or shouldn't.

Since then they had spent as much time together as possible – which was really no different to how it had been before, when they seemed to be the only people who didn't realise, or acknowledge, that their friendship was merely a prelude to something else.

'Blind Freddy could see that you two are on,' Darryl had said to her one day when Hamish was rostered on a different shift and, therefore, not in earshot.

'We are not!' Rita had protested, and it had sounded insincere even to her.

'All right, all right, whatever you want to believe.' Darryl had raised an eyebrow and taken a drag on his cigarette. 'Ten bucks says I'm right by the end of the month.'

Several days later Rita had paid him his ten dollars without fanfare. It wasn't the first day Darryl had turned out to be more perceptive than she'd given him credit for. He'd looked almost disappointed as he put the note in his pocket.

'I guess that'll keep me in cigs for a while,' he'd muttered. 'I shoulda put more on it.'

'Too late now, Daz,' she'd said, patting him on the shoulder. 'I thought you'd be happier about it – you won, after all.'

'Yeah.' He'd nodded and folded his arms across his chest. 'Just didn't think you'd go for a city bloke.'

'Oh?' She would never have imagined that Darryl would have given her personal life further thought.

'Yeah,' he grunted. 'You don't have any airs and graces, y'know?'

'And city people do?'

He'd shrugged and looked away. 'Maybe he does.'

'He's just polite, Dazzle.' She'd pinched his cheek and he'd simply gazed down at her. 'Something you could learn a thing or two about.'

'Yeah, yeah, all right.' He'd pulled his packet of cigarettes out of his shirt pocket and lit one. Rita had made a performance of coughing and moving away from him. Afterwards she'd wondered if he was right: if Hamish had airs and graces. She didn't think he had more than he should – certainly not too many for her.

'Are you working today?' Hamish said, taking her hands in his and kissing her palms. She loved it when he did that because she'd always thought her hands were too rough to be deserving of tenderness. All those years of scrubbing, of working them hard, had not made them ladylike.

'No,' she said, smiling. 'Are you?'

'No.' He placed her hands on his chest. 'So I think we should go back to bed.'

She took one hand to his hair and smoothed it down.

'Where did you come from?' she whispered.

He gave her a quizzical look. 'What do you mean?'

'I didn't . . .' She squeezed her eyes shut, wondering if she opened them again whether she'd find him gone.

She opened them – and he was still there.

'I really didn't think I'd meet a man I liked so much. You're an exceptional fellow.'

He smiled mysteriously, as he did sometimes.

'And you're an extraordinary woman,' he said, his eyes holding hers. She'd come to love those eyes.

'I don't wish to alarm you,' he said then – and of course her first reaction was to be alarmed.

She pushed his chest gently. 'Don't tease me.'

'I'm not teasing. Just preparing. So I don't wish to alarm you but . . .' He took her face in his hands and kissed her. 'I love you,' he said.

Rita's first instinct was to flinch. Hamish had always taken every opportunity to touch her, to kiss her, to tell her she was beautiful, to say that he couldn't wait until they were alone. She was not half as demonstrative with him, and it was because she felt ashamed that she had wanted Charles so much and it had ended the way it did. It was shame that had stopped her from telling Hamish what he meant to her, because she never wanted to feel that way again: so exposed, so vulnerable, in her love for a man who did not love her back.

Except Hamish did.

'I love you too,' she said.

He looked surprised – almost startled.

'I wasn't sure if you were going to say it,' he said, a smile at the edges of his lips. 'I was worried.'

'No need to worry,' she said, feeling like a million moths were in flight in her body.

'No.' He kissed her again, and this time his hands were on her back, on her hips, taking hold of her arms. He kissed her throat, her collarbone, and her lips once more.

She slid her hands up the inside of his old T-shirt and let her fingertips flutter over his skin, making him gasp.

'Ticklish?' she said against his lips.

'A bit,' he said, laughing as he pinched her bottom and she squealed.

'Good,' she said and he kissed her again, his body pressed against hers, his arms encasing her.

She let him pick her up and carry her to bed. They could stay there all day. There was nowhere else to be. And nowhere else she wanted to be.

CHAPTER TWENTY-NINE

Now that she was home, Della could see how much of her family's ranch looked like Ghost River Station. That was to say, there were similarities that made her realise why Ghost River had appealed to her. The trees and the grass were different, but Texas could look just as brown as the Territory, and just as wide. Except there were mounds here – hills, maybe. Hills with outcrops that popped up and marked the limits of how far you could see. At Ghost River there had been so little to get in the way of the horizon.

While she was fond of Ghost River, it was on Fairvale that her best memories had been made. Fairvale wasn't as desolate; there was more of a sense that you could make it home if you got lost, whereas on Ghost River she'd often had the feeling that they could ride for days on a muster and never be seen again.

It was on Fairvale that she had last seen Stan. He had asked her to visit because he was going to see his family, as he'd told her he might. He hadn't reckoned on the fact that she was about to do the same and she hadn't really known how to tell him, so instead she'd held out her mother's letter, the thin airmail paper fluttering in the light breeze that was playing around the creek. The river red gums formed a canopy above them. She remembered their colours, and the smell of the earth.

'What's this?' Stan had said.

'A letter from my momma.' Della had tried to smile but she couldn't.

'What's it say?'

She held it out to him again but he'd shaken his head.

'Not my business to read that letter,' he'd said solemnly.

She'd been naïve to think she might get out of actually telling him.

'My daddy's sick,' she'd said. 'It looks bad. They think it's cancer.'

Immediately Stan had put his arm around her and pulled her to his side. 'That's no good, Del,' he'd said. He'd kissed the top of her head. She remembered what his lips had felt like on her skin.

'I have to go home. Daddy can't work and my brothers are . . .' She'd shrugged. 'Let's just say Daddy alone is worth all four of them when it comes to work. He's asked for me. To go home and help out.'

Stan was holding her arms and he'd bent his knees so his head was almost level with hers. He was looking at her so intensely that the whites of his eyes seemed to have disappeared.

'You're leaving.'

'I don't want to,' she had whispered.

'You have to,' he'd said, although his voice had caught a little. 'It's your family. Just like I have to leave for mine.'

'But you're coming back,' she'd said, knowing that she could make no such commitment. If her father died, who knew what would happen after that?

'And so are you,' Stan had said, starting to smile.

'What are you smiling at?' she'd asked, confused.

'You'll be back because you love this Territory, Della girl,' he'd said, winking. 'And I reckon you love me too.'

It was the first time he'd said that word, *love*, and it had seemed like a dare. She had felt brave, right then, but not reckless. She had known for a long time that she loved him, and that it was changing her, making her see the world in shades she had never witnessed before. Shades of hope, of expectation, of opportunity – of the future.

'I do,' she'd said, her hands by her side, one clutching the letter. 'I do love you.'

Stan had gazed at her. She tried to guess the emotions playing out in him, the thoughts that were in his head, but he could be hard to read when he wanted to be.

'And I love you,' he'd said, his face serious. 'I'll still love you when you're gone. And when you come back.'

Coming back might not be all that easy, however. Nothing would be certain after she left – not even Stan. She couldn't ask for him to wait for her.

'If I go I lose my job,' she'd said. 'That makes it harder to come back, when I don't know where I'm heading.'

'You'll get another one. You got this one, didn't you?' He'd taken hold of her free hand. 'And I can take care of you.'

'Maybe I want to take care of you,' she'd said. He pulled her towards him and she pressed her head against his chest.

'Let's work it out later,' he'd said into her hair. 'When you're back.'

She thought about those moments a lot now that she was far away from him. She marvelled at how much her heart had expanded since. She had worried that once she left Stan, once she didn't have the anticipation of seeing him and the excitement of being with him, her feelings might shrivel up. Instead they had grown. She hadn't heard from him – he had left Fairvale not long after she'd flown home and, besides, he'd told her he wasn't a letter writer. But he'd also told her that each time she looked up and saw the sun shining, that was the sign that he was thinking of her. So every day when she walked out and saw the sun, she thought of him, and thought of him thinking of her, and knew she could wait.

'Della?' she heard her mother call from the back door of the house.

'Yes, Momma?' she said, keeping her gaze on the landscape.

'Your daddy's asking to speak to you.'

'Okay, Momma – I'll be in.'

'I need some help with your grandmammy later,' her mother said, and Della could tell that her mother wasn't going to let her enjoy any more moments of peace.

'What can I do?' she said resignedly.

'Her sheets need changing and I think her hair needs washing.'

Della's grandmother had lived in the back room of their house ever since Della's grandfather had died. She wasn't quite as infirm as she made out – with all the housework being done for her, though, she had little reason to correct anyone's impression. But she knew Della was wise to it and, accordingly, ever since Della had arrived home, Grandmammy had made sure to ask for Della to do just about everything for her.

'Sure, Momma,' Della said, trying not to sound annoyed. She'd do those chores and then there'd be more. Always more. And since her arrival her brothers had suddenly decided that they needed to be out on the ranch every day, with the cattle, instead of doing what needed to be done in the office, ordering supplies, fixing things – everything her father did, basically.

'It's good to have you home at last, Della,' her mother said, smiling sweetly.

Della loved her mother and didn't resent her asking for help; she was positive Momma was tired of taking care of everyone. Della was already tired. She wasn't going to stay forever, though, even if that's what her mother hoped for and talked about. She wasn't going to 'find a nice boy in the town', as her grandmother suggested at least once a day. She'd found her nice boy – her more-than-nice boy. And she was determined to return to him, even if she had no idea how she was going to extricate herself from the family web that had enmeshed her once more.

CHAPTER THIRTY

After two years of living on Fairvale, Kate was used to receiving mail every two weeks during the dry season if they were lucky and not for months at a time during the wet. After the first Christmas her mother had learnt to send her present so it would reach Kate in October, otherwise she wouldn't receive it until March or April.

The arrival of the mail had its own ritual. Sybil would greet the truck and then sort out who had what before delivering everything by hand.

'I feel like Father Christmas,' she'd said once, cheerily.

With Ben gone the mail had taken on more than its usual significance, but it was too soon for him to have sent anything. So she had a letter from her mother and a thick parcel from Della.

The parcel beckoned first and Kate ripped open the plain brown paper to find four copies of a book of short stories by Flannery O'Connor.

I wish I could be there for your next meeting, her note read. *Instead I thought I'd provide the books. Flannery O'Connor, just like I mentioned – and I had a darned hard time rounding up these copies, so make sure you read them! Please tell Sybil that although O'Connor was from Georgia,*

I think these stories of the South have something to say about where I am now. Love to all, Della.

There were two different editions, and only one of the copies was not secondhand; Della probably had to scrounge around to find them. Kate felt simultaneously delighted that Della had been so thoughtful and sad that she wouldn't be there to talk about the book with them. It was a combination of emotions that wasn't unfamiliar: since Ben left she'd had a low level of sadness mixed with the satisfaction of her life on Fairvale. She felt useful here; wanted. She was productive. She could see that the efforts she made each day were contributing to the greater whole. When she'd been working in London, just a little secretary to an important man in a bank, she had never felt like this.

Putting the books to one side, she opened her mother's letter. There was family news: Georgia and Charlie were moving to Cornwall, which was a surprise given how much her cousin loved London, but Charlie wanted to become a farmer and they could buy more land in a better climate.

Kate's parents were thinking of selling their home and moving to Bath, which they'd always loved. This was the house that Kate had grown up in; the only other house she'd known apart from Fairvale. It was a house she'd left happily when she'd moved to London, and she hadn't really thought about it since, but now that her parents wanted to move . . .

Kate let the letter drop. She supposed she should feel upset; show some sign that part of her missed England so much that the news of the impending loss of her family home would upset her. There was no such sign.

She could hear Sybil talking on the radiotelephone in the office. It was almost time for tea. She and Sybil would chat; she would tell her about the books Della had sent. Then an hour would have passed and she would be due back in the kitchen to help Ruby with lunch.

The talking had stopped.

'Sybil!' she called out, standing up to walk from the sitting room towards the office.

'Yes?' came the terse reply.

As Kate reached the office door she could see Sybil frowning, one hand on her hip, tapping her foot.

'What's going on?' Kate said.

'That was Felicity. Ruby's daughter . . .' As Sybil's eyes met hers, Kate could see concern. 'She's been hurt.'

'What do you mean? She's injured?'

'Yes, she . . .' Sybil took a sharp breath in. 'She was climbing a tree for some reason. Fell off. Managed to impale herself on a fallen branch.' Sybil looked ashen. 'It doesn't sound good. And Rose's husband is out with the cattle for a few days so he doesn't even know.'

Kate put a hand to her throat; she didn't know why, unless it was to contain her distress. Ruby adored Rose – this news would almost kill her.

'Ruby has to go there right away.'

'Yes.' Sybil looked out the window. All the men were away on a muster; the yards were still. 'I'll take her.'

As she turned back Kate could see what she'd come to recognise as Sybil's 'business face': it wasn't unemotional so much as emotionless, as if Sybil was making an effort to be professional towards people who either were family or whom she considered to be family.

'I need you to run the station kitchen,' Sybil said. 'I'll see if I can get one of the girls from the camp to help you. I'm sorry to do this to you, but—'

'It's fine,' Kate said. 'I know what to do.'

Sybil nodded, her eyes flitting around. 'I have to think about what else needs to be done.'

'Don't worry about it,' Kate said confidently. 'I can look after the office and the kitchen.'

'It's a lot of work,' Sybil said, frowning again.

Kate shrugged. 'It's not as if I have to worry about my husband getting annoyed that I'm working too much.'

Sybil's face relaxed.

'True,' she said.

'Can I come with you to see Ruby now?'

'Yes. Please do.'

Sybil started for the door and stopped abruptly as she reached Kate. She kissed her on the cheek and Kate looked at her quizzically.

'Thank you,' Sybil said. 'I wouldn't be able to do this without you.'

Kate nodded, feeling wildly pleased, then guilty that she could feel like that when they were about to give Ruby bad news. But this marked something: Kate felt properly like one of the family now. An equal partner in the enterprise that was Fairvale.

'Thanks for letting me help,' she said, standing back for Sybil to walk ahead of her, already making a list in her head of everything she needed to do today.

CHAPTER THIRTY-ONE

It was Rita who told Sallyanne about Della's departure when she called to ask how Sallyanne was. She'd been doing that fairly regularly of late – 'Just checking in,' she'd say, sounding breezy.

'What does *she* want?' Mick would ask after each call.

'She's my friend,' was Sallyanne's response that wasn't really an answer.

'What do you say to her?' he'd added once, standing so close to Sallyanne that she had curled into herself, trying to be smaller, less noticeable, so she didn't anger him.

'We're just chatting about nonsense,' she'd said, keeping her voice light. And it was true: if anyone was listening – and she knew Mick was – it would sound like they were talking about characters in a book or movie. She and Rita used code: 'I don't like the way the hero has been written' meant that Sallyanne was having a bad week; 'He's no Errol Flynn' conveyed that Mick hadn't been misbehaving.

Soon, though, Rita started phoning just on weekdays, when she knew Sallyanne would be home with only Gretel for company. It was on such a call that Rita said that Della had returned to Texas and they didn't know if she'd be back.

That night, knowing that one of his friends was looking for a job, Sallyanne told Mick that Ghost River was down a worker.

'How do you know that?' he said, his voice hard, and she could see the trap she'd laid for herself.

'I, uh—'

'Did that nurse call you again?' He stood up and stormed to the kitchen, yanking open the fridge and pulling out a beer.

'You need to go to the shops,' he said when he sat down again, while Sallyanne was trying to come up with a suitable explanation that didn't involve Rita.

'Oh?' she said, stalling.

'There's only five beers left. I'll be out by tomorrow night.'

'Okay.' She picked up the embroidery sitting in her lap and wondered if it was wise having a hobby that required needles. Mick was unpredictable: there was nothing to stop him picking up the needle and doing something to her with it. She hated that she thought these things; he might never do it, or he might, with terrible consequences. It was the uncertainty – the fear of it – that was the hardest thing to deal with.

'You didn't answer my question,' he said after he'd drained half the can.

'Sybil wrote to tell me,' she said.

'Oh yeah? Where's the letter?'

She thought quickly. 'I threw it out. You know I don't like clutter.'

With a quick glance she saw that he was looking at her just like a crocodile might: eyes slitted, face set. She felt a chill up her spine and tried not to shudder.

The next week he arrived home from work later than usual, after she'd put the children to bed, and she could sense something different about him. He didn't move as heavily; his shoulders weren't slumping, and he wasn't glowering.

'Did you have a good day?' she said as he passed the fridge without opening it. That, too, was different and she felt a twinge of hope. She had never stopped wanting the old Mick to return even if she'd stopped believing he would.

He smiled at her. She couldn't remember the last time she'd seen his smile. Then one side of his mouth curled. It looked like a snarl and her hope shifted to fear so quickly that the reaction was automatic now.

'I've got that job at Ghost River,' he said.

'What do you mean? What job?'

'You said that someone left,' he said. 'I went out there today to talk to them about the job.'

'But . . .' She tried to think yet her brain wasn't working. She might have wanted him gone – she'd almost prayed for it some nights, even though she wasn't religious – but that didn't mean she had any idea what her life might look like without him there.

'You've never worked with cattle,' she managed at last.

He shrugged, then leant against the wall and cocked one leg over the other.

'Can you even ride a horse?'

'Yeah,' he said. 'Not for a while but I can catch up.'

'But you're a plumber.' She was still trying to figure this out. Why was *he* leaving? She should be the one to leave. She was the one who had no power, no control, and no prospect of that changing.

'And now I'm not,' he said, and she thought he was laughing at her.

'Why?' she said.

'Why what?'

'Why are you leaving?'

Mick looked around the sitting room and made a noise that sounded like exasperation.

'Why would I stay?' he said, and as his eyes met hers she expected to see contempt, as she so often did. But there was only sadness there. 'The kids get all your attention. I don't even rate.'

He pushed off the wall and came towards her slowly.

'Why do you think I drink?' he said, his eyes dark. 'You won't even give me the time of day.'

'That's not true,' she said.

His laugh sounded empty as he stopped in front of her, fists on his hips.

'After Tim was born I thought you were just getting used to having a kid. All that time you spent with him. He—'

'I told you that he'd need all my attention for a while. It wasn't like I didn't warn you,' Sallyanne said so quickly she could barely understand herself.

'*I know what you said.*'

She flinched and his eyes widened. He leant back and she exhaled slowly.

'But you should have known what you were doing after one,' Mick said, now sounding weary. 'Then there was Billy, and *he* got all that attention too.' His eyes narrowed as he looked at her. 'How come you couldn't cope by then? Why did you need to spend all that time with them when you could have been with me?'

Sallyanne thought back over those early years. She had never not coped with the children; she'd loved having them. Loved those delicious months when they were new and soft and smelled like babies. The time she spent with them was the time they needed because they were completely dependent on her. She could see now, though, that Mick had interpreted it differently. For years, then, they had been living in two different marriages: his was a union of time sacrificed to his children; hers was a life of every moment full of being a mother and trying her best to be a wife.

'They needed me,' she said, because it was the simplest truth she could offer.

'I needed you,' he said.

'I know,' she admitted. 'But they were helpless. They needed everything done for them.'

'But what about me?' he said mournfully.

What about him indeed – and what about her? There was no one to take care of her. She had never complained. She hadn't drunk ten cans of beer each night and yelled at Mick for not helping her around the house. Nor would she ever do that, because she was the mother and the wife and this was her lot in life. There was no way out for her – but Mick had created his own exit.

'I'm sorry,' she said. 'I hadn't realised.' She closed her eyes and felt the most profound urge to lie down. If she didn't lie down, she feared that the responsibility she was carrying – for the children, for Mick, for apparently ruining Mick's life – would press her down.

'What are you going to do about it?' Mick said, hardness back in his voice.

Sallyanne's eyes opened.

'It's probably for the best that you go away for a while,' she said. 'We obviously . . . aren't getting along.' She forced a smile. To appease him. That's how it went, didn't it? Keep the man happy. All her romance novels had taught her that. 'A break will give me some time to work out how to make it up to you.'

She almost choked on the lie. She might not ever be able to give him the attention he wanted – not until the children were grown and had left home – nor was she convinced she wanted to.

'When do you start the job?' she said.

'Next week. You could come with me,' he said, sounding surprisingly gentle.

She didn't hide her reaction quickly enough. She knew she looked startled instead of pleased: she could see it on his face.

'That's what I thought,' he said, turning away from her. 'You just want to be with those kids. Without me.'

She watched his shoulders roll like a fighter about to step into a ring; his fists clenched and unclenched. He hadn't hit her yet but maybe today everything would change. He knew he was leaving – what was to stop him giving her a souvenir? She was surprised that she felt calm, as if she was waiting for an inevitability.

He turned back and she saw that his face was hard, his shoulders still moving, his eyes glittering. She swallowed as he took a step towards her.

She had a fleeting vision of Scarlett O'Hara standing in the broken fields of Tara, dirt in her hand, promising herself that as God was her witness she'd never be hungry again. Sallyanne had always loved that scene. She'd always wanted to be like that – to be able to make a promise with such conviction and see it through. That was one of the reasons why she read books and watched movies: so she could find something she could use in her life. If she didn't have examples to draw on around her, there was always the library she stored in her brain.

Except, Sallyanne realised, she did have examples. She had Sybil, who managed to do a thousand different things and made it look easy; whose fiancé had died – Rita had told her about him – and she had managed to get on with her life. And she had Rita, who saw awful things in her work and still believed that people were good and life was graceful. She could almost hear what they would tell her to do right now.

She stared at him and felt resolve coming over her, hardening into steel.

'That's not true,' she said, making her voice as strong and clear as she could. 'But we need some time apart, Mick. I think you will like it out there. Della did.'

'So you're tossing me out?' he said, his voice low.

'I'm not tossing you out,' she said calmly. This might be the last thing she ever said to him and she wanted it to count. 'You're leaving.'

He held her stare.

'In fact,' she said, 'you can leave now.'

He opened his mouth as if to speak. She lifted her chin and folded her arms across her chest.

'I'm better off without you anyway,' he muttered.

'Fine,' she said.

She turned away from him, hurrying towards the children's rooms. She would stay there until he left, protecting her babies, her heart hammering in her chest, her mouth dry, with her new carapace in place and a sense that while she had no idea what her life would look like now, it had to be better than it had been with Mick in it.

CHAPTER THIRTY-TWO

'We're not going into town, are we?' Kate said as she came to stand next to Sybil, who was looking out the sitting-room window at the rain that was falling too hard and too early.

The wet season was meant to be a month away – except it was here and Sybil knew what that meant. She'd seen it once before: a hard dry, an early wet. The wet would be over too soon and after that they wouldn't have enough water to last them until the next one. The cattle would be dehydrated and thin – unsaleable.

'The creek will be too swollen,' Sybil said with an air of resignation. 'No book is worth us getting carried downstream.'

'I'd hoped it would stop,' Kate said wistfully, looking up at the sky.

Ben had left two weeks ago and Kate had done an admirable job of acting like she was fine, but Sybil could tell that she wasn't. How could she be? Her husband had gone away for months and they didn't even have a telephone line to themselves if he wanted to call and say hello.

'Me too,' Sybil said quietly. 'But we've got the radio here. Rita will have the Flying Doctor radio. If Sallyanne can get to a radio, we can still talk to each other.

'I know you were looking forward to seeing them all in person,' she continued. 'So was I. We'll have to organise something another time.'

'I thought we'd be able to see each other before . . .' Kate gestured to the sky. 'That started. I'm still getting used to it – how it affects everything.'

'So am I,' Sybil said drily. She smiled tightly at Kate and turned from the window. 'I'll start making calls. I need to stop Rita getting on the plane – mind you, her pilot's probably not that keen to fly into this weather anyway. I'll come and find you when I've finished.'

Sybil headed for the office, admiring its neatness as she picked up the two-way radio's handset. Kate was meticulous, she had to give her that: she found order in their papers where Joe tended to introduce chaos.

She couldn't use the radiotelephone to call the Flying Doctor in Alice Springs – they were on the two-way. It was how she and Rita often communicated, although they could never talk for long, Rita not wanting to tie up the Flying Doctor radio. But Sybil had come to appreciate how meaningful short, regular bursts of conversation could be.

'RFDS Alice, go ahead,' said a voice over the airwaves and Sybil got on with organising the day.

~

There hadn't been time to distribute Della's books to everyone before this meeting; Sybil had hoped to hand them out in person so they could read them for next time. But the rain had ruined that idea, and now the mail wouldn't be working for a while either. Della might be back in the Territory before they read her books – and perhaps that was as it should be.

Instead today's novel was *The Far Pavilions*, suggested by Sallyanne, who had heard about it from a friend she'd made at the CWA. She'd turned into quite the stalwart at CWA meetings, even baking the scones that were the staple of every gathering. Sybil was pleased: Sallyanne brightened every occasion. Yet she knew she was also covering her distress and confusion about her marriage. It was an effort, a strain, to maintain a facade. To be always cheerful so that you didn't inflict your own worries on others. What would happen, Sybil wondered, if they all stopped pretending?

She and Kate were squashed together in the office, crouched over the radio, Barney lying over their feet in his usual manner.

Sallyanne had managed to convince someone at the Katherine fire station to let her use their two-way; she'd told the others when they'd started the meeting that she'd said to the firemen that as it was the wet season there were unlikely to be any fires, so they wouldn't need the radio.

'Wasn't it such a romantic book?' Sallyanne said. 'And so dramatic. They were like Romeo and Juliet, weren't they?'

'That wasn't romantic,' Kate said, and Sybil thought she saw the briefest roll of Kate's eyes. 'They died.'

'Yes, yes, I know,' Sallyanne said almost testily and Kate and Sybil raised their eyebrows at each other.

'You sound cross, Sal,' said Rita.

'I'm not,' came a crackling voice. 'I just . . . I just like those stories. There's so much keeping them apart but they try to find a way to be together.'

They all knew that Mick had moved to Ghost River but Sybil hoped Sallyanne wasn't trying to create her own semi-tragic narrative. Mick was no romantic hero, from everything Sallyanne had said; Sybil wasn't convinced the story would end the way Sallyanne might intend, if that's what she was planning.

'A fair point,' said Kate.

'Except I guess sometimes they shouldn't be together,' said Rita, and Sybil knew that the statement was loaded. 'Sometimes it's not good for them.'

'But wouldn't it be nice,' Sallyanne said, 'if they were?'

'You've been reading too many romance novels, Sal,' Rita said. 'You know I suggested that you try something else.'

'This isn't a romance novel!' Sallyanne protested. 'It's an historical saga.'

'Fine,' said Rita. 'Sybil, help me. I'm causing offence left, right and centre.'

'You're not,' Sallyanne said in a conciliatory tone.

'Darryl, I'll be off in a minute,' Rita said.

'What's going on?' Sybil said.

'Daz wants the radio,' Rita said, sounding cross. 'Said he has a mate who's going to place a bet on a race in Brisbane for him and he needs to get onto him.'

'Doesn't he realise that literature is more important than racing?' Sybil said.

'He's a boofhead who doesn't even read the newspaper,' Rita said, and Sybil could hear a man's raised voice in the background.

'What's Darryl saying?' Sybil said.

'He told me I'm a philistine who doesn't appreciate the sport of kings.'

'Do you want to let him have the radio and rejoin us afterwards?' Sybil said.

'Good idea. Back in a sec.'

'Sallyanne, how are the children?' Sybil said.

'Oh fine,' Sallyanne said with what Sybil identified as false breeziness.

'Are they enjoying school?' Kate said.

'As much as they can.' They could hear a noise in the background. 'Sorry – there's someone telling me I'm not supposed to be in here. The man says it's all right,' she said, her voice sounding more distant. 'No, I'm not breaking rules.'

'I'm here,' Rita announced. Then she launched in, putting the case that Ashok was a weak hero, and Sallyanne insisted that he was not.

'I liked him,' said Kate, 'although I don't know that I'd fall in love with him. And aren't we meant to want to? Isn't it hard to believe in the story if we don't like the hero?'

'Maybe that's the point,' said Rita. 'He's not an obvious hero, but neither are the men we meet in life. So we can relate our own experiences to the book.'

'Oh, who wants to do that?' said Sallyanne. 'I like to escape.'

Sybil smiled at Kate. 'And there's nothing wrong with that. Well, I liked your choice, Sallyanne.'

'Me too,' said Kate. 'I didn't love the hero but it was an interesting story. It made me slightly homesick, in a funny way.'

After a few more minutes of conversation, the call was over.

'That was the shortest meeting ever,' Kate said.

'It's not quite the same when we're not all together,' Sybil said, smiling sadly. 'I really like seeing them. I've grown used to it.'

'We'll see them soon,' Kate said, standing up and dislodging the sleeping dog, who barked once. 'The advantage of doing it this way is that we're home and we can have an early glass of something. What do you think?'

Sybil and Kate had become used to having a drink together in the evening, and Sybil was enjoying her daughter-in-law's company a great deal. She pressed Kate to tell her stories of her home, of her early life. Apparently a friend of a friend knew Princess Anne and Sybil had felt a ridiculous thrill to have a tangential connection to the Royal Family.

'I think that's a very good idea,' Sybil said. 'Come on, Barney,' she said, whistling to the slow-moving dog.

As the women walked slowly to the sitting room, Sybil felt Kate's arm loop through hers.

'So you're feeling a bit homesick?' Sybil said.

Kate nodded and yawned. 'And a bit tired.'

'We're working you too hard.' Sybil watched Kate's face for her reaction.

Kate shook her head. 'It's fine.' She withdrew her arm. 'I'll fix the drinks.'

As an hour slipped by easily, Sybil realised that Ben's absence had brought an unexpected gift: she had made a friend right where she least expected to – at home.

CHAPTER THIRTY-THREE

The air was so thick with humidity that Kate thought she'd have to stand over the dough while it rose to make sure it didn't explode. Even as she kneaded it, she could feel the change in her hands: the dough got puffy and hot, and if she paused even for a few seconds it changed. She still thought it was alchemy and that baking of any kind had its own sort of magic. She was good at it now, though – she knew that by Ruby's proud smile each time she pulled a cake out of the oven.

In the weeks since Rose's accident Ruby had returned to Fairvale sporadically – mainly, Sybil told Kate, because Felicity was being difficult about 'an extra mouth to feed' – and Kate had managed in the kitchen with help from one of the girls. She'd had the occasional disaster: once with an overdose of curry powder in a stew when she was too busy chatting to remember she'd already put the powder in, and another time when she had forgotten to put salt in the bread. Otherwise, things had run smoothly, everyone had been fed, and Kate had been exhausted but pleased with herself.

Now Rose was recovered, if weak; Ruby had brought her back to Fairvale for a while so she could convalesce without being badgered to work, and because her husband had to work himself. Kate had never seen Ruby so happy.

'Whew-ee.' Ruby waddled over to where Kate was standing, frowning at the balls of dough. 'That bread looks ready to pop, girl,' she said, her cackle starting to rise.

'I know. I'm almost afraid to leave it.'

'You have to leave?' Ruby looked concerned.

'Just to go to the house to check on some accounts that Joe asked me to look over.'

'He can't look over them himself?'

Kate felt like laughing – Ruby was often audacious when it was just the two of them in the kitchen but Kate knew she'd never say anything like that to Joe's face. For one thing, Joe was the boss; for another, Ruby adored him.

'He gave me a home when no one else would,' Ruby had told her once, going on to say that because she had a child and no husband, other people judged her. She'd had to leave where she was living, on a station near the Gulf of Carpentaria, just after Rose was born, and, after trying to find a home on two other stations, a cousin had told her to journey to Fairvale, where 'young Joe' had just taken over. By car Fairvale was a solid day's drive from the Gulf Country; hitching rides, as she had done, it took her a week.

When she'd arrived, with her baby, it had been Sybil who'd come out to talk to her. Ruby had asked to see 'Mister Joe' and Sybil had fetched him.

'You know what he said?' Ruby had told Kate. 'He said, "You've arrived at the right time! I need a cook. Do you know how to cook?"' Ruby had cackled and covered her eyes. 'I didn't know. But I learnt!' Another cackle. 'He gave me a place to live and a job. He's a good man. So is his boy.'

Ruby had smiled and Kate had known by 'boy' she had meant Ben. Ruby had already made her opinion of Lachie clear, shocking Kate once by saying that Sybil and Joe's eldest 'should never have been born'.

'What on earth do you mean?' she'd asked.

Ruby had shaken her head vigorously. 'He's a bad fella,' she'd said. 'Nothin' but trouble. All those years he used to sulk round here – didn't like the food, didn't like the horses, didn't like the rain, didn't like the dry.' She had shaken her head again. 'Sure didn't like his brother or his parents. Used to beat up Ben good.'

This was information Ben had already given Kate but it still hurt to hear it – to learn that other people had known.

'When he went away to school,' Ruby had continued, 'we were all happy then. We had a party the day mister and missus left with him!' She giggled. 'Big cow in the coal pit. Lots of singing that night.' She'd winked. 'Even a bit of grog.'

'So nothing happened to make him that way?' Kate said, still unable to believe that Lachie could have been so destructive without a reason.

'Bad spirit in him,' Ruby had said seriously, nodding slowly.

Kate had been tempted to laugh – it seemed like such an easy answer. There were easy answers in Roman Catholicism: the Devil was possessing someone or God had worked a miracle. But she'd never believed them when she was growing up and she didn't believe them now.

'What . . .' Kate started then paused. She didn't want to sound disrespectful so she had to phrase this carefully. 'What makes you think that?'

'Don't think it, girl,' Ruby responded with authority. '*Know it*.' She nodded again. 'Mister Joe's father, he killed a man.'

Kate gasped – this was something she hadn't been told.

'He killed that man for no good reason,' Ruby went on. 'That man was stealing cattle and Mister Joe's father caught him. He fired a shot. He said it was a warning. But that man, he was shot in the middle of the back.'

Ruby's eyes blazed as they held Kate's. 'What kind of warning is that?'

'So you think that Lachie was ... born bad because of that? As retribution?'

Ruby pressed her lips together until they almost disappeared, her cheeks puffing out at the same time.

'That fella who was killed,' she said, 'he is in Mister Lachie.'

Then Ruby's eyelids half closed; from previous experience Kate knew the discussion was over. The chill that ran up her spine, however, lasted quite a while.

Since then she and Ruby had passed many days in the kitchen sharing information about each other's lives and countries. Sometimes Kate thought Ruby knew more about her than Ben did.

'He could look over them himself,' Kate said now, casting an eye over the dough, thinking of what waited for her in the office, 'but he and Stan are talking about what they can do with the cattle.'

'It's a good thing that Stan came home before the rain,' Ruby said, picking up a potato. 'He could have been stuck!' That cackle again. 'Stuck for months!'

Kate smiled at Ruby's ability to find laughter in everything.

'With the rain coming early they have to work out how to get the cattle here and out to the meatworks.' She frowned. 'It's made things difficult.'

Ruby's face turned serious and she shook her head slowly. 'It's no good when the rain comes now.'

'What do you mean?'

'Rain comes early, rain stops early. Then we have long dry. No water. Animals can't eat. No good.'

Kate had never experienced an abnormality in the weather pattern, although she'd heard plenty of talk about such things. Weather was a regular topic of conversation at night when they were all in the sitting room.

'I guess we'll wait to see what happens,' Kate said lamely. 'But would you mind keeping an eye on the bread while I pop into the house?'

'Off you go, Katie girl.' Ruby nodded solemnly.

'Thanks.' Kate pulled off her apron, not wanting it to get wet as she dashed between buildings.

She pressed her hat onto her head – it would be her only protection against the rain – then pulled open the screen door and made a run for the big house.

Her boots slid on the muddy ground as she moved as fast as she could, through the garden gate and up the path, kicking them off when she reached the door. She couldn't bring that mud into the house, even if it meant she'd have to check for snakes before she put the boots back on. That sort of thing was automatic for her now.

She headed for the office and hung her hat on the back of a chair to dry. The desk was a mess: Joe had obviously made a start on things then decided to leave them for her.

As Kate pulled out the chair to sit down she heard a commotion towards the front of the house. There was a noise outside, like someone was shouting, but she couldn't make it out properly over the rain.

She headed for the sitting room just as there was a loud banging on the front door. It couldn't be Sybil or Joe – they'd come in through the back.

'Hello! Hello, hello!'

She recognised Stan's voice and trotted to the door, opening it to see him looking sodden, his hat in his hand, his breathing fast.

'Are you all right?' she said.

'Mister Joe,' he said, starting to gulp his breaths, turning to point towards the stables. He had a desperate look in his eyes and Kate felt her throat constrict.

'Missus Sybil,' he panted. 'Where is she?'

Kate thought quickly: that morning Sybil had said she wanted to check on one of the families in the Aboriginal camp. It was five hundred metres away.

'Go back to Joe. I'll get Sybil.'

'Kate, he's . . .' His eyes told her the information she hadn't wanted to know.

'Go,' she ordered, and she ran in the opposite direction, through the back door, ignoring her boots. She didn't care about rain. She didn't care about mud. She didn't care about sticks or anything else that might be on the ground.

She ran down the path to the garden gate, fleetingly wondering if she should jump over it, shoving it open instead.

She ran, trying not to slip.

She ran, feeling rain on her head, on her neck, sticking her shirt to her skin.

'Sybil!' she yelled as she came to the first humpies, hoping that the sound would carry loudly enough that it would flush her mother-in-law from wherever she was.

'Sybil!' she tried again, her voice catching.

She was almost at the third house when she saw Sybil emerge from the doorway, a child on her hip.

'What is it?' Sybil called. The boy was laughing.

'Put him down!' Kate said.

'What?' Sybil frowned as Kate stopped in front of her,

feeling like she couldn't breathe, her clothes soaking, her hair in her eyes.

'Joe,' Kate said roughly. Now the child's mother appeared behind Sybil.

'It's Joe,' she tried again. Wordlessly, the woman took the boy from Sybil, whose eyes never left Kate's even as they widened, even as her mouth opened without sound.

'Come with me,' Kate said, holding out her hand, hauling Sybil into the rain.

As they ran, Kate wasn't sure if she was pulling Sybil, or Sybil was pulling her, but they arrived together at the stables to see Stan standing by a chair, and Joe slumped in it with his hat askew, his eyes closed and his mouth – Kate knew she would never forget the contortion of that mouth, or how grey Joe looked, or how tightly Sybil squeezed her hand just before she let it go.

'Missus Sybil,' she heard Stan say and she watched as Sybil walked swiftly to her husband, immediately putting two fingers against his neck.

Kate felt a stab of hope: if Sybil was checking his pulse, maybe there was a—

'No use, missus,' Stan said, and his voice was so sad that Kate wanted to cry. Except she was already crying. She had started as soon as Sybil had taken her hand and only realised it when they reached the stables.

'I know, Stan,' Sybil murmured. 'I know. But I had to check.'
Stan bowed his head.

'What happened?' Sybil said, putting a hand on his arm and Kate wondered at her ability to care for Stan in this moment when they should both be caring for her. If only she didn't feel stuck to the spot.

'He, um . . .' Stan sniffled and rubbed his eyes. 'He said he wasn't feeling well. Then he was lifting that saddle.' He nodded at a saddle lying on the ground, stirrups splayed. 'He was grey, missus. He said he had a pain. I . . .' Stan sniffled again. 'I took the saddle from him and he came to this chair. He was trying to get his breath. He told me to get you.'

Stan's face was almost unrecognisable, his brow furrowing deep into itself, his mouth twisting and turning as he tried to talk.

'I didn't make it, missus,' he said, his breathing ragged now. 'I got to that door and Mister Joe, he called out. I ran back to him.'

Stan shook his head and dropped it into his hands as Sybil slid an arm around him. Kate couldn't understand how she could be so calm.

'It wasn't your fault, Stan,' Sybil said. Then her eyes met Kate's and Kate could see why Sybil was so calm: all the roiling emotion, the disbelief, that shock was in those eyes. Sybil's eyebrows and lips started to quiver then she looked away and released Stan's shoulders.

'I'm going to need your help to get him to the house,' she said to him. 'Will you help me?'

Stan nodded slowly and wiped his nose with the back of his hand.

'Thank you,' Sybil said.

She put her hand against Joe's cheek and kissed his forehead. As Joe's eyes stayed closed Kate felt a jolt, as if tectonic plates were moving against each other.

Stan went to fetch one of the stockmen so they could carry Joe to the house. Sybil came towards Kate and took her hand. Silently, they walked – not to the front door of the house, which was closest, but down the side, into the garden, where Sybil stopped and turned her head to the sky.

Rain cascaded onto her face, and then Kate, too, lifted her face and felt the warm splodges on her skin. She felt her shirt sticking to her skin and her hair plastered onto her skull. She didn't care.

After minutes had passed, maybe hours, Sybil turned to her.

'Now it begins,' she said.

CHAPTER THIRTY-FOUR

In the first few days after Joe's death Sybil searched her memory for clues she might have missed. He'd been tired for a while, but she'd put it down to him getting older. He'd looked pale from time to time – he'd told her he wasn't sleeping well. He'd been eating normally, as far as she could tell. Or maybe he hadn't and she hadn't known because there were plenty of times when she wasn't with him at lunch, in particular.

Even if she had noticed more definitive signs, however, she doubted she could have made Joe see a doctor – he always said there was nothing that sunshine and a day on horseback couldn't fix. Morever, they hadn't been able to leave Fairvale for weeks now, nor could the doctor get to them in order to examine Joe's body. So she'd told him what she suspected had killed her husband: a heart attack. She relayed what Stan had told her about how Joe had died and the doctor had concurred with her assessment, saying he'd post her a death certificate as soon as the weather cleared.

It was no comfort at all for the doctor to tell her that proximity to town, to help, wouldn't have made a difference – wouldn't have kept Joe alive. No – none of it was a comfort, and she suspected it was because she didn't want to be comforted. She wanted to feel guilty – to feel as though she'd failed him. She wanted to feel anything, and instead it was as if she lived inside a sphere that kept her insulated from the world around her, and paralysed within. Even the air seemed to change shape as she moved through it; it didn't touch her, it avoided her.

They buried Joe past the stables, near a stand of river red gums that had been growing since before he was a boy. The whole population of Fairvale was there, the rain bowing the brims of their hats. A flock of black cockatoos, larger than Sybil had ever seen, flew past and Ruby had turned to her and waggled her eyebrows. Sybil knew what she was trying to say: Joe had taken flight. It was a tempting thought, even if she didn't quite believe it.

Now Fairvale was her responsibility. Ben would want to run it when he could finally return but she didn't want his name on the bank documents. That's what she'd told him when she'd finally been able to speak to him. He'd been out on a horse for days, unaware that his father had died. Once she'd told him, he'd immediately said he'd come home but she'd told him the truth: the roads weren't passable, and he should finish what he'd started there. Why should he hurry back to a responsibility that wasn't meant to be his yet? He'd inherit the debt one day, if they still had it; for now he should be allowed to be young, to make mistakes as he learnt what to do.

She was the one who should know what she was doing. But all these years she had occupied herself with the house or what was close to the house: the kitchen, the school, the women and children who lived on Fairvale while their men went out to work. Joe had tried to tell her but she didn't know anything about cattle – not really. Not enough to know how many head they should muster at a time, and how fat or thin the beasts should be to fetch the best price. She didn't even know what all the horses were called, or where their tack came from, and she had no idea if Joe was breeding the dogs himself or getting them from somewhere else. She didn't know where on Fairvale the drovers went when the cattle needed to feed. She didn't know the names or locations of any of the bores apart from the one that was closest to the house, and only then because she'd heard Joe talking about it.

Trying to learn everything she didn't know, to keep the place running, to listen to the grief of everyone else who wanted to come and talk to her about how much they missed Joe, was exhausting her. Despite the bone weariness that drove her to bed each night, she wasn't sleeping much. Certainly, she would fall asleep hard – then wake up two hours later, and sleep would not return.

One night she had a nightmare about Lachie holding his father under water and Joe accepting his fate, smiling up at his son. She awoke violently and found the sheets tangled around her legs. She was shaking, and she knew she couldn't stay in this room, with that dream still pressing on her brain, compounding the distress she felt that she had been unable to let Joe's eldest son know that his father had died. He should be told; she wanted to tell him. But he still hadn't been found.

In the kitchen she filled the teapot and took it to the table along with her favourite cup and saucer. She waited for the tea to brew; she poured it carefully. She always drank it black and strong. Probably not a good idea if she wanted to get back to sleep. But she didn't. The night held only terrors and loneliness for her right now.

A noise in the hallway made Sybil look up and Kate walked in, came over and put her arm around her.

'The nights are the worst,' her daughter-in-law said, sitting down, placing two books on the table.

Sybil smiled gratefully. Kate had helped her so much over the past few days. More than helped – she was insisting on taking care of the accounts, including all the parts that Joe used to check, until Sybil was ready to talk about them. She was baking special cakes for Sybil, doing wonders with the meagre stores they had. Sybil didn't feel like eating anything but she made an effort because Kate had – and perhaps this was what Kate had planned on.

'What do you have there?' Sybil said, nodding at the books.

'Well . . .' Kate looked pleased with herself. 'Ben called and told me to pull these off your shelves. I meant to give them to you this afternoon but I forgot. When I heard you in here . . .' She smiled, although Sybil could see the same fine red capillaries in her eyes and hollowed-out space below her eyes that Sybil herself saw in the mirror. They had clearly both become nocturnal.

Kate pushed the books towards her. 'He told me that you'd know why he suggested them.'

Sybil picked them up: collected poems of Banjo Paterson and *We of the Never Never* by Jeannie Gunn.

'That rascal,' she murmured.

'Why?' Kate said, frowning. 'What is it?'

Sybil shook her head. 'It's his way of telling me to get on with things.' She held up the volume of poetry. 'When the children were little, Joe used to love reciting "The Geebung Polo Club". He thought it was hilarious. He would threaten to start playing polo in the cattle yards. Ben tried to hold him to it.'

'I don't know the poem, I'm afraid.'

'Oh, you will – I am quite sure Ben wants me to read it to you. And then give you the book so you can read some other poems. It's your education in Australiana.'

Her son might be far away but Sybil felt suddenly grateful to him. That he could remember this brought him closer to her. He knew that the poetry would cheer her up, and bring her happy memories of his father.

'My father loved Banjo Paterson too,' she said, thinking of the tall, gruff man who would pull out his pipe of an evening and read to her as he puffed away. It wasn't until she was older and away from home that she realised how much that time meant to her. Her father wasn't a demonstrative man; he'd never once told her that he loved her. He'd shown her instead. After she'd moved to the Territory he would send her clippings from *The Bulletin* and Column 8 from *The Sydney Morning Herald*. Her mother, also not prone to declarations of affection, would send copies of *The Australian Women's Weekly* with roses from their garden pressed between the pages. They were both dead now and she hadn't been there to say goodbye. She hadn't been there with Joe to say goodbye either. At the moment Sybil felt numb about that; later – maybe in a few months' time – it would haunt her, the way it had with her parents.

'And the other book?' Kate said gently.

'Sorry – did I drift off?'

Kate reached over to pat her hand. 'A little bit. But I don't mind.'

Sybil smiled gratefully. 'The other book is for you, I'd say. It's about a young woman from Melbourne who married and came to live in the Northern Territory – the "Never Never", as it used to be called. Sometimes it still is – not by me, though.'

'Why not?' Kate said, picking up the book and opening it to look at the inside flap.

'Let's just say it's a phrase from a time when some people understood less than they do now. Anyway – happy reading.' She gave the book back to Kate. 'I should have given it to you when you arrived. I just didn't . . .' She stopped, regret pushing its way into her brain. 'I didn't think. It had been so long since I moved here that I forgot what it's like. That book helped me – a lot. I think it will help you too.'

'Do you think I need help?' Kate said, her face showing uncertainty.

'No,' Sybil said quickly. 'I just meant that it helps explain this place. I've lived here for decades and so much of it is still a mystery. I think Joe felt that way too. We will never see most of the Territory. You and I will never even see most of Fairvale – and that sounds quite strange when I say it out loud, doesn't it?'

She and Kate sat looking at each other, the vastness of Fairvale containing only silence at this time of night.

'Anyway, that book helped me realise that I wasn't strange for not understanding the Territory straightaway. And I'm sure you feel about as bewildered as I did for my first few years.'

Kate had a faraway look.

'It's funny, isn't it?' she said. 'How we find out more from books than we do from life sometimes?'

Sybil thought of the books she'd read over the course of her life: as a child; during snatched hours while she was between shifts at the hospital; late at night when her boys were babies and she couldn't sleep for worrying about these precious new lives that were her responsibility. Those books had been her escape and her solace; from them she had learnt how to be a woman and a wife and a parent, more than she had from any humans.

'Books give us the benefit of a lot of people's experiences,' she said slowly. 'They give us more options to choose from – more ways to live – than we could ever find on our own.'

Kate seemed to be considering what she'd said.

'I think we should read, then,' Kate said after moments had passed. 'Since we both can't sleep.'

'You don't want to hear me recite a poem?' Sybil said, wishing she hadn't made the suggestion. Even if she wouldn't be able to sleep for the rest of the night, she was too tired to do justice to Joe's favourite poem.

'I'm fairly sure,' Kate said, 'that Ben would want you to read it to yourself first. I'll read it when you're finished.'

Sybil smiled, although she felt her mouth wanting to drag down at the corners.

'May I have some tea?' Kate said softly.

'Of course.' Sybil stood, moving to the cupboard for another cup and saucer, handing them to Kate.

As she sat down again she opened the book and sought out not 'The Geebung Polo Club' but her own favourite poem: 'Clancy of the Overflow'. When Sybil was a teenager she had found Clancy to be a romantic figure: the wild bush man who had no interest in city life. Once she was an adult and living on Fairvale, she realised that she had, quite to her astonishment if not surprise, married her very own Clancy. It was in his memory, then, that she turned to the right page and began to read.

The teapot was exhausted by the time the sun started to rise. Sybil read on, with Kate beside her, until the kitchen clock struck six and a new day had to begin.

1980

1 January	Princess Victoria of Sweden is made heir to the throne after a change to the law of succession
29 January	The Rubik's cube makes its public debut
13 February	The Winter Olympics commence in Lake Placid, New York
19 February	AC/DC lead singer Bon Scott dies
3 March	Pierre Trudeau once more becomes prime minister of Canada
4 March	Robert Mugabe is elected prime minister of Zimbabwe
21 March	President Jimmy Carter announces the US boycott of the Summer Olympics in Moscow
30 April	Queen Juliana of the Netherlands abdicates and is succeeded by her daughter, Queen Beatrix
18 May	The volcano Mt St Helens erupts in the US state of Washington
21 May	*The Empire Strikes Back* is released
17 August	Baby Azaria Chamberlain is taken by a dingo from a campsite at Uluru
18 October	Malcolm Fraser is re-elected as prime minister of Australia
4 November	Ronald Reagan is elected as US President
8 December	John Lennon is assassinated in New York City

CHAPTER THIRTY-FIVE

Rita put her elbows on the topmost log of the cattle-yard fence. It was just a bit too high but she liked the feeling of leaning into it; she imagined she could haul herself on top of the fence as she saw the young men do, but she'd never been that agile and this wasn't the time of her life to start trying.

Sybil was standing beside her, gazing out across Fairvale's plains.

'You shouldn't have driven all that way,' she said vacantly. 'Where did you stay last night?'

'Daly Waters.'

Once the rains had stopped long enough for the Stuart Highway to be opened all the way to Katherine, Rita borrowed Hamish's car and set off for Fairvale.

Sybil nodded slowly and Rita scrutinised her face. She looked different – as if she'd arrived from another country and didn't know her way around.

'Can you stay for a few days?' Sybil smiled at her now, but Rita couldn't find her anywhere in that smile. It was the expression of someone who wanted to be polite, and Rita had the distinct impression that she shouldn't have come.

'Yes,' Rita said. 'If that's all right.'

Sybil blinked and Rita saw something change. Or snap.

'Of course,' she said. 'It's so good to see you.'

'Are you sure?'

Sybil frowned. 'Why wouldn't I be sure?'

'I've just landed here. And you have a lot to do.'

'Ben will be home very soon,' Sybil said, and her tone of voice suggested the subject was closed. 'He has to finish up some things where he is and then he'll be back. So we're fine. Not much longer now.'

She looked once more across the yards, down behind the stables, towards the river. She'd told Rita that Joe was buried there but she hadn't suggested they go to the grave.

'Do you want to talk – about Joe?' Rita said.

Sybil's eyes glittered as they met hers and Rita had the uncomfortable feeling that she'd made Sybil angry.

'I suppose we could,' Sybil said, an edge to her voice.

So she was angry. Or upset. But Rita had also known her long enough to be able to speak frankly.

'It's not about could or should,' Rita said. 'It's about what you want, Syb.'

Sybil's jaw hardened. 'What I want,' she said, 'is for my husband not to be dead. What I want is for my sons to be here. Both of them.'

She took a breath in and exhaled it to the sky. 'I'm so angry, Rita, I don't know what to do with myself. Poor Kate has to put up with me going quiet but it's so I don't yell at her when nothing is her fault. I've been left with this—' she moved her hand in an arc over the horizon, 'and I have no idea what to do with it. Joe didn't train me up the way he did Lachie. He had barely trained Ben. Now he's gone.'

She put her hands on her hips and looked down to the earth. Rita noticed that her hair was now almost completely grey and it was longer than Rita had ever seen it. Sybil usually had Ruby cut it every six weeks; perhaps, in the wake of Joe's death, she had forgotten.

'A heart attack,' Sybil said to the ground. 'How could I not have noticed that was a possibility?'

'Sybil,' Rita said firmly and Sybil lifted her head. 'Do not, for a second, blame yourself.'

'Why not?'

'Because you were his wife, not his bloody doctor.'

'He didn't go to the doctor.'

'Precisely!'

'I should have made him,' Sybil said, her breath coming faster.

'And I should have married Kerry Packer so I could have a nice big house in the eastern suburbs, but I missed that boat too.'

Sybil turned away and kicked the dirt.

'I'm angry,' she said again.

'Yes, you are, and that's normal.'

'I never wanted to be normal,' Sybil said, the heel of her boot digging a hole in the ground. 'I wanted to be exceptional.'

Rita chortled. 'You're that, too.'

She felt a wet tongue on her leg and a glance confirmed that Sybil's dog had found his way to her.

'Barney!' she said. 'Get off me.' She jiggled her leg to shoo him away but he kept licking.

'He likes you,' Sybil said, her voice sounding more relaxed.

'A little too much.' Rita reached down to push him away.

'I like you, too,' Sybil said.

As their eyes met they smiled at each other.

Sybil looked at her watch. 'Is it too early for a drink?'

'Well . . . it's two o'clock.'

'I guess that makes it all right.'

Sybil offered her arm to her friend. As Rita took it, Sybil led her towards the house, Barney frolicking around their feet.

The garden gate gave way to a shove from Sybil's hip. Barney slipped through ahead of them, and as they entered Sybil's domain Rita could see that it, too, was suffering from inattention: normally Sybil kept it neat, with not a stray fallen leaf or weed to be found. The plants and bushes were now looking as raggedy as Sybil's hair.

'What's going on here?' Rita said, letting go of Sybil's arm.

'What do you mean?' Sybil said wearily.

Rita used her arm to indicate the circumference of the garden. 'This place is a mess, Syb.'

She knew that the look of hard shock on Sybil's face was her reward for being rude but she wasn't going to stay silent.

'I – I've been distracted,' Sybil said.

'I know,' Rita said firmly, 'but that is no excuse to not look after your garden. Or yourself.'

'Fairvale takes up a lot of my time,' Sybil said through thinned lips.

'And so does grief. I'm aware of that. But you *need* this garden. You've always needed it. Remember why you started it – to give you a place to be on your own? To think? Maybe dream a little?' Rita dared to smile. 'I think that's what you told me.'

'Perhaps I don't want to be alone or to think,' Sybil said, and once again Rita found it hard to read her tone: was she cross with her? Sad?

'I've done enough thinking since Joe died to last me the rest of my life,' Sybil went on. 'I'm sick of thinking. It never goes anywhere.'

'So what have you been doing to switch it off – drinking?' Rita frowned.

'I tried that,' Sybil said with a heavy sigh. 'I don't make it very far.' She made a face. 'A couple of glasses of whisky and I start falling apart.' She took hold of her elbows and bowed her head as she turned away from Rita, towards the largest tree in the garden: a tall frangipani.

'What, then?' Rita said, more gently. She reached out and tugged the back of Sybil's shirt. 'Hey,' she said, 'turn around.'

Sybil turned and looked crestfallen as she did so. 'Nothing,' she said. 'There's nothing. I'm going quietly mad, I think.'

'Have you talked to Kate about this?'

Sybil looked out past the trees to the stables. 'No. She's been doing so much. She doesn't need to worry about me too.'

'She might want to worry about you, though.'

Sybil shook her head and bit her bottom lip, closing her eyes. She needed to cry, Rita thought, but she also knew Sybil rarely did that. After Ray's death and the tears that for a while had almost overwhelmed her each day, Sybil had told her that she felt as if crying meant losing control. Rita had thought that losing control wasn't such a bad thing. But she knew why it scared Sybil: it had taken her so long to recover from Ray's death and she didn't have the luxury she'd had then, of no responsibilities of the order she had here on Fairvale.

'How am I going to do this?' Sybil whispered hoarsely.

'What do you mean?'

'This.' Sybil gestured to the house, then turned and flung her arm towards the cattle yards. 'All of this. How am I going to do it without him?'

Their eyes met and Rita saw what was really going on: fear. Stronger than grief, more crippling than loneliness, and written all over her friend's face.

'You're doing it already,' Rita said. 'Can't you tell?'

Sybil started to laugh but there was no mirth in it. 'Then how can I make myself *want* to do it?'

Rita glanced around the garden, hoping she'd find a good answer there – something witty or inspirational.

'Well, old friend, that's the tricky question, isn't it?'

She stepped closer to Sybil and pulled her into a hug. Sybil let herself be enfolded and for the first time in their friendship Rita had the sensation of supporting Sybil more than Sybil was supporting her.

'But I reckon we start with this garden,' Rita said into Sybil's hair before taking hold of her elbows.

'This—' she nodded to one of the weedy beds, 'is not you. Your world might be out of order because Joe is gone but there are ways to bring it back under control. If you can't manage to keep this garden orderly I'm not surprised that you're lacking the motivation to do other things. Everything would feel messy to you. Not right. So . . .'

She dropped Sybil's arms.

'We're going to put this garden to rights. Then we're going to make you a list of things to do that you enjoy. Maybe even things that can make you happy. And you're going to promise me that you'll come into this garden every day to keep it tidy, and sit long enough to enjoy it, and that you'll do at least one other thing on that list every day. I'm going to tell Kate about the list so she can enforce it.'

Sybil made a sound.

'No arguments,' Rita said. 'When I can't be here Kate can keep an eye on you, and I'll check in with her – and, if you're lucky, I'll also call you from time to time.' She grinned.

'Barney!' Rita whistled to the dog, who padded towards her, his long tongue hanging out and his big black-patched eye turned in her direction. Rita bent down and scratched behind his ears. 'Can you look after Sybil for me? Can you? Can you?' She laughed as he sat on her feet and was pleased to see that Sybil was smiling.

'Do you have a bucket?' Rita said. 'I'll get started on those weeds. And you'll need some secateurs so you can start pruning.'

Sybil tilted her head to one side. 'Where did you learn to be like this?' she said with a faint smile.

'What – bossy?' Rita winked. 'Where do you think, Sister?'

Sybil nodded and walked slowly towards Rita as she crouched beside the garden bed.

Rita smiled up at her as Sybil kissed the top of her head.

'My world's not ended,' Sybil said, 'while I have you.'

As Sybil looked down at her, Rita held her smile and was sure – or she could almost be sure – that she saw tears in Sybil's eyes.

Then Sybil blinked, and sniffed, and they were gone.

CHAPTER THIRTY-SIX

Della closed the door to the shack that held the office and walked across the yard back to the house, her eyes squinting against the sun which was setting over the rocky ridges that marked one of the boundaries of their ranch. She'd wanted to climb those ridges when she was a child but she'd never made it – they were too steep and far more dangerous than she'd imagined. Even her brothers left them alone.

She pushed through the kitchen door into the house and stopped dead.

'Daddy – what are you doing in here?' she squeaked.

Her father was sitting up at the kitchen table, leaning on his elbows. He had rarely left the guest bedroom since she'd arrived five months ago and she hadn't been sure if he'd ever make it down the hallway again. He beamed at her as she rushed towards him, and as she went to put her hand on his shoulder he took it and squeezed it.

'Having you home has made me feel a whole lot better,' he said, squeezing again. 'I was sick of that old room. Thought I'd come out here, see what y'all were doing.'

'That's good,' Della said.

'Sit down, honey,' her mother said. 'Your father asked for a cup of coffee. Would you like one?'

'Sure,' Della said, smiling weakly. She had work to do but she supposed she could stay a while.

'Is there any for me?'

At the sound of her brother's voice Della looked to the doorway.

'Of course, Teddy,' their mother said, her grin so wide it looked like it would split her face. 'Take a seat.'

Ted was the eldest and least favourite of Della's brothers, mainly because he was their ringleader when it came to shirking his responsibilities and shifting them on to Della. He was also the recipient of most of their mother's forgiveness – she would always excuse him. He could be lots of fun but Della had watched him get away with so much as they were growing up that she was convinced he was carefree because he'd never had to worry about getting into trouble, or doing his fair share of work around the ranch. Their father had tried to make him work more and Ted had always gone to their mother to complain.

'Ain't you meant to be hauling hay, Della?' Teddy said with a slight smirk. 'It's just sittin' out there, waitin'.'

'That's your job, Ted,' her father said sternly. 'Della's got enough to do.'

'Hmmm.' Ted frowned. 'Well, Della's been away so long I just thought she could pull a bit more weight around here.'

'She's doing enough,' their father repeated. 'Where are your brothers? Maybe they could do it.'

'They've gone into town,' Ted said, smiling sweetly at his mother as she put a mug of coffee in front of him.

'You're not going with them?' she said.

'I've got a date,' Ted said, looking pleased with himself. 'Gotta make myself pretty before I go.'

Della knew that if she sat quietly they were unlikely to notice her. Her whole life, it had been this way: when Ted was in the room, she might as well be invisible.

'So, Della – the hay?' Ted said, taking a sip of his coffee. 'This is good joe, Momma, thank you.'

'Ted,' their father said warningly and was met by a glare from his son. 'Della's been running the place ever since she got back. She's helping your mother around the house and with your grandmother. You boys could lend a hand, you know.'

'A woman's work is never done – isn't that what people say?' Ted winked at his father and Della shot a glance at her mother, who blanched momentarily. Della had occasionally wondered if her mother knew exactly who her son had turned out to be and pretended not to notice just to keep the peace.

'That's enough, Ted,' their father barked. 'Now, I'm feeling better but I'm not up to getting back to work. Della's exhausted. You and your brothers have to help out more instead of riding off into the goddamn sunset all the time.'

Ted glared at his father and Della held her breath. Despite his illness, her father still ruled their family and she didn't think Ted would challenge him – but she didn't want a scene. Her mother would hate it and her father didn't have enough strength for it.

'Fine,' Ted said, pushing back his chair as he stood. 'That's fine. I'll go on my date now. Tomorrow I'll start my shift at the salt mines.'

'There's no need for drama, Teddy,' their mother said, her tone conciliatory.

Ted looked at Della then at his parents. 'Looks like I should go away for a while. Seems like that's the only way anyone gets appreciated round here.'

'Ted,' her mother said pleadingly but it didn't help: her son was gone.

'We've spoilt that boy,' her father muttered and Della was shocked to hear it.

'He just needs a good woman,' her mother said. 'Then he'll settle down.' She looked at Della. 'I do appreciate all you're doing here, Della. I do. We need you here.'

Della looked down at the table and swallowed. All the nights she had lain awake thinking of Ghost River, of Fairvale, of the people and land she missed – all that homesickness, for that's what it was. She couldn't stay here but she didn't know how to leave.

'The girl might have other ideas, honey,' her father said, pulling his coffee cup towards him. 'We can't jail her here. She was doing just fine without us.'

Della's eyes met her mother's. She saw uncertainty there, and sadness too.

'I suppose not,' her mother half whispered. 'Della, why don't you sit down?' She attempted a smile as she nodded towards Della's coffee.

Taking a seat, Della grasped her cup and felt the heat of it. The three of them sat in silence for a while.

⌒

The mornings were so still that if Della closed her eyes she could almost imagine she was back at Ghost River in the minutes between the sun rising and the animals and people starting to move around, men calling to each other, horses whinnying, cattle bellowing. Even some of the noises were the same here in Val Verde County. But as soon as she opened her eyes the illusion was ruined. So she drank her weak coffee and wished it was sweet black tea from a billy, and she ate the pancakes her mother had made her and wished they were damper, although she didn't want to be ungrateful.

The wet season would be over now, in the Territory. She had missed a book club meeting; she'd told herself she would read the book they'd discussed, as a way of keeping up with them, but there was no bookstore in town. Her life here was very different, in spite of the surface similarities of the work. No friends, no books. No Stan.

She looked up as the side door opened. Her mother walked in, holding envelopes.

'Forgot to get the mail yesterday,' she said, looking apologetic.

'That's okay, Momma,' Della said, standing to put her mug and plate in the sink. She should wash it now, before her mother attempted to. It was her job, she kept saying when Della tried to get her to sit down for a few minutes, to take a break from looking after them all. She could see her mother wearing out. She was the same age as Sybil but she looked so much older.

'There's one here for you.' Her mother held out an envelope that was covered in stamps and markings.

Della's heart leapt as it did each time she recognised a letter from Australia. She quickly turned it over and couldn't help the disappointment as she saw the return address: *Sybil Baxter, Fairvale Station, near Katherine, NT, Australia.*

'Thanks, Momma.' She kept her voice neutral. Her mother didn't know about Stan and she didn't intend on telling her.

'Your friends are good with the letters,' her mother said as she eased herself into a chair. 'Better than you were.' She smiled weakly.

'I know,' Della said. She'd apologised so many times that she couldn't do it again – it would lose its meaning.

'There's some letters here for your father.' Her mother tapped several envelopes into a pile. 'I'll take them in to him.'

'He seems to be doing better, don't you think?'

Her mother's smile was hopeful. 'I do. He's always been strong, your father. Like you are.'

Never in Della's life had her mother ever said she was strong. Never had her mother even paid her many compliments. She wasn't mean; it just wasn't her way. Della wasn't sure what she was meant to say in response.

'You read your letter and I'll be back,' her mother said, saving her the trouble.

Della nodded and sat down, deciding to forgo coffee for the time being. Even if Sybil wasn't Stan, she still wanted to read her letter.

The onion-skin airmail sheets looked so insubstantial but it was clear from the first line that they held substantial news.

Joe has died, it said and Della felt the shock of it. She had barely known Joe but he had seemed healthy and Sybil had never said that he wasn't.

He had a heart attack. He hadn't seen a doctor in years so we don't know if there were any warnings that he had ignored.

Della read on, through the short details about what was happening on Fairvale. Then: *Kate might have told you that Ben went to work in New South Wales. He'll be returning soon but I also have to make decisions about our future here.*

I know you have family responsibilities, the letter continued, *but I really need help. Stan tells me that you are brilliant with horses and you can tolerate cattle. Would you consider returning to the Northern Territory to work on Fairvale?*

Della re-read the last paragraph, disbelief and excitement whipping around each other in her mind.

She looked around the kitchen. She could hear her parents talking, the noise carrying from near the back of the house. Now she could hear her grandmother calling out to her mother. The constant motion of her family's life had prepared Della well for life on Ghost River, even if she hadn't realised it. She loved them, even her brothers – sometimes especially her brothers, because she was sure that living in reaction to them had made her into the woman she was.

She'd never been a big believer in fate or destiny or kismet, whatever the term of the day was. People who grew up around nature rarely were. Animals lived and died. People lived and died. Nature changed in cycles, and each year it all went round again. Fate was a concept for people who needed a reason for everything, a bigger sense of purpose, and so often there was neither reason nor purpose.

Yet Sybil's letter had the air of fate about it and now fate was in Della's hands. She could change the seasons of her life. She could swap the hemispheres. She'd need to be brave enough to disappoint her parents and strong enough to leave them again. Strength she had. Maybe determination, too.

She didn't know if the time was right, though – if it was too soon for her to leave. As happy as the idea of returning to the Northern Territory made her, she would think on it a while. She'd take a horse and go out for a few hours, have a good look around this land she would have to leave again and ask herself if she could. Because if she went, she might not be back for a very long time. She had to be able to live with that.

CHAPTER THIRTY-SEVEN

The last few months without Mick had been a revelation for Sallyanne. She felt like a flower unfurling, its face towards the sun, its perfume released. The children were happier, too. She was having trouble managing financially because Mick was sending money only sporadically but that didn't seem so difficult when she could greet each day with anticipation rather than dread.

Now she had a CWA meeting to attend. People to talk to; conversations to be had. She had missed the last meeting because her father wasn't available to look after Gretel. One of the women had called and asked where she was – when Sallyanne had told her the reason she'd offered her eighteen-year-old daughter as a babysitter.

'I've had five more kids since her,' the woman had said, 'so she knows a lot about littlies.'

So it was with her new teenaged minder that Sallyanne had left Gretel, who had seemed delighted to be spending time in a house full of girls' toys and fairy dresses.

Carefully balancing her plates of freshly baked scones, Sallyanne pulled open the back door of the CWA hall and walked into the usual din. She focused on getting to the table to put the scones down, then was brought to a stop by someone stepping into her path.

'May I help you with those?' said a voice she knew instantly. She looked up to see Sybil, who was smiling at her as though Sallyanne was the best thing she'd ever laid eyes on.

'Sybil!' she gasped, grateful that Sybil took hold of the plates before she dropped them. Sallyanne immediately knew she was going to cry – all the sadness she had felt for Sybil and Kate, and for Ben, even though she didn't really know him, was pushing its way up through her. But it was his father who had died, and Sallyanne was sorry for that.

As Sybil embraced her, Sallyanne couldn't help a little sob escaping, especially when she saw Kate walking towards them.

'I'm so sorry,' she said into Sybil's ear. 'I'm so sorry about Joe.'

Sybil stepped back as Kate kissed Sallyanne's cheek, her eyes also filling with tears.

'It's so good to see you,' Kate said. 'We've missed you.'

Sallyanne sniffled, aware that her cheeks would be turning blotchy like they always did when she cried.

'We have indeed,' said Sybil, who was as upright and stoic as ever, which Sallyanne found comforting. 'Phone calls just aren't the same.'

Sybil had called her once a week since Mick left, even in the wake of Joe's death, to check on her and see how she was managing on her own. Sallyanne had felt bad that she hadn't been able to get to Fairvale, even if it was the wet season that had kept her away, just as it had kept Sybil and Kate from coming to town.

The chairwoman of the Katherine CWA called the meeting to order and Sallyanne glanced quickly at her friends.

'Do you have time to come over after this?' she said softly. 'I would love to catch up properly.'

'I was counting on it,' Sybil said, and Sallyanne wanted to cry all over again.

After the meeting the two cars travelled in convoy the short distance from the CWA hall to Sallyanne's home. Sallyanne could see Sybil and Kate in her rear-vision mirror, Sybil behind the wheel.

As they entered her street, Sallyanne put on the blinker to indicate that her house was near; ordinarily she wouldn't bother because there were so rarely other cars in this street. She pulled into her driveway and went into the house to wait for them to arrive.

It had been so long since she'd had visitors that she hesitated inside the kitchen. Should she put the kettle on now? Or wait until they had chatted a bit? What did Sybil do when they all went to Fairvale? Sallyanne was sure Sybil waited a while before making tea. Although she was usually too caught up in the conversation to really notice.

'Hello?' Sybil called at the screen door and Sallyanne pulled it open.

'Come in!' she said, feeling a bit breathless with the excitement of having actual guests. 'Please – sit down.' She gestured to the couch in the sitting room. 'I'll, um . . .' She was still dithering about the timing of the tea.

'We don't need anything,' said Sybil. Of course Sybil would know what she was worrying about.

'Not even water?' Sallyanne said.

'We're fine, honestly,' Kate said.

'So,' Sybil said, 'a lot has happened to all of us since we last saw each other.' She smiled tightly at Kate. 'I think we've all been living through difficult circumstances. Although I must say, Sallyanne, you look happier than when I last saw you.'

Sallyanne wished she could say the same about Sybil, who seemed to have lines across her forehead and around her mouth where there hadn't been any before. Her eyes were still bright, although Kate's looked smaller, almost as if she was keeping them half closed the whole time. They looked tired, that was it.

'The house is quite different now,' Sallyanne said. 'In a good way. I didn't realise the kids were walking on eggshells around Mick too. Now . . .' She couldn't help smiling as she thought of her rambunctious boys, not having to worry about upsetting their dad when he had a hangover. 'No more eggshells.'

'I'm so glad,' said Sybil.

'And how are you?' Sallyanne looked from Sybil to Kate and back again. 'How are you going . . . out there?'

She wanted to say 'since Joe died' but it sounded so blunt and she didn't want to upset them.

The corners of Sybil's mouth turned down momentarily and she shrugged. Sallyanne saw the look she exchanged with Kate – saw the bond that was so clearly between them now.

'It's . . . been hard,' Kate said, flattening the 'a'. She was sounding more like an Australian each time Sallyanne saw her. 'With Ben away.' She glanced at Sybil. 'But we're managing. Sybil knows such a lot.'

'Kate has been magnificent,' Sybil said, and the smile she gave her daughter-in-law told Sallyanne just how wonderful Kate had been. 'She's doing the work of at least two people.'

'It must be strange, though,' Sallyanne said, looking only at Sybil.

'Suffice to say that things are very different,' Sybil said wearily. 'We'll be adjusting for a while. But there's nothing else we can do. Fairvale has never stayed the same in all the

time I've been there. It expands. It contracts. People live.'
A flash of pain crossed her face. 'People die.'

Then Sybil's eyes met Sallyanne's and Sallyanne saw
something shift in them.

'What are you doing about money?' Sybil said. 'That was
a rapid change of subject, wasn't it? And I know we're not
meant to talk about money.' She waved her hand dismissively.
'But you're here on your own, you have three children ...
Mick could hold onto his money out there and you'd never
tell anyone. So I'm asking.'

Sallyanne wasn't sure how much to say, except she felt
Sybil would settle for nothing less than the truth.

'Dad's helping out, but things are ... tight,' she admitted.

'I bet they are,' Sybil said. She glanced at Kate, who nodded
once.

'We have an idea,' Sybil went on. 'There are a couple of
children living on Fairvale who will be ready to start school
next year. We need to organise distance education for them.
School of the Air. And there's some little ones who will need
it in due course too.

'I was planning to run the school,' Sybil continued. 'But
now ... I have to do what Joe used to do. Ben and I are
running Fairvale. With Kate's help, of course.' She nodded at
her daughter-in-law. 'So we need someone to run the school.
We can provide a cottage, and of course all the meals would
be taken care of. Although we might ...'

She glanced at Kate.

'We might need your help there too from time to time, if
you don't mind. But there are horses for the children to ride.
Built-in babysitting, because there's always a mob of people
around to watch children. School starts in February, and I
know that's nearly a year away but it would be ideal if you

could come out before the next wet season begins, just to make sure everything's ready. Actually, you could move out whenever you want to.' Sybil's face was full of hope.

'Me?' Sallyanne said, still confused. She had no experience teaching, let alone organising distance education. Sybil couldn't be talking about *her* doing this.

'You.' Sybil grinned.

'I . . . I can't teach.'

'Of course you can,' Sybil said. 'You teach your children things every day, don't you?'

Sallyanne frowned, her brain starting to race. Was that true? Was she already teaching? But that was different to teaching someone else's children. And what would it mean, to live on Fairvale? Would Mick object? *Could* he object, given that he had moved to a station anyway?

'Tim and Billy would be your students at the school too,' Sybil said, interrupting her thoughts. 'And Gretel, in time. In fact, she'll be ready to start then as well, I imagine.'

Sallyanne felt her mouth drop open and she looked over to Kate, who was smiling encouragingly.

'We'd love to have you living with us,' Kate said.

'You would?'

'Of course.' Kate was still smiling. 'I've never met anyone like you, Sallyanne. You cope with such a lot and you are always smiling. And you're so *interested* in things. You know more about books and films and music than anyone I know. Well, maybe not books – Sybil knows a lot about those.'

Her laugh was light.

'I think we could all have a lot of fun,' Kate added.

'And we wouldn't all be in one another's pockets,' Sybil picked up. 'Your cottage would not be right next to the main house. You'd have privacy.'

They looked at her expectantly but Sallyanne didn't feel ready to give an answer. She would have to tell Mick, and maybe he wouldn't let her leave Katherine – maybe he'd come back just to spite her. To keep her here.

'You can take some time to think about it, obviously,' Sybil said. 'It would be a big change.'

Sallyanne looked at Sybil, then Kate, then Sybil again. She felt warmth take over her body.

'You really want me to live on Fairvale?' she said, still wondering if she'd heard them correctly.

'You know I'm not given to jokes, Sallyanne,' Sybil said with a serious expression.

Sallyanne blinked. 'Oh,' she said, then she smiled as she saw Sybil's face relax.

'I realise you'll need to talk to your father,' Sybil went on.

'And there's your house to think of,' Kate said, nodding. 'We know that Fairvale won't be as appealing as town.'

Sallyanne thought of all that space for her children, that fresh air, the trees and the birds, and the kind people she had seen and met each time she'd been to that grand cattle station.

'I think it might be more appealing,' she said quietly, and she saw Kate smile tentatively. 'But I will need to work some things out. I'll have to talk to Mick.'

Sybil nodded and Sallyanne couldn't read her expression.

'We should probably head back,' Sybil said, getting to her feet.

'I have to cook dinner,' Kate said. 'Ruby decided to retire so the kitchen is all mine.' She smiled apologetically as she also stood and walked towards Sallyanne, throwing her arms around her. 'It really is lovely to see you,' Kate murmured.

Next Sybil gave her a less effusive but no less warm embrace.

'I don't want you to feel pressured,' she said as she pulled her car keys out of her handbag. 'The invitation is there *if you want it.* And if not, we shall look forward to seeing you soon, either at the CWA or to talk about books.'

Sallyanne nodded quickly. 'I'll see you soon,' she said.

As they drove off, Sybil honking the horn once, Sallyanne felt a swarm of emotions: sadness that she wouldn't see them again for a while, excitement at the prospect Sybil had offered her, dread about telling Mick about it, and doubt that she was able to teach children anything. There was no way for her to tell, right now, which of those was going to emerge on top.

CHAPTER THIRTY-EIGHT

The ingredients for the stew were on the kitchen bench: a pile of potatoes, one large pumpkin, some jealously guarded onions, salt, pepper – and a big side of beef. It was the standard Fairvale dish and when Ruby had taught it to Kate she had said the trick to making it delicious was all in the timing.

'Put that pumpkin in too early – mush!' she had declared, her face screwing up as she laughed. 'Put him in once those potatoes are starting to sweat.'

Kate had learnt that Ruby's definition of a sweating potato meant one that had been boiling for five minutes.

She'd learnt how to make the stew by repetition but she wished she'd made more notes before Ruby had decided not to continue working in the kitchen.

'It's my feet, Katie girl,' she'd explained with a loud sigh accompanied by a roll of her eyes. 'I'm wearing out. Can't stand all day no more. My feet hurt.' Another roll. 'Even my back! Bad back!' She had cackled and half bent over, pretending to hobble around.

There had been no arguing with that: if the cook couldn't stand to work then she couldn't be a cook. Not that Ruby had been too upset, especially since Sybil had told her that her cottage was hers for life and they would take her to Ghost River to see Rose whenever she wanted to.

'All yours now, love,' Ruby had said on her last day and Kate had thought – *presumed* might be the better word – that she'd remember everything she'd been taught. There were so many little things, though, that Ruby would do and Kate couldn't remember them all, nor did she want to ask. Sybil had told her that she should come up with her own recipes. She didn't feel experienced enough for that.

There hadn't been any complaints at meal times, and her cakes were particularly popular, yet she still felt like the apprentice. It was good motivation, though: every day she got out of bed wanting to do better. It had helped her through the last few months since Joe had died. It was good to have a purpose; even better to have one that took up most of the day.

'I'm here,' Sybil said, rushing in the door, sounding breathless.

Kate felt immediately relieved to see her. The work Kate had been sharing with Ruby was almost overwhelming now she was on her own. She wasn't as fast as Ruby, nor as skilled; everything seemed to take twice as long. So Sybil was helping her when she could and when the girls in the camp could not. Peeling, chopping, cutting. They'd developed their own rhythm.

'Thank you for coming,' Kate said.

'Don't you dare thank me.' Sybil tied an apron over her thick cotton work pants and tucked her shirt more firmly in. 'We'd starve without you. I feel bad that you're managing this and the office and the housework too.'

'We're managing the housework together,' Kate said, trying to sound upbeat, although she was exhausted. She and Sybil didn't want anyone else on Fairvale to feel as though things were being missed – including their meals – but it was on the pair of them to make it work seamlessly. They were both down to their last reserves of energy, hoping that Ben could make it back soon. He'd had to keep delaying his return, his friend proving less friendly and more intransigent than anyone could have predicted – when the wet had ended early Ben had told him that he had to leave and he'd been informed that he was expected to work through to the middle of the year. Their negotiations had taken weeks and Kate still wasn't sure if they were over.

Kate rolled up the sleeves of her old house dress so that they were over her shoulders. As soon as that oven went on she'd turn into a pile of damp, and the more skin she could expose to the air, the better. The dress had seen far better days – it had been a bright yellow and was now faded to what could only be described as pale lemon – but it was good for kitchen work because it kept her cool and she could wash it easily.

'Now,' Kate said, pushing some potatoes, a small knife and a cutting board towards Sybil, 'if you could peel those, I'll start on the pumpkin.'

'The pumpkin's the hard job,' Sybil said. 'How about I do it? You're due an easy task.'

Kate smiled gratefully. She was perennially worried that she'd take off a finger each time she hacked away at pumpkin skin.

The door opened behind them and Kate had a second of wondering who on earth would come to the kitchen – she rarely had visitors.

'Ladies,' said a man's voice and she thought her heart would actually stop.

She spun around to see her husband standing in the doorway: thinner and less tanned than when he'd left, but his eyes were still big and bright and shining, and his grin was still cheeky.

'B-Ben,' she gasped.

'Miss me?' he said. She heard a knife drop beside her.

She flew towards him.

'Darling,' he said to Kate, holding out one arm to her, kissing her full and hard on the lips, keeping her with him as he held out his other arm to Sybil.

'Mum,' he murmured, kissing Sybil's forehead, pulling her close.

'Don't cry, Mum,' Ben said in a cheeky tone. 'I'm here now. It's the best day of your life, right?'

Sybil was shaking, and Kate realised it was from laughter.

'It took you long enough to get here,' Sybil said, kissing her son's cheek and drawing back.

'Tell me about it.' He winked, then turned completely towards Kate.

She wanted to pinch his cheeks to see if it was really him. He didn't smell like him: his clothes had been washed with a different detergent; he'd been living with different trees and dirt, sleeping in different swags. She missed the smell she'd always associated with him – the smell, she realised, of all of Fairvale combined. But she was confident it would come back.

'You look beautiful,' he said, taking her in both of his arms, his expression serious for once in his life. 'I've missed that amazing smile.'

She hugged him so hard she thought he'd complain. But he didn't. He kissed the top of her ear and stroked her cheek with his finger, and as he held her, and she held him, she felt the memory of his body return to her skin.

'You're back,' she said, and he laughed.

'You bet I am,' he said.

He kept one arm around her as he turned to look at Sybil.

'I'm sorry, Mum,' he said.

Sybil looked surprised. 'What for?'

The corners of his mouth turned down. 'For not being here.'

Kate had never seen Ben look sad before. Cross, yes; sometimes frustrated. But never sad – never what was on his face now.

'We're all sorry he's gone, darling,' Sybil said. 'But you don't have to be sorry about that.'

Ben stared at his mother. 'Thank you,' he murmured, 'for keeping on top of things here.'

Sybil nodded towards Kate. 'You should thank your wife too. She's been at least half of the equation and sometimes more.'

'And Stan,' Kate said, resting her head into the side of Ben's neck. 'We couldn't have coped without Stan.'

'I thanked him already,' Ben said, winking. 'Gave him a new Akubra.'

Kate pinched Ben's side and he yelped. 'Then you'd better have diamonds for me.'

'I'm the diamond, baby,' he said.

'Wait,' Kate said, 'when did you see Stan?'

'Ah, so you didn't catch him sneaking the truck away this morning,' Ben said, looking pleased. 'He told me he thought he'd got away with it.'

'He's meant to be on a muster,' Sybil said, slightly indignantly.

'He's my head stockman,' Ben said. 'He has to do what I say. And I told him to come to the airport to get me.'

'I had no idea he was so stealthy,' Kate said.

'I did,' said Sybil. 'Watch him tracking snakes and you'll find out.'

She sighed – a noise of release and relief.

'I think I'll leave you two alone,' Sybil said, patting her son's cheek. 'But I can't give you too long, Ben – Kate and I have to get the stew on for dinner.'

She smiled at Kate and quickly made her exit.

'Where's Ruby?' Ben said, looking around the kitchen.

'Not here,' Kate said, almost giggling. She felt light-headed with the surprise of having him home. 'She retired.'

Ben took hold of her arms, concern on his face.

'So you've been doing everything here?' he said and Kate nodded.

'Your mum's been helping me,' she said. 'We just get up each day and keep going until we fall over.'

He hugged her fiercely, kissing the top of her head.

'I'm sorry I haven't been here,' he said. 'That's more work than either of you should have to do.'

Kate felt her body sagging against his and she had the strangest sensation of wanting to fall asleep right here, standing up. Maybe because she knew he'd catch her if she fell.

'I love you,' he said, looking into her eyes. 'I can't tell you how much I missed you. It was . . .' He drew a ragged breath. 'It was bloody hard being without you.'

He stroked her cheek with his thumb, as he so often did. But it was harder to look at him than it was before: there were flashes of Joe in him, reminders of what they'd all lost.

It was nothing, though, compared with what he must be feeling: to come home knowing he would never see his father here again.

'Kiss me,' she whispered, wanting them both to have the best salve she knew.

'I already did,' he said, laughter on his lips. 'When I arrived, remember?'

She rolled her eyes.

'How about *you* kiss *me*,' he said.

She smiled up at him and slid one hand around his waist as the other moved up underneath his shirt. He always wore his shirts loose.

Her hand remembered his skin, the light covering of hair on his torso, the way he liked to be tickled just a little. She brought her lips to his and let herself luxuriate in them.

Then he was taking her head in his hands and bending her backwards, his mouth opening hers, his body pressed against hers. She had missed him, more than she'd let herself realise. She had been holding herself together all these months, just waiting for him, and now he was here, and she released herself to him.

Making dinner could wait for a little bit longer.

CHAPTER THIRTY-NINE

The newspaper was faded and more than a little crumpled, but it contained the first news from the outside world that Sybil had seen in about three weeks. The vet had brought it with him that morning before heading off to inspect the horses and Sybil had waited until she'd completed a few tasks before sitting down to read it.

'What's the news, Mum?' Ben said as he pushed open the kitchen flyscreen door, hanging his hat on the hook that Joe had used instead of dropping it on the furniture as he used to do.

'Pierre Trudeau was re-elected as prime minister of Canada,' she said, looking up from the article she was reading. 'And . . .' She turned back to the first page and held it up to show him. 'The USA aren't going to the Moscow Olympics but we are.'

'Right.' He took the paper and scanned the piece. 'Fraser's not happy.'

'Obviously the Australian Olympic Committee doesn't care what prime ministers think.'

'And prime ministers don't care about the Territory, so . . .' Ben shrugged. 'What goes around comes around.'

Sybil laughed. Ben was becoming a more passionate Territorian with each passing day, to the point that she was starting to tease him about running for parliament.

'There's mail here,' Ben said, picking up a stack of envelopes from the kitchen bench.

'Yes, the vet brought that too. I haven't gone through it yet.'

Ben frowned as he quickly checked each envelope. 'There's one from Geoffrey.'

He caught his mother's eye. After Joe's death Sybil had told Ben that Geoffrey had been trying to find Lachie.

'Don't you want to read it now?' Ben said, holding it out to her, not really giving her a choice.

Her heart started beating faster as she took the envelope and opened it carefully. She quickly read the first paragraph and stopped, her eyes lifting to Ben's.

'He doesn't have any news about Lachie,' she said. 'But . . .' She read the next paragraph and felt something like relief mixed with sadness overtake her. 'He's found Amelia,' Sybil added, her hands trembling. 'And her son. Lachie's son.'

She stared at Ben – her lovely boy who wanted children of his own so badly. It didn't seem fair that Lachie could have a child he didn't even want and Ben did not. Not that, in her experience, life had ever been fair.

'Are you sure it's his, Mum?' Ben said quietly.

She looked down at the letter and read further. 'Geoffrey's seen a photograph. He says that—' She inhaled sharply. '"If you saw him, Syb, I think you'd agree that he is the spit of Joe. Quite uncanny. And he has Ben's curls. I really don't doubt that the boy is Lachlan's."'

Putting the letter down, she pinched the end of her nose, not wanting to cry.

She quickly read the rest of the letter as Ben came and put his hand on her shoulder.

'They're in the Riverina,' she said. 'A town called Coolamon. Amelia has a cousin there, he says.'

'How did he find all this out?'

'I don't ask,' Sybil said. 'But I need to go. I need to find them.'

'Mum . . .' Ben's voice was full of warning.

'It's not about Lachlan anymore,' she said, pushing back from the table and standing up.

'Then who is it about?'

'This child,' she said, knowing she sounded shrill and defensive.

'Mum, what if Amelia doesn't want to be found?' Ben put his hands on his hips, the way he always did when he was trying to make a point.

'Then she can tell me that herself. But I have to at least try to see her – don't I? Isn't that the right thing to do?'

He glared at her – and Ben had never once glared at her in his whole life.

'If Dad was still alive,' he said slowly, 'would you be so keen to run off after this kid?'

It was a valid question – and one to which she didn't have an answer. Hypotheses meant nothing to her in a world that had left her without a son and a husband in short order. She wanted sureties – and Lachie's son was real.

'I'm going to Sydney,' Sybil said, her voice as resolute as she could make it. 'Then I'm going to take Geoffrey with me and find them. I'm not asking for your approval, Ben – only your understanding.'

He blinked and dropped his hands. 'I'm just worried, Mum,' he murmured.

She frowned. 'About what?'

'That this will be a disaster. That you'll get there and you won't be able to see this kid and then . . .' He looked away, scratching his head.

'I can take care of myself,' she said. 'And I need you to take care of Fairvale.'

'I can do that,' he said.

'I know you can. Now, I have to make some arrangements.'

He nodded. 'When will you leave?'

'As soon as I can. And I'll be back sooner. All right?'

'Just get back,' he murmured, and she was touched to see worry so clearly etched on his features.

'Of course I will,' she said, although she didn't yet know how far this new road would take her.

CHAPTER FORTY

Everything beneath the aeroplane was orangey-red and green – what looked like kilometres of flat country, although Della knew that there were always little secrets in this land. Nothing was ever really flat, or really solid, for that matter.

Further out was the opal blue of the Timor Sea, land and water creating a palette that was unique to this place. When she'd flown out of Darwin, on the first leg of the long journey back to the United States, she had hoped – dreamt – that she would return but she knew nothing was certain. Now, it was.

She had considered Sybil's letter for a few days – going for a ride late each day, mulling over her offer even though she'd wanted to accept straightaway. She'd needed the time because she was uncertain how to broach the subject with her parents. Della had suspected that she wanted a miraculous solution to appear: that the path would be clear for her to leave Texas once more. Rationally, though, she just wanted to find the sentence she'd need to start the conversation. She had kept stalling, feeling more like a coward than she was comfortable with, until her father had declared that he was well enough to make it to San Antonio for some medical tests, as his local doctor had suggested. Della knew she couldn't say

292

anything while they waited to find out the results – if he was really sick, if he was going to die, she would not take off to the other side of the world.

A couple of weeks after that she came back to the house for lunch and found her parents had been waiting for her.

'We have good news, honey,' her mother had said, her smile radiant. 'Your daddy's not as sick as the doctor thought.'

Her father had nodded then winked at her. 'It's a good thing we went to San Antonio. Turns out that doctor here in town doesn't know as much as he says he does.'

'So . . . what is it?' she'd said, hardly able to believe that what had seemed so serious could be something else so easily.

'Got to have my gall bladder out,' her father had said. 'Then I should be just fine. I'll be back working with y'all in no time.'

At that point Della had known she could smile and say nothing about Sybil's letter, allowing her parents to think she was sticking around. Then . . . what? She would let more weeks go by, let them and her brothers get more used to having her around, relying on her to do things, before announcing she was leaving? There was never going to be a good time to tell them, and now seemed as appropriate an occasion as any.

'That's great news, Daddy,' she'd said. 'I'm so happy for you.' She'd swallowed. Despite her conviction, the words didn't come out as smoothly as she'd hoped.

'What is it?' her father had said.

'What do you mean?'

'I can see it on your face, honey: you're worried about something.'

So she'd told them, and felt guilty for causing her mother's happiness to disappear. But Della's own happiness was just as important – and for that she had to return to the place and the people she loved. To Stan, even if her parents didn't know about him.

Her father had understood, more than her mother.

'That's fine, Della,' he'd said. 'I know we can't offer you much here. You work so damn hard and in return I can't promise this place to you. I wish I could.'

In truth he could, if he wanted to. But family tradition and social pressure meant he'd leave it to Ted, and Ted knew it, which was why he also knew he didn't have to work to earn it. Della had worked that ranch because she'd felt it was her duty and she'd returned for the same reason. She was old enough now, though, to put her duties to herself first.

The next day she had organised her plane ticket and two weeks later she'd kissed her parents goodbye.

She retraced her steps from her first arrival in Australia, taking a flight to Sydney – because there was no other option – before travelling on to Darwin. She stayed a couple of days in Sydney, in a small hotel in the city, and walked around Circular Quay to the Royal Botanic Gardens, past the Opera House. She looked across the harbour to Kirribilli, with its densely packed apartment buildings, and knew she could never live in a place like that. She couldn't feel free when her neighbours could see everything she was doing. She'd grown up with space and she would always need it.

The harbour was a different matter: it sparkled with sunlight, and Della could tell that it would be easy to fall in love with this city if the harbour looked like this every day. It had grandeur and beauty. But it would never be as lovely as the red-dust palace that awaited her in the north, as the black-soil plains that beckoned her to travel over them.

When she'd first arrived at Ghost River she had been almost overwhelmed by the different plants, the strange animals.

There were birds that she could never have imagined: black cockatoos with red tails that would fly back to the trees by the river at sunset, screeching so loudly that she often couldn't hear herself think; birds called black kites that had distinctive forked tails. One of them had spooked a stockman when he saw it flying near the big house.

'Fire coming,' he had whispered, his eyes wide.

Della had sniffed the air and smelled nothing sinister. 'What do you mean?'

He'd pointed towards the bird. 'That fella, he comes with the fire.'

The stockman had taken off at speed towards where the horses were tethered in the yard, and a minute later all she saw was hooves receding along the riverbank. That afternoon Felicity had told her that a lightning strike had caused a few acres to burn and they'd lost several head of cattle. That stockman had arrived in time to rescue the others.

That day she'd had her first inkling that the trees and the birds, and other things besides, told stories to people if they just paid attention. She'd been paying attention ever since.

Della wanted those stories again, and down below this aeroplane another story was waiting to unfold: her own. Hers and Stan's. She knew he would be waiting for her – Sybil had written to tell her so.

As the plane landed she felt that same nervousness she had whenever she was about to see him. Stronger, this time – it felt like it had taken over her whole body.

Walking down the steps to the tarmac, she almost didn't dare look towards the terminal in case he wasn't there, after all. Loving him had made her vulnerable to fear. When she finally looked up, though, she could see him. His smile was bigger than ever. His hands were on his hips, his head leaning to one side. It looked like he was laughing, and she wanted to laugh too. Being here was so improbable, yet it felt like the most natural thing in the world.

'Della girl,' he said softly as she reached him, and she knew he was resisting putting his arms around her, as she was around him. They couldn't be on display here – it wasn't something they could risk.

'Hello,' she said, smiling at him, hoping he could see everything that was in her heart.

He picked up her suitcase and walked her to the truck. They looked at each other but didn't speak. She could wait to talk to him. There were miles between here and Fairvale. There were years between now and the end of their lives.

Once they were in the truck, though, she didn't want to resist anymore.

'I'm so happy to see you,' she said.

Stan smiled, that big grin she loved so much. 'You're home,' he said, sliding one arm around her.

She kissed him, but not for long. She would kiss him again soon; now she wanted to put her head against his chest and listen to him breathing, the way she used to do, they way she hoped she would always do, before he started the engine and their next adventure began.

CHAPTER FORTY-ONE

It had been so many years since Sybil had been home to Sydney that she hadn't seen the by-now famous Sydney Opera House in its completed form, so she made sure to look at it as Geoffrey's car drove along the Cahill Expressway and onto the Sydney Harbour Bridge. The last time she'd visited, when Ben had finished school in 1972, the project had become controversial and there were doubts that it would ever be completed.

The years of the boys' schooling – those frantic years of working hard at Fairvale, missing the boys dreadfully, running back and forth to Darwin to get them on and off planes, rarely able to visit them in Sydney due to the demands of the station, liaising with her parents as they kept an eye on things, trying to keep track of the boys' academic progress and minor sports injuries – raced through Sybil's brain as Geoffrey took her across the bridge, carrying her to where they had both grown up, in Gordon Street, Mosman.

'Are we driving down tomorrow?' she said to him as they swept past the distinctive Greenway building in Kirribilli. Everything was so close here: buildings and people all jammed together. She was so unused to it now; Sydney seemed so noisy and bright compared with the silence and shifting light of the Northern Territory.

'Day after,' Geoffrey said, his old sports car complaining as they rattled up towards Military Road. 'I have a case wrapping up tomorrow – I hope you don't mind a delay.'

'That's fine,' Sybil said, trying to contain her irritation. She wanted to go *now*. Who knew if Amelia and her little boy were still in Coolamon? What if they left today and went somewhere else? She shouldn't be ungrateful, though – Geoffrey had done so much for her already.

'Roger's joining us for dinner – I hope you won't mind that either,' Geoffrey said, keeping his eyes on the road.

'Of course I don't mind. It will be lovely to see him. It's been – how long since you visited us? Four years?'

Geoffrey smiled tightly, the way he always did. She had never seen her brother engage in a full-throated chuckle. 'Yes, four years.'

Roger was Geoffrey's 'friend', as their parents had insisted on calling him. Sybil had always known that Roger was far more significant than that but if it had helped her parents to use a neutral term, she hadn't felt it right to correct them. As Geoffrey had said to her once, it was to their great credit that they'd stopped asking him when he was going to get married not long after he'd met Roger, and he had never expected more. Their mother used to say that Lachie and Ben were more than enough grandchildren for her and she didn't care if she didn't have others; that, too, had been her way of accepting the direction Geoffrey's life had taken.

'I don't want you to get your hopes up,' Geoffrey said. 'It's likely that even if Amelia agrees to see you, she won't want anything further to do with you. She's very angry at Lachlan.'

'I don't blame her,' Sybil said, gazing out the window as the car stop-started its way along one of Sydney's busiest roads, past some buildings that were familiar and others that were not. 'I am too.'

'It's about time,' Geoffrey muttered.

'Hm?' Sybil said, turning to look at him. It could be her father sitting at the wheel, they were so alike: thick, wavy, grey hair worn slightly long; trim sideburns; a jaw that verged on being lantern-like; the Roman nose that she had luckily avoided inheriting.

'I think it's fair to say,' Geoffrey said as a sign reading 'Taronga Zoo' appeared ahead of them, 'that Lachlan has given you a few reasons to be angry and you've never taken them.'

Geoffrey had never commented on her parenting before now. Sybil didn't know whether to be shocked or annoyed.

'Remember how he used to just not turn up to Gordon Street when Mum and Dad were meant to have him for the weekend, and Ben would have to make his own way there?' Geoffrey said, shaking his head.

'Of course I do,' Sybil snapped. There had been frantic phone calls trying to locate Lachie and she had felt so helpless being so far away. Lachie had always turned up at some friend's beach house or country weekender, blithely uncaring about how many people were worried about him.

'He never tried at school,' Geoffrey went on. 'He had a good brain but he seemed determined not to use it.'

'What's your point?' Sybil said, still cross.

Geoffrey turned left onto Middle Head Road. Not long now until they'd be home.

'You were always understanding, Sybil. You never punished him.'

'So this is my fault, is it?'

'Not at all,' Geoffrey said. 'What I'm trying to say – clumsily, perhaps – is that you gave that boy everything, including that understanding, and you've never once been angered by the fact that he didn't seem to care.'

He pulled the car to a stop outside the pretty semi in which they had grown up. They'd had a simple, fun life here; a carefree life. She missed it sometimes, in the way only a perfectly preserved childhood memory can be missed.

'I'm just glad you're human,' he said, turning to her with that tight smile. 'And all this time I thought you were a saint.'

She could hardly believe that was what he'd really wanted to say, but she wasn't going to push it. They had a long drive southwest in two days' time and they needed to get along.

As she walked through the front door that was so familiar to her, Sybil felt exhaustion seeping into her bones. She'd been travelling for hours to make a journey that had taken years – ever since Lachie had left them. Now she understood the real reason Geoffrey didn't want to leave tomorrow: he knew she would need time to rest and ready herself for whatever lay ahead.

Up close the Opera House was more impressive than it had seemed, even set against the drama of the harbour. The gleaming off-white tiles reflected sun and water; the building's graceful arcs resembled the sails of boats going by. It was beautiful and majestic – a modern cathedral. And it made her miss Fairvale, which was more impressive than anything a city could conjure.

With her day off Sybil had decided to take a ferry into the city. She had already been to David Jones on Elizabeth Street and found absolutely nothing that was appropriate for the life she lived now, although she'd enjoyed looking at all the beautiful, useless things.

She walked slowly along the concourse that wrapped around the Opera House and watched as seagulls waited patiently for humans to discard food. She hadn't seen seagulls since her last trip to Sydney; certainly, she never saw them in the Territory. Their flapping and squawking seemed a little pathetic next to the often aggressive birds of the north.

The path past the Opera House took her into the Botanic Gardens. Sybil saw the spot where she and Joe had taken the boys for a picnic, that first year of Ben's high schooling. It had been their last day together; he was due to go into the boarding house that afternoon. Lachie had declared he was bored and taken off into the gardens. They'd lost him for a bit but he'd come back that time. Ben had stayed with them, bright-eyed, funny. Mindful, she could tell, of how his parents were feeling.

A giant Manly ferry cut its way past Farm Cove, en route to Circular Quay. There were so many ferries and boats criss-crossing the harbour – even the water was busy here.

Sybil realised she should get back: her own ferry would be leaving soon to take her to the wharf at Mosman Bay, where she had left Geoffrey's car.

She increased her pace as she neared the quay, checking her watch: five minutes to go. She had to buy a ticket and headed for a window at wharf four.

While she felt around in her handbag for her purse, a man stepped so close to her that she reared back.

'Excuse me,' she said but he carried on, walking quickly, his dark hair curling over the back of his neck, his broad shoulders encased in a suit jacket, his gait so familiar that for a second she thought it was Joe's ghost that had almost stepped on her.

Then she knew. With ice-cold conviction and a searing surge of pain, she knew.

'*Lachlan!*' she cried.

She saw him slow, then stop. She was sure she wasn't breathing. She was sure that time had dropped into a fissure in the ground and she wasn't really here, in this moment. It couldn't be him. After all this time, how could it be?

As the man turned, she saw the eyes and nose and chin and brow that were so familiar and that she loved so much. There were people passing between them but she saw only him.

Those eyes stared into hers. She saw nothing in them: no recognition, no fear, no dislike or affection. But it was him. This man, looking at her as if he didn't recognise her, was her son.

'Lachie?' she called as she dared to take a step towards him, as if he was a dog she didn't want to anger. Or a snake in her path that she didn't want to have striking her.

Lachie's eyes narrowed. His mouth set into a line. Sybil felt time moving so quickly that she was sure she was about to run out of it. And there was something she had to tell him.

'Lachlan, your father is dead,' she said. A stranger moved in front of her so she did not see what was on his face before he turned it away.

'Lachie – please.' She knew she sounded like she was begging; she *was* begging.

He looked at her and she saw no emotion in his eyes, on his face, anywhere. 'He's been dead to me for a while,' he said flatly and in the space between them were the words he had left unsaid: *And so have you.*

But she couldn't accept that. He was still her son.

She reached a hand towards him, wanting to touch him one more time, to feel the son she had raised with love even if he couldn't return it.

Someone jostled her and pushed her back, away from Lachie. For a moment she thought he had vanished. Then she saw him – heading for the adjacent train station, his long legs carrying him away from her.

She started to run after him, keeping sight of his dark hair, his height making him visible. Her breath was coming fast now, and her brain seemed to be empty. She had no thoughts, only instinct driving her on.

As she reached the ticket gates she looked around frantically. She needed to buy a ticket – she had to get through. Did he have a ticket? Was he already in there?

She looked wildly between the staircases that led steeply up to opposite platforms. She heard a train arriving. She still couldn't see where the tickets were being sold.

She checked the staircases again but she couldn't see him.

And as her breathing grew faster still, her eyes felt like they were turning themselves inside out, her armpits were damp even as her mouth felt dry, and her thoughts came back to life to tell her one thing: he was gone. That, and not only that: he wanted to be gone.

She bent over, her hands to her sides, feeling as though she was getting a stitch. Her breathing was ragged and high in her chest. She wondered if she might faint. She might want to faint. Then she could wake anew and pretend the whole episode had never happened.

'Are you all right, love?'

Sybil felt a hand on her arm and straightened to see the kind, concerned face of a weathered old man.

She gulped a breath and nodded. 'I am,' she said. 'Thank you.' She faked a smile. 'I ran too fast for a train and I missed it anyway.'

He looked as if he didn't believe her but patted her arm. 'All right, then,' he said. 'I hope you make the next train.'

'Thank you,' she said, trying to smile. 'I appreciate your concern.'

He nodded and raised a hand in farewell. As he walked away she looked up at the platforms overhead as if there was some way they could bring Lachie back to her. But even if she'd kept track of him, even if she'd bought a ticket in time, even if she'd managed to follow him onto a train, he would still have evaded her, just as he had been doing for years. Just as he had that day in the Botanic Gardens. And he wasn't coming back this time. She knew it now. He was never coming back.

The quay, the city, the world grew still. She stood in front of the ticket gates with people walking past her, people hurrying on to whatever they were doing next, and she felt only the certainty of this moment, this breath, this thought: she had to let him go.

Sybil turned away from the train station. Her wharf was just there, next to it. She had been so close to getting on the ferry and not seeing Lachie at all. A few seconds earlier or later and she wouldn't have seen him. She wouldn't have watched him almost run away from her.

The past year had brought more sadness than Sybil had ever wanted to feel. But she had survived it. She felt it still, yet each day was easier to bear than the last. She had proved that she could live without Joe, even if she didn't want to. She would live without Lachie, too. She would have to.

She had come to know exactly how strong she was, and how loved. For all the love that had left her life, there was so much left in it. She could live the rest of her life with that knowledge. And she was now more determined than ever that she was going to find the son Lachie had left behind, just as he had left her.

CHAPTER FORTY-TWO

In half an hour's time Kate and Della would converge on the house, back from their ride, and Sallyanne was due to turn up too. So there wasn't much time for Sybil to have Rita to herself, because her friend would be returning to Alice Springs later today, Darryl only able to give her a few hours while he did whatever it was he did in Darwin.

Rita was helping her organise the crockery for morning tea, because she was so far behind, and Rita had noticed. Usually Sybil would set out everything early in the day, if not the night before, but when Rita had arrived nothing had been done and Sybil had no good reason why apart from the fact that her mind was still in Sydney.

'Syb, you're daydreaming again,' Rita said sharply. Sybil blinked and realised she was standing at the window, holding a tea towel.

'Have I been daydreaming a lot?' she said vaguely.

Rita appeared next to her and took the tea towel. 'What's going on?' she said.

Sybil exhaled. 'I . . .' How did she start this? *Where* did she start this?

'Sybil! It's not like you to dither and if you keep doing it I'll get a doctor up here. Or examine you myself.'

Rita looked more annoyed than Sybil had seen her since she'd once ordered her to clean up a row of bedpans, and Sybil couldn't help but laugh.

'All right,' Sybil said. 'Sorry – I'm just trying to work out what to say.'

Rita frowned. 'Well, while you figure it out we can talk about something else if you like. What do you think about that Chamberlain baby?'

The story of Azaria Chamberlain had been preoccupying the Territory since mid-August and Sybil knew it was likely to be discussed today once everyone was gathered. The whole thing had made her feel sad, more than anything, but most people were convinced that Azaria's parents had harmed her, and there was no persuading them differently.

'I think,' Sybil said, 'that the story has probably been even bigger in Alice Springs than it has been here.'

'You're not getting out of it like that – come on, did a dingo take that baby or not?'

'I think it was a dingo, yes,' Sybil said. 'They go for calves – why not a baby? A baby's a lot smaller.'

'It's all a bit weird, though, isn't it?' Rita's brow furrowed. 'Those parents must have—'

'Your tactic's worked, all right?' Sybil said, sighing loudly. 'I'll tell you my news. Such as it is.'

Rita smiled.

Sybil took a deep breath; her lungs felt tight and she felt oddly nervous.

'I saw Lachie.'

She watched as Rita registered the news, her eyes and eyebrows dancing.

'How?' Rita said, sitting on the kitchen table, putting the tea towel aside.

'You know that I asked Geoffrey to find him?'

Rita nodded.

'I went . . . This is going to get complicated,' Sybil said. 'I went to Sydney—'

'Why didn't you tell me? I could have come with you.'

'It all happened quickly. Geoffrey found out that – we believe that Lachie has a son,' Sybil rushed on. 'That he was . . . involved with Amelia, who used to be Felicity's cook.'

'How on earth . . .' Rita stopped and frowned again. 'Go on.'

'Geoffrey sent word that he believed Amelia and the boy were living in the Riverina. Near Wagga. With a cousin.'

She took a breath as Rita stayed silent.

'So I went to Sydney. Geoffrey and I were going to drive down together. I had a day to myself before we left. I went for a walk around the harbour. Circular Quay.'

Sybil felt a pain in her chest, as if her heart was trying not to let something out. But she'd already confronted the truth, so why shouldn't Rita know it?

'I bumped into him,' she continued. 'Quite literally. He almost trod on me. As he walked past I realised who he was and I called out.'

As she looked at Rita she saw trepidation and concern, and she realised that Rita knew how this story was going to end. Perhaps she'd always known.

'Did he see you?' Rita said.

Sybil nodded.

'And he didn't want to,' Rita stated.

It hurt to hear it said aloud.

'Yes,' she said.

'What about the child?'

'We drove down. Six hours.' Sybil remembered how caught

up in her thoughts she had been, wound so tight that she had barely said a word the whole way there.

Rita nodded for her to continue. 'Yes.'

'We got to the house. Amelia's cousin . . .' She stopped, the disappointment still causing her pain, the dismay still fresh. 'She said that Amelia and her son had gone the day before. The cousin had no idea where.'

'Did you believe that?'

'I had no choice but to.' She had come so close to answers, she'd thought, and left with only loss. 'She said that Amelia had been moving around a bit. She thought she might come back but she couldn't say how long it would take.'

'And why hadn't she called you?'

'I don't know.' Sybil could still see the well-meaning young woman who'd seemed genuinely upset that Amelia had gone; she hadn't wanted to make her more upset.

'Oh, Syb.' Rita was looking at her with concern. And Sybil felt that concern herself: concern that she would never see her son again, never meet his son, and her husband was gone, and all the things she couldn't change or solve were right there in that room, swirling around her, crowding in on her.

Sybil put her hands on her hips, feeling her chest tightening, her breath trying to get deeper into her lungs and not succeeding.

In a second Rita's strong hands were on her forearms and Rita was looking into her eyes.

'Breathe slowly,' Rita commanded.

Sybil tried to take a deep breath and coughed.

'*Not* deeply,' Rita said. '*Slowly.*'

Sybil held Rita's gaze.

'This has – this has never happened before,' she gasped out, hating this feeling of her body running away from her.

'I'm not surprised,' Rita said matter-of-factly. 'You've never had such a particular combination of events before.' She patted Sybil's arm. 'Let's cancel the book club.'

'No!' Sybil said vehemently. 'I've been looking forward to it all week.'

'Syb,' Rita said warningly, 'you need to rest.'

Sybil shook her head. 'No, I don't. I need to have something to take my mind off things.'

'Yoohoo!' called a voice from the garden and Sybil saw Sallyanne's head bobbing along past the window.

'Well,' said Rita, arching an eyebrow, 'it's like magic.'

Sybil made a face. 'Don't say anything, please.'

'Of course not.'

'Thank you.' Sybil stood up.

'When is Sallyanne moving here?' Rita asked Sybil as they both went to the door.

'Before the wet begins,' Sybil said. 'I'm fixing up one of the cottages for her and the children.' She coughed and took half a breath. 'Did you have a hand in her making this decision?'

Rita tried on an expression of innocence but Sybil didn't find it convincing.

'Thank you.' Sybil opened the door. 'Sallyanne, welcome.'

Sallyanne bustled in the door and her face lit up as she saw Rita. Sybil could also see that she'd cut her hair.

'Hello!' Sallyanne cried and almost flung herself into Rita's waiting arms. 'I'm so happy to see you.'

'I love your new look, Sal,' Rita said, nodding at Sallyanne's head.

'Do you?' Sallyanne beamed as she touched the underside of the bob that was level with her ears. 'I decided it was time for something new.'

'Mu-um!' called Kate from the front of the house.

Rita turned to Sybil with a questioning look.

'She's calling me "Mum" now,' Sybil said quietly, with a brief smile. 'It just started one day. I guess she misses her own mother.'

'I loved the book,' Sallyanne said, waving her copy of *The Harp in the South*. 'Rita, was it your choice?'

'It was,' Rita said. 'It's one of my favourites. All about hardship and love and surviving both. Isn't it, Sybil?'

'I suppose so,' Sybil said softly.

Rita put her hand on Sybil's shoulder, just for a second, and Sybil breathed out slowly.

The trio moved towards the sitting room, where Kate and Della were standing close together, laughing.

As Kate turned her head she immediately looked concerned.

'Mum, are you all right?'

'Yes, I'm fine.' Sybil felt uncharacteristically self-conscious.

Kate didn't look convinced and Sybil saw her glance at Rita, who gave a tiny shake of her head.

'I'll make the tea,' Kate declared. 'Sallyanne, why don't you help me? We have to get you used to the kitchen so you can pop in whenever you like and make a cuppa.'

'Oh – yes.' Sallyanne's face shone. 'I'm looking forward to that.'

Della gazed after them. 'I think I'll help,' she said, starting to walk away.

Sybil and Rita looked at each other and as they began to laugh Sybil felt something in her body letting go.

'Alone again,' Rita said.

'So it seems.' Sybil smiled at her oldest friend.

'Let's sit down.' Rita nodded at the couch. 'And you can shut your eyes for a few seconds.'

Sybil complied. 'You want me to "regroup", is that it?'

'I do.'

Sybil leant her head against the cushions and felt Rita's hand resting on hers. She sighed, so heavily that she felt as though she might sink into the couch and through to the floor.

'You've had a hell of a time, Syb,' Rita murmured. 'But I'm here, and you have other people who love you too.'

'I'm lucky,' Sybil murmured and she realised it was true.

'We're lucky too.'

Sybil felt Rita squeeze her hand.

'Everything will be just fine,' Rita said softly.

And for a few seconds, Sybil believed her.

CHAPTER FORTY-THREE

The single-engine plane jerked around on the air currents and Rita tried to keep her face calm, out of habit – she didn't want her young patient to see that she was nervous. All the times she'd flown in this little plane and turbulence still frightened her, just a bit. But the child was so sick, lying on a gurney with her eyes closed, that she was unlikely to notice.

They'd received the call two hours ago, to a station a half-hour's flight away. The girl had a fever but her mother said they had no thermometer, so there was no way of telling how sick she was.

When they'd arrived Rita had taken one look at the child and marched straight out to tell Kevin to keep the engine running.

The girl was septic, she was sure of it. Forty degrees on the mercury and a cut on her leg that was surrounded by bright red flesh. They needed to get her into Alice Springs or she'd lose her leg, if not her life. The call should have come in days ago and now it might be too late, but they'd try. They'd always try.

The plane jerked again, more violently.

'What's going on, Kev?' she called over the engine noise.

'Bit of a willy-willy,' he called back.

'Up here?' Willy-willies hugged the ground, not the sky.

'Nah, but it feels like it.'

She could see that his knuckles were white as he held the controls.

On this flight there was no doctor: Hamish was rostered off and the other, newer doctor hadn't turned up to his shift in time. For the third day in a row. She'd have a word to HQ about it when they got back. They hadn't been able to wait for him this morning and Rita was confident enough in her skills that she reckoned she could do without him anyway. Certainly, she hadn't needed him to make the diagnosis.

At the thought of doctors, of Hamish, Rita felt a twinge of embarrassment. She'd picked a fight that morning when he'd said he was heading back to Brisbane for a few days to see his children. His birthday was coming up and they wanted to see him.

'Aren't they grown up?' she'd said a bit meanly, and she'd only understood why when she saw the look of surprise on his face: she was jealous. He wasn't to know that Rita had plans for his birthday too. She had asked if the roster could be arranged to let them both off for three days in a row so they could drive to Ayers Rock. He'd told her he wanted to go camping there and she'd squirrelled away the information, wanting to use it at the right time. And she had longed to see sunset on the Rock with him – she'd thought it would be romantic.

'They still want to see me,' he'd said in response to her question, his tone mild.

'I guess you should go, then,' she'd said, and she was being mean that time because she was sheepish that she'd been mean the first time. She had felt petulant, not like a teenager but like a toddler, yet it was as if she'd had no control over it – and

314

that alarmed her more than anything, that she could feel so strongly about this man that she could almost forget herself.

'Rita, I won't be gone long,' he'd said, and he'd sounded so understanding, so reasonable, that she'd wanted to shout at him: *Can't you tell that I don't want to share you with anyone?* But she hadn't. Instead she'd sniffily picked up her handbag, kissed him primly on the cheek and wished him luck booking the tickets as she'd swept out the door to go to work.

What a selfish, self-absorbed idiot she had been. And now she was stuck in an aircraft that was being bounced around like a tennis ball on a dry grass court, wishing she had behaved quite differently.

The plane dropped suddenly and Rita reached an arm across her prone patient, trying to hold her steady because the straps that were holding the gurney weren't doing a good enough job. With her other hand she tightened her seatbelt.

'Cripes, Kev, what the hell's going on?'

'Um . . .'

Rita could hear Kevin swearing. She shouldn't talk to him again – he needed to concentrate as the plane bucked and swerved from side to side. These small planes were agile but they didn't insulate passengers from conditions the way the big ones did. This was the worst turbulence Rita had ever been in and for the first time ever on the Flying Doctor she started to feel queasy.

She looked down at the girl, whose eyes were shut. She was breathing, that much was clear, but her yellow–grey pallor betrayed her condition. The poor little thing – they might get her through this awful flight, take her to the hospital in Alice, see her treated with all the antibiotics they could find and she could still die. In fact, she probably would. And all because, as the girl's parents had said, they 'hadn't wanted to bother' the Flying Doctor, which was why they hadn't called earlier.

Rita really should not begrudge Hamish the opportunity to see his children. She would tell him that, and tell him she was sorry for her behaviour, as soon as this bloody flying tin can landed.

'Hold on!' Kev yelled.

Did he mean 'hold on' as in 'wait' – or 'hold on to something'?

'What? Why?' she called back. The noise was so loud that she didn't think he'd heard her.

She checked her patient – there was nothing the girl could hold on to, if that's what he'd meant. What was she supposed to do with her?

'I'm taking her a bit lower,' Kevin yelled. 'We need to get out of this crap.'

Rita peered out the window and saw the desert beneath them, closer than it would usually be on one of these flights. She wondered if Kevin was planning to ditch into the sand without telling her.

Suddenly, where there had been noise there was nothing. It felt as if they were floating on the currents of air. Perhaps the turbulence was over.

Then the plane started to drop.

'Kevin?' she shouted. No response.

There was a sputtering noise, then nothing again. The nose of the plane drifted downwards and Rita finally understood what it meant to feel her heart in her throat. Gravity rapidly pulled them towards the earth and in an instant she understood what was happening and also refused to believe it.

As she felt the metallic taint of adrenaline flood her mouth she still believed that Kevin would fix this. She believed that he'd get the plane going again and they'd pull up any second. They'd laugh about it later and he'd tell the story of their close call over the Simpson Desert.

Rita believed it all in the few seconds it took for the plane to plummet towards the earth, for her to lie over her patient and hold on tight, and for her consciousness to become nothingness as the plane hit the ground.

CHAPTER FORTY-FOUR

Sybil looked out the car window but barely registered what she was seeing. Although she should, because she'd never been to Alice Springs; there had been no opportunity to come here before now. She was a Top Ender and Alice was central, and even though it was all the Northern Territory that didn't mean they had anything else in common. And the demands of life on Fairvale had kept her away.

She exhaled sharply and looked ahead through the windshield.

'Not far now, darl,' Darryl said, his face grim.

It was funny that they had never met before when Sybil felt like she knew him. No, not funny; just odd. Rita had talked about Darryl so often that Sybil had known him instantly when he'd jumped out of his plane at Tindal to greet her. She'd waited for a joke. She knew he liked jokes. But it wasn't the time for them. They both knew that.

She'd been in the kitchen the previous afternoon when she'd heard the radiotelephone ringing in the office. Kate had picked it up and come into the hallway.

'Mum, come quickly,' she'd called, although her voice had been calm, so Sybil had taken time to wipe her hands on a tea towel and hang it up.

'Who is it?' she'd said softly as she entered the office.

Kate's eyes were round. 'Darryl,' she whispered.

'Darryl?' Sybil's first thought was that he must have been organising a surprise for Rita and he wanted her help. It wasn't a logical thought but it was the first one.

Sybil had taken the phone. 'Hello?'

'Yeah, Darryl here,' he'd said, then fallen silent.

'How are you, Darryl?' Sybil had asked.

'There's been an accident,' he'd said quickly.

Sybil's brain had whirred through its gears: if he was calling about an accident, it could only mean . . .

'Is she all right?' Sybil had blurted as nausea flooded her gut. *Not Rita.*

'She's banged up pretty good.'

Sybil took a few seconds to process the news, then she'd wanted to howl with relief, knowing that was the wrong response but it felt like the right one to her.

'The plane went down. Not far from here. The other pilot, he . . .' Darryl had breathed out and sounding like he was hiccupping. 'Anyway,' he'd gone on, 'I know she'd want to see you. She talks about you all the bloody time.'

'How did you find me?' Sybil had said.

'If I heard "Fairvale" once I heard it twenty bloody times a week,' he'd said. 'It wasn't too hard. So I can come up and get you in the morning. Too late now – the sun'll be gone soon. Can you get to Tindal?'

'Of course,' she'd said. 'But please tell me – what sort of injuries does she have?'

'Um . . . something about a spleen. Think she broke a leg. Maybe two? Honestly, after they told me she was alive I stopped paying attention.' He'd laughed drily. 'She'll kill

319

me if she finds that out. Always going on about how I never listen to anyone.'

'It's understandable,' Sybil had said. 'So I'll see you tomorrow?'

'Nine o'clock, eh?'

'Yes. Thank you, Darryl. I appreciate this so much.'

'Rightio. See ya tomorrow.'

After the call Sybil had hurriedly packed a bag and then found herself in stasis, not able to go to her friend but with thoughts about Rita churning in her head through the night. Thoughts that didn't go anywhere useful either.

Now Sybil was in Darryl's old Valiant and her relief that Rita was alive had turned into concern that she hadn't yet woken up since the crash.

'That doctor bloke's with her,' Darryl said.

'Hamish?' Rita had given her some details about Hamish in between telling her that she was 'too superstitious' to believe it was going to last. Given that Rita had never been superstitious in her life, the remark had been strange. At the time.

'Yep.' Darryl's face tightened.

'Don't you like him?' Sybil said. It seemed ridiculous not to be upfront with someone who saw more of Rita than she did.

Darryl had shrugged. 'He's all right.'

They were silent as the car entered the hospital grounds.

'Here we are,' he said as he pulled into a parking spot.

Sybil walked quickly into the hospital, trailed by Darryl. As a young nurse she had been trained never to run in hospitals because it alarmed the patients; she wasn't going to break that training now, not even when she was seeing Rita.

At the door to Rita's room, Darryl paused.

'I'll leave you here, eh?' he said.

'You don't want to come in? Have you seen her already?'

He shook his head. 'Not my place.'

'Darryl,' Sybil said, her face softening. 'Of course it's your place.'

He jerked his chin at the door. 'Her doc's in there. I'll see ya round.'

Sybil watched him go as he put his shoulders back to walk down the corridor and she wondered at the small emblems of pride that people wore. Darryl didn't want Hamish to see how much he cared about Rita – and he probably didn't want Rita to see it either. That was the limit of his pride. She couldn't argue with it.

She pushed open the door and saw Rita lying in bed, cannulas in each arm, her face slack and bruised. Rita, who was always so animated and vivacious, now inert – Sybil felt something like an electric shock go through her.

Next to the bed was a man with thick blond hair, sitting forwards on a hospital chair that looked inadequate for his height.

'Hamish?' she said.

His head whipped around and she saw that he was distraught, his mouth half open, his eyes hooded, his face lined.

'Yes?' he said, standing.

'I'm Sybil.' She extended her hand. Instead of taking it he moved towards her and put his hand on her arm, his eyes meeting hers with an understanding, before he hugged her stiffly. She hugged him back and felt him softening against her.

'Thank you for coming,' he said, sniffing and wiping his eyes with the back of his hand. 'Darryl said he would try to find you.'

'He did,' she said.

A noise from the bed made them both look. Rita was moving her mouth as if she was trying to taste something.

'Darling?' Hamish said, putting his hand on her leg as Sybil moved to the other side of the bed.

Rita groaned and tried to move her arm only to have it tethered by the drip. Sybil felt the release of all her worry and the overwhelming urge to sit down, but she kept herself standing. She could be strong now. She had to be.

'Rita,' Sybil said, taking her hand, 'you're in hospital.'

Rita sighed and turned her head to one side, flinching as she did so, her mouth still moving like a baby bird's.

'Darling? Darling, I'm here. And Sybil's here.'

Rita's eyelids fluttered and Hamish stroked her brow with his thumb. His love for her was clear in every small gesture of care.

Then Rita opened her eyes, blinking into the fluorescent light above her.

'Rita, do you know where you are?' Hamish said and Sybil heard the shift of tone to 'doctor'.

Rita tried to move her arm again and winced.

'If I had to hazard a guess,' she said, her voice hoarse but still unmistakably Rita's, 'I'd say hospital.'

Hamish's face relaxed. 'It is,' he said, kissing her forehead. 'I've been so worried about you.'

'She was always going to be fine,' said Sybil, bending down to kiss Rita's forehead. 'Weren't you?' She smiled as reassuringly as she could.

'Syb,' Rita croaked, smiling with one half of her face, 'what the hell are you doing here?' She scowled. 'Ow. Why does my face hurt?'

Hamish glanced at Sybil with a worried expression. She thought he would likely be wondering if Rita remembered anything and, if she didn't, how much they should tell her. It

322

was the calculation of a medical professional, and of someone who cared deeply for the patient.

'You gave us all a fright,' Sybil said, opting not to explain the injuries. 'Darryl came and got me this morning.'

'Darryl,' Rita murmured, then recognition dawned on her face. 'Kevin?' she said. 'What happened to him?'

Rita looked to each of them in turn. Hamish half raised his eyebrows to Sybil, who nodded once.

'Darling . . .' Hamish said slowly, taking her hand. Rita gasped and looked as if she was trying to sit up.

'Don't do that, Rita,' Sybil said, putting a hand on her shoulder to try to keep her down. 'You need to lie down.'

'But I'm going to be sick,' she said. 'Can you get me a bowl?'

Sybil squeezed her shoulder. 'You're all right,' she said, but she turned to pick up the bowl from the bedside cabinet.

'The girl?' Rita said, her eyes wide and blinking rapidly.

Hamish shook his head and Sybil wanted to turn hers away.

'Why am I still here?' Rita said as tears rolled down her cheeks, her eyes half closing.

'You stayed with the wreckage,' Hamish said sadly. 'The others were thrown clear.'

'How – how did they find us?' Rita moved around again, her fingers playing over one of the cannulas.

'Rita, try to calm down,' Sybil said gently. 'Your spleen ruptured in the crash and I don't want it rupturing again.' She had treated other patients in Rita's condition: people who could be lucid but still disoriented; who could appear to take in the information they were being told and then do something irrational.

'I was in the office waiting for you,' Hamish said, 'when it happened. Kevin made a mayday call. We took off . . . They found you not long after it happened. You were . . .' His face seemed to collapse. 'You were only fifty kilometres away.'

Rita looked past Sybil, out the window of the room.

'They died out there,' she murmured.

'And you didn't,' said Sybil.

Rita's eyes met hers but Sybil could barely see them through Rita's tears.

'I don't want to stay here,' Rita said quietly, her eyes pleading with Sybil.

'You have to, darling, you know that,' said Hamish. 'You're not well enough to leave.'

Rita turned her head towards him. 'I mean I don't want to stay in Alice Springs.'

Hamish frowned and looked at Sybil.

'You need to get some rest now,' Sybil said, patting her arm. 'We'll leave the big decisions for another day.'

'Don't leave me, Syb,' Rita said, her voice breaking. Sybil had never seen her so vulnerable – so broken. It made Sybil want to scoop her up and take her home to Fairvale where she could look after her for as long as it took to get her right.

'I won't.' Sybil looked at Hamish, hoping he wouldn't mind if she stayed. 'Hamish and I will stay with you.'

He nodded and moved to perch on the windowsill, leaving the sole chair for Sybil.

She pulled it up to the bed, took hold of Rita's hand and watched as Rita's eyes fluttered to a close.

CHAPTER FORTY-FIVE

The hotel on The Esplanade in Darwin wasn't as fancy as anything Kate had seen in London but it had luxuries not available to her at Fairvale: water that didn't come out of a bore, for one thing, and there were people who cleaned her room for her. She should be enjoying it – she was only here for a couple of nights – but instead she was worrying about what lay ahead.

The doctor's appointment was in half an hour; he was a gynaecologist, or a 'lady doctor', as her mother might have said. For the first time since she was a little girl, Kate wished her mother was here to hold her hand and tell her that everything would be all right.

At least she had the novelty of a ten-minute drive to look forward to; the quickest drive from Fairvale to anywhere was the one hour to Ghost River, and Darwin took a lot longer than that. She'd driven up the day before so she didn't have to leave Fairvale in the dark, and she'd been encouraged to stay an extra night, seeing as it was so long since she'd left Fairvale.

'You could have a bit of time to yourself,' Sybil had said with a smile. 'Have a break from all of us.'

Yet she didn't want a break from them. She'd only been gone a night and she already missed the silence of the early morning broken by the first whinnies of the horses, closely followed by the dogs letting everyone know they were awake. She missed Ben's legs tangled in hers, and his scratchy morning beard when he woke her up with a kiss. She missed knowing that Della was a short walk away if she wanted a chat after dinner. She even missed the now-daily sense of achievement she derived from cooking for everyone.

She had to be here in Darwin, though. There had been no sign of another pregnancy – not that she and Ben weren't trying for one as often as they could – and while Kate had almost forgotten about it for a while, in the midst of all the change on Fairvale, a letter from her cousin Georgia had prodded her into action. Georgia and Charlie were going to have another baby, even though their first seemed barely to have arrived. So, clearly, fertility ran through one branch of the family; Kate wanted to find out why it wasn't running through hers. She might have other things in her life now that gave her purpose, but her desire to be a mother had not dimmed – and Ben was as keen as ever to have 'baby Baxters' running around.

Looking at her watch, Kate chewed her bottom lip. Still twenty-five minutes to go but she couldn't sit here any longer. Better to be early than late anyway; that's what she'd been taught. She could sit in the doctor's waiting room for a while.

～

The doctor was efficient although not warm. Which seemed strange – shouldn't someone who dealt with the most intimate body parts of women be a little friendlier? Maybe he was worried that his patients would construe it the wrong way if he was, or that they'd find it creepy. Actually, that was a good point: she didn't want him telling jokes while he was poking around inside her.

'Just relax, Mrs Baxter,' he said as he put one hand on her abdomen.

Kate breathed out through her mouth. She hadn't realised that she wasn't relaxed. Probably normal not to be relaxed, though, given what was happening. She focused on breathing steadily.

The doctor abruptly withdrew both hands.

'Thank you, Mrs Baxter,' he said. 'You may get dressed now.'

He opened and closed the curtain before Kate had registered that he was leaving her alone. Was that all he was going to do? Prod her and then write up his notes or something? How was he going to tell what was wrong with her if he didn't do more than that?

Kate obediently dressed, gently opened the curtain and sat on the chair across the desk from the doctor's own. He smiled at her – finally, she thought, a sign of humanity.

'So we've established that menstruation is normal, yes?' he said, glancing at a piece of paper in front of him. 'No abnormally heavy bleeding. A fairly regular cycle. No undue amount of pain. You've recovered well from your miscarriage.'

She nodded slowly and had a vague sensation of disappointment that he wasn't telling her that she had something horrendous wrong with her – some never-before-seen cause for her lack of children.

'Yes, that's right,' she squeaked.

'I couldn't find anything out of place in my pelvic examination,' he said. 'So . . .' His smile was brief and tight. 'I don't believe that there's any reason why you cannot fall pregnant.'

What a strange person she was, Kate thought, not to be happy to hear that news. But she had so wanted there to be a reason – something to name and something to fix.

The doctor interlaced his fingers and placed his hands on

the desk. 'Perhaps it's your husband who needs to be examined, Mrs Baxter.'

She blinked at him. 'Oh no, I don't think so,' she said, flushing with embarrassment that she should have to discuss Ben like this.

The doctor gave her a funny look. 'Why not?'

'Because I was the one who had the miscarriage,' she said, the words tumbling over themselves, her sense of failure returning when she'd thought it tucked away into a neat little compartment inside her.

'That's because you're the only one who can get pregnant.' The doctor tilted his head slightly to the side. 'The cause of the miscarriage might not have been you.'

Kate tried to understand what he was saying but it didn't fit with anything she'd learnt about pregnancy. When her mother's friends had had miscarriages, her mother had always talked about them in terms of the friends having the problems. Surely the woman was always to blame?

'How do you know?' she said.

'I don't,' he said briskly. 'One rarely does. But it's usually because there's a problem with the foetus, not the mother's body, and as the foetus is created by both mother and father, there is no way of knowing with whom the exact cause lies.'

'I see.' Kate frowned as she looked into her lap, where her hands were tightly clutching the handbag she'd borrowed from Sybil. 'So what should I do now?'

'You should keep trying,' he said, now sounding cheerful. 'Which is, no doubt, not what you wanted to hear as you may be sick of trying.'

'I'm not!' she said forcefully.

He looked amused. 'I'm sure your husband will be pleased to hear that, Mrs Baxter. So, keep trying, and try not to worry too much – worry is an enemy. Have you had much to worry about lately?'

Kate thought of the past few years and the enormous events and changes that had occurred.

'A bit,' she said.

'Hopefully that will abate?'

'I believe so, yes.' Kate gave him a small smile. She had no idea what the future held for any of them but at least she knew that she was settled in her life, so the stress of becoming used to Fairvale was over.

'There you go,' he said cheerfully. 'Just try not to add to those worries and I believe all will be well.'

Kate felt a flash of irritation that he could issue such a trite instruction, but she hadn't exactly given him details of her life so he didn't have much to go on.

'Thank you, Doctor,' she said, pushing back her chair as she stood.

'Thank you, Mrs Baxter.'

He walked around the desk to open the door for her.

'And do call me when you fall pregnant,' he said. 'We can discuss where you want to have the baby – here or Katherine.'

Kate was nonplussed, wondering how he could be so confident about her prospects, but she thanked him anyway.

Once she reached the car she sat behind the wheel for several minutes, grappling with the fact that there was absolutely nothing wrong with her. All this time, all the ways she had blamed herself, and she'd had no reason for it. And, still, she had no answers.

Sighing, she clipped the seatbelt into place and decided she would check out of the hotel early and drive back to Fairvale tonight. She had a life waiting for her there.

CHAPTER FORTY-SIX

The cottage was smaller than the house in Katherine but Sallyanne didn't mind: as soon as they'd arrived at Fairvale and deposited their suitcases the boys had run outside, just as Sybil had said they would, and when they were out there was plenty of space.

Even Gretel was intrigued by what lay beyond their front door: she had taken to sitting on the steps that led down to the little garden, watching as Tim and Billy hurtled past either in pursuit of some of the camp children or in flight from them, all hooting or screaming, everyone laughing. They'd never been able to do this at home – there had only been one other child their age in the street and her mother had kept her inside most of the time.

The boys were already outside this morning, heading to who knew where, but whereas Sallyanne would have worried if they'd done this in Katherine, out here there were eyes everywhere. There were eyes on Gretel, too: Ruby's. She might have retired from the kitchen but she'd decided to take up babysitting and she had declared that Gretel was her special charge since she didn't have any grandchildren yet.

Sallyanne had needed a couple of weeks to get used to how the community of Fairvale worked; so much time and affection was offered and no one seemed to expect anything in return. She was still adjusting to having so many people interested in her comings and goings, when she'd been relatively anonymous in her street. And she hadn't yet become comfortable with the silence that permeated most of the day when the stock camp was off on a muster. She preferred it when everyone was back; she found herself enjoying the way the place tended to sound like a nonstop party: mealtimes were full of animated conversation and at night there were singalongs around campfires.

In the beginning she'd found it strange that she not only couldn't run to the shops when she had forgotten something but that she didn't need to: all their food was being taken care of – and sometimes cooked by her. When Sybil had mentioned that Kate would need help in the kitchen, Sallyanne hadn't realised how huge the undertaking could be, but the two of them had found their rhythm.

The only thing that had niggled at her, really, was that she hadn't been able to see Rita. After Rita had been discharged from hospital Sallyanne had called her but the first couple of times Hamish had answered and said that Rita wasn't able to come to the phone. Once Sallyanne finally managed to speak to her, Rita had sounded distant and weak. Not at all herself. Not at all as she was when she'd talked Sallyanne into moving to Fairvale.

'So Sybil's made you an offer,' Rita had said chirpily down the phone not long after Sybil and Kate had visited her.

'Yes,' Sallyanne had said hesitantly, wondering how much Rita knew.

'Are you going to take it?'

'Should I?' By that stage Sallyanne had thought of lots of reasons why she shouldn't move – the fact that she had never lived in the bush being primary amongst them – and she hadn't let herself consider why she should. Not because the thought wasn't appealing; it was more that she had no idea what the shape of her life on Fairvale would be.

'I think you'd love it there,' Rita had said. 'And if the only thing you're scared of is change, well . . .'

'I don't know if I am. I guess – I guess I haven't had enough change to know.'

Rita had laughed. 'You don't call marriage and three kids change?'

Sallyanne had known Rita was right but also not: she'd been in the one town all her life and she hadn't even moved that far away from her childhood home, because nothing in Katherine was very far, so she couldn't claim to be adventurous. And wasn't adventure part of living in the bush? Katherine was a country town but it was still a town and Sallyanne didn't know if she was cut out for living with animals and having dirt get into everything even more than it did now.

'Look,' Rita had continued, 'I think you're not risking much if you go. The kids are young enough to be flexible and you and Mick own the house, don't you? So put in a tenant or leave it empty – or tell him he can move back into it – and it will still be there if you decide that Fairvale isn't for you.'

'I suppose so,' Sallyanne had said meekly.

'Sa-a-a-l,' Rita had said, 'stop sitting on the fence. Mick's gone now. You're free. You can make decisions like this.'

'But what if he wants to come back?' The words had been out of her mouth before she'd thought them through and as soon as she'd said them she knew the real reason why she'd been hesitating about Fairvale: she still had hope, fragile but persistent, that Mick would come back sober, and maybe even kind, and they could try again.

Rita had been silent for a while. 'Do you want him to?' she'd then said.

'I—' Sallyanne had thought about how to phrase it. 'What if he's changed? Since he's been working away?'

'Has he been in touch?'

Sallyanne felt a thud of disappointment. 'Not really. A couple of letters to the kids.'

More silence.

'If he cleans himself up and he wants to find you,' Rita had said after several seconds had passed, 'he will. But that doesn't mean you should hang around. You could be hanging around for years waiting for that.'

Sallyanne had ended the conversation not entirely convinced but after another week of her life being the same – taking the boys to school, housework, shopping, looking after Gretel – and the prospect of all the weeks for the next few years being exactly the same, for her and the children, she realised that change was less scary than monotony. And she already knew Fairvale, and Sybil, and Kate and Della. She wouldn't be leaving home so much as joining friends. She had called Ghost River to tell Mick what she had decided – figuring that it was only right that he be told his children were moving – but she'd been told he wasn't available. So she'd written, and received no reply.

'Knock, knock!' Ruby called from the open front door.

'Come in,' Sallyanne replied, walking to the door as Gretel jumped up and down on her spot on the steps.

'Ruby! Ruby! Ruby!' she squealed and Sallyanne smiled to see her daughter so happy. The children had all become more relaxed after Mick had left but she hadn't seen them happy until they moved to Fairvale.

'It's all right, love,' Ruby said, chuckling as Gretel pulled on her dress. 'I'll just take her now. She's not going to wait, eh?'

'She always looks forward to seeing you.' Sallyanne smiled broadly at this woman she barely knew who was being so kind to her family.

'Ah, she's a sweet little thing. I look forward to seeing her too. Don't I, little Gretel? Come on, lovey.'

Ruby took Gretel's hand and Sallyanne watched them walk off towards Ruby's home, Ruby swaying from side to side on what she called her 'funny feet'. Sallyanne marvelled that Gretel, who had been so clingy before, barely gave her a backwards glance.

Sallyanne pulled the front door closed behind her and headed towards the kitchen. She'd have a few hours with Kate, then a couple giving the boys their lessons – her warm-up for teaching them and the other children next year. Then there would be people to see, dinner to eat, and early to bed. But while the structure of each day was the same, Sallyanne never knew what to expect out here – and it made her feel more alive than ever before. While she was living with Mick and uncertainty was a permanent state, it had unsettled her. She knew why she didn't have the same feeling here: the people were constant. It was only the work and the land that changed. She was finally living with people who cared about her; life could throw anything at her now and she would be ready for it.

CHAPTER FORTY-SEVEN

At odd times Rita felt as if she had ants crawling inside her body and she had to shake vigorously to get them out. She was almost sure this wasn't a physical problem; she believed, rather, that it was a manifestation of what was going on in her mind. Which was why she didn't tell Hamish about it – he would try to look for a medical explanation and if he couldn't find something he might think she was going crazy. But Rita knew it wasn't that. It was that her heart had been broken.

The yawning grief that marked the days after the plane crash – her anguish that Kevin had died and her guilt that her patient had died, even if it wasn't her fault – had given way to a pulsing restlessness. The ants. It was as if they had poured out of that crack in her heart and taken her over. Rita had never felt like this before. She had been terribly upset when her parents died but she hadn't felt responsible, guilty, the way she did now. She hadn't survived their cause of death, the way she had in that plane.

'What's in the paper today?' Hamish said, jerking her back to awareness. She'd been sitting in front of the newspaper for several minutes and hadn't read a word.

'Not much,' she fibbed. She forced herself to smile at him. She wanted to smile at him – she loved him – but for the past few weeks she had to make herself do it. Smiles weren't spontaneous anymore. Hamish had said that she'd take some time to recover, to adjust to life again. He just hadn't been able to predict how much time, and Rita thought she should know anyway. All those occasions on which she'd blithely counselled other people, telling them that their sadness would alleviate *with time*, haunted her now. She'd been a fool. An ignorant, unthinking fool.

'You weren't really reading it, were you?' he said, looking as if he'd been forcing his own smile.

Rita shook her head.

'What are we going to do with you?' Hamish reached over and took her hand. She caught his quick expression of sadness and felt guilty about that, too.

She coughed once, stalling. 'I don't know,' she said.

He started to say something.

'I know you're worried,' she said hurriedly, not wanting to hear him say it for the thousandth time. 'I'm worried too. Sybil's worried. Sallyanne's worried. Everyone's worried.'

Hamish sighed. 'You don't have to go back to work next week,' he said, his face showing his concern. 'It's only been six weeks.'

Her return to work had been postponed several times now but she couldn't keep putting it off: the Flying Doctor needed a permanent nurse. Nor had Rita forgotten that instinctual reaction she'd had on waking in the hospital: she wanted to leave Alice Springs. This place would forever mean nothing more to her now than tragedy.

'I've been thinking about that.' She took a breath, nervous about how he would react to what she was going to say next. 'I don't think I should go back at all.'

Hamish glanced down and then back to her, nodding slowly. 'I thought you might feel that way.'

'So you won't try to talk me out of it?'

Now he shook his head. Once. Twice. 'Not if it's what you really want.'

She had asked herself this, over and over, wanting to be sure she was making her decision with as clear a head as she could muster.

'I don't know what I really want,' she said slowly. 'I may never know that.'

'You can take some more time,' he urged.

She tried to smile but knew it looked more like a grimace.

'I feel stuck here,' she said. 'And taking more time would just make that worse.'

'So . . . what's next?' he said uncertainly.

She'd asked herself this too, and only one answer recurred.

'I'm going to apply for jobs in Sydney,' she said. 'I need to go home.'

In the weeks since the crash she had lain awake at night, thinking of the bright comfort of the city of her birth. She thought of waking to magpies and kookaburras; of green lawns in summer, the Christmas tree in Martin Place, and beaches where she could lie for hours on end, snoozing in the afternoon sun and plunging into the water that was everywhere – the harbour, the coastline, the fingers of river reaching deep into the city. She still thought Alice Springs was beautiful but it was the antithesis of what she needed now.

Hamish flinched and withdrew his hand from hers.

'Sydney,' he stated quietly.

'I can't stay here, Hamish. I can't go back on a Flying Doctor plane, and there's no other work for me here.'

'What about the hospital? I'm sure they'd be delighted if someone of your calibre asked them for a job.'

'No,' she said firmly. 'I have to leave Alice Springs.'

'But . . .' He sighed heavily. 'I'm here,' he said.

Rita knew she was being selfish, wanting to move, but she also knew she wouldn't recover if she only did what other people wanted her to do. She could stay in her job because she'd made a commitment to it; she could stay in Alice Springs because Hamish wanted her to, and because it was closer to Sybil and the friends she had made because of Sybil. But none of those things meant that she was putting herself first. She'd been so dutiful all her life – a good daughter, a good nurse, a good employee, a good friend, even a good mistress – even though sometimes it made her want to scream, because fundamentally what she really wanted to do for herself could be at odds with her duties. Coming to Alice Springs had been the first time she had done something unusual, and now that decision had almost destroyed her.

'I love you,' she said, wanting him to know that before she said anything more. 'But I have to look after myself.'

'I'd look after you,' he said pleadingly.

'You do look after me,' she said. 'I don't want to leave you but I don't want to stay here. I hope you can understand. I *need* to go home.'

Hamish breathed in and seemed to hold onto that breath while he stared into her eyes.

'I don't want to live without you,' he said. 'My life . . . it is so much better with you in it. You're unique. Magnificent.'

She put her hands across the table with her palms up and he placed his hands in hers.

'I don't think this is the end of our story,' Rita said softly. 'But I have to start a new one of my own. I hope that makes sense.'

He looked at her with a certain wonder and she watched his frown melt. Then he brought the back of her hand to his lips and kissed it.

'It does,' he said.

Rita leant across the table and kissed him. She could always lose herself in these kisses, in his embrace. But she didn't want to lose herself now; as much as she loved this man, that love wasn't enough to sustain her here. She didn't know what form their story would take next. All she had was uncertainty about her future. Strangely, though, it felt safer than all the certainties she had known in her life to date.

CHAPTER FORTY-EIGHT

The horses were stirring up dust that plumed towards the riders, who coughed and tucked their chins into their chests. Della started laughing, thinking she'd never been so happy to see dust in her life. It was the red dust that told her exactly where she was: home.

'How're you going, Del?' Ben called back to her from his place at the head of the pack of riders.

'I'm fine,' she responded. 'Don't worry about me.'

'Oh, I wasn't worrying,' Ben said, and she could see his smile through the red fog. 'Just being polite.'

Stan was slightly ahead of her and she gazed at his straight back, the hair just brushing the back of his neck, squashed down by his old hat. He was holding the reins in one hand, as usual, his body moving in sync with the horse.

She'd had a new horse to get used to, because Arthur was still at Ghost River. As much as he'd annoyed her at first, Della had grown used to Arthur: he was solid and calm, and he never tired when other horses did. She was happy with her new mount, though, a chocolate-coloured quarter horse called Phoenix. He wasn't as tall as the part-Clydesdale Arthur but she liked his temperament.

They were heading out in search of some feral cattle Ben believed were at least a day's ride away. Della loved the freedom of roaming beneath these big skies, on horseback, with so much country to explore. She hadn't counted on the joy of being able to see Stan every day as they worked together – joy that was allowed because Ben had no rule prohibiting relationships amongst workers. Not that the matter had really come up before: she was his first female stockman.

'Just name your firstborn after me, okay?' he'd said, winking, when the subject had been raised over dinner on her first night on Fairvale. 'Benjamina for a girl.'

Della had blushed when he'd said it; Stan had looked pleased. Kate had merely raised her eyebrows and smiled mysteriously.

She gave Phoenix a nudge and caught up to Stan, who gave her a funny look rather than his usual broad smile.

'Long way to go today,' he said.

'I'm looking forward to it.' She smiled at him. 'I don't know this country as well as you do yet. It's exciting.'

Stan's laugh came from deep in his chest. 'Not a lot of people find this country exciting. Some say it's boring.'

'Nuh-uh,' she said. 'Not to me. It's . . .' She took a deep breath as she searched for the right word. 'Spectacular.'

She glanced at him sideways and he was looking at her curiously.

'So you want to stay here?' he said.

'Of course!' she said. She was surprised he had to ask – she had come back, hadn't she?

'With me?' He sounded uncertain.

'Yes, with you,' she said confidently, knowing it was what she wanted.

He didn't look at her, and Della wondered if she'd been too forthright in her answer; maybe Stan had wanted her to hesitate, seem a little less eager. She'd had friends in school who told her that boys didn't like girls to be forward; it made the girls seem fast, and no one wanted a girl who went with a boy too eagerly.

'We'll be all right while we're here,' he said, lifting his chin towards the hill in the distance. 'But I worry, Della girl.' His eyes clouded as he looked at her. 'I worry about what happens when we're not.'

'What are you talking about?' she said.

Stan's eyes flickered sideways and then his chin dropped.

'Is this about what that stupid boy said?' Della pressed him. They had a new stockman named Mark whom Ben had reluctantly taken on because he was the younger brother of the friend near Tamworth who had given Ben a job. Yesterday, while they were preparing for the camp, Mark had been sorting gear when he'd hurled a swag at Stan, hitting him in the chest.

'Hey,' Stan had said, looking confused. 'What did you do that for?'

'It's your job, isn't it?' Mark had said. 'Packing people's swags?'

'Nah, you got it wrong, mate,' Stan had said, putting the swag on the ground. 'We pack our own around here. And I'm the head stockman so if anyone's packing anyone's swag, you're packing mine.'

Mark's laugh was brittle. 'Head stockman? In your dreams, mate. No one who looks like you is ever going to be my boss.'

Della had felt the air become instantly taut as Stan had put his face into neutral, which she knew from experience could be his most dangerous expression. When Stan didn't want his emotions to show, it usually meant he was saving them up so he could unleash them at the right time.

'Well, he's *my* boss,' she had said, hoping to defuse the tension.

'Yeah, and that's not all he is, is it?' Mark had stared at her then looked her up and down slowly. 'That's a waste, if you ask me.'

'No one did,' came a sharp retort from the stable door. Della turned to see Ben there, his hands on his hips, his face like thunder. That had been the end of the trouble with Mark but Della was wary of him. She hadn't realised that Stan might feel wary too.

Now Mark was up ahead, near Ben. Since yesterday Mark had been trying to be teacher's pet, although as far as Della could tell Ben wasn't impressed. That didn't mean she could forget what had happened, though.

She saw Stan looking ahead, as if his eyes were drilling holes in Mark's back.

'Lots of people out there – away from here – don't want to see a fella like me with a girl like you,' he said. 'They don't think it's natural.'

She had thought about this – of course she had. Mostly just after she'd realised she was falling in love with him. It wasn't as if there weren't problems in her own country when black men and white women wanted to be together. But it happened anyway. People got through it. They simply had to try harder and want it more. She could do that. And she could certainly ignore a flea like Mark.

'I know,' she said, taking a deep breath of Territory air as she smiled at him. 'But I'm not afraid.'

Phoenix tossed his head and pulled on the reins.

'He wants to catch up to the others,' Stan said.

Again, Della wondered if Stan was hiding what he really wanted to say. He hadn't answered her and for the first time since she'd met him, doubt grabbed hold of her insides. Maybe he'd changed his mind about her since she'd returned; maybe the incident yesterday had given him an excuse to let her down gently. That wasn't a logical thought but she was keenly aware of how much she had at stake now.

'Stan?' she said hesitantly.

His face had no expression.

'I don't want you to get hurt,' he said after seconds that had passed too slowly, his voice cracking on the last word.

She swallowed, knowing she had to make her case with her next sentence.

'I'll only get hurt if you say you don't want to be with me anymore,' she said.

Stan was chewing his lips. 'I love you,' he said and she almost cried out with relief. 'But we . . .' He shook his head so quickly he almost lost his hat. 'I need to think about it. About what might happen.'

Della knew she should react strongly: Stan seemed to be telling her that he needed time away from her. Instead she felt like molasses – her brain was working slowly, her lips didn't move fast enough to retort anything, her heart didn't seem to be beating anymore.

'So what do we do now?' she said, so quietly she wasn't sure he'd heard it.

They rode in silence for a minute or so.

'Can you give me time?' he said, not looking at her.

The expanse of her life – backwards, forwards – was nothing but time already spent or time waiting for her. Of course she could give him time, but she thought the question he was really asking was: did she want to?

'All right,' she said, although it was a lie: she had waited for him all those months she was away, not hearing from him, missing him. But she didn't know what he'd do if she forced him to make a decision now: she might wake up tomorrow and find he had gone back to the big house and handed in his notice.

'You go ahead,' he said quietly.

For a second Della didn't understand what he meant. Then, with a cloud of uncertainty blooming inside her, she nudged Phoenix into a trot and left Stan behind.

CHAPTER FORTY-NINE

The decision to go ahead with their next book club meeting had Sybil going back and forth in her mind for days. None of them had had much time to read, and Rita was still not fully recovered from her injuries. However, despite the arguments against a meeting, Sybil felt that they all needed one. Only she had seen Rita since her accident; Sallyanne, in particular, was keen to have visual reassurance that Rita was in one piece.

When Sybil had asked if she would be able to come to Fairvale, Rita had said she would fly up, as nonchalantly as she had always said it.

'Are you sure?' Sybil had asked.

There was silence for several seconds.

'No,' Rita had said finally. 'But if I can't get into a plane I'll never go much further than Alice Springs, will I? I can't drive everywhere.'

'True.'

'Darryl will fly me,' Rita had said, and Sybil could hear a note of forced levity in her voice. 'In his own plane. Not the same as the Flying Doctor plane at all. So . . .' Sybil had heard a sound like a hiccup. 'Nothing to worry about there.'

'Very well,' said Sybil. 'I'll come and get you at Tindal.'

And so she had, while Kate and Sallyanne made the preparations for morning tea.

Rita had taken the plane's short steps slowly, with Darryl holding onto her elbow, and Sybil could see that her bravado had disappeared, if it ever existed. By the time Rita reached her, though, her smile was broad and Sybil decided not to ask about the flight.

Now, settled in Fairvale's living room, with the teapot, cups and saucers, and one of Kate's cakes laid out on the table, Sybil finally felt able to relax. She looked over at Della, who was frowning.

Della had been quiet lately – not that she was normally loud, but they had all reached a point of familiarity which meant that conversation flowed casually between them. But today Kate had asked Della a question about Stan and Della had barely answered. Sybil knew nothing about Della and Stan's relationship, nor did she want to unless either one of them was miserable and she could do something about it. She feared that things might have reached that stage but, then again, she might never be told.

The only discussion Della would have was about the book, which she had enjoyed because she saw parallels with her own experience. *My Brilliant Career* by Miles Franklin had been chosen to make things as easy as possible for this book club meeting. Sybil had read it years ago; so had Sallyanne and Rita. It was short enough for Kate and Della to read quickly, passing Sybil's copy between them. In truth, the book was just a device to bring them together – a nod to their stated reason for meeting. Sybil hadn't expected it to provoke much discussion.

'I still don't understand why she had to change her name,' Della was saying as Sybil kept a close eye on Rita, who was looking pale yet cheerful.

'It's because women weren't allowed to use their names then,' Sallyanne said.

'Huh?' Della said.

'That's not quite true, Sal,' Rita said, adjusting the cushion behind her. 'She thought she'd have a better chance of getting the book published if she used a man's name.'

'And she was right,' Sybil observed.

'Like Henry Handel Richardson,' Rita said. 'Remember her?'

'Her?' said Della, frowning.

'Another time,' said Sybil.

'I'm amazed Jane Austen didn't have to use a fake name,' said Kate, sipping her tea and making a face. Sybil tried hers and understood why: it had been stewed too long.

'Sallyanne, may I have some sugar?' Sybil asked.

The sugar bowl was plonked down in front of Sybil and immediately afterwards tears welled in Sallyanne's eyes.

'Sal, what's the matter?' Rita said.

'This is all wrong,' Sallyanne wailed.

'Sallyanne,' Sybil said, leaning towards her, 'everything's not wrong. We're all quite content here.'

'Well, I'm in pain,' Rita said, shrugging listlessly. 'And your son's still who knows where.'

Sybil made a face like she was tasting something sour. 'Let's not talk about that,' she said.

Rita shrugged again. 'I thought it was worth mentioning. It's a bit of a constant sore and you put up with it. And . . .' She looked away. 'Everything else.'

Sybil knew she was talking about Joe but she didn't want to even start on that topic. The best method she had to cope with living without Joe was to think about him always and talk about him seldom.

Sallyanne sniffed. 'That's what I mean. Everything's *wrong*. I was so happy on Fairvale and Rita – Rita—' Her face crumpled. 'Rita was in a terrible plane crash.' She held up a limp hand in Rita's direction. 'And people *died*.'

Sybil glanced quickly at Rita, who blanched.

'We know people died,' Sybil said quietly.

'I've said the wrong thing, haven't I?' Sallyanne breathed out and in through her mouth.

Kate got up and sat next to Sallyanne on the couch, putting an arm around her.

'You're having a bad day,' Kate said. 'There've been a few of them, but you're at Fairvale now. And we all love you.'

'Hey,' Rita said sharply, 'what about me? I'm the one whose spleen blew up. *And* I broke a leg.'

'And you fractured a bone in the other one, didn't you, Rita?' Sybil said.

Rita glared at her, then winked, and Sybil knew with a surge of relief that her old friend was feeling more like herself again.

'I love you,' Sallyanne said, extracting a tissue from her dress's breast pocket and sniffling into it. 'I love you all too.'

Improbably, Sybil felt a laugh escaping her. 'Maybe I should have chosen a more light-hearted book. It seems as though we could have done with the distraction.'

Four women looked at her expectantly.

'Oh, I'm not going to suggest one,' Sybil said. 'I haven't read anything light-hearted since . . .' She paused.

'Since primary school, wasn't it, Syb?' Rita said.

'Oh, stop it,' Sybil said, narrowing her eyes at her friend. 'Although you might be right.'

'Maybe next time we could read something not so serious?' Sallyanne said.

'I'd like that,' Della said, smiling tightly. 'Just not a romance novel, okay?'

'You don't like romances?' Sallyanne said, looking hurt.

'Not at the moment,' Della said, not looking at any of them.

Sybil and Kate shared a glance and then Sybil broke it off before Della could see it.

'All right, Sallyanne,' Sybil said, 'you choose something fun for us. And you have time – we'll take a break now for the wet season.'

She watched as Rita took a sip of tea and screwed up her face.

'I think we need a drink,' Rita said.

'It's midday,' said Kate, looking amused.

'Perfect,' said Rita.

Sybil nodded, then pushed off the couch to stand up. 'Come and help me, Sallyanne. It's been so long since I had a drink I may need you to organise a search party for the whisky.'

Trailing Sallyanne into the kitchen, Sybil could hear Gretel calling from another room.

'I'll get her,' Sybil said. 'It must be her lunchtime.'

Sallyanne smiled gratefully and Sybil turned to go, leaving Sallyanne fossicking in a cupboard and Rita's laugh ringing from the sitting room.

CHAPTER FIFTY

The sun had set like a stone dropping into a pond and Kate saw its last remnants as she looked out of the office window and yawned. She stood up and stretched, arching her back and then curling forwards, her body cramped from sitting for hours.

The days seemed to be getting longer and harder. She was finishing later in the office than she used to, sometimes too late to eat the dinner that she had prepared for everyone. She was getting skinny, Ben said, and he wasn't pleased about it.

'You know I like those curves just how I found them,' he'd said the night before, nuzzling her neck, moving one hand over her hip.

'I'm not going to apologise for being busy working on *your* station,' Kate had said with an instinctual indignation that had surprised her.

Ben had laughed.

'You're getting more fiery the longer you live here,' he'd said, and pulled her into a kiss that had turned into something more. Something they hadn't had for a while, both of them so tired at the end of the day that they would often fall asleep as soon as they lay down. There was no mystery, now, why she wasn't pregnant: it would almost be a miracle if she was.

On the odd morning that she awoke before Ben, she would lie next to him and imagine what their little boy might look like: just like him, she hoped. Kate never thought about a little girl, for some reason. Perhaps because having a baby, for her, did not involve replicating herself. She thought of their child as something she and Ben would share, a living embodiment of the lives they had created and the love that grew stronger between them all the time.

There was a knock on the open office door and she spun around.

'Hi,' Ben said, smiling at her but not in his usual cheeky way.

'Hi,' she said, grinning at him with his shirt collar half up and one sleeve rolled shorter than the other. He always left in the mornings looking immaculate and every day something went awry.

'Mum wants to talk to us,' Ben said, stepping inside and giving her a quick kiss.

'That's unusual,' Kate said, tickling his waist. 'How was your day?'

Ben cocked his head to one side and narrowed his eyes as they walked slowly into the hallway. 'I've got a problem with Mark,' he said. 'He's a hard worker but I don't think Stan likes him.'

They entered the sitting room to find Sybil looking pensive, holding a letter.

'Hello,' she said absent-mindedly. It sounded oddly formal, given how often they all saw one another each day.

As Kate and Ben took up their usual positions on the couch, Kate looked at him expectantly and he shrugged in reply.

'Geoffrey's written,' Sybil said and Kate noticed that the letter shook a little. 'He's found Amelia and the boy again.

And he's, um . . .' Sybil closed her eyes briefly. 'He's persuaded her to go to Sydney so he – so I – can meet her. Meet the boy.'

Kate watched the play of emotions on Ben's face: incredulity, worry, a flash of what looked like happiness, then worry again. She felt them all herself, as she had done when Ben had first told her that Lachie's child existed. She loved the idea of having a nephew, although she could not believe she'd ever get to meet him. The whole pursuit of Amelia and her boy had been surreal, almost like a game that was being played on Sybil. On them.

'How do you know the same thing won't happen as last time?' Ben said, his voice full of concern.

'I don't,' Sybil said with a smile that didn't reach her eyes. 'But I have to try.'

'Do you?' he said.

'Don't I?' Sybil's nostrils flared. 'That boy is part of our family. So is Amelia, for that matter. I can't give up on them just because Lachie can. And I won't.'

Kate swallowed, wishing she could do something to break the tension between Sybil and Ben, knowing that the only solution was for this script to play out.

'I know it may seem insane to you, Ben,' Sybil said, 'but I'm being selfish. And I want to be selfish. I want to see this boy. I *need* to see this boy. Joe is dead, Lachlan is gone, and I—' She took a breath. 'I feel like I don't have a lot of family left. I have to do what I can. For me. And for you, too.'

'I'm doing all right,' Ben muttered.

'Are you?' Sybil said. 'You look happy enough, but are you really all right?'

Ben leant back and lifted his chin. Trying to shut out his mother, Kate thought, but it wouldn't work.

'Anyway,' Sybil said, 'the reason I wanted to talk to you is not so you can try to talk me out of going. I'm going.' She nodded once, firmly. 'It's because we need to discuss the options.'

'Options?' Ben said.

Kate was surprisd to see Sybil focusing her attention on her. 'What if we could bring them both here? What if Amelia needs help, and that's why she's been moving around so much?'

'Who says she even wants to be here?' Ben said, sounding tired.

'No one. But it's a possibility. Kate, I would really like to know what you think. There would be two other people in the house.'

Kate paused to think, feeling stuck: Sybil had a point but her role, she thought, was to support her husband.

'It's not my house,' she said finally, the only response she could think of that was vaguely neutral.

'It *is* your house,' said Sybil. 'Now, and in the future. We're all sharing it. Your opinion matters as much as mine.'

Kate thought again. 'I would be happy to welcome them here,' she said, 'as long as Ben is.' She turned to look at her husband, and he turned to her.

'I would be,' he said slowly. 'And I think we need to consider something else: what if she doesn't want to keep the child?'

'Why would that even be a consideration, Ben?' Sybil said with a degree of passion.

'How do we know she wanted him in the first place? Or that she still wants him? She's young. She's on her own. It would be hard.'

Sybil's face looked pinched. She interlocked her fingers and pulled them against each other, her shoulders tensing.

'I just can't imagine any woman giving up her child,' she said softly.

Ben reached across to put his hand over hers. 'Some women don't have a choice, Mum,' he said gently.

Kate sympathised with Sybil's reaction but she also knew that she had no understanding of what Amelia's life was like. Ben was right: they had to consider everything.

'I would be happy for the boy to come here,' Kate said. 'I would be happy to take care of him.' She glanced from Sybil to Ben. 'I think it would be an honour.'

Sybil gave her a grateful half-smile as Ben sat back in the couch.

'So we know what we're prepared to do,' he said. 'Let's talk about the logistics.'

Sybil smiled at him, too, and Kate saw a look of understanding pass between them. They had come this far; now they would find out where Sybil's quest would take them next.

CHAPTER FIFTY-ONE

Sitting in the room she knew so well, in which she had spent all of her younger years, reading, dreaming, talking to her parents, being teased by Geoffrey, Sybil felt none of the safety or reassurance that she would have expected. She had hoped that being in a familiar environment might help her to stay calm; instead she couldn't stop fidgeting and she felt as if something the size of an apple was wedged into her chest, right on her sternum.

She had become used to managing things on her own, without Joe, although in her mind she would often ask him for advice. For guidance. Today was not the first time she had wished he was with her – that she had reached for his hand, or turned hoping to see him smile – but it was the first time she felt that he wasn't with her somehow. She was on her own.

Geoffrey was being no help, calmly smiling at her whenever he passed. And now that there was a knock at the door, he smiled again as he walked towards the front of the house.

Sybil stood, her stomach feeling twisted, her hands nervously stroking the sides of the sensible skirt she had decided to wear. She'd bought it nearby yesterday after her long journey south, the wet season almost stopping her getting here. Almost preventing her from meeting her grandson.

She heard the door open, murmured voices, and then footsteps.

'Sybil,' Geoffrey's stentorian voice declared, 'I believe you remember Amelia from Ghost River Station.'

Amelia walked into the room holding a little boy, and Sybil wanted to look at her first, but her eyes flew to the child. He was her Lachie, but he was not. He looked almost exactly like the boy she had kept safe, loved, fed, sent off to school, yet he wasn't that boy. Of course he wasn't, even if her heart was beating as if he was.

'Hello, Amelia,' Sybil said, tearing her eyes away from the boy.

'Hello, Sybil,' Amelia said flatly. Sybil could see how tired this young woman was. She was pale, and her long, mouse-brown hair was pulled back in a ponytail, looking like it hadn't been brushed in days. Sybil remembered when she'd seen Amelia at Ghost River: she had seemed healthy, vital. Lachie had done this to her: he had worn her out, simply by vanishing.

'This is Archie,' Amelia said, bending down to put him on the floor. 'Archie, this is your grandma.'

Sybil's mouth opened with the shock of hearing that word. She had thought it to herself but she hadn't expected Amelia to use it, or to think of her that way.

'Hello, Archie,' Sybil said, getting down onto her knees.

'Say hello, Archie,' Amelia urged. She smiled weakly at Sybil. 'He's a bit shy with new people.'

'That's perfectly reasonable,' Sybil said. 'Thank you so much for coming. Please – take a seat. Would you like tea? Water?'

Amelia shook her head. 'I'm fine.'

She sat and Archie sat by her feet. Sybil picked up the set of building blocks that she'd bought for him and pushed them along the floor.

'I thought he might like something to play with,' she said to Amelia, seeking her approval. Amelia nodded once.

Geoffrey also sat and crossed one leg over the other, folding his arms across his chest. He'd told Sybil that he wouldn't speak unless necessary – he was just a facilitator, not an actor in this scenario.

'I'm sorry that Lachlan left you to manage all of this,' Sybil said and Amelia's face hardened. 'You haven't heard anything from him?'

'Not lately.' Amelia glanced down at her son. 'He didn't even wait for Archie to be born. He just took off.'

Sybil watched as Archie played with the simple toy.

'I'm sorry,' she said. 'I wish I'd known. I could have helped.'

Amelia shrugged. 'You can help me now,' she said, glancing at Sybil then looking away. Geoffrey had told Sybil to prepare for this – Amelia was likely to ask her for money. She would give it, she had no qualms about that. She would put no conditions on it, either; she'd merely express the wish to see Archie sometimes.

'Yes, I can,' Sybil said. 'What do you need?'

Something in Amelia seemed to sag then – almost as if she had been waiting for a battle and now, with the battle not eventuating, she realised how heavy her weapons were.

'I can't look after him,' Amelia said, her voice firm despite her demeanour.

'What do you mean?'

'I'm just . . .' Amelia's face showed resignation, steel and sadness. 'I'm not cut out to be a mum. I didn't want this. But I didn't have a choice, right?'

She looked at her son, who kept playing, his awareness only of the toy in his hands.

'No one wants to take us in.'

'You can live with us,' Sybil said, glad she had discussed this with Ben and Kate. She would happily take Amelia and Archie home with her, right away.

Amelia laughed, caustically.

'I don't want to go anywhere near the bloody Northern Territory,' she said, her face hard. 'My life was ruined there. By your son.'

She exhaled sharply and glanced away.

'My family don't want us because they're worried about what people will think or something. I can't support us, though, if I don't get work. And if I don't have someone to watch him, I can't work.' She looked at Sybil with weariness in her eyes. 'I've tried. For two years. It's not working. He'd be better off somewhere else.'

Sybil thought about the home she had created, how it was filled with love even though Joe was gone. She thought of the horses, the dogs, the open spaces that a boy could enjoy as her own boys had once done, before their differences revealed themselves.

'Can he come to Fairvale?' Sybil said. 'Can we . . . have him?'

Amelia stared at her.

'You could visit whenever you want, of course,' Sybil added hurriedly. 'He's your son.'

Amelia's face became pinched.

There were key moments in every life when decisions had to be made in a second even though they had the potential to irrevocably alter everything that came after them. Sybil had experienced them before. She remembered how they felt: how the world became quiet and narrow. How each breath seemed momentous. Time changed form and sometimes it never changed back. She was sure, if she searched the crevices of her memory, she had anticipated that this moment would arise, now. She could only hope that Ben meant what he had said when they spoke before she left.

'My son,' she said, 'my other son, Ben, and his wife – they want a child. They haven't . . . had any luck. I know they would look after Archie as if he was their own. You wouldn't have to give him up completely. Although, of course, it's an option.'

Sybil glanced at Geoffrey, whose face was impassive, then back at Amelia.

Time was slowing down, Sybil could feel it. And then—

'Yes,' Amelia said. 'That makes sense. And I think I do want to give him up. For good. I want to do things, you know? Things you can't do with a kid.'

'I do,' Sybil said, because her own life had changed when Lachie then Ben had arrived. She had been prepared for it, and still it had been a shock.

'We'll take good care of him,' she said, and Amelia nodded, then looked out the window. Her face was less pinched now. Sybil wondered how long she had wished she didn't have to be a mother anymore.

'Thank you,' Sybil said. 'It's inadequate, but . . . thank you.'

Amelia looked at her again. '*You're* doing *me* a favour,' she said. 'I thought I was going to have to give him to the government.'

She bent down and picked up her son, then stood and walked over to Sybil, holding him out.

'Archie, go to Grandma,' she said.

Archie squirmed as Sybil opened her arms. But as she put him on her lap, he stopped, and rested his head against her chest.

Sybil felt everything become still. The world was narrowing further, tighter, around her. Then she felt it expand. Colours, sounds, all growing larger, brighter. Even as it happened, she knew she had to say goodbye to Lachie, in her heart, where her hopes lived, forever.

'Are you sure?' she said haltingly, barely able to believe the gift Amelia was bestowing on her so willingly. The gift of a child she hadn't even dared to think she might hold one day.

Amelia put a hand on Archie's head and stroked it slowly while Sybil held her breath, terrified that Amelia would change her mind.

'I am,' Amelia said faintly. Then she smiled, and Sybil saw the girl she had first met five years ago when she was the new young cook at Ghost River. 'I love him – will you tell him that I love him?'

Sybil felt tears become stuck in her throat and she gasped, trying to let them loose. 'Yes,' she said. 'Of course.'

Amelia let her hand drop. 'Tell him that I loved him so much I realised I couldn't look after him properly.'

Her eyes met Sybil's and Sybil saw no trace of sadness. Instead there was something that looked remarkably like freedom.

'I know you'll take good care of him,' Amelia said, her voice strong. 'That you'll love him. Maybe one day, when he's grown up, if he wants to find me . . .' She smiled. 'Anyway, I'll send you a letter every now and then. Maybe . . .' Her smile faltered. 'Maybe you could write me back.'

'Of course,' Sybil said quickly. 'We can never repay you.' She held Archie tightly against her, feeling him squirm, still marvelling that Amelia would let her take him back home, to Fairvale.

'I don't want you to,' Amelia said. 'Archie will be happy.' She sighed lightly. 'And so will I.'

Sybil felt the tears again, pushing against her throat. This time she gave them permission to rise; she let them fall down her cheeks, sliding towards her collarbone. All her loss, and all her love, released.

'What happens now?' Amelia said, looking to Geoffrey.

As Geoffrey took over, all Sybil could see was the boy in her arms, and all she could feel was the cracking open of her heart, to let Archie in.

CHAPTER FIFTY-TWO

Kate heard the truck's whiny engine and looked at Ben. Together they stood up from the couch in the sitting room, where they'd been waiting for half an hour, barely speaking. As they both headed for the front door Ben stood back so Kate could go first. Kate rubbed her fingertips over her palms and swallowed. She couldn't remember ever feeling as nervous as this.

As the truck's engine went quiet Ben took hold of her arm and kissed her on the cheek.

'Ready?' he said and she nodded, pulling open the door.

She saw Sybil holding a little boy whose head was resting on her shoulder. The boy had dark brown hair in loose curls, long-lashed brown eyes and a strong nose. She saw Ben in this child, although Sybil had seen only Lachie, or so she had said.

'Damn,' Ben breathed.

'What is it?'

'He looks like Lachie, all right,' Ben said.

Kate smiled back at him, realising he was just as nervous as she was. 'I think he looks like you.'

His eyes were shining as they met hers. He held out his hand and she took it, using him to steady herself as they walked down the steps to meet Sybil.

'Hello, darling,' Sybil said, kissing Ben on the cheek. 'Hello to you too, darling.' She kissed Kate, who was sure that Sybil was looking at her differently. She'd never called her 'darling' before, either.

'This,' Sybil said, jiggling the boy up and down, eliciting giggles, 'is Archie.'

Kate heard Sybil talking as if she was in a dream. Or maybe she had dreamt it. She'd been dreaming so much the past few nights, ever since Sybil said she was coming home. She'd had dreams of children she'd never seen before and Ben with grey in his hair, his eyes dancing, as he twirled her around a parquet floor. She'd had dreams of Sybil, older, more wrinkled, sitting on the verandah and telling her stories. And of her own parents sitting with them, talking about how far away Fairvale was from anything. She'd never had conscious thoughts about any of these things; it was only at night that they occurred to her, and they were so vivid that she remembered them all.

'G'day, Archie,' Ben said, tickling the child under his chin. Archie wriggled and turned his head away; Ben looked at Kate with apology. Normally small children loved Ben: Joe had sometimes called him the Pied Piper for the way the Fairvale camp children followed him around.

Kate wasn't sure what she was meant to do now: she had no idea if rules existed for the first time you met your child. Should she ask if she could take him from Sybil? Was Sybil meant to suggest it?

Then Archie turned his head and grinned at her. An impish grin that looked just like Ben's when he was trying to make her laugh, or about to say something rude.

Something happened to her right then. Something she couldn't have prepared for. Her heart felt as though it was being squeezed, wrung out like a sponge. It was such a strong sensation that she put one hand on her chest and tried to gulp for a breath, even though she was breathing normally.

There it was again: a pain, but not. A sensation of the contents of her chest rearranging themselves. Archie grinned and her heart responded.

She opened her mouth to say something to Ben. Or maybe to Sybil, who knew more about how bodies worked. But what would she say: *My heart feels like it's changing shape?*

Sybil bounced the boy up and down again, and Archie giggled. Now Kate felt tears spring into her eyes and she wanted to turn away. She didn't know what was happening to her but it was becoming too hard to hide.

'Kate?' Sybil said softly and Kate felt a gentle hand on her arm.

She turned to look at Sybil, feeling a thousand emotions and not able to articulate any of them.

'Ben, why don't you take your son?' Sybil said. Ben opened his arms and Archie's eyes lit up. He went willingly to Ben, who swung him onto his shoulders and held onto him tightly. Archie giggled and dug one hand into Ben's hair.

'Ow!' Ben said, making a face at Kate, who started to laugh. This was such an improbable day. A week ago Archie didn't exist – not really. Now he was sitting on Ben's shoulders, and the two of them were approaching the front door as Kate stood still, watching.

'You coming, Katie?' Ben called. He reached the top of the stairs and looked down at her. Archie looked down at her too. And there it was again, that exquisite pain in her heart.

'What's wrong with me?' she whispered hoarsely to Sybil.

Sybil's smile was kind and knowing.

'Oh, darling,' she said, placing a hand on Kate's cheek. 'You've fallen in love.'

Kate didn't understand at first.

'*With Archie*,' Sybil said and kissed her quickly on the other cheek. 'You're done for now, my girl. Welcome to motherhood.'

Sybil winked at her.

'But I—' Kate shook her head. 'I didn't know it felt like this.'

Sybil smiled wryly. 'Oh, it does. And it will feel better and worse than this.'

Kate didn't know how things worked. If God was real. If prayers had any effect. If no longer wishing for something meant that it was more likely to happen. She had stopped wishing – had looked away from the life she wanted – and here it was.

If all the pain Lachie had caused Ben and Sybil, and Joe, could amount to this – one boy they could all love – Kate thought it just might have been worth it. She would spend each day of the rest of her life being thankful, even if her thanks were shouted into the dark, the unknown, the mystery of this great big world that had never seemed more bright and alive than it did now.

As Kate stepped into the house, Ben turned around.

'Here's your new mummy,' he said to Archie, whose eyes were darting around the room.

'It may take him a while to get used to a different mummy,' Kate whispered. She had prepared herself for that, but not for how much she didn't want it to be true.

'Yeah, it may.' Ben stepped towards her and put Archie in her arms. 'Or it may not.'

He grinned and kissed her, and as Kate held her new son, and felt her husband's soft lips on hers, she knew that it all wasn't really a dream. No dream could ever feel as full and big and joyous as her real life felt at that exact moment.

1981

24 February   The announcement of the engagement of Charles, Prince of Wales to Lady Diana Spencer

30 March   US President Ronald Reagan is shot by John Hinckley, Jr in an attempted assassination

11 April   There is a three-day race riot between protestors and police in Brixton, South London

12 April   The first space shuttle, *Columbia*, launches

11 May   Reggae legend Bob Marley dies

21 May   François Mitterrand becomes President of France

13 June   Blanks are fired at Queen Elizabeth II during the Trooping the Colour ceremony in London

7 July   Sandra Day O'Connor, the first woman to serve on the US Supreme Court, is nominated to her role by President Ronald Reagan

29 July   Charles, Prince of Wales marries Lady Diana Spencer and more than 700 million people around the world watch on television

CHAPTER FIFTY-THREE

A new morning in the kitchen and the same old routine greeted Sallyanne. She had practically trilled her hellos to Kate and was now merrily pounding into the dough.

'I've never known anyone so happy to make bread,' Kate said, and Sallyanne noticed again how the younger woman's accent had changed. It was clear that Kate's vowels were flattening and she was learning how to barely move her mouth when she spoke, just like a real Australian.

'How's Archie?' Sallyanne said. She had purposely not visited the big house too much while Archie settled in. He had enough new people to get used to, even if she loved the idea that Kate and Ben had a child and couldn't wait for the day that Archie could run around with her own children. They'd have their own little Fairvale pack.

Kate lifted her head, smiling from ear to ear.

'He's wonderful,' she said. 'And with Sybil. She's going to take him while I'm here, then I'll keep an eye on him when I'm working in the office. Although he may end up with Ruby from time to time. So much for her retirement!' Her laughter filled the kitchen.

'Ruby is so good with Gretel. I'm lucky she can take her,' Sallyanne said.

'I think Gretel's got her well organised.' Kate winked. 'So how did your trip into town go? Did you see your father?'

The day before, Sallyanne had asked if she could run into town. Her father had asked to see her and she was worried that he was sick – he'd never seemed so interested in having a visit from her. Sybil had offered to drive her in, saying she needed to pick up a few things and drop in on a friend. So Sybil knew what had happened, and clearly she was a good keeper of secrets because Kate did not.

'I did,' Sallyanne said, keeping her voice light. What had happened was so momentous that she didn't want to sound dramatic when she told it. She liked drama in her novels but not in her life. Which was funny, considering what had happened to her marriage.

Kate stopped peeling potatoes.

'Is that all you're going to give me?' she said. 'You've been to town and you have no news for me?'

Sallyanne tried to laugh and instead she coughed. She wasn't good at subterfuge; she never had been. Her mother had always known when she was lying.

'He offered me money,' she blurted.

Kate frowned. 'What?'

'Dad had a pub. A while ago.' Sallyanne tried laughing again, suddenly self-conscious about her new circumstances. Another cough ensued.

'When he sold the pub he just kept the money. It's been in the bank the whole time. In a term deposit.' She remembered her father telling her the figure. She had almost stopped breathing. 'Anyway, he wanted me to have it.'

'What did he say?' Kate was wide-eyed. 'Exactly?'

'He, um . . .' She briefly closed her eyes and saw her father's face. He was a serious man and he'd grown more serious since her mother died, but this time his expression had been different: it had care and concern but it lacked the gravity he so often displayed. Opening her eyes again, she saw that Kate was waiting for her to answer.

'He said he thought I should have it,' she continued, 'to do what I want in life.' Her voice caught. 'He said I've never really been able to do that. It's enough . . .' She paused. 'It's enough, really, to do whatever I want to do.'

Kate placed the paring knife onto the bench.

'So what do you want to do?' she said kindly.

On the drive back to Fairvale, after she and Sybil had stopped laughing with incredulity at what had transpired, Sallyanne had thought about taking a long holiday overseas or sending the boys away to a boarding school, as everyone who could afford it did. She wondered if she should move to Darwin, or perhaps even further away. But her thoughts kept returning to one truth: she wanted to stay on Fairvale. She wanted the community she'd found there. She wanted to work. And she wanted her children with her.

'I want to stay here,' she said to Kate, stuffing dough into bread tins. 'And now I can afford to divorce Mick.'

'Oh,' Kate said, her eyes growing wider still. 'I didn't realise it was money stopping you doing that.'

'That was part of it. I couldn't afford a place on my own. I couldn't even afford a solicitor. Mick was the only one earning money. That's why—' She stopped, the emotions of the last few months – the ones she had been trying not to feel because she didn't want to get upset around the children – catching up to her.

'That's why it was so kind of you and Sybil to invite me to come here,' Sallyanne finished. 'It helped me so much.'

'Nonsense,' Kate said. '*You're* helping *us*.' She pointed to the bread. 'Look at what I don't have to do now that you're here.'

Sallyanne bit down on her bottom lip as she remembered how relieved she'd felt when they'd first come here.

'So Mick gets the flick,' said Kate, and Sallyanne gasped.

'I guess so,' she said. Kate made it sound so easy. She wished it could be, but she'd have to talk to him face to face at some stage. She had already decided that if he wouldn't leave Ghost River, she would go to him.

'He hasn't visited us once,' she said, feeling sad about it for her children, if not for herself.

'I've noticed,' Kate said, raising her eyebrows. 'Hardly winning a blue ribbon for fatherhood, is he?'

'No.' But Sallyanne remembered the young man she'd married and the hopes she'd had for their future, so deeply embedded inside her. It had taken her a long time to let go of those, and even now she would find them popping back into her head, or she'd have to pull a little root out of her heart and throw it away. They had been married for a long time. It wasn't so easy to say goodbye to him.

'I don't know anyone else who's divorced, though,' Sallyanne continued. 'People in town might have something to say about it.'

'But you don't live in town anymore, do you?' said Kate. 'You live here now. And we won't have anything to say about it. Well, nothing bad.'

'Do you think Sybil will help me find a solicitor?'

'Of course she will. Now, let's stop talking about Mick,' Kate said briskly. 'Let's talk about something else. There's a new American president, isn't there? That actor fellow, Reagan?'

Sallyanne wiped her hands on her apron and looked around for her next task as Kate chatted on, grateful for the change of subject but already thinking ahead to the next steps of her life: talking to Sybil about a lawyer, meeting the lawyer, then a divorce. And beyond that: a life that would be entirely hers to make.

CHAPTER FIFTY-FOUR

The wet season was starting to make everyone grumpy. The cattle were roaming free, the younger stockmen had been sent home for the season and those remaining either had too much time on their hands or they were spending it repairing saddles and equipment.

Della had been surprised when Ben had kept Mark on after the rain started. But Kate had explained to her that Mark's brother – Ben's friend – had said that he thought it would be good for the young man to experience both wet and dry in the Territory, so that he didn't complain so much about the odd thunderstorm at home. There had been something about Kate's expression that told Della there might have been another truth at work, but she hadn't pressed.

So the situation was good for Mark, maybe, but not good for her, or for Stan. After their initial run-in with him, Mark had been behaving himself, but Della found that she was constantly bracing herself for him to say something to Stan. And she knew that Stan was coiled, waiting for an opportunity to strike. He hadn't found one yet because Mark kept his racism confined to certain looks in Stan's direction, and that sneer. But no words. Never anything that Ben might observe or hear.

Della had never seen Stan like this before – because there had never been anyone on Fairvale to provoke him. She supposed it should have made her careful around him – worried, maybe, that he had anger in him when she'd always found him to be so calm – but instead she respected him for it. And it had made her love him more. Not that she'd had the chance to tell him. His 'time to think' had lasted for months now. She had thought it would get easier to be around him each day and not be able to smile at him the way she used to, the way she wanted to, but it was only getting harder. Which was why she had resolved to talk to him, regardless of how much more time to think he might want.

She went to seek him out just before dinner, when he'd be in the stables having a smoke. It had been his ritual always, and everyone else on Fairvale respected it, leaving him alone.

'Hey,' she said as she found him, his long torso draped over the edge of a stall, cigarette in one hand, whickering to the horse. She let herself enjoy the sight of him in a way she hadn't been able to do when they were at work.

He pulled back and turned to look at her. In his eyes she saw the way he had felt about her, before – then a hood came down and she could see only gloom.

'Hello, Della girl.'

At least he still called her that.

'It's been a long time since we talked,' she said, shoving her thumbs into her jeans pockets and rocking back on her heels.

'I reckon,' he said, taking a drag of his cigarette. 'But I've been thinking about you.'

'So why haven't you come to see me?' she said quickly. The question had been bottled up inside her for so long.

Stan pursed his lips. 'That fella's still here.' His eyes flickered away from hers.

'*Mark* is the reason?'

His eyes met hers briefly. 'Yeah,' he said. She had suspected that but she hadn't suspected how disappointed she would feel that he'd let a man they barely knew come between them.

'But he's a nobody,' she said. 'He's not even staying here. Once the wet ends he's—'

'He can hurt me,' Stan said, pain flooding his face. 'He can hurt you. Us.'

'He's already hurting us because you don't want to be with me!' She was almost shouting but she didn't care if anyone heard.

Stan flicked his cigarette onto the cement and trod on it. He stepped towards her and Della felt the long-ago thrill of him being near her, the anticipation that he might take her in his arms, that they would be together.

'I do want to be with you,' he said, his voice low and fire in his eyes. 'But it's not going to work.'

'I love you, dammit!' she said. She almost stomped her foot. 'How can that not work?'

He took her arms then and she relaxed in his grasp, even though he looked more fierce than she had ever seen him. 'Because there's too much that can go wrong, Della,' he said. 'What's going to happen to us if we leave here? If people make trouble for us?'

'Don't you love me too?' she said, wishing she didn't sound so desperate. But that's what she was, and she had already decided not to be embarrassed by how much she wanted him.

He brought his face close to hers and she could hear him breathing hard. 'You know I do,' he said.

'I don't understand, then,' she whispered. 'Won't that be enough?'

She stared into his eyes until he pulled her into his chest. She relished the heat of him, after so long without it. She wanted to put her hands on his skin, but this wasn't the place.

'It's not enough, Della,' he whispered, and she pushed back from him as if he'd told her that, in truth, he hated her.

'You can't say that!' she cried. 'You can't tell me it's not enough!' She wasn't a dreamer – the conviction that their love for each other could be strong enough to get past what Stan was worried about came from deep inside her. It was a belief she had formed by his side. Because of him. If he felt as strongly about her as she did about him, there was nothing they couldn't do together. Love had made her braver than she had ever been. She refused to believe that it couldn't make him brave too.

'It's not about you, Della!' he said, his voice raised for the first time since she'd met him. 'I'm the one who has to cop it. If someone sees us together – if someone doesn't like it – it's *me* who ends up with a boot to my head. Not you.' He gave a cry like a felled animal. 'Not you.'

His chest was heaving and she saw – she understood acutely – how naïve she had been. He had been protecting her from his reality while they were cocooned here in the bush. But now it had intruded and he couldn't change it. Nor could she. And by insisting that she could, that they could, that he should, she was making it worse.

The question over their future, she knew now with the same clarity that had brought her to Australia in the first place, was whether or not she loved him enough to leave him, no matter what it cost her.

'I understand,' she said quietly.

She put a hand on his cheek and kissed him softly on the lips.

'If things change,' she said, 'know that I will still love you. Come find me.'

He took her elbows and put his forehead against hers. 'I don't want to do this. But I . . .' His chest heaved again.

'You're not doing this,' she said, stepping back, summoning all the courage she had acquired since she left home. 'I am.'

She left him standing in the stables, his hands by his sides, his shoulders slumped, as she turned and walked as briskly as she could towards the big house. She wasn't going to her quarters. She was going to see Kate. And Sybil. And maybe she'd even rouse Sallyanne and see if she would sit for a while.

As the life she had wished for herself dissolved behind her, Della decided not to make any wishes – not for the time being. Life would come for her, and she would step up to meet it, and that was the only thing she knew for sure.

CHAPTER FIFTY-FIVE

The noise in the sitting room had passed the point of dull roar and reached the level of actual din. Ever since Archie had arrived Ben had taken to doing everything at top volume and Sybil's peaceful house had become a sideshow.

'Kate!' she called, but there was no response.

'*Kate!*'

She heard heavy footsteps in the hallway and Kate appeared in the doorway, flustered but radiant. She had never looked more beautiful than she had over the past few weeks.

'What is my son doing to your son to make all that noise?' Sybil said, working to open a stubborn cake tin. Although Archie was not officially Kate and Ben's child yet, Geoffrey had begun the processes and Amelia had firmly indicated that she wasn't going to change her mind. So Sybil had started calling Kate and Ben 'Mummy' and 'Daddy' in front of Archie, and he had been using those names, much to Sybil's delight.

'He's, uh . . .' Kate smiled. 'He's tickling him.'

'Does Ben not have any work to do?' The cake tin lid wouldn't budge so she held it out to Kate. She was the one who'd made the cake, after all, so she might have better luck with the tin.

'He wants to join us for the book club, he says.' Kate prised open the tin and handed it back to Sybil, who put her nose to the contents.

'That smells delicious. What does he mean, he wants to join us? The book club is not for him. And I've lined up Ruby to take care of Archie, so he can't use that as an excuse.'

'He said he's curious about what goes on.'

Sybil arched an eyebrow. 'Then he'll just have to remain curious. Ben!'

She took off towards the sitting room, arriving in time to see a mound of cushions, Archie nowhere to be seen and her son looking like the Cheshire cat.

'You'll suffocate that child if he's under those cushions,' Sybil said crossly. Ben was nothing if not an enthusiastic parent but she did worry that he tended to forget that Archie was child-sized and not built for roughhousing with an adult.

'He's tough,' Ben said to a background of giggles emanating from beneath the mound. 'Aren't you, mate?'

'You can't stay when the others arrive,' Sybil said.

'Why not?' Ben pulled Archie out and held on to him as he stood up. Sybil smiled at her grandson, whose curls had not long ago been clipped short even as everything else seemed to grow daily.

'Because you'll ruin it.'

Ben looked taken aback.

'Ruin it?'

'Make fun of it,' Sybil said impatiently.

'No, I won't. I just want to sit and have a chat.' He tickled Archie's belly. 'We both do, don't we, mate?'

'Then you can stay for a few minutes but after that Ruby will come to take Archie so Kate can switch off for a while.'

Ben made a conciliatory noise and put Archie on the

floor. 'Go and find Mum, Arch,' he said, gesturing towards the kitchen. 'Do you share secrets or something?' he asked, a glint in his eye.

'No. We talk about books but they're not the sorts of books that would interest you, and I don't want you voicing your opinions. Now, I have to get back to the preparations.' Sybil pivoted on her heel and was only stopped by Ben's hand on her arm.

'Thank you,' he said quietly and Sybil turned back.

'For what?'

He looked serious, so she knew he wasn't about to gee her up again.

'For . . . this.' He gestured to the room. 'Doing everything. That book club – it's been so good for Kate. When you started it she really looked forward to it. It made her feel . . . less alone, I guess. And now Della and Sallyanne are living here – she has friends, Mum. And Archie.' His voice caught and Sybil wanted to scoop him into her arms as she had when he was small. He would always be her son; she would always want to make things better for him.

'What you've done for us,' he said, then he dropped his head and Sybil couldn't read his face.

'What you've done for *me*,' she said, hugging him.

'We're managing okay, aren't we?' Ben murmured.

'More than okay,' Sybil said, kissing the side of his head. 'Your father would approve.'

Ben's laugh was short. 'I reckon he would.'

'Sybil?' It was Della's voice.

'Come in, Della. Was Kate in the kitchen?'

'She's getting Archie changed into some outside clothes. Hi, Ben.'

'Del,' he said. Sybil caught the look he gave her: concern mixed with caution. He knew full well that Stan and Della were no longer in a relationship – he had been the one to tell Sybil – but he hadn't said a word to Della about it, and Sybil could see that he was going against his better, caring instincts. She'd advised him to say nothing, though, reasoning that Della would talk about it if and when she wanted to.

Della held up her copy of the book they would discuss.

'I've learnt how to be a woman of substance,' she said, grinning in a slightly forced way.

Ben turned to Sybil with a small look of horror. 'Are you on that self-improvement craze or something?'

'No, Benjamin. It's a novel. *A Woman of Substance* by Barbara Taylor Bradford. It's a sweeping saga of a woman setting up a business and going on to glory, despite challenges and dangers and whatever else you can imagine.'

He smiled at her, his eyes so dark and with so much love in them. 'So it's almost a book about you, is it, Mum?'

Sybil considered what he had said. Certainly, she'd had challenges in her life. But the business had not been set up by her and by no means did she feel she was living in glory. Not yet.

'We'll see,' she said. 'I hear a car.'

Through the window she saw Stan pull up outside with Rita in the passenger seat.

'If you're going to stay for a while,' she said to Ben, 'you might as well make the tea. And would you mind letting Sallyanne know that we're about ready to start?'

'Rightio, Mum,' he said, grinning.

Della took her usual spot on the couch as Sybil moved to open the front door just as Kate arrived, her face alight.

'Welcome,' she said as Rita reached the front door, 'to the seventh meeting of the Fairvale Ladies Book Club.'

'Syb,' Rita said, hugging Sybil before kissing her on the cheek. They shared a look – only Sybil knew that Rita had news to announce and that it would upset Sallyanne, in particular.

'It's good to see you,' Sybil said softly.

Sallyanne bustled into the room and flung her arms around Rita. 'I've missed you!' she said.

'I've missed you too, Sal,' Rita said, catching Sybil's eye over Sallyanne's shoulder.

Cups of tea were poured and Rita asked about Archie. Sybil had told her about Della and Stan, knowing that Rita had discretion enough not to raise the subject unless invited. Della looked smaller than usual, though, almost curling into the corner of the couch while Kate spoke. She hadn't seen Della cry once or say a bad word about Stan, but she couldn't believe she was unaffected. Stan was certainly looking miserable, not that she was going to raise the issue with him either.

'Now, I have something to tell you all,' said Rita.

'Yes?' Sallyanne looked excited. Sybil was sure Sallyanne believed that Rita was going to say she was marrying Hamish and she felt a pang of guilt for knowing the truth and keeping it from her.

'I've been thinking about moving back to Sydney,' Rita said, her smile faltering as Sallyanne's face fell. 'And I've been looking for work accordingly.' She grimaced. 'Turns out that your late forties is not a great time for a woman to find a new job.'

'But – why?' said Sallyanne, the corners of her mouth turning down.

'Oh, Sal.' Rita lightly pinched her cheek. 'I can't stay in Alice Springs. Not after what happened.' Now it was Rita's turn to look sad. 'I can't go back to that job. And I can't ask Hamish to keep supporting me financially.'

'Why not?' said Sallyanne.

'I want to go home,' Rita said. 'And that's a decision I've had to make for myself.'

'But what . . . what does Hamish think?'

'He's not happy. But he understands. Anyway, I've finally been offered a job. I start in six weeks' time. It's a government job so nothing moves quickly.'

'You're not going to be a nurse?' Kate said.

Rita shook her head. 'I'll be in administration. I think I'll like it.' She grinned quickly. 'For a while.'

For Sybil, hearing it said aloud to Sallyanne made it imminent and, for the first time, real. She had taken her relative proximity to Rita for granted and now she would have to live without it.

Sybil took a deep breath. 'So we'll have one more book club meeting after this. With all of us here, that is. After that . . .' She looked around at four sad faces. 'We'll see.'

'I didn't realise the book would be so appropriate,' Sallyanne said mournfully.

'What do you mean, Sal?' Rita said, summoning a laugh.

'You're going off to pursue your work.' Sallyanne clasped her hands in her lap. 'Just like Emma in the book.'

'I think we're all pursuing work in our own way, aren't we?' said Rita. 'I just have to move far away for mine.'

'I don't want you to go,' said Sallyanne.

'Oh, Sal.' Rita sighed.

Sybil decided to get the meeting back on track before they all became maudlin.

'You'll see her again before she goes,' Sybil said. 'Come on, let's talk about whether or not we actually finished this great big book.'

Rita's eyes met hers and Sybil hoped that Rita could see what she was feeling: she didn't want her to go either. Not that she would try to stop her; instead she would send her off with love, and miss her always. Her friend had made her decision, and she'd had a choice, and that was a freedom Sybil never underestimated.

CHAPTER FIFTY-SIX

For the past two weeks Rita had been staying with Hamish. She'd let her rental house go; because she wasn't working, and therefore had no income, she didn't think it was fair that he kept paying her rent. When he'd offered her the money initially she'd thought it wouldn't be for long. She had expected that with her qualifications she'd have no trouble finding a job in Sydney. She couldn't find anything in a hospital, though, even when she had contacted old colleagues; everyone was younger than her, with years of hard work ahead of them. She had never thought of herself as old until now.

The government job had been the last thing she wanted but, as it turned out, the first thing she needed. The hours were far more civilised and Rita was looking forward to not being around sick and dying people. Ever since she had been sick and almost dying herself, she didn't want to be around it any more.

Since the accident she had spent her time either applying for jobs, calling Sydney or sleeping. She had told herself that the years of shift work were catching up with her but she knew the truth: she didn't want to be awake most of the time. She had flashes of memory: of the girl on the gurney, of Kevin in the cockpit. She remembered the pain; she didn't feel it in her body but she remembered her response to it. She remembered that at times it was powerful enough to make her want to go to sleep and never wake up again.

'I took the last of your boxes to the post office,' Hamish said as he came back from his outing. When he was rostered off he'd been helping Rita pack up her things, which hadn't amounted to much in the end. The house had come furnished and all that was left were her clothes and books and a few photo frames.

'Thank you,' she said, moving around the kitchen to prepare lunch for him. It was the least she could do given his generosity to her.

They had been gentle with each other, these past few weeks. Rita couldn't escape the knowledge that she was doing something hurtful to him but it would have been more hurtful to her to stay. He seemed to have accepted that, telling her he would visit her in Sydney as soon as he could.

'Are you still planning to go to Brisbane?' she said. He'd talked about visiting his children; his earlier plans had been put aside after her accident. She thought it was proper that he would see them before coming to visit her, although she was surprised that she still felt slightly jealous about that.

'Yes,' he said. His smile was as endearing as ever, even if these days the expression in his eyes seldom matched it. She was the cause of that, but she still wasn't going to change her plans. She had become ruthless in her need to take care of herself.

'I'm going to head up just after you leave,' he said, moving behind her and putting his hand on her waist as he kissed her behind the ear. She shuddered at the pleasure of it, wishing she could preserve the sensation to keep her company once she was back in Sydney.

'Then,' he said, taking up a spot next to her so she could see his face, 'I thought I'd move to Sydney too.'

Rita stopped peeling the boiled egg that was in her hand. 'What did you say?' She put the egg down.

His eyes were more alive than she had seen them for weeks.

'I didn't want to say anything until I heard officially,' he said. 'I've been offered a job in Casualty at Royal North Shore Hospital.'

Rita could never remember being at a loss for words. She always had something to say or to add or to slip into a conversation. In this moment, however, she had nothing.

He laughed. It was such a light sound – she hadn't heard that in ages either.

'I've stumped you,' he said.

'You have,' Rita managed.

'Do you mind?' he said.

They had talked about the possibility of him moving to Sydney but he had maintained that Brisbane would always be his first preference, because of his children. So Rita hadn't let herself believe that he might join her, for all his assertions that he loved her and wanted to be with her. She had thought it too greedy, to want to do something for herself and have him do it too.

'Quite the opposite,' she said, turning her body towards his so she could wrap her arms around his neck. 'Why are you doing this? What about Brisbane?'

He put one hand on her hair and stroked it with his fingers, the way he knew she loved. He could send her to sleep, doing that; standing up, she felt like he was almost hypnotising her.

'My children have their own lives,' he said. 'They're already living quite successfully without me. If I go there, I would have my old life back, and that would be fine. But if you're not there it's not what I want.'

Up close, she could see the fine wrinkles on his face. He wasn't yet what could be called weathered but he was worn in. As was she.

'I'm glad,' she said, kissing his chin. 'Actually, I'm incredibly happy. I didn't want to ask you to move. It seemed like it would be too much.'

'You could have,' he said, stroking the other side of her head. 'I wouldn't have minded.'

He kept stroking her head as she kissed him, relishing the prospect that she didn't have to store this memory to retrieve later. There were, now, an infinite number of kisses ahead of them.

'I just have one request,' he said as the kiss ended.

'Mmm?' she said dreamily.

'I'm quite traditional,' he said. 'I don't want to ask you to live with me in Sydney.'

She pulled back and stared at him. They were living together quite happily now – she couldn't foresee there would be a problem in Sydney.

'If we're making a life together, Rita,' he said, reaching back to unclasp her hands and hold them in his, 'I'd like to start it properly. I'd like you to marry me. And I'd like to marry you.'

She felt strangely weightless yet secure; giddy but serious; loved and loving.

'I'd like that too,' she said, smiling so widely that she felt her cheeks ripple.

Hamish let out a long breath. 'I've been holding that breath for weeks,' he said, his laughter starting slowly.

'Keep breathing,' she said, hugging him tightly and quickly. 'I need you to stay around.'

She kissed him again and let herself relax into it; she felt the memories of her pain tucking themselves away into recesses she didn't know she had. There were brighter days ahead; they had already started.

CHAPTER FIFTY-SEVEN

The lesson plans had taken most of her Saturday but Sallyanne was pleased to be organised so far in advance. The children were playing in Sybil's garden – she could hear them, asking Stan to give them piggybacks. She could hear Stan's laugh too, and now Ben's, as they pretended to refuse. Then the squeals as they obviously acquiesced and small children were hoisted onto their backs.

She smiled as she picked up her pen again, almost finished with a list of books for them all to read – books she'd have to order from town when someone next drove in. She was now used to the pace of getting things done out here: write a list, wait for someone to go into town, accept that they might not return for a few days, be patient with it all. It was a pace she'd grown used to in the kitchen. She wasn't there as much anymore; the school was taking up the majority of her time. Sybil was helping Kate as she searched for someone to hire.

'Hello?' called a soft voice from outside the schoolroom's screen door.

'Are you waiting for an invitation?' Sallyanne said lightly, walking towards the door. 'You know you don't need one.'

'I don't like to barge in,' Kate said as she stepped inside, holding Archie on one hip.

'You're not barging.' Sallyanne grinned at Archie, who giggled then turned his face into Kate's shoulder.

'I've come to ask a favour,' Kate said, glancing at Archie.

'Oh?'

'You've probably noticed that Archie likes to go where Tim and Billy go.'

Sallyanne nodded. 'Little children love older boys. My mother always said that.'

'Would you mind if . . .' Kate looked around the schoolroom. 'Would you mind if he sat in here a bit each day while they're at school? Not the whole time, of course. Just enough so that he doesn't feel like he's missing out.'

'Sure,' said Sallyanne. 'Gretel would love to not be the youngest anymore.' She smiled. 'And she loves Archie.'

'He's very lovable.' Kate smiled.

'Mummy,' Archie said now, patting Kate's cheek.

'Did Sybil tell you about the television?' Kate said, her eyes still on Archie.

'No. What?'

'She wants to watch the royal wedding so she's told Ben he needs to work out a way to get a television here and hook up an aerial so we can see it.'

'When is it?'

Kate looked at her strangely. 'July the twenty-ninth. I'd have thought you'd know that. It's a big love story.'

'Oh . . . I don't pay as much attention to those anymore,' Sallyanne said, thinking of the novels she had given away to some of the CWA women. Since moving to Fairvale she found she hadn't needed love stories as much as she used to.

'Really? Well, it's a big day for my people,' Kate said, grinning. 'We thought Charles would never find anyone.'

'Let alone that lovely Diana.'

'She can have him.' Kate put Archie on the ground and held onto his wrist while he danced around her feet.

'You've never wanted to be a princess?'

'I think every girl in England wanted to be the Princess of Wales at one time. I mean, if they weren't wishing Paul McCartney would leave Linda.' Kate grinned. 'But no – I'm happy where I am.'

She crouched down next to Archie and looked up at Sallyanne.

'More than happy,' she said.

Sallyanne nodded.

'Are you?' Kate said.

Sallyanne swept her gaze around the schoolroom and out the window to what she could see beyond: one side of Sybil's garden, now riotously green after the long wet; the cattle yards; two of the stockmen talking to each other while they held onto their horses; Barney loping along in the dirt.

'I am,' Sallyanne said. 'I never thought I'd be able to say that, but I am.'

Kate stood, picking up Archie with her.

'I'm glad,' she said.

'Mummy,' he said again, pulling Kate's hair this time.

'All right, time for a snack.' She grinned at Sallyanne. 'See you – and thanks.'

Sallyanne waved goodbye to Archie. He would probably be a handful in the classroom but she would find a way to make it work. She had surprised herself with how practical she'd become out here.

She put her papers into drawers and the pens and pencils into a cup. Everything was now ready for Monday.

The screen door opened again and she laughed.

'Did you forget something?' she said, turning around to find Mick standing there instead.

'Oh,' she said.

It had been over a year since she'd seen him. He hadn't tried to visit her or the children in the meantime and the children had stopped asking about him. She didn't want to ask them if they missed him; she was afraid of how happy she'd be if they said 'no'.

The Mick standing before her wasn't the one who had left her, though. He looked different now – better. Healthier. The puffiness that alcohol had given him had gone; his skin was tanned. He was standing up straighter. He even looked handsome, the way he used to.

'Aren't you going to say hello?' he said, stepping closer.

'Hello,' she said, trying to sound breezy.

'You cut your hair,' he said, sounding uncertain.

'Yes,' she said. 'I've wanted to for years.'

He stared at her and she stared back.

'What are you doing here?'

'Your solicitor sent the papers,' he said. She had almost forgotten about the divorce; the visit to the solicitor's office had taken place weeks ago and she'd been caught up in Fairvale life since then. Perhaps because, in her mind, the marriage was already over.

'Yes,' she said, 'and you need to sign them.'

'I don't want to,' he said. 'I thought we were going to try again.'

He'd been telling himself stories for years, about the effect the children had on their marriage, about how neglected he thought he was. She saw those stories now as a sad loop that he'd caught himself in. But it wasn't her loop.

'We're not, Mick,' she said, trying to look sympathetic when she really just wanted him gone. 'The kids and I are doing well here.'

'But I could move here,' he said, and she resisted the instinct to yell *No* in his face.

'There's nothing for you here,' she said. 'And – and I don't want you here.'

'What about the kids?' It almost sounded like a whine.

'You didn't care about them when you were getting drunk all the time,' she said, sounding as close to snappy as she ever did.

'Don't you love me anymore?' He sounded like a little boy who'd been scolded by his mother.

Did she or didn't she? When she remembered the way he used to be she loved him – then she had to tell herself that it was an echo, nothing more. She didn't love him now. She knew it because she barely thought about him.

'I'll always feel something for you,' she said truthfully. 'But I can't stay married to you, Mick. We both need to start again. Not with each other.'

He looked away from her, down at the floor, scuffing it with the toe of his boot.

'Yeah,' he said, and as his eyes met hers once more she saw the stranger he had become. 'I reckon we do.'

'So you'll sign the papers?' she said, trying not to sound as if she was unsure of his answer. She needed him to believe she was resolute.

'Yep,' he said, scratching his head. 'Can I see the kids before I leave?'

'Of course,' she said. 'You can probably hear where they are.' The sound of squeals continued to float through from the garden.

'Can I come and visit?' he said.

'Yes. Just call first,' she said. 'There's always a lot going on here.'

He nodded. 'It was good for a while, wasn't it?' he said.

She smiled, thinking of him when they had first met. She'd been so impressed by him. 'Yes, it was,' she said. 'Goodbye, Mick.'

She nodded towards the door and watched as he left without another glance at her. She saw the back of his head disappearing. She felt as though one plane of her life overlapped another and then separated; almost like time had split. That conversation could have gone differently and one possible future was already disappearing into the ether while another was coming into being.

Mick was really gone. Her past was really past. As she sat at her desk, she felt the last few years – all her concern about him, about her life, about what would become of them – flow out of her. Tears flooded her eyes and dripped onto her lips. All she could taste was relief. And freedom. And the future before her, as boundless as Fairvale's sky.

CHAPTER FIFTY-EIGHT

The nausea had started two weeks before and Kate had put it down to some unseasonal rain they'd had: the barometric pressure was all over the place. She was sure that was it. She'd felt nauseated during her first build-up – this had to be the same, even though they were in the dry season.

The rain had gone, however, and she was still unwell. Archie was keeping her busy, so she must be tired. That was it.

Then Ben had remarked on her pallor and told her that he'd heard her retching in the bathroom.

'I must have picked up something from a visitor,' she told him.

One morning the nausea woke her before dawn and she fled to the bathroom, horrified that in the quiet house the noise of her trying to be sick would likely be heard by Sybil as well as Ben and Archie.

She almost crawled to the kitchen to make herself a cup of tea. It was the only thing she could bear to drink. Even the water tasted foul until it was boiled. She had been feeling like a neurotic, boiling all her drinking water and keeping it in a jug. Ben had looked at her strangely the first couple of times she'd done it but he hadn't asked why.

At this time of morning there was no hiding the noise of

the kettle either, so she wasn't surprised to see Sybil appear, still in her nightdress.

'You're up early,' she said, looking at Kate as if she suspected her of something.

'Sorry if I woke you.' Kate pressed her lips together as a wave of sickness tried to rise up again.

'It's fine. May I?' Sybil nodded at the kettle.

'Of course.'

Silently Sybil made herself a cup of tea and sat next to Kate at the table.

'Milk?' she said and Kate wanted to vomit.

'Um – no. Thank you,' Kate picked up her black tea and took a small sip as Sybil watched.

'How long have you been feeling sick?' Sybil said, her face expressionless.

Kate felt guilty: she'd have to ask Sybil to watch Archie while she went into town to see the doctor, and if she continued to feel unwell Sybil could be looking after Archie for a while. Not that she ever minded, but Sybil had enough to do and with Stan about to go on a long muster, Ben would be too busy with his job to watch him.

'Stop worrying about whatever it is you're worried about,' Sybil said, 'and tell me: how long?'

'About a fortnight,' Kate said. 'I'm not improving. I'm starting to think it's something serious.'

'Oh, I'm sure it's not,' Sybil said pragmatically, to Kate's astonishment.

Sybil looked at her as if she had a third eye.

'You're pregnant, Kate,' she said with a small smile.

No, she couldn't be. It had been years since the miscarriage and there had been nothing since then. Not even a hint that she'd be able to get pregnant again. Not a single period missed. Since Archie arrived she and Ben hadn't even thought about having a baby. They'd stopped thinking about trying and had grown much happier as a result – although she believed Archie had a lot to do with that.

'When was your last period?' Sybil said.

'It was only—' Kate stopped. When was it, indeed? She was so caught up in what she was doing every day that she barely noticed anymore.

She counted back. She was sure it had only been a week or so ago. No, that wasn't right. It was just after their last book club meeting, which was . . .

'Six weeks ago,' she said, noting Sybil's slightly triumphant expression.

'There you have it,' Sybil said.

'But I can't be pregnant. I didn't feel sick the last time.' As much as she wanted to believe Sybil, Kate was scared that she was right – scared, and not a little exhilarated.

'The same woman can have morning sickness with one pregnancy and not with another. It doesn't mean anything.' Sybil smiled as she brought her teacup to her lips.

'How did you know?' Kate said, almost whispering in wonder.

'Your bum dropped.'

'My what?'

'Pregnant women's bottoms drop right from the start of pregnancy. I learnt to identify it when I was nursing. Not that I was *looking*, of course – I just happened to notice.'

Kate was flabbergasted that Sybil could pick up such a detail about her when she had no idea herself. Who knew what else her mother-in-law had noticed about her over the years?

'I'm guessing you're having a tough time in that kitchen,

cooking meat.' Sybil looked at her questioningly. Kate felt ill even thinking about the meat.

'Yes,' she said feebly.

'Right, well, Ruby can come back for a while. She'll just have to sit down every now and again.' Sybil had a funny look on her face, as if she was trying not to reveal something.

'Does Ruby know too?'

There was that triumphant expression again. 'We might have discussed our theory.'

Kate felt like giggling. If Sybil thought she was pregnant, and Ruby thought she was pregnant, she might actually *be* pregnant. The giggle erupted.

'I can't believe it,' she said. 'Can I?'

'You can. And by the second trimester you'll be right as rain so you might even be able to enjoy it.'

The second trimester. A few minutes ago she hadn't even thought about a first trimester. She hadn't thought about babies at all for quite a while.

'If I make it that far,' Kate said, her face falling as the memory of what happened last time blasted into the front of her brain. The memory, and the pain that came with it. She looked at Sybil and knew that she was remembering too. Impossible for either of them not to.

'If you don't, you'll cope,' Sybil said, quietly but determinedly. 'First of all we need to make sure you're not overdoing it, which means you stick to making bread and cakes, and Ruby will take over everything else. I'll ask Sallyanne if she can add Archie to her tribe for a while.'

'Oh, that's not—'

'Kate,' Sybil said gently, 'you're not meant to handle this on your own. You have one child and you're expecting another – that's when you let old ducks like me take over and tell you what to do, and you smile and nod and say "Yes". That's your sole job for the next few weeks, all right?'

It was all right. And it was a relief. It was enough to make Kate want to cry. In fact, she was crying. On Sybil's shoulder, and she didn't even remember laying her head there. She was glad for it, though, as a maelstrom of hope, love, doubt, dismay and wonder swirled inside her.

'Tears,' Sybil said, rubbing her arm, 'are good. And there will be a few of them, just because your hormones will be all over the place.'

Kate nodded, aware that she was rubbing the tears into Sybil's nightdress.

'Everything will be wonderful,' Sybil said soothingly. And as the light in the kitchen began to change with the dawn, Kate believed her.

CHAPTER FIFTY-NINE

It was weird, watching something and knowing it might be the last time you ever saw it. Della had felt that way when she was last at home, watching her mother make coffee in the kitchen. She couldn't be sure it would be the last time she'd see it happen, but it might have been. Just as she wasn't sure that this was the last time she'd see Stan talking to Ben by the cattle yards – but it might be.

He'd come to tell her himself, a week ago, that he was going back to his country for a while because his family needed him, and after that he didn't know what he was doing. They had been cordial with each other since they had formally parted ways; Della had tried not to be stiff, conscious that people were watching them. She didn't want Ben to feel uncomfortable around them. It wasn't his fault that they couldn't be together and it shouldn't affect their work.

Except Della knew it had. She and Stan had become quiet, whereas before they used to banter. Now Della rode with Ben on the stock camp and Stan stuck to the back, on his own. Della didn't like the arrangement, and she was pretty sure he didn't either. But they were apart now, in everything.

So she hadn't been surprised when he'd knocked on her door with his news, although she had been devastated.

'I wanted to tell you myself,' he'd said, and she could tell he wanted to lean in her doorway like he always had when he used to take his time coming into her room, drawing it out until desire made her practically yank him in.

'When are you leaving?' She felt like this was her fault – that he was moving away to avoid her. It wasn't as if she hadn't considered doing the same thing but Della had decided that she'd have been running away from a central truth in her life: she loved Stan and she had decided to let him go, and the pain of seeing him every day felt like a penance.

'Coupla weeks,' he'd said. She could hardly see his eyes in the gloomy light, so she didn't know if he was happy or sad. She'd lost her right to know, anyway.

'Okay. Well, thanks for telling me.' She'd used her bravest voice, then she'd shut the door on him and cried until she fell asleep.

Now the day of his departure had arrived and he was saying his goodbyes to Ben while she hovered, determined to have a last word with him.

He and Ben shook hands, their faces serious.

'Your job's always here for you,' she heard Ben say, and Stan nodded before tipping his hat. He turned away and she thought he was going to head to the big house. Instead he pivoted and came straight towards her.

She stepped out of the doorway.

'I didn't think you'd see me here,' she said, nervously fluttering her hands by her sides as he came to a stop in front of her.

He gave her a curious, sad smile. 'I'd see you anywhere, Della girl,' he said.

'I'm going to miss you,' she said, not looking him in the eye. She'd decided to tell him the truth but that didn't mean it was easy.

'I'll miss you too,' he said, his face serious now.

She could smell him: earth and rain and fire. That's what he'd always smelled like to her. In twenty years' time, fifty, to the end of her life, she would know that smell anywhere.

'Take care of yourself,' she said, knowing it sounded lame but how could she say what she really wanted to: *Keep yourself safe. Keep yourself healthy. I can't bear the thought of anything happening to you.*

'Are you going to stay here, Della girl?' he said, taking one of her hands, causing her to suck a breath in and feel it catch in her chest.

She nodded quickly. 'I don't have plans to leave.'

'Then I might see you again. Later.'

Was that a promise of something? Or was it just his way of saying goodbye? She couldn't read him. But if he was offering her the chance of a way back to him, she would take it.

'You might,' she said.

He nodded slowly and let her hand go.

'Stan!' Ben called from a few metres away. 'Truck's ready.'

He tipped his hat to her. 'I'll see you round, Della girl.'

'Goodbye, Stan,' she whispered.

She watched him walk to the truck that was parked in front of the big house. Saw him hug Kate and Sybil, then hop in next to the stockman who was going to drive him to town.

She waited as the truck half circled to get onto the gravel road. She saw his hand out the window, his fingers waving once, and knew she was the only person who could see it.

So he was gone. And she was not. That was the only truth she had right now.

CHAPTER SIXTY

Rita had finished asking Darryl for one last flight to Katherine. She'd told him why she needed it: for her final gathering of the book club, and to say goodbye to Fairvale. But not to Sybil, even if she didn't know when she'd see her again. And not to the others either, because she didn't want it to be goodbye.

'You're leavin',' he said, a tinnie in one hand and a Benson & Hedges in the other. She'd come to see him at the end of his shift and he was marking it in his traditional way.

'I am,' she said. 'And I'll miss you, Daz.'

'You'd better,' he said, drinking from the can. 'Never thought of you as the type.'

'For what?'

He turned towards her, one eye squinting. 'To run after a man.'

'I'm not running after him. I've decided to leave and he's going to join me.'

'Whatever you say,' he grunted and she felt a flash of annoyance that her plans could be so readily discounted by him.

'Everyone deserves to be loved, Darryl,' she said. 'Sometimes it doesn't always come in the form we expect.'

'Yeah, well.' He drank the last of his beer. 'He'd better take care of you. It's not every day a man finds gold in a swamp.'

Laughter bubbled out of her; she would miss his view on the world.

'I'll let him know,' she said.

'Don't worry – I'll bloody well tell him myself.' He stubbed out his cigarette.

'I need to fly up on Saturday and come back Sunday – is that all right?'

'Yep.' He turned to go, looping all the way around the scattered chairs in the office in order to leave.

'Darryl?'

He gave her a salute in response and departed quickly, not showing her his face. Rita didn't know if he was upset that she was leaving or annoyed that she'd asked him for a lift to Katherine. She'd probably never know.

That was the last piece of her departure planned. After she saw Sybil her Northern Territory life would be over and her Sydney life would begin.

~

The Fairvale guest bedroom had not changed much since Rita had first visited Sybil after she married. Sybil had updated the bed linen but the chest of drawers and the mirror were the same. So was the bed. Maybe the curtains were different; Rita couldn't remember what they were all those years ago.

She unpacked her clothes and then stood and looked at herself in the mirror. Things were starting to sag – she couldn't avoid that. Her hair was getting greyer and she should really try a new haircut. The fringe had had its day and she wasn't a spring chicken anymore. But Hamish loved her anyway.

'Cup of tea?' said Sybil, poking her head into the doorway.

'Something stronger, maybe,' Rita said, her smile tight. She already felt the pain of leaving and she wasn't going until tomorrow.

'Come on,' Sybil said, reappearing with two mugs in hand.

Rita raised a questioning eyebrow.

'Oh, it's whisky,' Sybil said. 'Cleverly disguised.' She whistled and Barney appeared as they walked out through the garden towards the yards.

'I love this time of day,' Sybil said as she and Rita held their mugs and leant against the fence of the cattle yard, as they'd done so many times over the years. 'The sun is high, everyone is busy. The dogs are barking, the children are squealing . . .'

Sybil took a sip from her mug. 'Friends are leaving,' she said, and Rita thought she saw her jaw clench.

'Are you all right?' Rita said.

'I really don't want you to go to Sydney,' Sybil said. She sniffed. 'I hate the idea of you being so far away.'

'Syb,' Rita said as she reached out to pat Sybil on the arm. 'We've lived far away from each other before.'

'I didn't like it then, either, and now you've got me so used to your regular visits. You've *ruined* me.' She sniffed more loudly then held the mug to her face for several seconds. Rita almost laughed – she'd never heard Sybil sounding childish before and she could barely believe she was hearing it now.

'Is there another reason?' Rita said, wishing Sybil would meet her eyes.

'I don't know – is there?'

'Don't be petulant.'

'Don't move to Sydney!' Sybil huffed.

'I didn't tell you not to move up here when you left Sydney with Joe,' Rita said, knowing this was the first time she and Sybil had come close to anything resembling a fight.

Sybil's face set. 'I know,' she said. 'But I'm selfish – more selfish than you.'

'And you think I'm making a mistake,' Rita said flatly, not wanting to know if Sybil thought the mistake was Sydney or Hamish.

'I don't know that.'

'But do you *think* it?'

Sybil turned to put her back to the fence and angled her eyes away from the sun.

'I think a lot of things,' she said. 'I think my eldest son is a terrible person. I think my second son is a better man than either his brother or his father. I think I'm going to be lucky if I can keep him and Kate and Archie here forever, so there's a good chance I'm going to die alone and one of the dogs will drag me out to the garden and bury me.'

'Sybil,' Rita said, trying not to laugh, 'don't be ridiculous.'

'Do you honestly think I'm ridiculous? Is there no truth in that?'

They stared at each other.

'There could be truth in it,' Rita said at last. 'Or not. None of us knows what's going to happen. I might move back to Sydney, hate it, and beg you to give me a room here until I die.'

'Unlikely.'

'But possible. Anything's possible.'

Rita tried to follow Sybil's gaze but its destination was indeterminate.

'Is it?' Sybil said finally. 'I tend to think we have a limited range of possibilities and we have so little time in which to decide which to take.'

'You'll drive yourself mad if you keep thinking like that,' Rita said. 'The what-ifs are deadly.'

They stared at each other again.

'I'll miss you,' Sybil said.

'And I'll miss you. But I'll call you. I'll visit when I can.'

'I'd offer to give Hamish a warning about taking care of you or else, but given that he's only met me once, it might not have any effect.' Sybil's voice sounded light, but she wasn't smiling. Neither of them was.

'Darryl's already offered.' Rita tried to match her friend's tone, except this was the last conversation she and Sybil were likely to have in person for a long time.

'I took a risk when I came here with Joe,' Sybil said, her voice husky. 'I've never regretted it. I know that after all this time it's probably strange to know you're getting married. But he loves you. I wouldn't have let you say yes to him if I thought otherwise. Selfish, remember?'

Sybil stepped closer to her. 'You will always be my dearest friend. I will always be your refuge, if you need it. You can come here whenever you want. So if you ever need us, if you have doubts or you just need some time away, pack your bags and Ben will meet you at Tindal.'

She blinked once. Twice. Rita saw tears at the bottom of her eyes.

'I could say,' Sybil continued, 'that I want you to be happy. But that sounds so trite, and we both know that life is more complex than that. What I want is for you to know that you are loved by me – by all of us here. That is your guarantee for the future. If things go right, if things go wrong, that guarantee will not change. If you get swept up in your new life and I don't hear from you for months, I will be mildly miffed but I will never stop loving you.'

Sybil put her mug on top of the fence rail.

'Now give me a hug,' she said.

As Rita held her friend close, she looked beyond to the plains behind her. She saw two young men on horses, and in front of them she was sure she could see Della, cantering towards the stables. She saw Ben talking to the stock inspector and Kate walking towards him holding a mug, Archie right behind her. Sallyanne's children were tearing down the track from the camp, their mother walking slowly along.

Fairvale wasn't her home, it would probably never be, but Sybil was. All of these people were – these friends she had made right here, one day in 1978. Rita would carry that with her to her new life, and she would never forget them.

CHAPTER SIXTY-ONE

That morning Sybil woke with her limbs feeling heavy. She decided she should stay in bed. If she didn't get up, she would miss the book club meeting but she would also miss saying goodbye to Rita. That was what she really wanted to avoid.

Sybil knew she should be used to separation by now. Lachie was long gone and she dealt with that by trying not to think about him anymore. He would pop into her mind – of course he did – and she could not choose when that happened or what the thought would be. So she tried to think of him with love and then let the thought go. And she focused on Archie, on the child who had changed all of their lives simply by existing.

A knock on her door made her sit up.

'Yes?'

The handle turned and Kate's smiling face appeared.

'Archie wants to say good morning to his Gran-Gran,' she said, stepping into the room, Archie clutching her hand.

He laughed when he saw Sybil and let go of his mother, jumping up onto the bed.

'Gran-Gran!' he squealed, bouncing up and down as he made his way to Sybil. She hugged him, pressing her cheek against his, until he wriggled away. They always wriggled away.

'Did we wake you?' Kate said.

'No, I was up. And I need to get up.' She smiled, trying to muster enthusiasm. 'It's a big day.'

She took Archie's hand. 'Would you like to help me get out of bed?' she said and he nodded, his face serious.

'You're going to have to pull me up,' she said, offering him both of her hands.

He giggled and took them, leaning backwards with effort. Sybil pretended that he was strong enough to get her all the way out from under the sheets. Then she was on her feet, and Kate was taking Archie away for his breakfast, and Sybil was left alone again to think about what came next.

~

Sallyanne drifted in last, full of apologies for her lateness.

'Billy was refusing to go to Ruby's,' she said, looking impatient. 'He seems to think he's big enough not to need babysitting. He says Tim's old enough to look after him. Honestly – children!'

She huffed a bit as she sat down and Sybil smiled in recognition. Ben had argued the same case when he was around the same age – except it hadn't been Lachie he wanted to watch him, it was Ruby's daughter, Rose.

'I guess I can look forward to Archie doing the same thing,' Kate said, although she didn't look worried about it.

'That child is an angel,' said Sallyanne. 'Can we swap?'

'Not on your life,' Kate said, laughing.

'So,' Sybil said, 'we should start.'

She glanced at Rita, who was sitting up very straight, holding her cup of tea so tightly that she looked as though she could break the handle.

'Rita is leaving us,' Sybil said, 'as we already know. That's why I didn't suggest a particular book for this meeting. I thought we could . . . talk. Like old friends do.'

'Lord, Syb, this is starting to sound like a wake,' Rita said.

Sybil knew she was right, and it was because it felt like a wake. Not for Rita, not for their friendship, but for the group they had formed that had seen them all through the last three years. They would never meet again like this – of that, she was sure.

'I'm going to miss you,' Sallyanne said, her voice wobbly.

'Sal, not you too,' Rita said, leaning towards her and squeezing her hand. 'I'm not going that far.'

'But we don't know when you'll be back.' Sallyanne bit her bottom lip and started to pull at her skirt.

'You can visit me,' Rita said, looking around the group. 'I will always be happy to see you. Even if it's not for years. I won't forget.'

Her eyes met Sybil's and Sybil saw the girl she'd met that day in the hospital, so sharp and eager. They had aged, they'd changed, but fundamentally they were the same. If she didn't see Rita for years, if none of them did, it would be as if no time had passed.

'Now come on,' Rita said, letting go of Sallyanne's hand. 'I want you all to tell me what your favourite book is and why. Sal, you start.'

Sybil tried to concentrate on what everyone was saying but she found her mind listing. She was tired. And relieved. This book club had been an idea, then it was real, and now it was about to be a memory. She felt it had done its job, though, and perhaps she could relax a bit now. She didn't have to be responsible for everyone all the time. She could let Kate and Ben take charge. At least for a little while.

CHAPTER SIXTY-TWO

The sun was already low in the western sky as cock-atoos screeched their way to the trees by the creek. There were cattle in the yards and Sybil listened as they moved against the fences and huffed and scratched.

She heard another huffing noise and looked down to see Barney coming her way, his tail wagging.

'Did you miss me?' she said, bending down to scratch his ears. He sat on her feet, as if he wanted to keep her from going anywhere. He did that a lot.

She didn't take enough time to stand here, by her garden, in front of her house, and contemplate just how enormous her life was – how grand this station was, and how much Joe had achieved. How much they had achieved together. There was so much she hadn't known, though, before he died.

She knew more now. Fairvale was a home and a workplace; it was also, for her, a living thing. It changed shape as people came and went, and the seasons turned. If she'd been asked to say where its heart was, where its brain resided, she could give answers but they would change too. Sometimes its heart was the distant hill that Joe used to gaze at as the sun set, his eyes half closed, his face taking on an expression of wonder.

'I used to think,' he'd told her once, early in their marriage, 'that I could run to that hill and back in a day. When I was a boy, that was my goal: to do that run.'

'And did you?' Sybil had asked, following his gaze.

'Syb,' he'd said, turning to her, those blue eyes laughing, 'it's a two-day ride.'

Before that moment she'd thought she'd known the limits of Fairvale. Joe had told her numbers – square kilometres – and they'd seemed to make sense. She just hadn't thought about how they worked in practice – she hadn't thought about calculating distance in a different way.

Out here distance was described as days in the saddle and the number of cattle mustered; time was measured between downpours; eternities were judged by stretches between wet seasons. She couldn't say that such a place was subject to the normal rules of biology and physics. So Fairvale was alive, and if in many ways it was more robust than her – than any human – in others it was more frail, in need of her protection.

No doubt if she told this to someone who didn't live here they'd say it was good that she was taking care of Fairvale 'in Joe's memory'. That was one way to look at it – except there was no such thing as Joe's memory, because Joe was woven into the dirt and the trees, into that hill and the fences in the yard; into the creek where he'd swum as a boy; into Ben's slightly lopsided grin and his charm, into Archie's love of Fairvale's dust. Joe was alive, even if he couldn't be seen. He was there for her to talk to every day, and he talked back.

She didn't speak about Joe much – but Joe was there. Every now and again she'd hear a deep laugh and she was sure she heard a man calling her 'Syb'. She never turned to look for him, though, because she knew she wouldn't be able to see him. He was a slip in time away from her – just there, just beyond her reach – and that's where he would ever be.

She missed being able to touch him, though. She missed his eyes. She missed his hair. She missed the smell of him after a shower. She missed the way he'd tickle her behind the ear when she became too serious about something. But he was still there, he would always be there, and she would care for Fairvale as if it was him, until it was time for her, too, to find her place amongst the trees.

ACKNOWLEDGEMENTS

This book would not have existed without two people at Hachette Australia: Daniel Pilkington and Rebecca Saunders. Thank you both for breathing it into life.

Rebecca is the book's publisher and biggest champion, and she is everything an author dreams of in a publisher: passionate, creative, smart, savvy, responsive, committed, and firm when needed.

Huge thanks to everyone at Hachette Australia – such a knowledgeable, dedicated, great group of people – and the following people in particular: Fiona Hazard, Louise Sherwin-Stark, Justin Ractliffe, Vanessa Radnidge, Ashleigh Barton, Sophie Mayfield, Sarah Brooks, Laura Boon and Anna Egelstaff. And many thanks to Manpreet Grewal, Andy Hine and the rest of the team at Sphere and Little, Brown in the UK for their belief in the Fairvale ladies.

I was so fortunate to have two of Australia's best editors working on this book – 'thank you' is inadequate to express my gratitude to Alex Craig and Fiona Daniels. It was a privilege to have Karen Ward managing the project in-house and casting her keen editorial eye over these pages. Nathan Grice kept the production train on the tracks with good humour and bad rock songs.

This novel is not my first and I would not be writing fiction at all without Rod Morrison, Jon MacDonald and Joel Naoum publishing me before this – thank you.

Christa Moffitt has designed many a beautiful book cover and I am so lucky that she was able to design this one too.

Thank you to Jen Bradley, who kept me going with tennis matches, laughter, and her incredible friendship; and to Isabelle Benton for our many years of book-based friendship, and her support and encouragement. Kylie Mason has been a kind and sympathetic listener throughout – thank you.

Thanks to Toni Tapp Coutts for sharing her love for the Northern Territory with me, and with readers across the country in her books.

To my parents, David and Robbie Hamley, and my brother, Nicholas: thank you for all the things for all the years. I love you.

I would not be here to write this book if it were not for the doctors and nurses working in Emergency and Intensive Care at Royal North Shore Hospital in early July 2011.

READING GROUP NOTES

SOPHIE GREEN TALKS ABOUT THE BOOKS CHOSEN FOR READING BY THE FAIRVALE LADIES BOOK CLUB

THE THORN BIRDS BY COLLEEN McCULLOUGH

This modern Australian classic was the natural and only choice as the first book for the Fairvale Ladies Book Club members to read. It is a sweeping saga that puts outback Australia at its core – the setting of *Fairvale* meant that there was a natural relationship between the two stories, even if they are otherwise completely unalike.

I also chose *The Thorn Birds* because it has loomed so large in my life as a reader: it was the first saga I read, and the fact that it was Australian was important – it was a big Australian story with an Australian heroine. Even though I was a child at the time and didn't understand all of it, the drama and scope of it has always stayed with me. It's also a book that was written for readers: it is clear that McCullough wanted her readers to be moved and entertained, something she achieved then and continues to achieve, as evidenced by the book's continuing life and resonance for generations of readers.

LOVE IN A COLD CLIMATE BY NANCY MITFORD

As one of the characters, Kate, is English, I wanted there to be a book that might mean something more to her than it means to the other characters. The world of *Love in a Cold Climate* may be somewhat outdated but the writing is still sharp and pertinent, and the reputation of this book endures accordingly. There was also a technical parallel between the fact that many of the characters in *Love in a Cold Climate* spend a lot of time sitting around, chatting – and the Fairvale book club largely involves sitting around, chatting.

PICNIC AT HANGING ROCK BY JOAN LINDSAY

Another esteemed Australian novel that uses landscape to great effect; the role the land plays in this story is just as powerful as it is in *The Thorn Birds* but more specifically creepy. The novel is more clear-eyed than the movie: it can be brutal, bloody and unsentimental. As with *The Thorn Birds*, it reminds Australian readers that if we think we have the measure of our landscape, we are fools. We will always be its subjects; its caprices and mysteries will always get the better of us, and the best we can do is accept that and live in awe of the natural world we see.

THE FAR PAVILIONS BY M.M. KAYE

This historical epic will be known to many readers who may already have been swept away by its scope, and the love story at its core. There are some parallels to one of the storylines in Fairvale, but the novel was chosen for the Fairvale book club mainly because of the timing of its publication and its subsequent fame. It would have been hard for anyone to escape its notoriety, regardless of how remotely they lived, and the 'exotic' nature of its setting – exoticism, of course, being a relative concept – gave its readers an opportunity to be carried away to a completely different place and time. So much of the value of fiction is to offer us an escape from our daily lives, and *The Far Pavilions* certainly does that.

THE HARP IN THE SOUTH BY RUTH PARK

If *Fairvale* had not been a novel for adults, I would have included *Playing Beatie Bow*, which is a book that preoccupied me for quite a while when it was released. However, Ruth Park's other novels had no less of an impact – her layered, emotional stories of Australian life (in the case of *The Harp in the South*, life in inner-city Sydney) are beloved by many. Ruth Park is a singular figure in Australian literature, a versatile writer who could not help but write books that not only offered the aforementioned escapism but which had meaning and depth. Park was prolific, and I could have chosen other novels, but the timing worked for *The Harp in the South* and given that two of the *Fairvale* characters (Sybil and Rita) are from Sydney, it seemed fitting.

MY BRILLIANT CAREER BY MILES FRANKLIN

This is perhaps an obvious inclusion, given how well known the book is, but the truth is that it fits the story: it's about a woman and her work, and all the women in Fairvale work. Women's work may seem like an unexciting topic – and the very term is loaded – but women's work is also constant: on Fairvale, as in other homes, women's work tends to go on for as long as a woman is awake each day. There is no knock-off time for running a household or caring for others.

My Brilliant Career does not cover that sort of work but it is no less relevant to the experience of the Fairvale women.

A WOMAN OF SUBSTANCE
BY BARBARA TAYLOR BRADFORD

This novel was a sensation when it was published – an historical saga that was about work and heartbreak, it carried readers away with it and did what the best fiction can: let them become absorbed into another person's story even as their own were reflected back. So much of the job of storytelling is to offer readers reassurance, solace, acknowledgement and occasionally a touch of *schadenfreude* with their entertainment. We want to know that we're not alone or we want to tell ourselves 'that won't happen to me' even as we collect clues for how to manage if 'that' did, in fact, happen. If all that can be wrapped up in a story that also causes us to lose track of time and impatiently wait to be with that story again, what can be better for the reader? Barbara Taylor Bradford, like Colleen McCullough and other exemplars of the saga, including Judith Krantz, achieved all of that. *A Woman of Substance* became famous for a reason.

OTHER BOOKS MENTIONED

THE GROUP BY MARY McCARTHY

This novel was well known, then it wasn't. It was recently revived with support from Candace Bushnell, the author of *Sex and the City*, and thus it can be more easily discovered by readers too young to remember its first publication. In some ways I see it as a companion piece to *Love in a Cold Climate*, but that's only my opinion and, no doubt, others may disagree.

What can't be doubted is the skill McCarthy used to handle many different characters and their interweaving lives.

SNUGGLEPOT AND CUDDLEPIE BY MAY GIBBS

Many Australian children have been introduced to native flora thanks to the work of May Gibbs. Gibbs's glorious illustrations and lively tales of the Gumnut Babies and the Banksia Men brought the landscape to life.

THE COMPLETE STORIES BY FLANNERY O'CONNOR

O'Connor did not live long but her stories set in the American South are still in print and even more revered. It seemed natural that Della, as a woman of the South, would cherish O'Connor and her dark tales.

THE POETRY OF A.B. 'BANJO' PATERSON

I tried to avoid including Paterson, mainly because he might be deemed too obvious, but it was that obviousness which meant he couldn't be left out: there was just no way that out of Sybil, Rita and Sallyanne, none of them would hold dear the work of a man who told stories of the bush and whose work was regularly taught in schools. For Henry Lawson fans, no doubt umbrage will be taken, but sorry, folks: I've always been a Banjo girl.

WE OF THE NEVER NEVER BY MRS AENEAS (JEANNIE) GUNN

This book was once very well known to Australian readers; it's to be expected that Sybil would have read it when she first moved to the Northern Territory, as there was little else available by way of stories that might reflect her experience, even in a small way.

QUESTIONS FOR DISCUSSION

1. It's not uncommon for women, in particular, to move for their husband's work. Sybil has her reasons for leaving Sydney behind to move to the Northern Territory, but was it an extreme response born of extreme circumstances, or a sensible decision?

2. Rita takes a job in Alice Springs because she wants a change. Would that be a powerful enough motive for you to take a job in a remote location?

3. It is more common these days for women to be unmarried and childless but in the 1970s Rita wouldn't have had much company – or would she? Do you know women who were 'unconventional' in this way at that time?

4. Despite great physical distances between them over the years, Rita and Sybil have maintained a close friendship. Are there friendships in your own life that have lasted the distance?

5. If your child were to make it clear that they didn't want to talk to you anymore, as Lachlan does to Sybil, would you respect their wishes or keep trying to make contact?

6. Sallyanne faces a terrible dilemma: her marriage becomes increasingly untenable but she does not have money of her own and, thus, leaving becomes almost impossible to contemplate. Should she have stayed, given those circumstances?

7. Kate and Della are far from home, and the new landscape is more different for Kate than Della. Have you ever

found yourself in a place that felt completely foreign, and difficult to adapt to?

8. Kate never placed much importance on having babies until she married and had difficulty becoming pregnant. Does she make too much of it, or is her concern about the implications of a childless life warranted?

9. *The Thorn Birds* is a novel that uses the Australian outback to dramatic effect as a setting, conveying its harshness as well as its grandeur – what other Australian novels that you've read have done this?

10. What books have helped you to understand an experience or cope with a difficulty?

11. What is your favourite Australian novel written by a woman, and why?

12. If you could have suggested a book for the Fairvale ladies – bearing in mind that the book had to be published before the late 1970s, well known enough that the ladies would have heard of it and easy enough for them to acquire – what would it have been?